WICKED AND THE WALLFLOWER

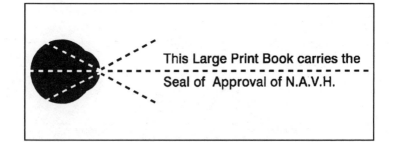

This Large Print Book carries the
Seal of Approval of N.A.V.H.

THE BAREKNUCKLE BASTARDS, BOOK 1

WICKED AND THE WALLFLOWER

SARAH MACLEAN

THORNDIKE PRESS

A part of Gale, a Cengage Company

Farmington Hills, Mich • San Francisco • New York • Waterville, Maine
Meriden, Conn • Mason, Ohio • Chicago

Copyright © 2018 by Sarah Trabucchi.
Thorndike Press, a part of Gale, a Cengage Company.

Thorndike Press® Large Print Romance.
The text of this Large Print edition is unabridged.
Other aspects of the book may vary from the original edition.
Set in 16 pt. Plantin.

LIBRARY OF CONGRESS CIP DATA ON FILE.
CATALOGUING IN PUBLICATION FOR THIS BOOK
IS AVAILABLE FROM THE LIBRARY OF CONGRESS

ISBN-13: 978-1-4328-6049-3 (hardcover)

Published in 2019 by arrangement with Avon Books, an imprint of HarperCollins Publishers

Printed in the United States of America
1 2 3 4 5 6 7 23 22 21 20 19

For my father,
who was the first to hear about my
Covent Garden crime lords,
and who never got to meet them.

Grazie mille, Papà.
Ti voglio tanto bene.

PROLOGUE

THE PAST

The three were woven together long before they were aware, strands of spun, silken steel that could not be separated — not even when their fate insisted upon it.

Brothers, born on the same day, in the same hour, at the same minute to different women. The high-priced courtesan. The seamstress. The soldier's widow. Born on the same day, in the same hour, at the same minute to the same man.

The duke, their father, whose arrogance and cruelty fate would punish without hesitation, stealing from him the only thing he wanted that his money and power could not buy — an heir.

It is the Ides of March the seers warn of, with its promise of betrayal and vengeance, of shifting fortune and inalienable providence. But for this sire — who was never more than that, never close to father — it was the Ides of June that would be his ruin.

Because on that same day, in that same hour, at that same minute, there was a fourth child, born to a fourth woman. To a duchess. And it was this birth — the birth all the world thought legitimate — that the duke attended, even as he knew the son who was to be his heir in name and fortune and future was not his own and still, somehow, was his only hope.

Except she was a daughter.

And with her first breath, she thieved future from them all, as powerful in her infancy as she would become in her womanhood. But hers is a story for another time.

This story begins with the boys.

CHAPTER ONE

THE PRESENT

May 1837

The Devil stood outside Marwick House, under the black shadow of an ancient elm, watching his bastard brother within.

Flickering candles and mottled glass distorted the revelers in the ballroom beyond, turning the throngs of people within — aristocrats and moneyed gentry — into a mass of indiscernible movement, reminding Devil of the tide of the Thames, ebbing and flowing and slick with color and stink.

Faceless bodies — men dark with formal dress and women gleaming light in their silks and satins — ran together, barely able to move for the craning necks and flapping fans waving gossip and speculation through the stagnant ballroom air.

And at their center, the man they were desperate to see — the hermit Duke of Marwick, shining bright and new, despite having held the title since his father had died. Since *their* father had died.

No. Not father. Sire.

And the new duke, young and handsome, returned like London's prodigal son — a head taller than the rest of the assembly, fair-haired and stone-faced, with the amber eyes the Dukes of Marwick had boasted for generations. Able-bodied and unwed and everything the aristocracy wished him to be.

And nothing the aristocracy believed him to be.

Devil could imagine the ignorant whispers running riot through the ballroom.

Why should a man of such prominence
   play the hermit?
   Who cares, as long as he's a duke?
Do you think the rumors are true?
   Who cares, as long as he's a duke?
Why hasn't he ever come to town?
   Who cares, as long as he's a duke?
What if he's as mad as they say?
   Who cares, as long as he's a duke?
I hear he is in the market for an heir.

It was the last that had summoned Devil from the darkness.

There had been a deal, made twenty years earlier, when they were three brothers in arms. And though much had happened since that deal had been forged, one thing remained sacrosanct: no one reneged on a deal with Devil.

Not without punishment.

And so, Devil waited with infinite patience in the gardens of the London residence of generations of Dukes of Marwick for the third in the deal to arrive. It had been decades since he and his brother, Whit — together known in London's nefarious corners as the Bareknuckle Bastards — had seen the duke. Decades since they'd escaped the country seat of the dukedom in the dead of night, leaving secrets and sins behind, to build their own kingdom of secrets and sins of a different sort.

But, a fortnight earlier, invitations had arrived at the most extravagant homes in London — the ones with the most venerable names — even as servants had arrived at Marwick House, armed to the teeth with dusters and wax, with irons and airing lines. One week earlier, crates had been delivered — candles and cloth, potatoes and port, and a half-dozen settees for the massive Marwick ballroom, each now festooned with the skirts of London's most eligible ladies.

Three days ago, the *News of London* arrived at the Bastards' Covent Garden headquarters and there, on the fourth page, a headline in smudged ink pronounced "Mysterious Marwick to Marry?"

Devil had carefully folded the paper and left it on Whit's desk. When he'd returned to his workspace the next morning, a throwing knife speared the newsprint to the oak.

And so it was decided.

Their brother, the duke, had returned, appearing without warning in this place designed for better men and filled with the worst of them, on land that he had inherited the moment he'd claimed his title, in a city they had made theirs, and in doing so, he revealed his greed.

But greed, in this place, on this land, was not permitted.

So, Devil waited and watched.

After long minutes, the air shifted and Whit appeared at his elbow, silent and deadly as a military reinforcement, which was appropriate, as this was nothing short of war.

"Just on time," Devil said, softly.

A grunt.

"The Duke seeks a bride?"

A nod in the darkness.

"And heirs?"

Silence. Not ignorance — anger.

Devil watched their bastard brother move through the crowd within, headed for the far end of the ballroom, where a dark corridor stretched into the bowels of the house. It was his turn to nod. "We end it before it begins." He palmed his ebony walking stick, its silver lion's mane, worn from use, fitting perfectly into his hand. "In and out, and enough damage that he cannot follow us."

Whit nodded, but did not speak what they were both thinking — that the man London called Robert, Duke of Marwick, the boy they'd once known as Ewan, was more animal than aristocrat, and the only man who had ever come close to besting them. But that was before Devil and Whit had become the Bareknuckle Bastards, the Kings of Covent Garden, and learned to wield weapons with precision to match their threats.

Tonight, they would show him that London was their turf and return him to the country. It was only a matter of getting inside and doing just that — reminding him of that promise they'd made long ago.

The Duke of Marwick would beget no heirs.

"Good chase." Whit's words came on a low growl, his voice ragged from disuse.

"Good chase," Devil replied, and the two moved in expedient silence to the dark shadows of the long balcony, knowing they would have to act quickly to avoid being seen.

With fluid grace, Devil scaled the balcony, leaping over the balustrade, landing silently in the darkness beyond, Whit following. They made for the door, knowing that the conservatory would be locked and off-limits to guests, making it the perfect entry point to the house. The Bastards wore formalwear — preparing to blend into the crowd until they found the duke and dealt their blow.

Marwick would be neither the first nor the last aristocrat to receive a punishment from the Bareknuckle Bastards, but Devil and Whit had never wished to deliver one so well.

Devil's hand had barely landed on the door handle when it turned beneath his touch. He released it instantly, backing away, fading into the darkness even as Whit launched himself back over the balcony and onto the lawn below without sound.

And then the girl appeared.

She closed the door behind her with urgency, pressing her back to it, as though she could prevent others from following with nothing but sheer strength of will.

Strangely, Devil thought she might be able to do just that.

She was strung tight, her head against the door, long neck pale in the moonlight, chest heaving as a single, gloved hand came to rest on the shadowed skin above her gown, as though she could calm her ragged breath. Years of observation revealed her movements unpracticed and natural — she did not know she was being watched. She did not know she was not alone.

The fabric of her gown shimmered in the moonlight, but it was too dark to tell what color it was. Blue, perhaps. Green? The light turned it silver in places and black in others.

Moonlight. It looked as though she was cloaked in moonlight.

The strange observation came as she moved to the stone balustrade, and for a mad half-second, Devil considered stepping into the light to have a better look.

That is, until he heard the soft, low warble of a nightingale — Whit cautioning him. Reminding him of their plan, which the girl had nothing to do with. Except that she prevented it from being set in motion.

She didn't know the bird was no bird at all, and she turned her face to the sky, hands coming to rest on the stone railing as she

15

released a long breath, and with it, her guard. Her shoulders relaxed.

She'd been chased there.

A thread of something unpleasant wove through him at the idea that she'd fled into a dark room and out onto a darker balcony, where a man waited who might be worse than anything inside. And then, like a shot in the dark, she laughed. Devil stiffened, the muscles in his shoulders tensing, his grip tightening on the silver handle of his cane.

It took all his will not to approach her. To recall that he'd been lying in wait for this moment for years — so long he could barely remember a time when he wasn't prepared to do battle with his brother.

He was not going to allow a woman to knock him off course. He didn't even have a clear look at her, and still, he could not look away.

"Someone ought to tell them just how awful they are," she said to the sky. "Someone ought to march right up to Amanda Fairfax and tell her that no one believes her beauty mark is real. And someone ought to tell Lord Hagin that he stinks of perfume and would do well to take a bath.

"And I should dearly love to remind Jared of the time he landed himself backside-first in a pond at my mother's country house party and had to rely upon *my* kindness to get him to dry clothes without being seen."

She paused, just long enough for Devil to think that she was through speaking into the ether.

Instead, she blurted out, "And must Natasha be so *unpleasant*?"

"That's the best you can do?"

He shocked himself with the words — now was not the time to be talking to a solo chatterbox on the balcony.

He shocked Whit more, if the harsh nightingale's call that immediately followed was any indication.

But he shocked the girl the most.

With a little squeak of surprise, she whirled to face him, her hand coming to the expanse of skin above the line of her bodice. What color was that bodice? The moonlight continued to play tricks with it, making it impossible to see.

She tilted her head and squinted into the shadow. "Who's there?"

"You have me wondering just that, love, considering you're talking up a storm."

The squint became a scowl. "I was talking to myself."

"And neither of you can find a better insult for this Natasha than *unpleasant*?"

She took a step toward him, then seemed

to think twice of approaching a strange man in the darkness. She stopped. "How would you describe Natasha Corkwood?"

"I don't know her, so I wouldn't. But considering you were happy to lambast Hagin's hygiene and resurrect Faulk's past embarrassments, surely Lady Natasha deserves a similar level of creativity?"

She stared into the shadows for a long minute, her gaze fixed to a point somewhere beyond his left shoulder. "Who are you?"

"No one of consequence."

"As you are on a dark balcony outside an unoccupied room in the home of the Duke of Marwick, it seems you might be a man of quite serious consequence."

"By that rationale, you are a woman of serious consequence."

Her laugh came loud and unexpected, surprising them both. She shook her head. "Few would agree with you."

"I am rarely interested in others' opinions."

"Then you mustn't be a member of the *ton*," she replied dryly, "as others' opinions are like gold here. Exceedingly cared for."

Who was she?

"Why were you in the conservatory?"

She blinked. "How did you know it is a conservatory?"

18

"I make it my business to know things."

"About houses that do not belong to you?"

This house was almost mine, once. He resisted the words. "No one is using this room. Why were you?"

She lifted a shoulder. Let it drop.

It was his turn to scowl. "Are you meeting a man?"

Her eyes went wide. "I beg your pardon?"

"Dark balconies make for excellent trysting."

"I wouldn't know."

"About balconies? Or trysting?" Not that he cared.

"About either, honestly."

He should not have experienced satisfaction at the answer.

She continued, "Would you believe that I enjoy conservatories?"

"I would not," he said. "And besides, the conservatory is off-limits."

She tilted her head. "Is it?"

"Most people understand that dark rooms are off-limits."

She waved a hand. "I'm not very intelligent." He did not believe that, either. "I could ask you the same question, you know."

"Which?" He didn't like the way she wove the conversation around them, twisting it in her own direction.

"Are you here for a tryst?"

For a single, wild moment, a vision flashed of the tryst they might find here, on this dark balcony in the dead of summer. Of what she might allow him to do to her while half of London danced and gossiped just out of reach.

Of what he might allow her to do to him.

He imagined lifting her up onto the stone balustrade, discovering the feel of her skin, the scent of it. Uncovering the sounds she made in pleasure. Would she sigh? Would she cry out?

He froze. This woman, with her plain face and her unremarkable body, who talked to herself, was not the kind of woman Devil ordinarily imagined taking on walls. What was happening to him?

"I shall take your silence as a yes, then. And give you leave to tryst on, sir." She began to move away from him, down the balcony.

He should let her go.

Except he called out, "There is no tryst."

The nightingale again. Quicker and louder than before. Whit was annoyed.

"Then why are you here?" the woman asked.

"Perhaps for the same reason you are, love."

20

She smirked. "I have trouble believing you are an aging spinster who was driven into the darkness after being mocked by those you once called friends."

So. He'd been right. She had been chased. "I have to agree, none of that sounds quite like me."

She leaned back against the balustrade. "Come into the light."

"I'm afraid I can't do that."

"Why not?"

"Because I'm not supposed to be here."

She lifted a shoulder in a little shrug. "Neither am I."

"You're not supposed to be on the *balcony*. I'm not supposed to be on the *grounds*."

Her lips dropped open into a little O. "Who are you?"

He ignored the question. "Why are you a spinster?" Not that it mattered.

"I'm unmarried."

He resisted the urge to smile. "I deserved that."

"My father would tell you to be more specific with your questions."

"Who is your father?"

"Who is yours?"

She was not the least obstinate woman he'd ever met. "I don't have a father."

"Everyone has a father," she said.

"Not one they care to acknowledge," he said with a calm he did not feel. "So we return to the beginning. Why are you a spinster?"

"No one wishes to marry me."

"Why not?"

The honest answer came instantly. "I don't —" She stopped, spreading her hands wide, and he would have given his whole fortune to hear the rest, especially once she began anew, ticking reasons off her long, gloved fingers. "On the shelf."

She didn't seem old.

"Plain."

Plain had occurred to him, but she wasn't plain. Not really. In fact, she might be the opposite of plain.

"Uninteresting."

That was absolutely not true.

"I was tossed over by a duke."

Still not the whole truth. "And there's the rub?"

"Quite," she said. "Though it seems unfair, as the duke in question never intended to marry me in the first place."

"Why not?"

"He was wildly in love with his wife."

"Unfortunate, that."

She turned away from him, returning her

gaze to the sky. "Not for her."

Devil had never in his life wanted to approach another so much. But he remained in the shadows, pressing himself to the wall and watching her. "If you are unmarriageable for all those reasons, why waste your time here?"

She gave a little laugh, the sound low and lovely. "Don't you know, sir? Any unmarried woman's time is well spent near to unmarried gentlemen."

"Ah, so you haven't given up on a husband."

"Hope springs eternal," she said.

He nearly laughed at the dry words. Nearly. "And so?"

"It's difficult, as at this point, my mother has strict requirements for any suitor."

"For example?"

"A heartbeat."

He did laugh at that, a single, harsh bark, shocking the hell out of him. "With such high standards, it's unsurprising that you've had such trouble."

She grinned, teeth gleaming white in the moonlight. "It's a wonder that the Duke of Marwick hasn't fallen over himself to get to me, I know."

The reminder of his purpose that evening

was harsh and instant. "You're after Mar-wick."

Over my decaying corpse.

She waved a hand. "My mother is, as are all the rest of the mothers in London."

"They say he's mad," Devil pointed out.

"Only because they can't imagine why anyone would choose to live outside society."

Marwick lived outside society because he'd made a long-ago pact never to live within it. But Devil did not say that. Instead, he said, "They've barely had a look at him."

Her grin turned into a smirk. "They've seen his title, sir. And it is handsome as sin. A hermit duke still makes a duchess, after all."

"That's ridiculous."

"That's the marriage mart." She paused. "But it does not matter. I am not for him."

"Why not?" He didn't care.

"Because I am not for dukes."

Why the hell not?

He didn't speak the question, but she answered it nonetheless, casually, as though she were speaking to a roomful of ladies at tea. "There was a time when I thought I might be," she offered, more to herself than to him. "And then . . ." She shrugged her shoulders. "I don't know what happened. I suppose all those other things. Plain, uninteresting, aging, wallflower, spinster." She laughed at the list of words. "I suppose I should not have dallied, thinking I'd find myself a husband, as it did not happen."

"And now?"

"And now," she said, resignation in her tone, "my mother seeks a strong pulse."

"What do you seek?"

Whit's nightingale cooed in the darkness, and she replied on the heels of the sound. "No one has ever asked me that."

"And so," he prodded, knowing he shouldn't. Knowing he should leave this girl to this balcony and whatever future she was to have.

"I —" She looked toward the house, toward the dark conservatory and the hallway beyond, and the glittering ballroom beyond that. "I wish to be a part of it all again."

"Again?"

"There was a time I —" she began, then stopped. Shook her head. "It doesn't matter. You've far more important things to do."

"I do, but as I can't do them while you're here, my lady, I'm more than willing to help you sort this out."

She smiled at that. "You're amusing."

"No one in my whole life would agree

25

with you."

Her smile grew. "I am rarely interested in others' opinions."

He did not miss the echo of his own words from earlier. "I don't believe that for a second."

She waved a hand. "There was a time when I was a part of it. Right at the center of it all. I was incredibly popular. Everyone wished to know me."

"And what happened?"

She spread her hands wide again, a movement that was beginning to be familiar. "I don't know."

He raised a brow. "You don't know what made you a wallflower?"

"I don't," she said softly, confusion and sadness in her tone. "I wasn't even near the walls. And then, one day" — she shrugged — "there I was. Ivy. And so, when you ask me what I seek?"

She was lonely. Devil knew about lonely. "You want back in."

She gave a little, hopeless laugh. "No one gets back in. Not without a match for the ages."

He nodded. "The duke."

"A mother can dream."

"And you?"

"I want back in." Another warning

sounded from Whit, and the woman looked over her shoulder. "That's a very persistent nightingale."

"He's irritated."

She tilted her head in curiosity, but when he did not clarify, she added, "Are you going to tell me who you are?"

"No."

She nodded once. "That is best, I suppose, as I only came outside to find a quiet moment away from supercilious smirks and snide comments." She pointed down the line of the balcony, toward the lighter stretch of it. "I shall go over there and find a proper hiding place, and you can resume your skulking, if you like."

He did not reply, not certain of what he would say. Not trusting himself to say what he should.

"I shan't tell anyone I saw you," she added.

"You haven't seen me," he said.

"Then it shall have the additional benefit of being the truth," she added, helpfully.

The nightingale again. Whit didn't trust him with this woman.

And perhaps he shouldn't.

She dipped into a little curtsy. "Well, off to your nefarious deeds then?"

The pull of the muscles around his lips

was unfamiliar. A smile. He couldn't remember the last time he'd smiled. This strange woman had summoned it, like a sorceress.

She was gone before he could reply, her skirts disappeared around the corner, into the light. It took everything he had not to follow her. To catch a glimpse of her — the color of her hair, the shade of her skin, the flash of her eyes.

He still didn't know the color of her gown.

All he had to do was follow her.

"Dev."

His name returned him to the present. He looked to Whit, once more over the balcony and at his side in the shadows.

"Now," Whit said. It was time to return to their plan. To the man he'd vowed to end should he ever set foot in London. Should he ever attempt to claim that which he had once stolen. Should he ever even think of breaking that decades-old vow.

And he would end him. But it would not be with fists.

"We go, bruv," Whit whispered. "Now."

Devil shook his head once, gaze fixed to the place where the woman's mysterious skirts had disappeared. "No. Not yet."

CHAPTER TWO

Felicity Faircloth's heart had been pounding for long enough that she thought she might require a doctor.

It had begun pounding as she'd slipped from the glittering Marwick House ballroom and stared at the locked door in front of her, ignoring the nearly unbearable desire to reach into her coif and extract a hairpin.

Knowing she absolutely mustn't extract a hairpin. Knowing she absolutely shouldn't extract two — nor insert them into the keyhole not six inches away and patiently work at the tumblers within.

We cannot afford another scandal.

She could hear her twin brother Arthur's words as though he were standing with her. Poor Arthur, desperate for his spinster sister — twenty-seven and high on the shelf — to be released into the care of another, more willing man. Poor Arthur, whose prayers would never be answered — not even if she

29

stopped picking locks.

But she heard the other words even more. The sniggering comments. The names. *Forlorn Felicity. Fruitless Felicity.* And the worst one . . . *Finished Felicity.*

Why is she even here?
  Surely she can't think anyone would have her.
Her poor brother, desperate to marry her off.
  . . . Finished Felicity.

There had been a time when a night like this would have been Felicity's dream — a new duke in town, a welcome ball, the teasing promise of an engagement at hand with a new, handsome, eligible bachelor. It would have been perfection. Dresses and jewels and full orchestras, gossip and chatter and dance cards and champagne. Felicity would barely have had free space on her dance card, and if she had, it would have been because she'd taken it for herself, so she might enjoy her place in this glittering world.

No more.

Now, she avoided balls if she could, knowing they offered hours of lingering around the edges of the room rather than dancing through it. And there was the hot embarrassment that came whenever she stumbled upon one of her old acquaintances. The memory of what it had been like to laugh with them. To lord with them.

But there was no avoiding a ball bearing a shining new duke, and so she'd stuffed herself into an old gown and into her brother's carriage, and allowed poor Arthur to drag her into the Marwick ballroom. And she'd fled the moment he had turned the other way.

Felicity had fled down a dark hallway, her heart thundering as she'd removed the hairpins from her coif, bending them carefully, and inserted one and then the other into the keyhole. When a quiet *snick* sounded, and the latchwork sprang like a delicious old friend, her heart had threatened to beat from her chest.

And to think, all that thunderous pounding was before she'd met the man.

Though, *met* wasn't precisely the correct word.

Encountered did not seem quite right, either.

It had been something closer to *experienced*. The moment he'd spoken, the low thrum of his voice wrapping around her like silk in the dark spring air as he tempted her like vice.

A flush washed across her cheeks at the memory, at the way he seemed to draw her in, as though they were connected by a string. As though he could pull her to him and she would go, without resistance. He'd done more than pull her in. He'd pulled the truth from her, and she'd offered it with ease.

She'd catalogued her flaws as though they were a change in the weather. She'd nearly confessed it all, even the bits she'd never confessed to anyone else. The bits she held close in the darkness. Because it hadn't felt like confession. It felt like he'd already known everything. And maybe he had. Maybe he wasn't a man in the darkness. Maybe he was the darkness itself. Ephemeral and mysterious and tempting — so much more tempting than the daylight, where flaws and marks and failure shone bright and impossible to miss.

The darkness had always tempted her. The locks. The barriers. The impossible.

That was the problem, wasn't it? Felicity always wanted the impossible. And she was not the kind of woman who received it.

But when that mysterious man had suggested that she was a woman of consequence? For a moment, she'd believed him.

As though it wasn't laughable, the very idea that Felicity Faircloth — plain, unmarried daughter of the Marquess of Bumble, over-looked by more than one eligible bachelor because of her own ill fortune and properly unfit for this ball, where a long-lost hand-some duke sought a wife — might be able to win the day.

The impossible.

So she'd fled, returning to her old habits and stumbling into the darkness because everything seemed more possible in the darkness than in the cold, harsh light.

And he'd seemed to know that, too, that stranger. Enough that she almost hadn't left him in the shadows. Enough that she'd almost joined him there. Because in those few, fleeting moments, she had wondered if perhaps it wasn't this world she wished to return to, but a new, dark world where she might begin anew. Where she might be someone other than Finished Felicity, wallflower spinster. And the man on the balcony had seemed the kind of man who could provide just that.

Which was mad, obviously. One did not run off with strange men one met on balco-nies. First off, that was how a person got murdered. And second, her mother would *not* approve. And then there was Arthur.

Staid, perfect, poor Arthur with his *We cannot afford another scandal.*

And so she'd done what one did after a mad moment in the dark; she'd turned her back and made for the light, ignoring the pang of regret as she turned the corner of the great stone facade and stepped into the glow of the ballroom beyond the massive windows, where all of London shifted and swirled, laughing and gossiping and vying for the attention of their handsome, mysterious host.

Where the world she'd once been part of spun without her.

She watched for a long moment, catching a glimpse of the Duke of Marwick on the far side of the room, tall and fair and empirically handsome, with aristocratic good looks that should have set her to sighing but in fact made no impact.

Her gaze slid away from the man of the hour, settling briefly on the copper gleam of her brother's hair on the far side of the ballroom, where he was deep in conversation with a group of men more serious than their surroundings. She wondered what they were discussing — was it her? Was Arthur attempting to sell another batch of men on Finished Felicity's eligibility?

We cannot afford another scandal.

34

They couldn't afford the last one, either. Or the one prior. But her family did not wish to admit that. And here they were, at a duke's ball, pretending that the truth was not the truth. Pretending that anything was possible.

Refusing to believe that plain, imperfect, tossed-over Felicity was never going to win the heart and mind and — more importantly — the *hand* of the Duke of Marwick, no matter what kind of potentially addled hermit he was.

There had been a time when she might have, though. When a hermit duke might have collapsed to his knees and begged Lady Felicity to notice him. Well, perhaps not *so* much collapsing and begging, but he would have danced with her. And she would have made him laugh. And perhaps . . . they might have liked each other.

But that was all when she'd never even dreamed of looking at society from the outside — when she'd never even imagined society *had* an outside. She'd been inside, after all, young and eligible and titled and diverting.

She'd had dozens of friends and hundreds of acquaintances and invitations for visits and house parties and walks along the Serpentine in spades. No gathering was worth attending if she and her friends weren't in attendance. She'd never been lonely.

And then . . . it had changed.

One day, the world had stopped glittering. Or, more aptly, *Felicity* had stopped glittering. Her friends faded away, and worse, turned their backs, not even attempting to shield her from their disdain. They'd taken pleasure in cutting her directly. As though she hadn't once been one of them. As though they'd never been friends in the first place.

Which she supposed they hadn't. How had she missed it? How had she not seen that they never really wanted her?

And the worst of all questions — *why* hadn't they wanted her?

What had she done?

Foolish Felicity, indeed.

The answer did not matter anymore — it had been long enough that she doubted anyone even remembered. What mattered was that now barely anyone noticed her, except to look upon her with pity or disdain.

After all, no one liked a spinster less than the world that made her.

Felicity, once a diamond of the aristocracy (well, not a diamond, but a ruby perhaps. A sapphire, surely — daughter of a marquess with a dowry to match), was a proper spinster, complete with a future of lace caps and invitations offered out of pity to look forward to.

If only she'd marry, Arthur liked to say . . . she could avoid it.

If only she'd marry, her mother liked to say . . . *they* could avoid it. For as embarrassing as spinsterhood was for the spinster in question, it was a badge of shame for a mother — especially one who had done so well as to marry a marquess.

And so, the Faircloth family ignored Felicity's spinsterhood, willing to do anything to land her a decent match. They ignored, too, the truth of Felicity's desires — the ones the man in the darkness had instantly queried.

The truth. That she wanted the life she'd been promised. She wanted to be a part of it again. And if she couldn't have that, which, frankly, she knew she couldn't — she was not a fool, after all — she wanted more than a consolation of a marriage. That was the problem with Felicity. She'd always wanted more than she could have.

Which had left her with nothing, hadn't it?

Felicity heaved an unladylike sigh. Her heart wasn't pounding any longer. She supposed that was positive.

"I wonder if I might leave without anyone noticing?"

The words were barely out of her mouth when the massive glass door leading into the ballroom opened, and out spilled half a dozen revelers, laughter on their lips and champagne in their hands.

It was Felicity's turn to press into the shadows, tucking herself against the wall as they reached the stone balustrade in breathless, raucous excitement. Recognition flared.

Of course.

They were Amanda Fairfax and her husband, Matthew, Lord Hagin, along with Jared, Lord Faulk, and his younger sister, Natasha, and two more — another couple, young and blond and gleaming like new toys. Amanda, Matthew, Jared, and Natasha liked to collect new acolytes. They'd once collected Felicity, after all.

She'd once been the fifth to their quartet. Beloved, until she wasn't.

"Hermit or not, Marwick is terribly handsome," Amanda said.

"And rich," Jared pointed out. "I heard he filled this house with furnishings last week."

"I heard the same," Amanda said with near-breathless excitement. "And I heard he's doing the rounds of the doyennes' tea-rooms."

Matthew groaned. "If that doesn't make the man suspect, I don't know what does. Who wants to drink tea with a score of dowagers?"

"A man in need of a bride," Jared replied.

"Or an heir," Amanda said, wistfully.

"Ahem, wife," Matthew teased, and the whole group laughed, making Felicity remember for half a second what it was to be welcome in their jokes and jests and gossip. A part of their glittering world.

"He had to meet the dowagers to get London here tonight, no?" the third woman in the party interjected. "Without their approval, no one would have come."

There was a beat of silence, and then the original foursome laughed, the sound edging from camaraderie into cruelty. Faulk leaned forward and tapped the young blond woman on her chin. "You're not very intelligent, are you?"

Natasha swatted her brother on the arm and offered a false, scolding, "Jared. Come now. How is Annabelle to know how the aristocracy works? She married so far above herself, the lucky girl never required it!" Before Annabelle could experience the full lash of the stinging words, Natasha leaned in and whispered, loud and slow as though the poor woman were unable to understand the simplest of concepts, "Everyone would have come to see the hermit duke, darling. He could have appeared in the nude and we all would have happily danced with him and pretended not to notice."

"With how mad everyone's made the man out to be," Amanda interjected, "I think we were all half-expecting him to appear nude."

Annabelle's husband, the heir to the Marquessate of Wapping, cleared his throat and attempted to bypass the insult to his wife. "Well, he's danced with a score of ladies already this evening." He looked to Natasha. "Including you, Lady Natasha."

The rest of the group tittered while Natasha preened — all, that is, but Annabelle, who narrowed her gaze on her laughing husband. Felicity found the response deeply gratifying, as the husband in question surely deserved whatever wicked punishment his wife was devising for not leaping to her defense.

And now it was too late.

"Oh, yes," Natasha was saying, looking every inch the cat that got the cream. "And I might add that he was a sparkling conversationalist."

"Was he?" Amanda asked.

"He was. Not a glimpse of madness."

"That's interesting, Tasha," Lord Hagin replied casually, drinking his champagne for dramatic pause. "As we watched the whole dance, and he didn't appear to speak to you once."

The rest of the group jeered as Natasha turned red. "Well, it was clear he *wished* to talk to me."

"Sparkling, of course," her brother jested, toasting her with his champagne.

"And," she went on, "he held me quite tightly — I could tell he was resisting the urge to pull me closer than was appropriate."

"Oh, no doubt," Amanda smirked, her disbelief plain.

She rolled her eyes as the rest of the group laughed. That is, the rest of the group, save one.

Jared, Lord Faulk, was too busy looking at Felicity.

Bollocks.

His gaze filled with hunger and delight in a way that sent Felicity's stomach straight to the stones beneath her feet. She'd seen that expression a thousand times before. She used to go breathless when it appeared, because it meant he was about to skewer someone with his wicked wit. Now, she went breathless for a different reason.

"I say! I thought Felicity Faircloth left the ball ages ago."

"I thought we drove her out," Amanda said, not seeing what Jared saw. "Honestly. At her age — and with no friends to speak of — you'd think she'd stop attending balls. No one wants a spinster lurking about. It's positively depressing."

Amanda had always had a remarkable skill at making words sting like winter wind.

"And yet, here she is," Jared pronounced with a smirk and a waved hand in Felicity's direction. The whole group turned in slow, gruesome tableau, a sextet of smirks rising — four well-practiced and two with a slight discomfort. "Lurking in the shadows, eavesdropping."

Amanda investigated a speck on one of her seafoam gloves. "*Really,* Felicity. So *tiresome.* Is there no one else you might skulk upon?"

"Perhaps an unsuspecting lord whose rooms you'd like to explore?" This from Hagin, no doubt thinking himself exceedingly clever.

He wasn't, although the group did not seem to notice, sniggering and smirking. Felicity loathed the wash of heat that spread across her cheeks, a combination of shame at the remark and shame at her past — at the way she, too, used to snigger and smirk.

She pressed back against the wall, wishing she could disappear into it.

The nightingale she'd heard earlier sang again.

"Poor Felicity," Natasha said to the group, the false sympathy in her tone crawling over Felicity's skin, "always wishing she were of more consequence."

And like that, with that single word — *consequence* — Felicity found she had had enough. She stepped into the light, shoulders back and spine straight, and leveled her coolest gaze on the woman she'd once considered a friend. "Poor Natasha," she said, mimicking the other woman's earlier tone. "Come now, you think I do not know you? I know you better than anyone else here. Unmarried, just as I am. *Plain,* just as I am. Terrified of being shelved. As I have been." Natasha's eyes went wide at the descriptor. Felicity went in for the final blow, wishing to punish this woman the most — this woman who had played so well at being her friend and then had hurt her so well. "And when you are, this lot won't have you."

The nightingale whistled again. No. Not the nightingale. It was a different kind of whistle, low and long. She'd never heard a bird like that.

Or perhaps it was the thrum of her heart that made the sound strange. Spurred on, she turned to the newest additions to the group, whose wide eyes were fixed upon her. "Do you know, my grandmother used to caution me to beware — she was fond of saying one could judge a man by his friends. The adage is more than true with this group. And you should watch yourselves lest you be tainted by their soot." She turned to the door. "I, for one, count myself lucky I escaped them when I did."

As she made for the entrance to the ballroom, quite proud of herself for standing up to these people who had consumed her for so long, words echoed through her from earlier:

You are a woman of serious consequence.

A smile played at her lips at the memory.

Indeed. She was.

"Felicity?" Natasha called to her as she arrived at the threshold.

Felicity stilled and turned back.

"You didn't escape us," the other woman snapped. "We *exited* you."

Natasha Corkwood was just . . . so . . . unpleasant.

"We didn't want you anymore, and we

tossed you out," Natasha added, the words cold and cruel. "Just like everyone else has. Just like they always will." She turned to the assembly with a too bright laugh. "And here she is, thinking she might vie for a duke!"

So unpleasant.

That's the best you can do?

No. No it wasn't. "The duke *you* intend to win, correct?"

Natasha smirked. "The duke I *shall* win."

"I'm afraid you are too late," she said, the words coming without hesitation.

"And why is that?" It was Hagin who asked. Hagin, with his smug face and noxious perfume and hair like a fairy-tale prince. And the question was asked with such condescension, as though he deigned to speak with her.

As though they had not all been friends once.

Later, she would blame the memory of that friendship for her reply. The whisper of the life she'd lost in an instant, without ever understanding why. The devastating sadness of it. The way it had catapulted her into ruin.

After all, there had to be some reason why she said what she said, considering the fact that it was pure idiocy. Absolute madness.

A lie so enormous, it eclipsed suns.

"You are too late for the duke," she repeated, knowing, even as she spoke, that she must stop the words from coming. Except they were a runaway horse — loosed and free and *wild.* "Because I've already landed him."

CHAPTER THREE

The last time Devil had been inside Marwick House was the night he met his father.

He'd been ten years old, too old to remain at the orphanage where he'd spent his entire life. Devil had heard rumors of what came of boys who aged out of the orphanage. He had been preparing to run, not wanting to face the workhouse where, if the stories were to be believed, he was likely to die, and no one would find his body.

Devil had believed the stories.

Each night, knowing it was a matter of time before they came for him, he'd carefully packed his belongings — a pair of too big stockings he'd nicked from the laundry. A crust of bread or hard biscuit saved from afternoon meal. A pair of mittens worn by too many boys to count, too filled with holes to keep hands warm any longer. And the small gilded pin that had been stuck to his swaddle when he'd been found as a babe, run through with a piece of embroidery, on which was a magnificent red M. The pin had long-ago lost its paint, turning back into rass, and the cloth that had once been white had turned rey with dirt from his fingers. But it was all Devil had owned of his past, and the only source of hope he'd had for his future.

Each night, he would lie in the pitch black, listening to the sounds of the other boys' tears, counting the steps to get from his pallet to the hallway, down the hallway to the door. Out the door, and into the night. He was an excellent climber, and he'd decided to take to the rooftops instead of the streets — they'd have been less likely to find him if they gave chase.

Though it had seemed unlikely anyone would chase him.

It had seemed unlikely anyone would want him.

He heard the footsteps ring out down the hall. They were coming for him, to take him to the workhouse. He rolled off the side of his pallet, crouching low and collecting his things, moving to stand flat at the wall beside the door.

The lock clicked and the door opened, revealing a thread of candlelight — never seen in the orphanage after dark. He made a run for it, weaving through two sets of legs, getting halfway down the hall before a strong hand landed on his shoulder and lifted him clean off the ground.

He kicked and screamed, craning to bite the offending hand.

"Good God. This one is feral," a deep baritone voice said, and Devil went perfectly still at the sound of it. He'd never heard anyone speak such perfect, measured English. He stopped trying to bite, instead turning to look at the man who held him — tall as a tree and cleaner than anyone Devil had ever seen, with eyes the color of the floorboards of the room where they were supposed to pray.

Devil wasn't very good at praying.

Someone lifted the candle to Devil's face, the bright flame making him flinch away. "That's him." The dean.

Devil turned to face his captor once more. "I ain't goin' to the workhouse."

"Of course you're not," the strange man had said. He reached for Devil's pack, opening it.

"Oi! Them's my things!"

The man ignored him, tossing the socks and biscuit to the side, lifting the pin and turning it to the light. Devil raged at the idea of this man, this stranger, touching the only thing he had of his mother. The only thing he had of his past. His small hands curled into fists, and he

49

took a swing, connecting with the fancy man's hip. " 'At's mine! You can't have it!"

The man hissed in pain. "Christ. The demon can throw a punch."

The dean minced. "He didn't learn that from us."

Devil scowled. Where else would he have learned it? "Give it back."

The well-dressed man summoned him closer, waving Devil's treasure in the air. "Your mother gave this to you."

Devil reached out and snatched it from the man's hand, hating the embarrassment that came at the words. Embarrassment and longing. "Yeah."

A nod. "I've been looking for you."

Hope flared, hot and almost unpleasant in Devil's chest.

The man continued. "Do you know what a duke is?"

"No, sir."

"You will," he promised.

Memories were a bitch.

Devil crept down the long upper hallway of Marwick House, the strains of the orchestra whispering through the dimly lit space from the floor below. He hadn't thought of the night his father had found him in a decade. Maybe longer.

But tonight, being in this house, which

50

somehow still smelled the same, he remembered every bit of that first night. The bath, the warm food, the soft bed. Like he'd fallen asleep and woken up in a dream.

And that night, it had been a dream.

The nightmare had begun soon after.

Putting the memory from his mind, he arrived at the master bedchamber, setting his hand to the door handle, turning it quickly and silently, and stepping inside.

His brother stood at the window, tumbler dangling in his hand, hair gleaming blond in the candlelight. Ewan did not turn to face Devil. Instead, he said, "I wondered if you would come tonight."

The voice was the same. Cultured and measured and deep, like their father. "You sound like the duke."

"I am the duke."

Devil let the door close behind him. "That's not what I meant."

"I know what you meant."

Devil tapped his walking stick twice on the floor. "Did we not make a pact all those years ago?"

Marwick turned to reveal the side of his face. "I've been looking for you for twelve years."

Devil sank into the low armchair by the fire, extending his legs toward the place

51

where the duke stood. "If only I'd known."

"I think you did."

Of course they had known. The moment they'd come of age, a stream of men had come sniffing around the rookery, asking about a trio of orphans who might have found their way to London years earlier. Two boys and a girl, with names no one in Covent Garden recognized . . . no one but the Bastards themselves.

No one but the Bastards and Ewan, the young Duke of Marwick, rich as a king and old enough to put the money to good use.

But eight years in the rookery had made Devil and Whit as powerful as they were cunning, as strong as they were forbidding, and no one talked about the Bareknuckle Bastards for fear of retribution. Especially to outsiders.

And with the trail gone cold, the men who came sniffing always dropped the scent and left.

This time, however, it was not an employee who came for them. It was Marwick himself. And with a better plan than ever.

"I assume you thought that by announcing your hunt for a wife, you'd get our attention," Devil said.

Marwick turned. "It worked."

"No heirs, Ewan," Devil said, unable to

use the name of the dukedom to his face. "That was the deal. Do you remember the last time you reneged on a deal with me?"

The duke's eyes went dark. "Yes."

That night, Devil had taken everything the duke had loved, and run. "And what makes you think I won't do it again?"

"Because this time I am a duke," Ewan said. "And my power extends far beyond Covent Garden, no matter how heavy your fists are these days, Devon. I will bring hell down upon you. And not just you. Our brother. Your men. Your business. You lose everything."

It would be worth it. Devil's gaze narrowed on his brother. "What do you want?"

"I told you I would come for her."

Grace. The fourth of their band, the woman Whit and Devil called sister, though no blood was shared between them. The girl Ewan had loved even then, when they were children.

Grace, who three brothers had vowed to protect all those years ago, when they were young and innocent, and before betrayal had broken their bond.

Grace, who, in Ewan's betrayal, had become the dukedom's most dangerous secret. For it was Grace who was the truth of the dukedom. Grace, born to the former duke and his wife, the duchess. Grace, baptized their child despite being illegitimate in her own way.

But it was Ewan now, years later, who bore that baptismal name. Who held the title that belonged to none of them by rights.

And Grace, the living, breathing proof that Ewan had thieved the title, the fortune, the future — a theft which the Crown did not take lightly.

A theft which, if discovered, would see Ewan dancing at the end of a rope outside Newgate.

Devil narrowed his gaze on his brother. "You'll never find her."

Ewan's eyes darkened. "I shan't hurt her."

"You are as mad as your precious aristocracy says if you think we'll believe that. Do you not remember the night we left? I do, every time I look in the mirror."

Marwick's gaze flickered to Devil's cheek, to the wicked scar there, the powerful reminder of how little brotherhood had meant when it came to claiming power. "I had no choice."

"We all had a choice that night. You chose your title, your money, and your power. And we allowed you all three, despite Whit wanting to snuff you out before the rot of our sire could consume you. We let you live, despite your clear willingness to see us dead. On one condition — our father was mad for an heir, and though he might get a false one in you, he would not receive the satisfaction of a line of them — not even in death. We will always be on opposite sides in this fight, Duke. No heirs was the rule. The only rule. We left you alone all these years with your ill-gotten title because of it. But know this — if you decide to flout it, I will tear you apart, and you will never find an ounce of happiness in this life."

"You think I am riddled with happiness now?"

Christ, Devil hoped not. He hoped that there was nothing that made the duke happy. He'd reveled in his brother's legendary hermitage, knowing that Ewan lived in the house where they'd been pitted against each other, bastard sons in a battle for legitimacy. For name and title and fortune. Taught to dance and dine and speak with eloquence that belied the shame into which the three of them had been born.

He hoped every memory of their youth consumed his brother, and he was consumed with regret for allowing himself to play the doting son to a fucking monster.

Still, Devil lied. "I don't care."

"I have searched for you for more than a

decade, and now I've found you. The Bare-knuckle Bastards, rich and ruthless, running God knows what kind of crime ring in the heart of Covent Garden — the place that birthed *me,* I might add."

"It spat you out the moment you betrayed it. And us," Devil said.

"I've asked a hundred questions a thousand different ways." Ewan turned away, running a wild hand through his blond hair. "No women. No wives. No sisters to speak of. Where is she?"

There was panic in the words, a vague sense that he might go mad if he did not receive an answer. Devil had lived in the darkness long enough to understand madmen and their obsessions. He shook his head, sending a word of thanks to the gods for making the people of the Garden loyal to them. "Ever beyond your reach."

"You took her from me!" Panic edged into rage.

"We took her from the title," Devil said. "The one that sickened your father."

"Your father, as well."

Devil ignored the correction. "The title that sickened you. The one that had you ready to kill her."

The duke looked to the ceiling for a long minute. Then, "I should have killed *you.*"

"She would have escaped."

"I should kill you now."

"You'll never find her, then."

A familiar jaw — an echo of their father's — clenched. Eyes went wild, then blank. "Then understand, Devil, I have no interest in keeping my end of the deal. I shall have heirs. I'm a duke. I shall have a wife and child within a year. I shall renege on our deal, unless you tell me where she is."

Devil's own rage flared, his grip tightening on the silver head of his walking stick. He should kill his brother now. Leave him bleeding out on the fucking floor, and finally give the Marwick line its due.

He tapped the end of his stick on the toe of his black boot. "You would do well to remember that with the information I have about you, *Duke*. A word of it would have you hanged."

"Why not use it?" The question was not combative, as Devil would have expected it. It was something like pained, as though Ewan would greet death. As though he would summon it.

Devil ignored the realization. "Because toying with you is more diverting."

It was a lie. Devil would have happily destroyed this man, his once brother. But all those years ago, when he and Whit had escaped the Marwick estate and made for London and its terrifying future, vowing to keep Grace safe, they'd made another vow, this one to Grace herself.

They would not kill Ewan.

"Yes, I think I shall play your silly game," Devil said, standing and tapping his walking stick on the floor twice. "You underestimate the power of the bastard son, brother. Ladies love a man willing to take them for a walk in the darkness. I'll happily ruin your future brides. One after another, until the end of time. Without hesitation. You never get an heir." He approached his brother, coming eye to eye with him. "I took Grace right out from under you," he whispered. "You think I cannot take all the others?"

Ewan's jaw went heavy with passionate rage. "You will regret keeping her from me."

"No one keeps Grace from anything. She chose to be rid of you. She chose to run. She didn't trust you to keep her safe. Not when she was proof of your darkest secret." He paused. "Robert Matthew Carrick."

The duke's gaze blurred at the name, and Devil wondered if perhaps the rumors were true. If Ewan was, indeed, mad.

It would not be a surprise, with the past that haunted him. That haunted them all.

But Devil didn't care, and he continued. "She chose us, Ewan. And I shall make certain that every woman you ever court does the same. I shall ruin every one of them, with pleasure. And in doing so, I shall save them from your mad desire for power."

"You think you haven't the same desire? You think you did not inherit it from our father? They call you the Kings of Covent Garden — power and money and sin surround you."

Devil smirked. "Every bit of it earned, Ewan."

"Stolen, I think you mean."

"You would know a thing or two about stolen futures. About stolen names. Robert Matthew Carrick, Duke of Marwick. A pretty name for a boy born in a Covent Garden brothel."

The duke's brow lowered, his eyes turning dark with clarity. "Then let it begin, brother, as it seems I have already been gifted a fiancée. Lady Felicia Fairhaven or Fiona Farthing or some other version of a stupid name."

Felicity Faircloth.

That's what the horses' asses on the balcony had called her before they'd shred her to bits, forced her hand, and inspired her to claim a ducal fiancé in a fit of outrageous cheek. Devil had watched the disaster unfold, unable to stop her from embroiling herself in his brother's affairs. In his affairs.

"If you think to convince me you aren't in the market for hurting women, bringing an innocent girl into this is not the way to do it."

Ewan's gaze found his instantly, and Devil regretted the words. What Ewan seemed to think they hinted at. "I shan't hurt her," Ewan said. "I'm going to marry her."

The unpleasant pronouncement grated, but Devil did his best to ignore the sensation. Felicity Faircloth of the silly name was most definitely embroiled now. Which meant he had no choice but to engage her.

Ewan pressed on. "Her family seems quite desperate for a duke — so desperate that the lady herself simply pronounced us engaged this evening. And to my knowledge, we've never even met. She's clearly a simpleton, but I don't care. Heirs are heirs."

She wasn't a simpleton. She was fascinating. Smart-mouthed and curious and more comfortable in the darkness than he would have imagined. And with a smile that made a man pay attention.

It was a pity he'd have to ruin her.

"I shall find the girl's family and offer them fortune, title, all of it. Whatever it takes. Banns shall post Sunday," Marwick said, calmly, as though he was discussing the weather, "and they will see us married within the month. Heirs soon on the way."

No one gets back in. Not without a match for the ages.

Felicity's words from earlier echoed through Devil. The woman would be thrilled with this turn of events. Marriage to Marwick got her what she wanted. A heroine's return to the aristocracy.

Except she wouldn't return.

Because Devil would never allow it, beautiful smile or no. Though the smile might make her ruination all the better.

Devil's brows lowered. "You get heirs on Felicity Faircloth over my rotting corpse."

"You think she will choose Covent Garden over Mayfair?"

I want back in.

Mayfair was everything Felicity Faircloth wanted. He'd simply have to show her what else there was to see. In the meantime, he threw his sharpest knife. "I think she is not the first woman to risk with me rather than spend a lifetime with you, Ewan."

It struck true.

The duke looked away, back out the window. "Get out."

CHAPTER FOUR

Felicity sailed through the open door of her ancestral home, ignoring the fact that her brother was at her heels. She paused to force a smile at the butler, still holding the door. "Good evening, Irving."

"Good evening, my lady," the butler intoned, closing the door behind Arthur and reaching for the earl's gloves. "My lord."

Arthur shook his head. "I'm not staying, Irving. I'm only here to have words with my sister."

Felicity turned to meet the brown gaze identical to her own. "Now you'd like to speak? We rode home in silence."

"I wouldn't call it silence."

"Oh, no?"

"No. I'd call it speechlessness."

She scoffed, yanking at her gloves, using the movement to avoid her brother's eyes and the hot guilt that thrummed through her at the idea of discussing the disastrous evening that had unfolded.

"Good God, Felicity, I'm not sure there's a brother in Christendom who would be able to find words in the wake of your audacity."

"Oh, please. I told a tiny lie." She made for the staircase, waving a hand through the air and trying to sound as though she weren't as horrified as she was. "Plenty of people have done far more outrageous things. It's not as though I took up work in a bordello."

Arthur's eyes bugged from their sockets. "A *tiny* lie?" Before she could reply he added, "And you shouldn't even know the word bordello."

She looked back, the two steps she'd already taken putting her above her twin. "Really?"

"Really."

"I suppose you think that it isn't proper, me knowing the word bordello."

"I don't think. I know. And stop saying bordello."

"Am I making you uncomfortable?"

Her brother narrowed his brown gaze on hers. "No, but I can see you wish to. And I don't want you to offend Irving."

The butler's brows rose.

Felicity turned to him. "Am I offending

you, Irving?"

"No more than usual, my lady," the older man said, all seriousness.

Felicity gave a little chuckle as he took his leave.

"I'm happy one of us is still able to find levity in our situation." Arthur looked to the great chandelier above and said, "Good God, Felicity."

And they were returned to where they'd begun, guilt and panic and not a small amount of fear coursing through her. "I didn't mean to say it."

Her brother shot her a look. "Bordello?"

"Oh, now it's you who are jesting?"

He spread his hands wide. "I don't know what else to do." He stopped, then thought of more to say. The obvious thing. "How could you possibly think —"

"I know," she interrupted.

"No, I don't think you do. What you've done is —"

"I *know,*" she insisted.

"Felicity. You told the world that you're marrying the Duke of Marwick."

She was feeling rather queasy. "It wasn't the world."

"No, just six of the biggest gossips in it. None of whom like you, I might add, so it's not as though we can silence them." The

64

reminder of their distaste for her was not helping her roiling innards. Arthur was pressing on, however, oblivious. "Not that it matters. You might as well have shouted it from the orchestra's platform for the speed with which it tore through that ballroom. I had to hie out of there before Marwick sought me out and confronted me with it. Or, worse, before he stood up in front of all assembled and called you a liar."

It had been a terrible mistake. She *knew*. But they'd made her so *angry*. And they'd been so cruel. And she'd felt so *alone*. "I didn't mean to —"

Arthur sighed, long and heavy with an unseen burden. "You never mean to."

The words were soft, spoken almost at a whisper, as though Felicity weren't supposed to hear them. Or as though she weren't there. But she was, of course. She might always be. "Arthur —"

"You didn't mean to get yourself caught in a man's bedchamber —"

"I didn't even know it *was* his bedchamber." It had been a locked door. Abovestairs at a ball that had broken her heart. Of course, Arthur would never understand that. In his mind it was brainless. And perhaps it had been.

He was on to something else now. "You

didn't mean to turn down three perfectly fine offers in the ensuing months."

Her spine straightened. Those she *had* meant. "They were perfectly fine offers if you liked the aging or the dull-witted."

"They were men who wanted to marry you, Felicity."

"No, they were men who wanted to marry my dowry. They wanted to be in business with *you,*" she pointed out. Arthur was a great business mind and could turn goose feathers into gold. "One of them even told me that I could remain living here if I liked."

Her brother's cheeks were going ruddy. "And what would have been wrong with that?!"

She blinked. "With living apart from my husband in a loveless marriage?"

"Please," he scoffed, "now we are at love? You might as well carry yourself up to the damn shelf."

She narrowed her gaze on him. "Why? You have love."

Arthur exhaled harshly. "That's different."

Several years ago, Arthur had married Lady Prudence Featherstone in a renowned love match. Pru was the girl who'd lived on the dilapidated estate next door to the country seat of Arthur and Felicity's father, and all of London sighed when they referred

66

to the brilliant young Earl of Grout, heir to a marquessate, and his impoverished, lovely bride, who'd immediately delivered her besotted husband an heir and was currently at home, awaiting the birth of his spare.

Pru and Arthur adored each other in that unreasonable way that no one believed existed until one witnessed it. They never argued, they enjoyed all the same things, and they were often found together on the edges of London's ballrooms, preferring the company of each other to the company of anyone else.

It was nauseating, really.

But it wasn't so impossible, was it? "Why?"

"Because I've known Pru for my whole life and love doesn't come along for everyone." He paused, then added, "And even when it does, it comes with its own collection of challenges."

She tilted her head at the words. What did they mean? "Arthur?"

He shook his head, refusing to answer. "The point is, you're twenty-seven years old, and it's time for you to stop dithering about and get yourself married to a decent man. Of course, now you've made it near impossible."

But she didn't want any old husband. She wanted more than that. She wanted a man who could . . . she didn't even know. A man who could do more than marry her and leave her alone for the rest of her life, certainly.

Nevertheless, she did not want her family to suffer for her wild actions. She looked down at her hands and told the truth. "I'm sorry."

"Your contrition isn't enough." The response was sharp — sharper than she would have expected from her twin brother, who had stood with her since the moment they were born. Since before that. She found his brown gaze — eyes she knew so well because they were hers, as well — and she saw it. Uncertainty. No. Worse. Disappointment.

She took a step down, toward him. "Arthur, what's happened?"

He swallowed and shook his head. "It's nothing. I just — I thought perhaps we had a shot."

"At the duke?" Her eyes were wide with disbelief. "We did not, Arthur. Not even before I said what I did."

"At . . ." He paused, serious. "At a proper match."

"And was there a team of gentlemen clamoring to meet me tonight?"

"There was Matthew Binghamton."

She blinked. "Mr. Binghamton is deadly dull."

"He's rich as a king," Arthur offered.

"Not rich enough for me to marry him, I'm afraid. Wealth does not purchase personality." When Arthur grumbled, she added, "Would it be so bad for me to remain a spinster? No one will blame you for my being unmarriageable. Father is the Marquess of Bumble, and you're an earl, and heir. We can do without a match, no?"

While she was wholly embarrassed by what had happened, there was a not-small part of her that was rather grateful that she'd ended the charade.

He looked as though he was thinking of something else. Something important.

"Arthur?"

"There was also Friedrich Homrighausen."

"Friedrich . . ." Felicity tilted her head, confusion flaring. "Arthur, Herr Homrighausen arrived in London a week ago. And he doesn't speak English."

"He didn't seem to take issue with that."

"It did not occur to you that *I* might take issue with it, as I do not speak German?"

He lifted one shoulder. "You could learn."

Felicity blinked. "Arthur, I haven't any desire to live in Bavaria."

"I hear it's very nice. Homrighausen is said to have a castle." He waved a hand. "Turreted."

She tilted her head. "Am I in the market for turrets?"

"You might be."

Felicity watched her brother for a long moment, something teasing about the edges of thought — something she could not put voice to, so she settled on, "Arthur?"

Before he could reply, a half-dozen barks sounded from above, followed by, "Oh, dear. I take it the ball did not go as planned?" The question carried down from the first floor railing on the heels of three long-haired dachshunds, the pride of the Marchioness of Bumble, who, despite having a red nose from the cold that had kept her at home, stood in perfect grace, wrapped in a beautiful wine-colored dressing gown, silver hair down about her shoulders. "Did you meet the duke?"

"She didn't, as a matter of fact," Arthur said.

The marchioness turned a disappointed gaze on her only daughter. "Oh, Felicity. That won't do. Dukes don't grow on trees, you know."

"They don't?" Felicity brazened through her reply, willing her twin quiet as she worked to fend off the dogs that were now up on their back legs, pawing at her skirts. "Down! Off!"

"You are not as amusing as you think," her mother continued, ignoring the canine assault going on below. "There is perhaps *one* duke available a year? Some years, no dukes at all! And you've already missed your chance at last year's."

"The Duke of Haven was already married, Mother."

"You needn't say it as though I don't remember!" her mother pointed out. "I should like to give him a firm talking to for how he courted you without ever intending to marry you."

Felicity ignored the soliloquy, which she'd heard a full thousand times before. She would never have been sent to compete for the duke's hand if not for the fact that other husbands weren't exactly clamoring to have her, so she didn't much mind that he had chosen to remain married to his wife.

Aside from the fact that she quite liked the Duchess of Haven, she'd also learned a piece of critical information about the institution of marriage — that a man wildly in love made a remarkable husband.

Not that a wildly in love husband was in Felicity's cards. That particular ship had sailed tonight. Well. It had sailed months ago if she were honest, but tonight was really the last nail in the coffin. "I'm mixing metaphors."

"What?" Arthur snapped.

"You're what?" her mother repeated.

"Nothing." She waved a hand. "I was speaking aloud."

Arthur sighed.

"For heaven's sake, Felicity. That certainly won't help land you the duke," said the marchioness.

"Mother, Felicity isn't landing the duke."

"Not with that attitude, she won't," her mother retorted. "He invited us to a ball! All of London thinks he's looking for a wife! And you are daughter to a marquess, sister to an earl, and have all your teeth!"

Felicity closed her eyes for a moment, resisting the urge to scream, cry, laugh, or do all three. "Is that what dukes are looking for these days? Possession of teeth?"

"It's part of it!" the marchioness insisted, her panicked words devolving into a ragged cough. She brought a handkerchief to cover her mouth. "Drat this cold, or I could have made the introduction myself!"

Felicity sent a quiet prayer of thanks to whichever god had delivered a cold to Bumble House two days earlier, or she would have no doubt been forced into dancing or some kind of ratafia situation with the Duke of Marwick.

No one even liked ratafia. Why it was at every ball in Christendom was beyond Felicity's ken.

"You could not have made the introduction," Felicity said. "You've never met Marwick. No one has. Because he's a hermit and a madman, if the gossip is to be believed."

"No one believes gossip."

"Mother, everyone believes gossip. If they didn't —" She paused while the marchioness sneezed. "God bless you."

"If God wished to bless me, he'd get you married to the Duke of Marwick."

Felicity rolled her eyes. "Mother, after tonight, if the Duke of Marwick were to show any interest in me, it would be a clear indication that he is indeed a madman, rattling around in that massive house of his, collecting unmarried women and dressing them in fancy dress for a private museum."

Arthur blinked. "That's a bit grim."

"Nonsense," her mother said. "Dukes don't collect women." She paused. "Wait. *After tonight?*"

Felicity went silent.

"Arthur?" her mother prodded. "How was

73

the evening, otherwise?"

Felicity turned her back on her mother and gave her brother a wide-eyed, pleading look. She couldn't bear having to recount the disastrous evening to her mother. For that, she required sleep. And possibly laudanum. "Uneventful, wasn't it, *Arthur*?"

"What a pity," the marchioness said. "Not a single additional bite?"

"Additional?" Felicity repeated. "Arthur, are you, too, looking for a husband?"

Arthur cleared his throat. "No."

Felicity's brows rose. "No, to whom?"

"No, to Mother."

"Oh," the marchioness said from far above. "Not even Binghamton? Or the German?"

Felicity blinked. "The German. Herr Homrighausen."

"He's said to have a castle!" the marchioness said before dissolving into another coughing fit, followed by a chorus of barks.

Felicity ignored her mother, keeping her attention on her brother, who did all he could to avoid looking at her before finally replying with irritation. "Yes."

The word unlocked the thought that had whispered around Felicity's consciousness earlier. "They're rich."

Arthur cut her a look. "I don't know what

you mean."

She looked up at her mother. "Mr. Bing-hamton, Herr Homrighausen, the Duke of Marwick." She turned to Arthur. "Not one of them is a good match for me. *But they're all rich.*"

"Really, Felicity! Ladies do not discuss the finances of their suitors!" the marchioness cried, the dachshunds barking and frolicking around her like fat little cherubs.

"Except they're not my suitors, are they?" she asked, understanding flaring as she turned an accusatory gaze on her brother. "Or if they were . . . I ruined that tonight."

The marchioness gasped at the words. "What did you do this time?"

Felicity ignored the tone, as though it was expected that Felicity would have done something to cause any eligible suitors to flee. The fact that she had done precisely that was irrelevant. The relevant fact was this: her family was keeping secrets from her. "Arthur?"

Arthur turned to look up at their mother, and Felicity recognized the frustrated plea in his eyes from their childhood, as though she'd nicked the last cherry tart or she was asking to follow him and his friends out onto the pond for the afternoon. She fol-lowed his look to where her mother stood on watch from high above, and for a moment, she wondered about all the times they'd stood in this exact position, children below and parent above, like Solomon, waiting for a solution to their infinitesimal problems.

But this problem was not infinitesimal.

If the helplessness on her mother's face was any indication, this problem was larger than Felicity had imagined.

"What's happened?" Felicity asked before shifting to stand directly in front of her brother. "No. Not to her. I'm at the center of it, obviously, so I'd like to know what's happened."

"I could ask the same thing," her mother said from up on high.

Felicity did not look as she called up to the marchioness. "I told all of London I was marrying the Duke of Marwick."

"You *what*?!"

The dogs began to bark again, loud and frenzied, as their mistress succumbed to another coughing fit. Still, Felicity did not look away from her brother. "I know. It's terrible. I've caused a fair bit of trouble. But I'm not the only one . . . am I?" Arthur's guilty gaze found hers, and she repeated, "Am I?"

He took a deep breath and exhaled, long

and full of frustration. "No."

"Something's happened."

He nodded.

"Something to do with money."

And again.

"Felicity, we don't discuss money with men."

"Then by all means, Mother, you should leave, but I intend to have this conversation." Arthur's brown eyes met hers. "Something to do with money."

He looked away, toward the back of the house, where down a dark corridor a narrow staircase climbed to the servants' quarters, two dozen others slept, not knowing their fate was in the balance. Just as Felicity had done, every night before now, when her brother, whom she loved with her full heart, nodded a final time and said, "We haven't any."

She blinked, the words at once expected and shocking. "What does that mean?"

Frustration flared and he turned away, running his fingers through his hair before turning back to her, arms wide. "What does it sound like? There's no money."

She came down off the staircase, shaking her head. "How is that possible? You're Midas."

He laughed, the sound utterly humorless.

"Not any longer."

"It's not Arthur's fault," the Marchioness of Bumble called down from the landing. "He didn't know it was a bad deal. He thought the other men were to be trusted."

Felicity shook her head. "A bad deal?"

"It wasn't a bad deal," he said, softly. "I wasn't swindled. I simply —" She stepped toward him, reaching for him, wanting to comfort him. And then he added, "I never imagined I'd lose it."

She reached for him, taking his hands in hers. "It shall be fine," she said quietly. "So you've lost some money."

"All the money." He looked to their hands, entwined. "Christ, Felicity. Pru can't know."

Felicity didn't think her sister-in-law would care one bit if Arthur had made a bad investment. She offered him a smile. "Arthur. You're heir to a marquessate. Father will help you while you restore your business and your reputation. There are lands. Houses. This shall right itself."

Arthur shook his head. "No, Felicity. Father invested with me. Everything is gone. Everything that wasn't entailed."

Felicity blinked, finally turning up to her mother, who stood, one hand to her chest, and nodded. "Everything."

"When?"

"It's not important."

She spun on her brother. "As a matter of fact, I think it is. When?"

He swallowed. "Eighteen months ago."

Felicity's jaw dropped. Eighteen months. They'd lied to her for a year and a half. They'd worked to wed her to a collection of less-than-ideal men, then sent her off to a ridiculous country house party to throw her lot in with four other women who were attempting to woo the Duke of Haven into accepting one of them as his second wife. She should have known then, of course, the moment her mother, who cared for propriety, her dogs, and her children (in that order), had presented the idea of Felicity competing for the hand of the duke as a sound concept.

She should have known when her father allowed it.

When her brother allowed it.

She looked to him. "The duke was rich."

He blinked. "Which one?"

"Both of them. Last summer's. Tonight's."

He nodded.

"And all the others."

"They were rich enough."

Blood rushed through her ears. "I was to

marry one of them."

He nodded.

"And that marriage was to have filled the coffers."

"That was the idea."

They'd been using her for a year and a half. Making plans without her knowing. For a year and a half. She'd been a pawn in this game. She shook her head. "How could you not have told me the goal was marriage at any cost?"

"Because it wasn't. I wouldn't marry you to just anyone . . ."

She heard the hesitation at the end of the statement. "However?"

He sighed and waved a hand. "However." She heard the unspoken words that followed. *We needed the match.*

No money. "What of the servants?"

He shook his head. "We've cut the staff everywhere but here."

She shook her head and turned to her mother. "All those excuses — the myriad reasons we did not take to the country."

"We did not wish to worry you," her mother replied. "You were already so —"

Forlorn. Finished. Forgotten.

Felicity shook her head. "And the tenants?" The hardworking people who worked the land in the country. Who relied upon the title to provide. To protect.

"They keep what they make, now," Arthur replied. "They trade for their own livestock. They mend their own homes." Protected now, but not by the title to which the land was tethered.

No money. Nothing that would protect the land for future generations — for the tenants' children. For Arthur's young son and the second on the way. For her own future, if she did not marry.

We cannot afford another scandal.

Arthur's words echoed through her again, unbidden. With new, literal meaning.

It was the nineteenth century, and bearing a title did not ensure the lifestyle it once did; there were impoverished aristocrats everywhere in London, and soon, the Faircloth family would be added to their ranks.

It was not Felicity's fault, but, somehow, it felt entirely so. "And now, they shan't have me."

Arthur looked away, ashamed. "Now, they shan't have you."

"Because I lied."

"What would possess you to tell such a stunning lie?" her mother called down, breathless with panic.

"I imagine the same thing that would possess you both to keep such a stunning secret," Felicity said, frustration coursing through her. "Desperation."

Anger. Loneliness. A desire to shape the future without thought of what might come next.

Her twin met her eyes, his gaze clear and honest. "It was a mistake."

She lifted her chin, hot rage and terror flooding her. "Mine, as well."

"I should have told you."

"There are many things we both should have done."

"I thought I could spare you —" he began, and Felicity held up a hand to stop his words.

"You thought you could spare *you*. You thought you could save yourself from having to tell your wife, whom you are supposed to love and cherish, the truth of your reality. You thought you could save yourself the embarrassment."

"Not just embarrassment. Worry. I am her husband. I am to care for her. For them all." A wife. A child. Another on the way.

A pang of sorrow thrummed through Felicity. A thread of empathy, tinged with her own disappointment. Her own fear. Her own guilt at behaving too rashly, at speaking too loudly, at making too much of a mistake.

In the silence that followed, Arthur added, "I should not have thought to use you."

"No," she said, angry enough not to let him off the hook. "You shouldn't have."

He gave another humorless laugh. "I suppose I've gotten what's coming. After all, you're not going to marry a rich duke. Or anyone rich for that matter. And you shouldn't have to lower your expectations."

Except now Felicity had told an enormous lie and ruined any chance of her expectations being met. And, in the balance, ruined any chance of her family's future being secure. No one would have her now — not only was she stained by her past behavior, she had lied. Publicly. About marriage to a duke.

No man in his right mind would find that a forgivable offense.

Farewell, expectations.

"Expectations aren't worth the thoughts wasted on them if we haven't a roof over our heads." The marchioness sighed, as though she could read Felicity's thoughts from above. "Good heavens, Felicity, what would actually possess you?"

"It doesn't matter, Mother," Arthur interjected before Felicity could speak.

Arthur — always protecting her. Always trying to protect everyone, the idiot man.

83

"You're right." The marchioness sighed. "I suppose he's disabused the entire *ton* of the notion at this point, and we are returned to our rightful place of scandal."

"Likely so," Felicity said, guilt and fury and frustration at confusing war in her gut. After all, as a female, she had a singular purpose at times like this . . . to marry for money and return honor and wealth to her family.

Except no one would marry her after to-night.

At least, no one in his right mind.

Arthur sensed her distaste for the direction of the conversation, and he set his hands on her shoulders, leaning in to press a chaste, fraternal kiss to her forehead. "We shall be fine," he said, firmly. "I shall find another way."

She nodded, ignoring the prick of tears threatening. Knowing that eighteen months had gone by, and the best solution Arthur had had was her marriage. "Go home to your wife."

He swallowed at the words — at the reminder of his pretty, loving wife, who knew nothing of the mess into which they'd all landed. Lucky Prudence. When Arthur was able to find his voice, he whispered, "She can't know."

The fear in his words was palpable. Horrible.

What a mess they were in.

Felicity nodded. "The secret is ours."

When the door closed behind him, Felicity lifted her skirts — skirts on a gown from last season, altered to accommodate changes in fashion rather than given away and replaced with something fresh. How had she not realized? She climbed the stairs, the dogs weaving back and forth in front of her.

When she reached the landing, she faced her mother. "Your dogs are trying to kill me."

The marchioness nodded, allowing the change of topic. "It's possible. They're very clever."

Felicity forced a smile. "The best of your children."

"Less trouble than all the rest," her mother replied, leaning down and collecting one long, furry animal in her arms. "Was the duke very handsome?"

"I barely saw him in the crush, but it seemed so." Without warning, Felicity found herself thinking of the other man. The one in the darkness. The one she only wished she'd seen. He'd seemed magical, like an invisible flame.

But if tonight had taught her anything, it

was that magic was not real.

What was real was trouble.

"All we wanted was a proper match." Her mother's words cut into her thoughts.

Felicity's lips twisted. "I know."

"Was it as bad as it sounds?"

You didn't escape us; we exited you.

Finished Felicity. Forgotten Felicity. Forlorn Felicity.

You are too late for the duke; I've already landed him.

Felicity nodded. "It was worse."

She made her way through the dark hallways to her bedchamber. Entering the dimly lit room, she tossed her gloves and reticule on the small table just inside the door, closing it and pressing against it, finally releasing the breath she'd been holding since she'd dressed for the Marwick ball hours earlier.

She crossed to the bed in darkness, tossing herself back on the mattress. She stared at the canopy above for a long moment, replaying the horrifying events of the evening.

"What a disaster."

For a fleeting moment, she imagined what she would do if she weren't herself — too tall, too plain, too old and outspoken, a proper wallflower with no hope of wooing an eligible bachelor. She imagined sneaking from the house, returning to the scene of her devastating crime.

Winning a fortune for her family, and the wide world for herself.

Wanting more than she could have.

If she weren't herself, she could do it. She could find the duke and woo him. She could bring him to his knees. If she were beautiful and witty and sparkling. If she were at the center and not the edge of the world. If she were inside the room, and not peering through the keyhole.

If she could incite passion — the kind she'd seen consume a man, like magic. Like fire. Like flame.

Her stomach flipped with the thought, with the fantasy that came with it. With the pleasure of it — something she'd never let herself imagine. A duke, desperate for her.

A match for the ages.

"If only I were flame," she said to the canopy above. "That would solve everything."

But it was impossible. And she imagined a different kind of flame, tearing through Mayfair, incinerating her future. That of her family.

She imagined the names.

Fibbing Felicity.

Falsehood Felicity.

"For God's sake, Felicity," she whispered.

She lay there in shame and panic for a long while, considering her future, until the air grew heavy, and she considered sleeping in her gown rather than summon a maid to help her out of it. But it was heavy and constricting, and the corset was already making it difficult to breathe.

With a groan, she sat up, lit the candle on the bedside table, and went to pull the cord to summon the maid.

Before she could reach it, however, a voice sounded from the darkness. "You shouldn't tell lies, Felicity Faircloth."

CHAPTER FIVE

Felicity leapt straight into the air with a little scream at the words, spinning to face the far side of the room, cloaked in darkness, where nothing looked out of place.

Lifting her candle high, she peered into the corners, the light finally touching a pair of perfectly polished black boots, stretched out, crossed at the ankle, the shining silver tip of a walking stick resting atop one toe.

It was him.

Here. In her bedchamber. As though it were perfectly normal.

Nothing about this evening was normal.

Her heart began to pound, harder than it had earlier in the evening, and Felicity backed away, toward the door. "I believe you have the wrong house, sir."

The boots didn't move. "I have the right house."

She blinked. "You most certainly have the wrong room."

"It's the right room, as well."

"This is my bedchamber."

"I couldn't very well knock on the door in the dead of night and ask to speak with you, could I? I'd scandalize the neighbors, and then where would that leave you?"

She refrained from pointing out that the neighbors were going to be scandalized in the morning anyway, when all of London knew she'd lied.

He heard the thought anyway. "Why did you lie?"

She ignored the question. "I don't converse with strangers in my bedchamber."

"But we aren't strangers, love." The silver tip of the walking stick tapped the toe of his boot in a slow, even rhythm.

Her lips twitched. "I have little time for people who lack consequence."

Though he remained in the dark, she imagined she could hear his smile. "And tonight you showed it, didn't you, Felicity Faircloth?"

"I am not the only one who lied." She narrowed her gaze in the darkness. "You knew who I was."

"You're the only one whose lie is big enough to bring down this house."

She scowled. "You have the better of me, sirrah. To what end? Fear?"

"No. I don't wish to scare you." The man's voice was heavy like the darkness in which he was cloaked. Low, quiet, and somehow clearer than a gunshot.

Felicity's heart thundered. "I think that is precisely what you wish to do." That silver tip tapped again and she turned her irritated gaze to it. "I also think you should leave before I decide that instead of fear, I shall feel anger."

Pause. *Tap tap.*

And then he moved, leaning forward into the circle of light, so she could see his long legs, tall black hat on one thigh. His hands were uncovered by gloves, and three silver rings glinted in the candlelight on the thumb, fore and ring fingers of the right one, beneath the black sleeves of his topcoat, which fit his arms and shoulders perfectly. The ring of light ended at his jaw, sharp and clean-shaven. She lifted her candle once more, and there he was.

She inhaled sharply, ridiculously remembering how she'd thought earlier that the Duke of Marwick was handsome.

Not anymore.

For surely, no man on earth should be as handsome as this one. He looked remarkably like his voice sounded. Like a low, liquid rumble. Like temptation. *Like sin.*

One side of his face remained in shadow, but the side she could see — he was magnificent. A long, lean face all sharp angles and shadowed hollows, dark, winged brows and full lips, eyes that glittered with knowledge that she'd wager he never shared, and a nose that would put the royals to shame, perfectly straight, as though it had been crafted with a sharp, sure blade.

His hair was dark and shorn close to his head, close enough to reveal the round dome of it. "Your head is perfect."

He smirked. "I've always thought so."

She dropped the candle, returning him to shadows. "I mean it's a perfect shape. How do you get your hair shaved so close to the scalp?"

He hesitated before he answered. "A woman I trust."

Her brows rose at the unexpected answer. "Does she know you are here?"

"She does not."

"Well, as she takes a blade to your head regularly, you'd best be going before you upset her."

A low rumble came at that, and her breath caught. Was it a laugh? "Not before you tell me why you lied."

Felicity shook her head. "As I said, sir, I do not make a practice of conversing with strangers. Please leave. Out the way you came in." She paused. "How did you come in?"

"You've a balcony, Juliet."

"I've also a bedchamber on the third floor, not-Romeo."

"And a sturdy trellis." She heard the lazy amusement in his words.

"You climbed the trellis."

"I did, as a matter of fact."

She'd always imagined someone climbing that trellis. Just not a criminal come to — what was he here to do? "Then I assume the walking stick is not to aid in movement."

"Not that kind of movement, no."

"Is it a weapon?"

"Everything is a weapon if one is looking for one."

"Excellent advice, as I seem to have an intruder."

He tutted at the retort. "A friendly one."

"Oh, yes," she scoffed. "Friendly is the very first word I would use to describe you."

"If I were going to kidnap you and carry you off to my lair, I would have done it by now."

"You have a lair?"

"As a matter of fact, I do, but I've no intention of bringing you there. Not to-night."

She would be lying if she said the additional qualifier was not exciting. "Ah, that will ensure I sleep well in the future," she said.

He laughed, low and soft, like the light in the room. "Felicity Faircloth, you are not what I expected."

"You say that as though it is a compliment."

"It is."

"Will it still be one when I hit you squarely in the head with this candlestick?"

"You aren't going to hurt me," he said.

Felicity didn't like how well he seemed to understand her bravado was just that. "You seem terribly sure of yourself for someone who does not know me."

"I know you, Felicity Faircloth. I knew you the moment I saw you on that balcony outside Marwick's locked conservatory. The only thing I did not know was the color of that frock."

She looked down at the dress, a season too old and the color of her cheeks. "It's pink."

"Not just pink," he said, his voice dark with promise and something else that she did not like. "It's the color of the Devon sky at dawn."

She didn't like the way the words filled

her, as though she might someday see that sky and think of this man and this moment. As though he might leave a mark she could not erase.

"Answer my question and I will leave."

Why did you lie?

"I don't remember it."

"Yes, you do. Why did you lie to that collection of unfortunates?" The description was so ridiculous that she nearly laughed. Nearly. But he didn't seem to find it amusing.

"They aren't so unfortunate."

"They're pompous, spoiled aristocrats with their heads shoved so far up each others' asses, they haven't any idea that the world is quickly moving on and others will soon take their place."

Her jaw dropped.

"But you, Felicity Faircloth." He tapped his stick on his boot twice. "No one is taking your place. And so I will ask again. Why did you lie to them?"

Whether it was the shock of his description or his matter-of-fact way of doing the describing, Felicity replied, "No one wishes my place." He did not speak, and so she filled the silence. "By which I mean to say . . . my place is nothing. It's nowhere. It was once with them, but then . . ." She

95

trailed off. Shrugged. "I am invisible." And then, because she couldn't stop herself, she added, softly, "I wanted to punish them. And I wanted them to want me back."

She hated the truth in the words. Shouldn't she be strong enough to turn her back on them? Shouldn't she care less? She hated the weakness he'd exposed.

And she hated him for exposing it.

She waited for him to reply from the darkness, strangely reminded of the time she'd visited the Royal Entomological Society and seen an enormous butterfly trapped in amber. Beautiful and delicate and perfectly preserved, but frozen in time, forever.

This man would not capture her. Not today. "I think I shall call a servant to come and take you away. You should know my father is a marquess, and it is quite illegal to enter a home of the aristocracy without permission."

"It's quite illegal to enter anyone's home without permission, Felicity Faircloth, but would you like me to tell you I am duly impressed by your father's title, and your brother's, too?"

"Why should I be the only one who lies tonight?"

A pause, then, "So you admit it."

"I might as well — all of London will

know it tomorrow. Flighty Felicity with her fanciful fiancé."

The alliteration did not amuse him. "You know, your father's title is ridiculous. Your brother's, too."

"I beg your pardon," she said, for lack of anything else.

"Bumble and Grout. Good Lord. When poverty at long last ensnares them, they can always become apothecaries. Selling tinctures and tonics to the desperate in Lambeth."

He knew they were impoverished. Did all of London? Was she the last to discover it? The last to be told, even by the family that intended to use her to reverse it? Irritation flared at the thought.

The man continued. "And you, Felicity Faircloth, with a name that should be in a storybook."

She cut him a look. "I did so wonder about your opinion of our respective names."

He ignored her set-down. "A storybook princess, locked in a tower, desperate to be a part of the world that trapped her there . . . to be accepted by it."

Everything about this man was unsettling and strange and vaguely infuriating. "I don't like you."

"No, you don't like the truth, my little liar. You don't like that I see that your silly wish is false friendship from a collection of poncy, perfumed aristocrats who cannot see what you really are."

She should be a dozen kinds of out-of-sorts with him so close and in the darkness. And yet . . . "And what is that?"

"Better than those six by half."

The answer sent a little thrill through her, and she almost allowed herself to be drawn in by this man who she might be convinced was made of magic with more champagne. Instead, she shook her head and put on her best disdain. "If only I *were* that princess, sirrah — then you would not be here." She moved to the wall, ready to pull the cord again.

"Isn't that the bit everyone likes? The bit where the princess is rescued from the tower?"

She looked over her shoulder. "That's supposed to be a prince doing the rescuing. Not . . . whatever you are." She reached for the cord.

He spoke before she could pull. "Who is the moth?"

She whirled back to him, embarrassment flaring. "What?"

"You wished to be a flame, princess. Who

98

is the moth?"

Her cheeks blazed. She hadn't said anything about moths. How did he even know what she had meant? "You shouldn't eavesdrop."

"I shouldn't be sitting in your dark bedchamber, either, love, but here I am."

She narrowed her gaze. "I take it you are not the kind of man who pays attention to rules."

"Have you known me to follow any of them in our lengthy acquaintance?"

Irritation flared. "Who are you? Why were you skulking about outside Marwick House like some nefarious . . . skulker?"

He remained unroused. "A skulking skulker, am I?"

This man, like all of London, seemed to know more than she did. He understood the battleground, had the skill to wage war. And she loathed it. She sent him her most withering look.

It had no effect. "Once more, love. If you are the flame, who is the moth?"

"Certainly not you, sir."

"That's a pity."

She didn't like the insolence in those words, either. "I feel quite satisfied with the decision."

He gave a little laugh, a low rumble that

did odd things to her. "Shall I tell you what I think?"

"I wish you wouldn't," she snapped.

"I think your moth is very difficult to lure." She pursed her lips but did not speak. "And I know I can get him for you." Her breath caught as he pressed on. "The one whose wings you've already bragged to half of London about singeing."

Felicity was grateful for the dimly lit room, so he couldn't see her red face. Or her shock. Or her excitement. Was this man, who had somehow found his way into her bedchamber in the dead of night, actually suggesting she had neither ruined her life nor her family's chances for survival?

Hope was a wild, panicked thing.

"*Could* you get him?"

He laughed then. Low and dark and barely humorous, sending an unwelcome thrill through her. "Like a kitten to the saucer."

She scowled. "You should not tease."

"When I tease you, love, you shall know it." He leaned back again, stretching his legs out, tapping that infernal stick against his boot. "The Duke of Marwick could be yours, Felicity Faircloth. And with London never knowing the truth of your lie."

Her breath grew shallow. "That's impossible." And still, she believed him, somehow.

"Is anything truly impossible?"

She forced a laugh. "Besides an eligible duke choosing me over every other woman in Britain?"

Tap tap. Tap tap. "Even that is possible, old, plain, opinionated, tossed-over Felicity Faircloth. This is the bit in the storybook where the princess receives everything she's ever wished for."

Except it wasn't a storybook. And this man couldn't give her what she wished for. "That bit typically begins with a fairy of some sort. And you do not seem at all spritely."

A low rumble of a laugh. "There, you are right. But there are creatures other than fairies who dabble in similar trade."

Her heart resumed its pounding, and she hated the wild hope there, that this strange man in the darkness could deliver on his impossible promise.

It was madness, but she advanced upon him, bringing him into the light once more, moving closer and closer, until she stood at the end of his impossibly long legs, at the end of his impossibly long walking stick, and lifted her candle to reveal his impossibly handsome face once more.

This time, however, she could see the

whole of it, and the perfect left side did not match the right, where a harsh, wicked scar marked him from temple to jaw, puckered and white.

When she inhaled sharply, he turned his head from the light. "A pity. I was looking forward to the set-down you appeared ready to deliver. I didn't think you would be so easily put off."

"Oh, I am not put off at all. Indeed, I'm grateful that you are no longer the most perfect man I've ever seen."

He turned back, dark gaze finding hers. "Grateful?"

"Indeed. I've never quite understood what one does with exceedingly perfect men."

A brow rose. "What one *does* with them."

"Besides the obvious."

He tilted his head. "The obvious."

"Looking at them."

"Ah," he said.

"At any rate, I now feel far more comfortable."

"Because I'm no longer perfect?"

"You're still terribly close to it, but you're no longer the handsomest man I've ever seen," she lied.

"I feel as though I should be insulted, but I shall get past that. Out of curiosity, who has usurped my throne?"

No one. If anything, the scar makes you more handsome.

But this was not the kind of man one said *that* to. "Technically, he had the throne before you. He's simply reclaimed it."

"I'll thank you for a name, Lady Felicity."

"What did you call him before? My moth?"

He went utterly still for a moment — not long enough for an ordinary person to notice.

Felicity noticed. "I thought you would have expected it," she said, her tone scoffing. "What with your offer to win him for me."

"The offer still stands, though I don't find the duke handsome. At all."

"We needn't debate the point. The man is empirically attractive."

"Mmm," he said, seemingly unconvinced. "Tell me why you lied."

"Tell me why you're so willing to help me fix it."

He held her gaze for a long moment. "Would you believe I am a Good Samaritan?"

"No. Why were you outside Marwick's ball? What is he to you?"

He lifted one shoulder. Let it drop. "Tell me why you don't think he'd be thrilled to find himself affianced to you."

She smirked. "First, he hasn't any idea who I am."

One side of his mouth twitched, and she wondered what it would be like to receive the full force of his smile.

Putting the wild thought to the side, she added, "And, as I said, exceedingly handsome men have no use for me."

"That's not what you said," the man answered. "You said you weren't sure of the use for exceedingly handsome men."

She thought for a moment. "Both statements are true."

"Why would you think Marwick would have no use for you?"

She frowned. "I should think that would be obvious."

"It's not."

She resisted the question, crossing her arms as if to protect herself. "It's rude of you to ask."

"It's rude of me to climb your trellis and invade your quarters, too."

"So it is." And then, for a reason she would never fully understand, she answered his question. Letting frustration and worry and a very real sense of impending doom pour over her. "Because I'm the epitome of ordinary. Because I'm not beautiful, or

104

diverting, or a stellar conversationalist. And though I once thought it impossible to believe I'd land myself an aging spinster, here we are, and no one has ever really wanted me. And I don't expect that to start now, with a handsome duke."

He was silent for a long moment, her embarrassment raging.

"Please leave," she added.

"You seem to be fairly stellar at conversation with me."

She ignored the fact that he hadn't disagreed with her other assessments. "You're a stranger in the darkness. Everything is easier in the dark."

"Nothing is easier in the dark," he said. "But that's irrelevant. You're wrong, and that's why I'm here."

"To convince me that I'm good at conversation?"

Teeth flashed and he stood, filling the room with his height. Felicity's nerves thrummed as she considered the shape of him, beautifully long, with a hint of broad shoulders and lean hips.

"I came to give you what you want, Felicity Faircloth."

The promise in his whisper coursed through her. Was it fear she felt? Or something else? She shook her head. "You can't, though. No one can."

"You want the flame," he said softly.

She shook her head. "I don't."

"Of course you do. But it's not all you want, is it?" He took a step closer to her, and she could smell him, warm and smoky, as though he'd come from somewhere forbidden. "You want all of it. The world, the man, the money, the power. And something else, as well." He came closer still, towering over her, his warmth flooding her, heady and tempting. "Something more." His words became a whisper. "Something secret."

She hesitated, hating that he seemed to know her, this stranger.

Hating that she wanted to reply. Hating that she did. "More than I can have."

"And who told you that, my lady? Who told you you could not have it all?"

Her gaze fell to his hand, where the silver handle of his walking stick tucked between his large, strong fingers, the silver ring on his index finger glinting up at her. She studied the pattern of the metal, trying to discern the shape on the cane. After what seemed like an age, she looked to him. "Have you a name?"

"Devil."

Her heart raced at the word, which

seemed somehow completely ridiculous and utterly perfect. "That's not your real name."

"It's strange, how we put such value on names, don't you think, Felicity Faircloth? Call me whatever you like, but I am a man who can give you all of it. Everything you wish."

She didn't believe him. Obviously. Not at all. "Why me?"

He reached for her then, and she knew she should have stepped back. She knew she shouldn't have let him touch her, not when his fingers ran down her left cheek, leaving fire in their wake, as though he were leaving his scar upon her, a mark of his presence.

But the burn of his touch was nothing like pain. Especially not when he replied, "Why not you?"

Why not her? Why shouldn't she have what she wanted? Why shouldn't she make a deal with this devil, who had appeared from nowhere and would soon be gone?

"I want not to have lied," she said.

"I cannot change the past. Only the future. But I can make good on your promise."

"Spin straw into gold?"

"Ah, so we are in a storybook, after all."

He made it all sound so easy — so possible, as though he might work a miracle in the night without any effort at all.

It was madness, of course. He could not change what she'd said. The lie she'd told, bigger than all of them. Doors had closed all around her earlier that evening, locking her out of every conceivable path. Shutting out her future. The future of her family. Arthur's helplessness flashed. Her mother's desperation. Their twin resignation. Unpickable locks.

And now, this man . . . brandishing a key.

"You can make it true."

His hand turned, the heat of him against her cheek, along her jaw, and for a fleeting moment he *was* a fairy king. She *was* in his thrall. "The engagement is easy. But that isn't all you wish, is it?"

How did he know?

His touch spread fire down the column of her throat, fingers kissing the swell of her shoulder. "Tell me the rest, Felicity Faircloth. What else does the princess in the tower desire? The world at her feet, and her family rich once more, and . . ."

The words trailed off, filling the room until her reply burst from her. "I want him to be the moth." He lifted his hand from her skin, and the loss was keen. "I wish to be the flame."

He nodded, his lips curling like sin, his colorless eyes dark in the shadows, and she wondered if she would feel less in his thrall if she could see their color. "You wish to tempt him to you."

A memory flared, a husband, desperate for his wife. A man, desperate for his love. A passion that could not be denied, all for a woman who held every inch of power. "I do."

"Be careful with temptation, my lady. It is a dangerous proposition."

"You make it sound as though you've experienced it as such."

"That's because I have."

"Your barberess?" Was the woman his wife? His mistress? His love? Why did Felicity care?

"Passion cuts both ways."

"It needn't," she said, feeling suddenly, keenly, strangely comfortable with this man whom she did not know. "I hope to eventually love my husband, but I needn't be consumed by him."

"You wish to do the consuming."

She wished to be wanted. Beyond reason. She wished to be ached for.

"You wish for him to fly into your flame."

Impossible.

She answered him. "When you are ignored

by the stars, you wonder if you might ever burn bright." Immediately embarrassed by the words, Felicity turned away, breaking the spell. Cleared her throat. "It does not matter. You cannot change the past. You cannot erase my lie and make it truth. You cannot make him want me. Not even if you were the devil. It's impossible."

"Poor Felicity Faircloth, so concerned about what is impossible."

"It was a *lie,*" she said. "I've never even *met* the duke."

"And here is truth . . . the Duke of Marwick shan't deny your claim."

Impossible. And yet, there was a tiny part of her that hoped he was right. If that, she might be able to save them all. "How?"

He smirked. "Devil's magic."

She raised a brow. "If you can make it so, sir, you will have earned your silly name."

"Most people find my name unsettling."

"I am not most people."

"That much, Felicity Faircloth, is true."

She did not like the warmth that spread through her at the words, and so she ignored it. "And you would do it out of the goodness of your heart? Forgive me if I do not believe that, *Devil.*"

He inclined his head. "Of course not. There's nothing good about my heart. When

110

it is done, and you have won him, heart and mind, I shall come and collect my fee."

"I suppose this is the part where you tell me the fee is my firstborn child?"

He laughed at that. Low and secret, like she'd said something more amusing than she'd realized. And then, "What would I do with a mewling babe?"

Her lips twitched at that. "I haven't anything to give you."

He looked at her for a long moment. "You undersell yourself, Felicity Faircloth."

"My family hasn't any money to give," she said. "You said so yourself."

"If they did, you would not be in this predicament, would you?"

She scowled at his matter-of-fact assessment. At the helplessness that flared with the words. "How do you know it?"

"That Earl Grout and the Marquess of Bumble have lost a fortune? Darling, all of London knows that. Even those of us who aren't invited to Marwick's balls."

She scowled. "I didn't know."

"Not until they needed you to."

"Not even then," she grumbled. "Not until I could do nothing to help."

He tapped his walking stick twice on the floor. "I am here, am I not?"

111

She narrowed her gaze on him. "For a price."

"Everything has a price, darling."

"And I assume you already know yours."

"I do, as a matter of fact."

"What is it?"

He smiled, the expression wicked. "Telling you that would remove the fun."

A tingle spread through her, across her shoulders and down her spine, warm and exciting. And terrifying and hopeful. What price her family, comfortable in their security? What price her reputation as an oddity, yes, but never a liar?

And what price a husband with no knowledge of her past?

Why not deal with this devil?

An answer whispered through her, a promise of something dangerous. And still, temptation thundered through her. But first, assurance.

"If I accept . . ."

That smirk again, as though he were a cat with a canary.

"*If* I accept," she repeated with a scowl. "He shan't deny the engagement?"

The devil inclined his head. "No one will ever know of your fabrication, Felicity."

"And he shall want me?"

"Like air," he said, the words a lovely promise.

It wasn't possible. The man was not the devil. And even if he were, not even God could erase the events of the evening and make the Duke of Marwick marry her.

But what if he could?

Bargains cut both ways, and this man did seem more exciting than most.

Perhaps in the loss of the impossible passion he promised her, she could win something else. She met his gaze. "And if you cannot do it? Do I collect a favor from you?"

He was silent, and then, "Are you certain you wish a favor from the Devil?"

"It seems that would be a far more useful favor than one from someone who is perfectly good all the time," she pointed out.

The brow above his scar rose in amusement. "Fair enough. If I fail, you may claim a favor from me."

She nodded and extended her hand for a proper handshake, one she regretted the moment his large hand slid into hers. It was warm and big, rough at the palm in a way that evoked work far beyond anything polite gentlemen performed.

It was delicious, and she released him immediately.

"You should not have agreed," he added.

"Why not?"

"Because nothing good comes from deals made in the dark." He reached into his pocket and brandished a calling card. "I shall see you two nights hence, unless you require me beforehand." He dropped the card to the little table next to the chair Felicity thought she might think of as his for the rest of time now. "Lock this door behind me. You wouldn't want a nefarious character coming in while you are asleep."

"Locks didn't keep the first nefarious character out of my room tonight."

One side of his mouth kicked up. "You're not the only lockpick in London, love."

She blushed as he tipped his hat and exited through the balcony doors before she could deny her lockpicking, his silver cane flashing in the moonlight.

By the time she reached the edge of the balcony, he was gone, snatched up by the night.

She returned inside and locked the door, her gaze falling to the calling card there.

Lifting it, she considered the elaborate insignia there:

The back offered an address — a street she'd never heard of — and underneath, in the same, masculine scrawl:

With the Devil's Welcome.

CHAPTER SIX

Two nights later, as the last rays of the sun faded into darkness, the Bareknuckle Bastards picked through the dirty streets of the farthest reaches of Covent Garden, where the neighborhood known for taverns and theaters gave way to one known for crime and cruelty.

Covent Garden was a maze of narrow, labyrinthine streets, twisting and turning in upon themselves until an ignorant visitor was trapped in its spider's web. A single wrong turn after leaving the theater could see a toff liberated of his purse and tossed into the gutter, or worse. The streets leading deep into the Garden's rookery were not kind to visitors — especially proper gentlemen dressed in even more proper finery — but Devil and Whit weren't proper and they weren't gentlemen, and everyone there knew better than to cross the Bareknuckle Bastards, no matter what finery they wore.

What's more, the brothers were revered in the neighborhood, having come up from the slums themselves, fighting and thieving and sleeping in filth with the best of them, and no one likes a rich man like a poor man with the same beginnings. It didn't hurt that much of the Bastards' business ran through this particular rookery — where strong men and smart women worked for them and good boys and clever girls kept watchful eye for anything out of sorts, reporting their findings for a fine gold crown.

A crown could feed a family for a month here, and the Bastards spent money in the muck like it was water, which made them — and their businesses — untouchable.

"Mr. Beast." A little girl tugged on Whit's trouser leg, using the name he used with all but his siblings. "It's 'ere! When are we 'avin' lemon ice 'gain?"

Whit stopped and crouched down, his voice rough from disuse and deep with the accent of their youth, which only ever came back here. "Listen 'ere, moppet. We don' talk 'bout ice in the streets."

The girl's bright blue eyes went wide.

Whit ruffled her hair. "You keep our secrets, and you'll get your lemon treats, don't you worry." A gap in the child's smile showed that she'd lost a tooth recently. Whit directed her away. "Go find your mum. Tell 'er I'm comin' for my wash after I finish at the warehouse."

The girl was gone like a shot.

The brothers resumed their walk. "It's good of you to give Mary your wash," Devil said.

Whit grunted.

Theirs was one of the few rookeries in London that had fresh, communal water — because the Bareknuckle Bastards had made sure of it. They'd also made sure it had a surgeon and a priest, and a school where little ones could learn their letters before they had to take to the streets and find work. But the Bastards couldn't give everything, and the poor who lived here were too proud to take it, anyway.

So the Bastards employed as many of them as they could — a collection of old and young, strong and smart, men and women from all over the world — Londoners and North Countrymen, Scots and Welsh, African, Indian, Spanish, American. If they made their way to Covent Garden and were able to work, the Bastards would provide it at one of their numerous businesses. Taverns and fight rings, butchers and pie shops, tanneries and dye shops and a half-dozen other jaunts, spread throughout the neighborhood.

If it wasn't enough that Devil and Whit had come up in the muck of the place, the work they provided — for decent wages and under safe conditions — bought the loyalty of the rookery's residents. That was something that other business owners had never understood about the slums, thinking they could hire in work while bellies in spitting distance starved. The warehouse on the far edge of the neighborhood now owned by the brothers had once been used to produce pitch, but had long been abandoned when the company that had built it discovered that the residents had no loyalty to them, and would steal anything that was left unguarded.

Not so when the business employed two hundred local men. Entering the building that now acted as the centralized warehouse for any number of the Bastards' businesses, Devil nodded to a half-dozen men staggered throughout the dark interior, guarding crates of liquors and sweets, leathers and wool — if it was taxed by the Crown, the Bareknuckle Bastards sold it, and cheap.

And no one stole from them, for fear of the punishment promised by their name —

one they'd been given decades earlier and stones lighter, when they'd fought with fists faster and stronger than they should have been to claim turf and show enemies no mercy.

Devil went to greet the strapping man who led the watch. "All right, John?"

"All right, sir."

"Has the babe come?"

Bright white teeth flashed proudly against dark brown skin. "Last week. A boy. Strong as his da."

The new father's satisfied smile was sunlight in the dimly lit room, and Devil clapped him on the shoulder. "I've no doubt about that. And your wife?"

"Healthy, thanks to God. Too good for me by half."

Devil nodded and lowered his voice. "They all are, man. Better than the lot of us combined."

He turned from the sound of John's laughter to find Whit, now standing with Nik, the foreman of the warehouse, young — barely twenty — and with a head for organization that Devil had never met in another. Nik's heavy coat, hat, and gloves hid most of her skin, and the dim light hid the rest, but she reached out a hand to greet Devil as he arrived.

"Where are we, Nik?" Devil asked.

The fair-haired Norwegian looked about and then waved them toward the far corner of the warehouse, where a guard reached down to open a door leading into the ground, revealing a great, black abyss below.

A thread of unease coursed through Devil, and he turned to his brother. "After you."

Whit's hand signal spoke more than words could, but he crouched low and dropped into the darkness without hesitation.

Devil went in next, reaching back up to accept an unlit lantern from Nik as she followed them in, looking up to the guard only to say, "Close it up."

The guard did as he was instructed without hesitation, and Devil was certain that the blackness of the cavernous hole was rivaled only by that of death. He worked to keep his breath even. To not remember.

"Fuck." Whit growled in the darkness. "Light."

"You have it, Devil." This, in Nik's thick Scandinavian accent.

Christ. He'd forgotten he was holding it. He fumbled for the door of the lantern, the dark and his own unsettling emotions making it take longer than usual. But finally, he worked the flint and light came, blessed.

"Quickly, then." Nik took the lantern from

121

him and led the way. "We don't want to make any more heat than necessary."

The pitch-black holding area led to a long, narrow passageway. Devil followed Nik, and halfway down the corridor, the air began to grow crisp and cold. She turned and said, "Hats and coats, if you please."

Devil closed his coat, buttoning it thoroughly as Whit did the same, pulling his hat low over his brow.

At the end of the corridor, Nik extracted a ring of iron keys and began to work on a long line of locks set against a heavy metal door. When they were all unlocked, she swung open the door and set to work on a second batch of locks — twelve in total. She turned back before opening the door. "We go in quickly. The longer we leave the door —"

Whit cut her off with a grunt.

"What my brother means to say," Devil said, "is that we've been filling this hold for longer than you've been alive, Annika." Her gaze narrowed in the lamplight at the use of her full name, but she opened the door. "Go on, then."

Once inside, Nik slammed the door shut, and they were in darkness again, until she turned, lifting the light high to reveal the great, cavernous room, filled with blocks of ice.

"How much survived?"

"One hundred tons."

Devil let out a low whistle. "We lost thirty-five percent?"

"It's May," Nik explained, pulling the wool scarf off the lower half of her face so she could be heard. "The ocean warms."

"And the rest of the cargo?"

"All accounted for." She extracted a bill of lading from her pocket. "Sixty-eight barrels brandy, forty-three casks American bourbon, twenty-four crates silk, twenty-four crates playing cards, sixteen cases dice. Also, a box of face powder and three crates of French wigs, which are not on the list and I'm going to ignore, other than to assume you want them delivered to the usual location."

"Precisely," Devil said. "No damage from the melt?"

"None. It was packed well on the other end."

Whit grunted his approval.

"Thanks to you, Nik," Devil said.

She did not hide her smile. "Norwegians like Norwegians." She paused. "There is one thing." Two sets of dark eyes found her face. "There was a watch on the docks."

The brothers looked to each other. While no one would dare steal from the Bastards' in the rookery, the brothers' overland caravans had been compromised twice in the last two months, robbed at gunpoint once they'd left the safety of Covent Garden. It was part of the business, but Devil didn't like the uptick in thievery. "What kind of watch?"

Nik tilted her head. "Can't say for sure."

"Try," Whit said.

"Clothes looked like dockside competition."

It made sense. There were any number of smugglers working the French and American angles, though none had such an airtight method of import. "But?"

She pressed her lips into a thin line. "Boots awfully clean for a Cheapside boy."

"Crown?" Always a risk for a smuggling operation.

"Possible," Nik said, but she didn't sound sure.

"The crates?" Whit asked.

"Out of view the whole time. Ice moved by flatbed wagon and horse, crates secure within. And none of our men have seen anything out of the ordinary."

Devil nodded. "The product stays here for a week. No one comes in or out. Get it to the boys on the street to keep an eye out for anyone out of the ordinary."

Nik nodded. "Done."

Whit kicked at an ice block. "And the packaging?"

"Pure. Good enough to sell."

"Make sure the offal shops in the rookery get some tonight. No one eats rancid meat when we've a hundred tons of ice to go around." Devil paused. "And Beast promised the children lemon ice."

Nik's brows rose. "Kind of him."

"That's what everyone says," Devil said, dry as sand. "Oh, that Beast, he's so very kind."

"Are you going to mix the lemon syrup, too, Beast?" she asked with a grin.

Whit growled.

Devil laughed and slapped a hand on a block of ice. "Send one of these round to the office, will you?"

Nik nodded. "Already done. And a case of the bourbon from the Colonies."

"You know me well. I've got to get back." After a wander through the rookery, he was going to need a wash. He had business on Bond Street.

And then he had business with Felicity Faircloth.

Felicity Faircloth, with skin that turned

gold in the light of a candle, brown eyes wide and clever, full of fear and fire and fury. And able to spar like none he'd met in recent memory.

He wanted another spar.

He cleared his throat at the thought, turning to look at Whit, who was watching him, a knowing look in his eye.

Devil ignored it, pulling his coat tight around him. "What? It's fucking freezing in here."

"You're the ones who chose to deal in ice," Nik said.

"It's a bad plan," Whit said, looking directly at him.

"Well, it's a bit late to change it. The ship, one might say," Nik added with a smirk, "has sailed."

Devil and Whit did not smile at the silly jest. She didn't realize that Whit wasn't talking about the ice; he was talking about the girl.

Devil turned on his heel and headed for the door to the hold. "Come on then, Nik," he said. "Bring the light."

She did, and the three exited, Devil refusing to meet Whit's knowing gaze as they waited for Nik to lock the double steel doors and return them through darkness to the warehouse.

He continued to evade his brother's watch as they collected Whit's wash and picked their way back to the heart of Covent Garden, weaving their way through the cobblestone streets to their offices and apartments in the large building on Arne Street.

After a quarter of an hour of silent walking, Whit said, "You lay your trap for the girl."

Devil didn't like the insinuation in the words. "I lay my trap for them both."

"You still intend to seduce the girl out from under him."

"Her, and every one that comes after, if need be," Devil replied. "He's as arrogant as ever, Beast. He thinks to have his heir."

Whit shook his head. "No, he thinks to have Grace. He thinks we'll give her up to keep him from whelping a new duke on this girl."

"He's wrong. He gets neither Grace, nor the girl."

"Two carriages, careening toward each other," Whit growled.

"He shall turn."

His brother's eyes found his. "He never has before."

Memory flashed. Ewan, tall and lean, fists raised, eyes swollen, lip split, and refusing to yield. Unwilling to back down. Desperate to win. "It's not the same. We have hungered longer. Worked harder. Dukedom has made the man soft."

Whit grunted. "And Grace?"

"He doesn't find her. He never finds her."

"We should have killed him."

Killing him would have brought London crashing down around them. "Too much risk. You know that."

"That, and we made Grace a promise."

Devil nodded. "And that."

"His return threatens us all, and Grace more than anyone."

"No," Devil said. "His return threatens him the most. Remember — if anyone discovers what he did . . . how he got his title . . . he swings from a noose. A traitor to the Crown."

Whit shook his head. "And what if he's willing to risk it for a chance at her?" At Grace, the girl he'd once loved. The girl whose future he'd thieved. The girl whom he would have destroyed if not for Devil and Whit.

"Then he sacrifices it all," Devil said. "He gets nothing."

Whit nodded. "Not even heirs."

"Never heirs."

Then, "There's always the original plan.

We rough the duke up. Send him home."

"It won't stop the marriage. Not now. Not when he thinks he's close to finding Grace."

Whit flexed one hand, the black leather of his glove creaking with the movement. "It would be glorious fun, though." They walked in silence for several minutes, before Whit added, "Poor girl, she couldn't have predicted how her innocent lie would land her in bed with you."

It was a figure of speech, of course. But the vision came nonetheless — and Devil couldn't resist it, Felicity Faircloth, dark hair and pink skirts spread wide before him. Clever and beautiful and with a mouth like sin.

The girl's ruination would be a pleasure.

He ignored the thin thread of guilt that teased through him. There was no room for guilt here. "She shan't be the first girl ruined. I'll throw the father money. The brother, too. They'll get down on their knees and weep with gratitude for their salvation."

"Kind of you," Whit said, dryly. "But what of the girl's salvation? It's impossible. She won't be ruined. She'll be exiled."

I want them to want me back.

All Felicity Faircloth wanted was back into that world. And she'd never get it. Not even after he promised it to her. "She's free to choose her next husband."

"Do aristocratic men line up for aging ruined spinsters?"

Something unpleasant coursed through him. "So she settles for someone not aristocratic."

A beat. And then, "Someone like you?"

Christ. No. Men like him were so far beneath Felicity Faircloth the idea was laughable.

When he did not reply, Whit grunted again. "Grace can never know."

"Of course she can't," Devil replied. "And she won't."

"She won't be able to stay out of it."

Devil had never been so happy to see the door to their offices. Approaching it, he reached for a key, but before he could unlock the door, a small window slid open, then closed. The door opened and they stepped inside.

"It's about damn time."

Devil's gaze shot to the tall, red-haired woman who closed the door behind them, leaning back against the door, one hand on her hip, as though she'd been waiting for years. He immediately looked to Whit, stone-faced. Whit's dark eyes met his calmly.

Grace can never know.

"What's happened?" their sister said, look-

130

ing from one to the other.

"What's happened with what?" Devil asked, removing his hat.

"You look like you did when we were children and you decided to start fighting without telling me."

"It was a good idea."

"It was a shite idea, and you know it. You're lucky you weren't killed your first night out, you were so small. You're both lucky I got in the ring." She rocked back on her heels and crossed her arms over her chest. "Now what's happened?"

Devil ignored the question. "You came back from your first night with a broken nose."

She grinned. "I like to think the bump gives me character."

"It gives you something, most definitely."

Grace harrumphed and moved on. "I have three things to say, and then I have actual work to do, gentlemen. I cannot be left lazing about here, waiting for the two of you to return."

"No one asked you to wait for us," Devil said, pushing past his arrogant sister toward the dark, cavernous hallways beyond, and up the back stairs to their apartments.

She followed, nonetheless. "First is for you," she told Whit, passing him a sheet of paper. "There are three fights set for to-night, each at a different place on the hour and half; two will be fair, the third, filthy. Addresses are here, and the boys are already out taking bets."

Whit grunted his approval and Grace pressed on. "Second, Calhoun wants to know where his bourbon is. Says if we're having too much trouble getting it in, he'll find one of his countrymen to do the job — really, is there anyone more arrogant than an American?"

"Tell him it's here, but not moving yet, so he can wait like the rest of us, or feel free to wait the two months it will take to get a new order to the States and back."

She nodded. "I assume the same is true for the Fallen Angel's delivery?"

"And everything else we're set to deliver from this shipment."

Grace's gaze narrowed on him. "We're being watched?"

"Nik thinks it's possible."

His sister pursed her lips for a moment, then said, "If Nik thinks it, it's likely true. Which brings me to third: Did my wigs arrive?"

"Along with more face powder than you can ever use."

She grinned. "A girl can try, though, can't she?"

"Our shipments are not designed as your personal pack mule."

"Ah, but my personal items are both legal and don't require tax payment, bruv, so it's not the worst thing in the world for you to receive three cases of wigs." She reached out to rub Devil's tightly shorn head. "Perhaps you'd like one . . . you could do with more hair."

He swatted his sister's hand away from his head. "If we weren't blood —"

She grinned. "We're not blood, as a matter of fact."

They were where it counted. "And yet, for some reason, I put up with you."

She leaned in. "Because I make money hand over fist for you louts." Whit grunted, and Grace laughed. "See? Beast knows."

Whit disappeared into his rooms across the hallway, and Devil extracted a key from his pocket, inserting it into the door to his own. "Anything else?"

"You could invite your sister for a drink, you know. If I know you, you've sorted out a way for *your* bourbon to arrive on time."

"I thought you had work to do."

She lifted a shoulder. "Clare can take care of things until I get there."

"I stink of the rookery and I have some-where to be."

Her brows shot together. "Where?"

"You needn't make it seem as though I've nothing to do in the evenings."

"Between sundown and midnight? You don't."

"That's not true." It was vaguely true. He turned the key in the lock, looking back at his sister as he opened the door. "The point is, leave me now."

Whatever retort Grace would have made — and Lord knew Grace always had a retort — was lost on her lips when her blue gaze flickered over his shoulder and into the room beyond, then widened enough for Devil to be concerned.

He turned to follow it, somehow, impossibly, knowing exactly what he was going to find.

Whom he was going to find.

Lady Felicity Faircloth, standing at the window at the far side of the room, as though she belonged there.

CHAPTER SEVEN

There was a woman with him.

Of all the things Felicity had expected might happen when she feigned illness and snuck from her house at twilight to summon a hack to take her to the mysterious location scrawled on the back of his calling card — and there were many — she hadn't expected a woman.

A tall, striking woman painted to perfection and with hair like a sunset, dressed in full, tiered amethyst skirts and a decorative corset in the richest aubergine Felicity had ever seen. The woman wasn't properly beautiful, but she was proud and poised and stunningly . . . stunning.

She was the kind of woman men fell for madly. That was no question.

Exactly the kind of woman Felicity so often dreamed of being herself.

Was Devil mad for her?

Felicity had never been happier about

standing in a dimly lit room than she was in that moment, her face blazing with panic and every inch of her wanting to flee. The problem was that the man who called himself Devil and his companion were blocking the only exit — unless she considered the possibility of leaping from the window.

She turned to look at the darkened panes of glass, gauging the distance to the alleyway below.

"Too far for jumping," Devil said, as though he was in her head.

She turned back to face him, brazening through. "Are you certain?"

The woman laughed and answered. "Quite. And the last thing Dev needs is a flattened titled lady." She paused, the familiarity of the nickname filling the space between them. "You are titled, are you not?"

Felicity blinked. "My father is, yes."

The woman pushed past Devil as though he was not there. "Fascinating. And which title would that be?"

"He is the —"

"Don't answer that," Devil said, coming into the room, setting his hat down on a nearby table and turning the gas up on a lamp there, flooding the space with lush golden light. He turned to face her, and she resisted the urge to stare.

And failed.

She properly stared, taking in his heavy greatcoat — too warm for the season — and the tall boots below, caked with mud as though he'd been cavorting with hogs somewhere. He shucked the coat and sent it over a nearby chair without care, revealing more casual attire than she'd almost ever seen on a member of the opposite sex. He wore a patterned waistcoat over a linen shirt, both in shades of grey, but no cravat. Nothing at all filled the opening of the shirt — nothing but the cords of his neck and a long, deep triangle of skin, dusted with a hint of dark hair.

She'd never seen such a thing before — could count on one hand the number of times she'd seen Arthur or her father without a cravat.

She'd also never seen anything so thoroughly male in her life.

She was consumed by that triangle of skin.

After a too long pause, Felicity realized she was staring, and returned her attention to the woman, whose brows were high on her forehead with knowledge of precisely what Felicity had been doing. Unable to face the other woman's curiosity, Felicity's gaze flew back to Devil's — this time to his face. Another mistake. She wondered if she'd ever get used to how handsome he was.

That said, she could certainly do without him looking at her as though she were an insect he'd discovered in his porridge.

He didn't seem like the kind of man who ate porridge.

He narrowed his gaze on her, and she'd had quite enough of that. "What do you eat for breakfast?"

"What in —" He shook his head as though to clear it. "What?"

"It's not porridge, is it?"

"Good God. No."

"This is fascinating," the woman said.

"Not to you, it isn't," he replied.

Felicity bristled at the sharp tone. "You shouldn't speak to her that way."

The other woman grinned at that. "I completely agree."

Felicity turned. "I think I shall go."

"You should not have come," he said.

"Oi! You *certainly* shouldn't speak to *her* that way," the woman said.

Devil looked to the ceiling as though asking for patience.

Felicity moved to pass him.

"Wait." He reached out to stop her. "How did you get here to begin with?"

She stopped. "You gave me your direction."

"And you simply marched over here from Mayfair?"

"Why does it matter how I arrived?"

The question agitated him. "Because anything could have happened to you on the journey. You could have been set upon by thieves. Kidnapped and ransomed by any number of ruffians."

Her heart began to pound. "Nefarious sorts?"

"Precisely," he agreed.

She feigned innocence. "The kind who might sneak into a bedchamber unannounced?"

He stilled. Then scowled.

"Oooh!" The other woman clapped her hands. "I don't know what *that* means but it is *delicious.* This is better than anything you could see on Drury Lane."

"Shut up, Dahlia," he said, all exasperation.

Dahlia. It seemed the right name for her. The kind of name that Felicity could never carry.

When Dahlia did not reply, he turned back to Felicity. "How did you get here?"

"I took a hack."

He cursed. "And how did you get *here?*

Into my rooms?"

She stilled, keenly aware of the pins threaded into her hair. She couldn't tell him the truth. "They were unlocked."

He narrowed his gaze on her; he knew it was a lie. "And how did you get into the building?"

She searched for an answer that might make sense — something other than the truth. Not finding one, she decided to simply ignore him. Moving to leave once more, she said, "I apologize. I did not expect you to be here with your . . ." She searched for the word. "Friend."

"She's not my friend."

"Well, that's not very kind," Dahlia objected. "And to think, you were once my favorite."

"I was never your favorite."

"Hmm. Certainly not now." She turned to Felicity. "I am his sister."

Sister.

A powerful wave of something she did not wish to name shot through her at the word. She tilted her head. "Sister?"

The woman smiled, bold and broad and for a moment, Felicity almost saw a resemblance. "His one and only."

"And thank God for that."

Ignoring Devil's snide remark, Dahlia approached Felicity. "You should come and see me."

Before she could answer, Devil leapt in. "She doesn't need to see you."

One red brow arched. "Because she's seeing *you*?"

"She's *not* seeing me."

The other woman turned to face her with a knowing smile. "I think *I* see."

"I *don't* see, if that helps," Felicity said, feeling as though she ought to interject to end the strange conversation.

The other woman tapped her finger to her chin, considering Felicity for a long while. "You will, eventually."

"No one is seeing anyone! Dahlia, get out!"

"So very rude," Dahlia said, coming forward, hands extended toward Felicity. When she set her own in them, Dahlia pulled Felicity close and kissed one cheek and then the other, lingering on the final buss to whisper, "72 Shelton Street. Tell them Dahlia welcomes you." She looked to her brother. "Shall I stay and play the chaperone?"

"Get out."

His sister smirked. "Farewell, brother." And then she was gone, as though the whole scenario were perfectly ordinary. Which of course it wasn't, as it had started out with Felicity sneaking out her back garden without a chaperone, walking three-quarters of a mile, and hiring a hack to bring her here, to the dead center of Covent Garden, where she'd never been before and for good reason — or so she imagined.

Except now she was here in this mysterious place with this mysterious man, and mysterious women were whispering mysterious directions in her ear, and Felicity could not for the life of her think of a good reason not to be there. It was all terribly exciting.

"Don't look like that," he said as he closed the door behind his sister.

"Like what?"

"Like it's exciting."

"Why not? It is exciting."

"Whatever she told you, forget it."

Felicity laughed. "I don't think that is going to happen."

"What did she tell you?"

"It occurs that if she wished you to hear what she told me, she would have said it so you were able to do so."

He pressed his lips together in a thin line, his scar going stark white. He did not like that answer. "You stay away from Dahlia."

"Are you afraid she shall corrupt me?"

"No," he said sharply. "I'm afraid you

shall destroy her."

Felicity's mouth dropped open. "I beg your pardon?"

He looked away, toward a sideboard where a crystal decanter sat, full of deep, amber liquid. Like a dog scenting the hunt, he went for it, pouring himself a glass and drinking deep before turning back to her.

"No, thank you," she said tartly. "I don't drink whatever it is that you did not offer me."

He drank again. "Bourbon."

"American bourbon?" He did not reply. "American bourbon is prohibitively expensive for you to be drinking it like water."

He leveled her with a cool look before pouring a second glass and walking it to her, extending it with one long arm. When she reached for it, he pulled it back, dangling it out of reach, the silver ring on his thumb glinting in the light. "How did you get in?"

She hesitated. Then, "I don't want the drink anyway."

He shrugged his shoulders and poured her glass into his. "All right. You don't wish to answer that. How about this one? Why are you here?"

"We have an appointment."

"I was planning to come to you," he said.

The idea of him climbing her trellis was not unwelcome, but she said, "I grew tired of waiting."

He raised a brow at that. "I am not at your beck and call."

She inhaled at the cool words, not liking the way they stung. Not liking him, much, if she were honest. "Well, if you did not expect me to come here, then perhaps you should not have left me a card with your direction."

"You shouldn't be in Covent Garden."

"Why not?"

"Because, Felicity Faircloth, you're looking to marry a duke and assume your rightful place as a jewel of the *ton,* and if some aging aristocrat saw you here, that would *never* happen."

He had a point, but oddly, at no time during her journey had she even considered the *ton.* She'd been too excited about what was to greet her at the other end of the calling card. "No one saw me."

"I'm sure not for lack of you sticking out like a daisy in dirt."

Her brows rose. "A daisy in dirt?"

His lips flattened. "It's a figure of speech."

She tilted her head. "It is?"

He drank. "Covent Garden isn't for you, Felicity Faircloth."

"Whyever not?" Did he know that saying such things made her want to explore every nook and cranny of the place?

He watched her for a long moment, his dark eyes inscrutable, and then nodded once, turned on his heel, and marched to the far end of the room, pulling a cord. Perhaps he *did* know.

"You needn't summon anyone to escort me out," Felicity said. "I found my way in —"

"That much is clear, my lady. And I've no interest in having anyone escort you out. I can't risk you being seen."

He was an irritating man, and Felicity's patience began to fray. "Afraid I shall destroy you, as well as your sister?"

"It's not out of the realm of possibility. Haven't you — I don't know — a ladies' maid or a chaperone or something?"

The question unsettled her. "I am a twenty-seven-year-old spinster. Very few people would think twice about me traveling sans-chaperone."

"I'm certain your brother, your father, and any number of Mayfair toffs would think far more than twice to find you traveling sans-chaperone to my offices."

Felicity brazened it through. "You think having a chaperone would make it more acceptable for me to be here?"

He scowled. "No."

"You think me more dangerous than I am."

"I think you precisely as dangerous as you are." The words, so forthright and without edge, gave her pause, sending a thread of something strange coursing through her. Something suspiciously like power. She inhaled sharply, and he leveled her with a look. "That's not exciting, either, Felicity Faircloth."

She disagreed, but thought it best not to say so. "Why do you insist on calling me by both of my names?"

"It reminds me that you are a fairy-tale princess. Faircloth indeed. The fairest of them all."

The lie stung, and she hated herself for letting it do so, more than she hated him for speaking it. Instead of saying so, however, she forced herself to laugh at his unwelcome jest.

His brows knit together. "You are amused?"

"Is that not what you intended? Did you not think yourself immensely clever?"

"How was I being clever?"

He was going to make her say it — and that made her hate him more. "Because I'm

146

the opposite of fairest." He did not speak, and did not look away, and she felt she had to continue. To make her point. "I am the plainest of them all."

When he still did not speak, she began to feel foolish. And annoyed. "Is that not our arrangement?" she prompted.

"Are you not to make me beautiful?"

He was watching her even more intently now, as though she were a curious specimen under glass. And then, "Yes. I shall make you beautiful, Felicity Faircloth." She scowled at the intentional use of both of her names. "Beautiful enough to draw the moth to your flame."

The impossible, made possible. And yet . . . "How did you do it?"

He blinked. "Do what?"

"How did you ensure he wouldn't deny it? Half a dozen doyennes of the *ton* turned up for tea this morning at our home, believing that I am the future Duchess of Marwick. *How?*"

He turned his back on her, moving to a low table laden with papers. "I promised you the impossible, did I not?"

"But *how?*" She couldn't understand. She'd woken that morning with a keen sense of impending doom, certain that her lie had been exposed, the Duke of Marwick had proclaimed her mad before all London, and her family had been ruined.

But none of that had happened.

Nothing near to that had happened.

Indeed, it seemed that the Duke of Marwick had tacitly confirmed the engagement. Or, at least, he had not denied it.

Which was *impossible.*

Except, this man, Devil, had made that precise promise, and made good upon it.

Somehow.

Her heart had pounded with each successive gawking well-wisher, and something like hope had flared in her chest, alongside another emotion — startlingly akin to wonder. At this man, who seemed capable of saving her and her family.

So, of course she'd come to see him.

It had seemed, frankly, quite impossible not to.

A knock sounded on the door and he moved to answer it, swinging it open and allowing a dozen servants in from the hallway beyond, each holding large pails of steaming water. They entered without a word — without looking at Felicity — marching through the room to the far wall, where a doorway stood open to a dark space beyond.

Her gaze flew to Devil's. "What is that?"

"My bedchamber," he said simply. "Did you not have a look when you picked my lock?"

Heat roared to life on her cheeks. "I didn't pick —"

"You did, though. And I don't understand how a lady procures the superior skill of lockpicking, but I hope you will one day tell me."

"Perhaps that will be the favor you ask of me once you've brought me my besotted husband."

One corner of his stern mouth twitched, as though he were enjoying their conversation. "No, my lady, that tale you shall offer freely."

The words were quiet and full of certainty, and she was grateful for the dim evening light lest the unexpected flush they brought with them be obvious. With a little uncomfortable cough, she looked to the door to his bedchamber, where a light had flickered to life, bright enough to make the shadows within dance, but not enough to reveal anything of the space beyond.

And then the servants returned, empty pails in hand, and Felicity knew exactly what they had done. Before they'd had a chance to file out and close the door behind them, Devil was shucking his waistcoat and making quick work of the buttons on the sleeves of the linen shirt beneath.

Her mouth fell open, and he turned to enter the room beyond, calling over his shoulder as he disappeared, "Well, we might as well begin."

She blinked, calling after him, "Begin what?"

A pause. Was he . . . *disrobing*? Then, from farther away, "Our plans."

"I . . ." She hesitated. Perhaps she was misunderstanding the situation. "I beg your pardon, but are you about to *bathe*?"

He peeked his head back around the edge of the door. "As a matter of fact, I am."

He was no longer wearing a shirt. Felicity's mouth went dry as he disappeared back into the room, and she watched the empty doorway for long minutes, until she heard the twin thuds of his boots, and then the splash of water as he took to the bathtub.

She shook her head in the empty front room of the apartments. What was happening? And then he called out, "Lady Felicity, do you wish to shout from out there? Or are you coming in?"

Coming in?

She resisted the urge to ask him to elaborate, and instead made her choice, knowing doing so could easily mark her a lamb to

slaughter. "I am coming in."
No, not lamb to slaughter.
Moth to flame.

CHAPTER EIGHT

He'd been teasing her. He'd wanted to make the innocent Lady Felicity Faircloth reconsider her rash decision to turn up in his rooms uninvited, knowing that there was no earthly way she would join him in his bedchamber, let alone in his bedchamber as he bathed.

And there he was, waist-deep in water in the copper tub, smirk upon his face, congratulating himself on delivering a proper lesson to the lady beyond — who would certainly never find cause to arrive, unchaperoned, on his Covent Garden doorstep again lest she be faced with proof of the baseness of the neighborhood — when the lady in question called out from the next room, "I am coming in."

He barely had time to hide his surprise before Felicity Faircloth flounced into his bedchamber, glass of his hard-won bourbon in hand, as though she belonged there.

To add insult to injury, he then found himself imagining what it might be like if she did, in fact, belong there. If it were perfectly normal for her to sit upon his bed and watch as he bathed the dirt of the day from his body, cleaning himself before he joined her there, on that bed.

Cleaning himself for her.

Shit. This had all gone sideways.

And there was no way to repair it, as he was naked in a pool of water, and she was fully clothed, hands clasped demurely in her lap, watching him with avid interest.

Hers was not the only interest that was avid, it should be said.

Not that his cock was going to have its interest slaked. This was not the kind of woman whom one fucked in the darkness. This was the kind of woman to be won over. Had she not waxed poetic about passion in her own bedchamber?

Seducing Felicity Faircloth away from his brother would take more than one night in his rooms in Covent Garden. And it wouldn't happen in Covent Garden at all — as she would never be here again.

He wasn't used to being concerned for people's safety on the Bareknuckle Bastards' turf, but with her, he was. Far too concerned. He still wasn't clear how she'd made it here without running into trouble.

The thought grated, and he found comfort in that, letting it overcome his first response to her. He was not the one who needed to be unsettled. She was.

He forced himself to lean back, pulled a length of linen from the edge of the tub, and moved it with purpose. "Once I am clean, I intend to return you to Mayfair."

Her gaze flickered to where his arm moved, lazily scrubbing up his chest. He slowed his pace when she swallowed, a faint flush creeping up her neck. She drank, her eyes going wide and slightly watery as a little hack sounded at the back of her throat — a cough she clearly refused to release. After she recovered, she met his eyes, narrowing her own on him. "I know what you are doing."

"And what is that?"

"You are trying to scare me away from this place. And you should have thought about that before summoning me here."

"I didn't summon you," he said. "I left you my direction so that you could get me a message, if necessary."

"Why?" she asked.

He blinked. "Why?"

"Why would I need to get a message to you?" The question set him back. Before he was required to fabricate an answer, she continued. "Forgive me if you are not exactly the type of man I would ask for assistance."

He didn't like that. "What does that mean?"

"Only that a man who climbs into one's bedchamber uninvited isn't the kind of man who assists one into a carriage or takes the empty slot on one's dance card at a ball."

"Why not?"

She cut him a look. "You don't seem the dancing sort."

"You'd be surprised by what sort I can be, Felicity Faircloth."

She smirked. "You're currently bathing in front of me."

"You didn't have to come in."

"You didn't have to invite me."

If he'd known what a difficult female she was, he would never have allowed this plan to go through.

Lie.

She sat back on the high bed then, letting her pink-slippered feet dangle, her hands settling to the counterpane. "You needn't worry, anyway," she said. "You are not the first man I have seen in a state of undress."

His brows shot up. He could have sworn she was a virgin. But she knew how to pick a lock, so perhaps there was more to Lady Felicity Faircloth than he imagined. Excitement warred with something else — something far more dangerous. Something that won out. "Who?"

She drank again, more careful this time, and the liquor did not burn as much. Or she was better at hiding it. "I don't see why that is any of your business."

"If you want me to turn you into a flame, love, I must know all the ways you've sparked before."

"I told you. I've never sparked before."

He didn't believe it. The woman was all spark — constantly threatening to flare.

"That's why I agreed to your offer, you see. I fear I shall never spark. I'm squarely on the shelf, now."

She didn't look on the shelf.

"And I was not blessed with porcelain beauty."

"There is nothing unattractive about you," he said.

"Please, sir," she said dryly, "you shall fill my head with your pretty compliments."

He didn't like how this girl could make him feel things he had not felt in decades. Things like chagrin. "Well, there isn't."

"Oh. Well, thank you."

He changed the subject, suddenly feeling

like a proper ass. "So, the extent of your witnessing men in a state of undress ends at who, your father in his casual, country attire?"

She smiled. "You are showing your lack of knowledge of the aristocracy, Devil. My father's casual country attire includes a cravat and coat, always." She shook her head. "No. As a matter of fact, it was the Duke of Haven."

He resisted the urge to stand. He knew Haven. The duke frequented The Singing Sparrow — a tavern two streets away owned by an American and a legendary songstress. But Haven was wild for his wife, and that wasn't gossip — Devil had witnessed it.

"I assume this is the duke who tossed you over for his wife?"

She nodded. "So it wasn't a state of undress that mattered," she said. "I was one of his bachelorettes."

She said it as though it would explain everything. "What does that mean?"

Her brow furrowed. "You don't know about Haven's search for a new duchess?"

"I know Haven has a duchess. Whom he loves beyond reason."

"She demanded a divorce," Felicity said. "Do you not read the papers?"

"I cannot articulate how little I care for

the marital strife of the aristocracy."

She stilled at that. "You're serious."

"Why wouldn't I be?"

"You really don't care what happened? It was in all the gossip pages. I was quite famous for a bit."

"I don't read the gossip pages."

One mahogany brow rose. "No, I don't imagine that you do, what with how very busy and important you are."

Devil had the distinct impression she was teasing him. "My interest extends to how it is relevant to you, Felicity Faircloth, and barely that far."

She cut him a look at the last. "Last summer, the Duchess of Haven demanded a divorce. There was a competition to become the second duchess. It was all foolish, of course, because Haven absolutely loved her beyond reason. Which he told me. While in his dressing gown and nothing else."

"He was unable to dress before telling you that?"

She smiled, soft and romantic. "I shan't allow you to make it sound ridiculous. I've never seen anyone so undone by love."

Devil's gaze narrowed. "And so we get to the heart of the impossible things you wish for."

She paused, myriad emotions passing over

her face. Embarrassment. Guilt. Sorrow. "Don't you wish for such a thing?"

"I told you, my lady, passion is a dangerous play." He paused. "So, Haven kept his duchess and what happened to the rest of you?"

"One of us left mid-competition to marry another. One of us became a companion to an aging aunt and is on the Continent, looking for a husband. The final two — Lady Lilith and I — we remain unmarried. It's not as though we were diamonds of the first water to begin with."

"No?"

She shook her head. "We weren't even diamonds of the second water. And now, our mothers' desperation to get us matched has become something of a vague black mark."

"How vague of a black mark?"

"The kind that makes us vaguely ruined." Another drink. "Not that I wasn't vaguely ruined before that."

It had always struck Devil that women were ruined either entirely or not at all. And she did not look ruined.

She looked perfect.

"Is that why your unfortunates passed you over for no apparent reason?" he asked. "Because that seems like a reason. An idiotic one, but one that the aristocracy would happily cling to in order to roast one of its own."

She looked to him. "What do you know of the aristocracy?"

"I know they like to drink bourbon and play cards." *And I know there was a time when I wanted very much to be one of them, just like you do, Felicity Faircloth.* He leaned back in the bath. "And I know it's better to be first in hell than simpering in heaven."

Her lips flattened into a straight, disapproving line. "Either way, your end of our bargain is more than a challenge. The Duke of Marwick might not care for a wife with such a sullied reputation."

The Duke of Marwick had no interest in a wife, period.

Devil did not tell her that. Neither did he tell her that her sullied reputation would be in tatters soon enough. He was suddenly uncomfortable, and he stood, water sluicing off him as he came to his full height.

He would be lying if he said he did not enjoy the way her eyes went wide or the little squeak she made as she hopped off the bed to turn her back to him. "That was very rude," she said to the far wall of the room.

"I've never been known for my politeness," he said.

She gave a little snort. "What a surprise."

He shook his head, amused. Even now, she remained smart-mouthed. "Are you regretting your earlier bravery?"

"No." The word cracked on its high pitch. She drank again. "Keep talking."

It was his turn to be suspicious. "Why?"

"So that I can be certain you are not approaching to take advantage of me."

"If I were going to take advantage of you, I would approach from the front, Felicity Faircloth. In full view, so you would have the joy of expecting me," he said. "But I shall talk, with pleasure." He moved to dress, watching her the whole time. "We are going to begin with a gown."

"A — a gown?"

He pulled on his trousers. "I promised that Marwick would be slavering after you like a dog, did I not?"

"I didn't say I wanted that," she said.

He grinned at the distaste in her words as he lifted a black linen shirt and pulled it over his head, tucking it in before fastening the stays of his trousers. "No, you said you thought him the handsomest man you'd ever seen, did you not?"

A pause. "I suppose."

Irritation flared, and he dismissed it. "You said you wanted him to come after you like

161

a moth to a flame. You do know what happens to moths when they get to the flame, don't you? You may turn around."

She did so, her eyes immediately finding him and tracking his clothing from shoulders to bare feet. The excitement in her gaze as she gave him her frank perusal sent a thread of awareness through him — and he shifted his weight at the sudden heaviness in his freshly pressed trousers.

"What happens?" He blinked at the words, and she added, "To the moths."

"They combust." He pulled on his waistcoat.

Her gaze was on his fingers as he worked the buttons of the coat, and he could not resist slowing his movements, watching her watch him. Devil had always loved the female gaze upon him, and Lady Felicity Faircloth watched him with pure, unadulterated fascination, making him want to show her everything she wanted.

"Combustion sounds better than slavering," she said, the words breathier than before.

"Says the woman who is doing neither." He finished the buttons and smoothed the waistcoat over his torso. "Now. If you'll let me finish . . ."

"By all means, slaver away."

He barely resisted the huff of laughter that threatened at her smart retort. "If you want him to desire you beyond reason, you must dress the part."

She tilted her head. "I am sorry. I am to dress for him?"

"Indeed. Preferably something with skin." He waved a hand at her high-necked shell pink gown. "That won't work." It was a lie. The gown worked quite well, as far as Devil's body was concerned.

She put her hand to her throat. "I like this gown."

"It's pink."

"I like pink."

"I've noticed."

"What's wrong with pink?"

"Nothing, if you are a mewling babe."

She pressed her lips into a thin line. "A different gown will do what, exactly?"

"Ensure he shan't be able to keep his hands off of you."

"Oh," she said. "I was unaware that men were so entirely susceptible to women's clothing that it rendered them unable to control their hands."

He hesitated, not liking the direction of her words. "Well, some men."

"Not you," she said.

"I'm more than able to control my urges."

"Even if I were to wear . . . what was it you suggested? Something with skin?"

And like that, he was thinking of her skin. "Of course."

"And is this a particularly male affliction?"

He cleared his throat. "Some might argue that it is a *human* affliction."

"Interesting," she replied, "because it could be said that you were just moments ago wearing *something with skin,* and my hands somehow, remarkably, remained quite far from your person." She grinned. "I slavered not at all."

The words were like a flag to a bull, and he wanted, immediately, to rise to the challenge and tempt Felicity Faircloth to slavering. But that way lay danger, because he was already far too intrigued by the lady, and that had to stop before it started.

"I shall have a dress sent round for you. Wear it to the Bourne ball. Three days hence."

"You do realize that dresses are not simply available in the dimensions of whomever you like, do you not? They are ordered. They are fabricated. They take *weeks* —"

"For some."

"Ah yes," she teased. "For mere mortals. I forgot that you have magic elves who make dresses for you. I assume they spin them from straw? In a single night?"

"Did I not tell you I would win you your duke?"

She shook her head. "I don't know how you've silenced his denial of our engagement, Devil, but it is impossible that he will remain silent."

He did not tell her there was no denial to silence. Did not tell her that she'd played directly into his hands two nights before, when he'd made it seem impossible for her to win the duke who had already decided she was a convenient mark. Did not tell her that he, too, had decided Felicity Faircloth was a convenient mark.

Suddenly, he was not so certain she was convenient after all.

"I told you, I have a skill for making the impossible possible," he said. "Here is how we begin: you continue to treat your lie as truth, you wear the gown I send, and he shall be in your path. Then it will only be a matter of winning him."

"Oh," she retorted, "just the simple matter of winning him. As though that's the easy bit."

"It is the easy bit." She'd won him already. And even if she hadn't, she could win whomever she wished. Of that, Devil had no doubt. "Trust me, Felicity Faircloth.

165

Wear the dress, win the man."

"I shall still need to be fitted, Devil Whatever-your-name-is. And even if I wear a magical gown, constructed by fairies and made to sweep men from their feet, I remain — how did you put it? *Not unattractive?*"

He shouldn't feel guilty about that. His purpose wasn't to make Felicity Faircloth think she was beautiful. But he couldn't seem to stop himself from approaching her. "Shall I elaborate?"

She raised a brow, and he nearly laughed at how surly she looked. "I wish you wouldn't. I don't know how I shall resist swooning in the fiery embrace of your compliments."

A smile twitched. "You are not unattractive, Felicity Faircloth. You have a full, open face and eyes that reveal every one of your thoughts, and hair that I imagine falls in rich, mahogany waves when it is pulled from its severe moorings . . ." He was standing in front of her now. Her lips had fallen open just a touch — just enough for her to suck in a little breath. Just enough for him to notice. ". . . and full, soft lips that any man would want to kiss."

He meant to say all that, of course. To lay it on thick and begin the seduction of Lady Felicity Faircloth. To punish his brother and win the day.

Just as he meant to be this close to her — close enough to see the freckles that dusted over her nose and cheeks. Close enough to see the little crease left by years of the dimple that lived there flashing. Close enough to smell her soap, jasmine. Close enough to see the ring of grey around her beautiful brown eyes.

Close enough to want to kiss her.

Close enough to see that if he did, she'd let him.

She's not for you.

He pulled away at the thought, breaking the spell for both of them. "At least, any proper toff in Mayfair."

One emotion after another chased through her gaze — confusion, understanding, hurt — and then nothing at all. And he hated himself just a little for that. More than a little, when she cleared her throat and said, "I shall wait in the other room for you to escort me home."

She pushed past him and he let her go, regret coursing through him, unfamiliar and stinging almost as much as the brush of her skirts against his legs.

He stood there for a long moment, attempting to find calm — the cool, unmoving center that had kept him alive for thirty years. The one that had built an empire. The one that had been shaken by the appearance of a single aristocratic woman in his private space.

And just when he found that calm once more, he lost it. Because the discovery was punctuated with the soft *snick* of the door to his chambers.

He was moving before the sound dissipated, tearing through the now empty exterior room to the door, which he nearly ripped from the hinges to get into the hallway beyond — also empty.

She was fast, dammit.

He went after her, down the stairs, determined to catch her. He headed through the maze of corridors to the exit, the door hanging ajar, like an unfinished sentence.

Except it was clear that Felicity Faircloth had said all she was interested in saying.

He ripped it open and burst through it, immediately looking right, toward Long Acre, where she would instantly find a hack to take her home. Nothing.

But to the left, toward Seven Dials, where she would instantly find trouble, her pink skirts were already fading into the darkness. "Felicity!"

She didn't hesitate.

"Fuck!" he roared, already heading back

through the building.

Goddammit, he'd miscalculated.

Because Lady Felicity Faircloth was heading into the muck of Covent Garden, in the dead of night, and his feet were bare.

CHAPTER NINE

Felicity moved as fast as she could away from the curving Arne Street, back toward the main thoroughfare where she had been deposited by the hack earlier in the evening. Turning the corner, she pulled up short, confident that she was out of sight of Devil's home, and finally able to catch her breath.

Once that happened, she'd find herself another hack and return home.

She'd be damned if she was going to allow him to escort her. She'd be just as likely to be ruined by him as she would be to be properly chaperoned by him.

Indignant irritation flared again.

How dare he speak to her in such a manner, discussing her hair and her eyes and her lips? How dare he nearly kiss her?

Why hadn't he kissed her?

Had it been a nearly-kiss, even? Felicity had never been kissed, but that certainly seemed to be the kind of run-up to kissing that she'd heard about. Or read about in novels. Or imagined happening to her. Many times.

He'd been so close — so close she could see the black ring around the velvet gold of his eyes, and the shadow of his beard, making her wonder how it would feel against her skin, and that scar, long and dangerous and somehow vulnerable, making her want to reach up and touch it.

She almost had, until she'd realized that he might be going to kiss her, and then *that* was all she wanted. But then he hadn't had any interest in doing it. Worse, he'd *told* her he had no interest in doing it.

"He'd leave kissing me to a Mayfair toff," she said to the night, her cheeks burning from embarrassment. She'd never been so proud of herself for taking the bull by the horns, so to speak, and leaving him right there, in his room, where he could ruminate on what one should and should not say to women.

She turned her face to the sky, inhaling deeply. At least coming here had not been a mistake. She didn't think she'd ever forget his sister — a woman who knew her worth, without question. Felicity could do with more of that, herself. She made a mental note to find her way to 72 Shelton Street —

whatever she would find there was sure to be fascinating.

And even now, on the streets filled with shadows, the craggy mountains of tightly packed buildings rising up around her, Felicity found herself feeling — unlocked. This place, far from Mayfair and its judgment and cutting remarks . . . she liked it. She liked the way the rain settled. The way it seemed to wash away the grime. The way it seemed to free her.

" 'Elp a gel out, milady?"

The question came close enough to shock her, and Felicity spun around to find a young woman standing behind her, wet from the rain that had started — a fine London mist that seeped into skin and clothes — in a ragged dress, hair stringy and loose around her shoulders. Her arm was extended, palm up.

"I — I beg your pardon?"

The woman indicated her open palm. "Got a bob? For somefin' to eat?"

"Oh!" Felicity looked to the woman and then to her hand. "Yes. Of course." She reached for the pocket of her skirts, where she kept a small coin purse.

A small coin purse that was no longer there.

"Oh," she said again. "I don't seem to —"

She stopped. "My purse is —"

The woman's lips twisted in frustration. "Aww, the blades 'ave already got to you."

Felicity blinked. "Got to me?"

"Yeah. Fine lady like yerself, cutpurse found you the heartbeat you landed in the Garden."

Felicity fingered the hole that remained in her skirts. Her purse was gone. And all her money. How was she to get home?

Her heart began to pound.

The woman scowled. "E'ryone's a thief 'round here."

"Well," Felicity said, "I've nothing left to steal, it seems."

The girl pointed to her feet. "Them slippers are pretty." And then to the bodice of her dress. "An' the ribbons there, the lace at yer neck, too." Her gaze stole to Felicity's hair. "And hairbits. E'ryone's after ladies' hairbits."

Felicity lifted a hand to her hair, "My hairpins?"

"Yeah."

"Would you like one?"

A gleam shone in the girl's eyes, and she looked as though she'd been offered jewels. "Yeah."

Felicity reached up and extracted one, extending it to the girl, who snatched it without hesitation.

"Got one for me, lady?"

"And me?"

Felicity spun to find two more standing behind her, one older and one no more than eight or ten. She hadn't heard them approach. "Oh," she said again, reaching for her hair once more. "Yes. Of course."

"And wot 'bout me, girl?" She turned to find a man beyond, reed-thin and smiling in a wolfish, toothless grin that made her skin crawl. "Wot you got for me?"

"I . . ." She hesitated. "Nothing."

A different gleam in a different eye. Far more dangerous. "You sure?"

Felicity backed away, toward the other women. "Someone's taken my purse."

" 'At's all right — you can pay me anovver way. You ain't the prettiest fing I've seen, but you'll do."

A hand touched her hair, fingers searching. "Can I have another?"

She blocked it from taking what she had not offered. "I need them."

"You got more at yer home, don't you?" the little girl whined.

"I — I suppose." She pulled another hairpin out and extended it to her.

"Fank you," the girl said, bobbing a little

curtsy, pushing the pin into her knotted mane.

"Get gone, girl," the man said. "It's my turn to deal wiv the lady."

Don't get gone, Felicity thought. *Please.*

Felicity looked down the dark street toward Devil's offices, out of sight. Surely he'd realized she was gone by now, hadn't he? Would he follow her?

"You fink a lady's going to deal wiv you, Reggie? She won't touch yer poxy pecker for a king's fortune."

Reggie's disgusting smile dropped, replaced by a menacing scowl. "You're askin' for a smack in the gob, girl." He moved toward her, arm up, and she scurried back, into the shadows. Satisfied with his exhibition of weak power, he turned back toward Felicity and came closer. She backed away, coming up against a wall as he reached out for her hair, now unpinned, falling down around her shoulders.

"That's pretty 'air —" He touched it, softly, and she flinched. "Like silk that is."

She edged to the side, along the wall, regret and fear warring in her gut. "Thank you."

"Ah-ah, lady." He closed his hand, catching a hank of hair in his fist, pulling tight. When she gasped at the pain, he said,

"Come back 'ere."

"Let me go!" she shouted, turning, shock and fear sending her into action, her hand fisted as she punched wildly toward him, skimming his bony cheek as he leaned away from the strike.

"You'll regret that swipe, you will." He tightened his grip, pulling her head back. She cried out.

Two taps replied from the distance, barely noticeable over the sound of her pounding heart.

"Shit," the man holding her said. He dropped her hair like it had burned.

"Oh . . . Reggie," the first woman cackled. "You've got yerself a bit o' trouble now . . ." She lowered her voice to a stage whisper as she backed farther into the darkness. "The Devil's found you."

For a moment, Felicity did not understand, too riddled with fear and confusion and immense relief that Reggie had unhanded her. She scurried to the side, away from those assembled, toward the sound of approaching footsteps.

"Look at her, heading for 'im," the woman narrated. "You've touched a Bastard's lady."

"I didn't know!" Reggie cried, his insolent bravado having escaped him.

And then he was there, the man they

called the Devil — wearing the clothes she'd seen him in moments ago, the sleek black trousers she'd heard slide over his skin. The black linen shirt. The waistcoat. And now, he was wearing boots.

He carried that walking stick in his bare hand, his rings and the silver lion's head glinting like wicked promise in the moonlight. It was a weapon, he'd assured her the night they met. And now, she had no doubt of it.

She let out a little exhale of relief. "Thank God."

He didn't look at her, too focused on Reggie as he twirled that stick menacingly. "God has no place here. Does he, Reggie?"

Reggie did not reply.

The stick spun, and Felicity could not tear her gaze from his face, where cold, hard angles had turned to stone and that wicked scar shone stark white against the darkness. "God has forsaken us here in the Garden, has he not, Reggie?"

Reggie swallowed. Nodded.

He kept moving, right past her, as though she were invisible. "And without God, whose benevolence allows you to remain here?"

Reggie's eyes went wide and he strained to look up at the other man. "Yours."

"And who am I?"

"Devil."

"And do you know the rules of my turf?"

Reggie nodded. "Yes."

"And what are they?"

"No one touches women."

"That's right," a woman crowed from the shadows, brave once more. *Safe, once more.* "Bugger off, Reggie."

Devil ignored her. "And what else, Reggie?"

"And no one touches children."

"Or?"

"Or they see the Devil."

Devil leaned in and said quietly, "Both of us."

Reggie closed his eyes. "I'm sorry! It weren't nuffin'. I weren't gon' do anyfin'."

"You broke the rules, Reggie." Devil grasped the silver tip of his cane and pulled, the ring of steel echoing against the bricks of the alleyway.

Felicity gasped at the appearance of the two-foot-long sword that came from within, cold steel glinting silver in the moonlight, the tip of which was immediately at Reggie's throat.

Reggie's eyes went wide. "I'm sorry!"

Felicity moved forward. "Wait!"

Devil did not look at her. Did not seem to

hear her. "I should cut your throat here, don't you think? Let the rain wash you away?"

"I'm sorry!"

Felicity put her hand on Devil's arm. "There will be no throat cutting! He didn't do anything! He pulled my hair! That's it!"

If anything, the words made Devil colder. His muscles went impossibly harder beneath her hand. And for a long moment, Felicity thought he might use that wicked blade. That he might slice the man's throat. That the blood might be on her hands.

"Please," she said, softly. "Don't."

He looked to her then, for the first time, fury burning in his black eyes, and she resisted the instinct to let him go. "You ask for his life?"

"Yes. Of course." She wished the man gone, but not dead.

He watched her for what felt like an age before he spoke, not taking his gaze from hers. "Thank the lady, Reggie. She buys your life from me tonight."

The sword point glinted as he returned it to its ebony sheath, and Reggie dropped to his knees in relief. "Fank you, lady."

He reached for her feet, and she backed away, avoiding his touch. "That . . . won't be necessary."

Devil stepped between them. "Get gone, Reggie, and stay gone. If I find you on Bastards' turf again, your angel won't be here to save you."

Reggie was gone before the words faded.

Devil turned to face the women, lurking in the shadows. "You three, too." He reached into his pocket and dug out a handful of coins. "No need to work tonight, Hester," he said to the first, dropping a bob in her hand before turning and giving two to the older woman and the girl. "Go home, girls, before you find more trouble."

The three did as they were told, leaving Felicity alone with the Devil.

She swallowed. "That was kind."

He remained silent, watching the place where the trio had disappeared as seconds stretched like hours, and then he said, "Nothing is kind here." He turned to her. "You shouldn't have wasted a bargain on that rat's life."

Uncertainty edged through her at the words. And still — "Was I to have let you kill him?"

"Others would have."

"I am not others," she said, simply. "I'm me."

He turned to face her, stepping close. "You traded for something that had very little value."

"I was not aware it was a trade."

"Nothing in the Garden is free, Felicity Faircloth."

She shook her head, forcing a little laugh. "Well, I haven't any money and I'm nearly out of hairpins, so I hope he wasn't worth very much."

He froze. "You ran without money? How did you think to get home?"

"I thought I had money," she said. She slid her hand into her skirts, revealing the hole there. "Someone stole it. I didn't even feel it."

He looked down at the place where her fingers wiggled through her pocket. "Our cutpurses are the best in town."

"You must be very proud." She tried for levity, unable to escape the relief that still coursed through her. When he did not reply, she said, quietly, "Thank you."

He turned to stone again. "He did not deserve lenience."

"Nothing happened. You came before it could. He barely touched me."

His scar went white and a muscle pounded in his cheek. "He touched you. Your hair." His gaze was locked on it where it fell around her shoulders, unpinned.

She shook her head. "Yes, but not much.

It's only down because I gave the women my hairpins."

"Not much?" he said, drawing closer to her. "I saw him with a lock of it in his filthy paw. I heard him describe it. *Like silk.* And I heard you cry out when he pulled it." He paused, his throat working to keep words back. Words that came anyway. "He touched it. And I haven't."

An echo came from earlier, from inside his bedchamber, the words he used to describe her hair. *Hair that I imagine falls in rich, mahogany waves when it is pulled from its severe moorings.*

Her eyes went wide. "I didn't know you wished to —"

He lifted his hand, then, and for a moment, she thought he would do it. Touch her. For a moment, she imagined what it would be like for him to slide his strong fingers into her hair and run them along her scalp, now free from the tight binds of hairpins and coifs. She imagined leaning into that touch. Leaning up to him.

Him leaning down to her.

"I should take it," he whispered. "My payment. I should touch it."

She blinked up at him. "Yes."

The decision warred in him. She could see it. And she saw him make it, too, saw him give in to the desire and reach for her. *Thank God.*

His touch was barely there, and the most powerful thing she'd ever experienced. Her breath caught in her throat as he sifted her hair through his fingers. Would his hand be warm? Would he let himself touch her? *Would he kiss her?*

"I should have killed him for touching it," he said, softly.

"It wasn't . . ." She hesitated, then whispered, "It wasn't like this."

His gaze found hers in the darkness. "What does that mean?"

"I won't remember him," she said. "Not when you are here now."

He shook his head. "Felicity Faircloth, you are very dangerous." Devil's fingers — work-rough and warm — moved to her cheek, traced down the curve of it, to her jaw. Lingered there.

She shivered. "Being here . . . with you . . . it makes me feel like I *could* be dangerous."

He tilted her face up to his glittering eyes, to the Covent Garden mist. "And if you were? What would you do?"

I would stay, she thought, madly. *I would explore this terrifying, magnificent world.* She didn't say those things, however. Instead, she focused on the third answer — the shocking one. The one that came on a flood of want. "I would kiss you."

For a moment he did not move, and then he took a deep breath and raised his other hand, cradling her face in his warm grasp before repeating, "You are very dangerous."

She did not know where the words came from when she said, softly, "Would you let me?"

He shook his head once, his gaze on hers. "I wouldn't be able to resist."

Later, she would blame the darkness for her actions. The rain on the cobblestone streets. The fear and the wonder. She would blame his warm hands and his beautiful lips and that scar on the side of his face that made him somehow impossibly handsome. She had to blame something for it, you see, as Felicity Faircloth, aging spinster wallflower, did not kiss men.

What's more, she absolutely did not kiss men who lived in Covent Garden and carried cane swords and were named Devil.

Except in that moment, when she rose up on her toes and did just that, pressing her lips to his full, soft ones. He was so warm, the heat of him coming through his linen shirt and waistcoat — the waistcoat she grabbed instantly and without thought, as though he might be able to keep her steady in the wild moment.

As though he weren't the reason it felt so wild, with the way he wrapped his arms around her and pulled her tight against him, the movement making her gasp her surprise. He growled — a deep, delicious sound, and his teeth nipped at her lower lip before he whispered, like darkness, "Take it then. Like you mean it."

And because he gave her permission, she did, taking her first kiss from this dangerous man who seemed the kind of man who gave nothing freely, and still gave all of himself to this moment . . . to her pleasure.

Not just hers, however. Devil licked over her lower lip, teasing her mouth open so he might claim it with a deep, unyielding caress. He groaned again, the sound sending a thrum of desire through her, pooling deep in her belly. Lower. That groan, coupled with his wicked, wonderful kiss, made her feel more powerful than she'd ever felt before.

As though he were a lock she'd picked.

He was ruining her.

Only it didn't feel like ruin. It felt like triumph.

She pressed closer to him, wanting him nearer, wanting more of this moment and its heady power. He lifted his head to look at her, his breath coming in short bursts, and with something like surprise in his eyes. He took a step away from her, rubbing the back of one hand over his lips. He shook his head. "Felicity Faircloth, you'll burn me down."

A scream sounded in the distance, followed by shouts and a collection of masculine voices. Felicity pressed closer to Devil, but he did not offer the comfort she sought, instead shaking his head firmly. "No."

Her brow furrowed. "No?"

Without reply, he took her arm in one impersonal hand and pulled her back toward his offices. When they rounded the curve, he stopped her in the street. "What do you see?"

"Your lair." Two nights earlier, she'd thought it a silly description. But now — it was a lair. The dominion of a man more powerful than she'd imagined. A man who could punish or protect at whim.

"What else?" he asked.

She looked about. She'd never thought much about the city at night. "It's beautiful."

He was taken aback. "What?"

She pointed. "See there? Where the mist and the light have turned the cobblestones gold? It's beautiful."

He stared at the spot for a moment, his scar white and angry. And then he smiled. But it wasn't a kind smile. Or a friendly one. It was something much more dangerous. "You think the wide world beautiful, don't you, Felicity Faircloth?"

Felicity stepped back from him. "I —"

He did not let her answer. "You think it's here for you, and why shouldn't you? You were raised in power and money without even a sense of anything ever going poorly for you."

"That isn't true," she said, hotly indignant. "Plenty has gone poorly for me."

"Oh, of course, I forgot," he said, snidely. "You've lost your terrible friends at the center of your silly world. Your brother can't keep coin in his pocket. Your father, neither. And you're stuck having to win a duke you don't want."

Her brow furrowed at the tone, as though she was a child without any sense of what was important. She shook her head. "I don't —"

He cut her off. "And here's my favorite bit of your sad story. You've never felt passion; you think passion is sweet and kind and good — love beyond reason. Protection. Care."

Resentment flared. "Not think. Know."

"Let me tell you about passion, Felicity Faircloth. Passion is *obsession.* It is desire beyond reason. It is not want, but *need.* And it comes with the worst of sin far more often than it comes with the best of it."

She tugged on her arm, where his fingers dug harshly into her flesh. "You're hurting me."

He released her, instantly. "Silly girl. You don't know what hurt is."

He pointed up toward the dark windows above, to the shadowed overhangs and gaping black wounds in the side of the brick structures. "Once again. What do you see?"

"Nothing," she said, anger making the word loud and harsh. "What next, you tell me that I don't understand how to look at a rooftop?"

He ignored her, pointing up the curving empty road, where the entrances to half a dozen alleyways lurked. "And there?"

She shook her head. "Nothing. Darkness."

He turned her in the opposite direction. "There?"

Unease threaded through her. "N-nothing."

"Good," he said. "That feeling? The fear? The uncertainty? Hold on to that, Felicity Faircloth, for it shall keep you safe."

He turned her back to him, pushing her

behind as he stepped forward and tapped his walking stick twice on the hard stones of the street. He looked up at the shadowed buildings and spoke, his words firm and clear, echoing against the stones. "No one touches her." Down the street, calling out to no one, "She is under my protection."

And the other way, once again, speaking to ether. "She belongs to me."

Felicity's gaze went wide. "I beg your pardon! Are you mad?"

He ignored her. Silver tapped against the ground, clear and crisp. Once. Twice.

Its echo came like thunder. Two taps, everywhere. Above her, on either side of her, against windowpanes and stone walls and the street itself, knocked with wood and steel, and the claps of hands and the stomps of boots.

There must have been a hundred of them, and not one of them seen.

She looked to him, shock coursing through her. She shook her head. "How could I not have known?"

His dark gaze glittered in the moonlight. "Because you've never had to. Go home, Felicity Faircloth. I shall see you three nights hence. Keep up your ruse until then — tell no one the truth about you and Marwick."

She shook her head. "He's going to —"

"I've had enough of this conversation. You wanted proof I could do as I promised, and I provided it. You remain unruined, do you not? Despite your best efforts to land yourself otherwise by traipsing through Covent Garden in the dead of night."

"I didn't traipse."

He turned away, and she thought for a moment that he cursed beneath his breath. He reached into his pocket and extracted a gold coin, pressing it into her palm before pointing up the road, the opposite direction from whence they had come. "That way for hacks. The other, for hell."

"Alone?" With a hundred pairs of eyes watching from the shadows? "You do not plan to escort me?"

"I don't, as a matter of fact," he said. "You've never in your life been safer than you are right now."

She did as she was told, walking to the high street. With every step, she lost her fear. Her nervousness.

At the end of the street, a man stepped from the shadows and hailed her a hack, opening the door, tipping his cap as he let her pass into the conveyance.

As the carriage rocked back and forth, clattering along the cobblestones, Felicity

watched the city beyond the window, turning dark to light, until she was home.

Devil had been right. Felicity had never
felt more safe.

Or more powerful.

Chapter Ten

Three evenings later, Devil was in the back gardens of Bourne House, watching the teeming masses highlighted in the massive ballroom windows beyond, listening to the music spilling out through the open doors, when his brother appeared at his elbow.

"You spend too much time watching her."

Devil did not turn to face the accusation. "Watching who?"

Whit did not reply. He didn't have to.

"How do you know how much time I spend watching her?"

"Because the boys tell me where you go."

Devil scowled. "I don't have the boys following you."

"I never leave the Garden."

"That doesn't seem like truth tonight." Unfortunately. Whit remained silent, and Devil added, "We have street runners to run the streets, not to skulk about spying on me."

"You're the only one allowed to spy on people?"

Devil ignored the logical reply. "I am making sure she's done as she was told."

"When was the last time you went unheeded?"

"Felicity Faircloth does not ascribe to the rules the rest of the world so intelligently follows." Whit made a low noise, and Devil cut him a look. "What does that mean?"

A massive shoulder lifted and dropped.

"You think it's a bad plan."

"I think it is a plan that will not end as you imagine."

"The Marwick line ends with Ewan. We agreed to that."

An affirmative grunt.

"And yet he is there, inside Bourne House, drinking tepid lemonade and eating crumpets and dancing the quadrille."

Whit cut him a look. "Crumpets?"

"Whatever they fucking eat," Devil growled.

"He's waiting for us to blink."

Devil nodded. "And we're not blinking."

"He hasn't met the girl yet. Felicity Faircloth."

"No." Devil had had a watch on Felicity and the duke since the night of the Marwick ball, and they'd still not met. But Marwick's silence on the subject had all London talking about the future marriage of the Duke of Marwick to a long-shelved lady.

"He has a plan, Dev," Whit said. "He always had a plan. And I like whatever this one is even less than I like yours."

Memory flashed — three young boys sitting side by side on one edge of a river, with matching eyes and matching puppies. He stopped it before it played through, shaking his head and letting his gaze return to the ball beyond.

"You won't like it, either, when it comes time to use the girl proper," Whit said.

"I don't care about the girl." The words didn't feel right in his throat, but Devil ignored them.

"I heard you banished Reggie from the Garden."

"Reggie is lucky I didn't banish him from the fucking Earth."

"That's my point. Hester said the lady begged you not to, and you went soft."

Devil shoved his hands in his pockets, ignoring the truth of the words. "I need her on our side, don't I? Can't keep her there if she sees me gut a man in an alleyway."

Whit's grunt made his thoughts clear. "Placing her under our protection?"

That bit had been unexpected. Born of

194

his own fury at the idea that she might have been hurt on their streets, and his frustration that he couldn't carry her to his bed and keep her there for a night. Or two. *Or more.* "I can't very well have an aristocratic chit turning up dead a stone's throw from our headquarters, can I?"

"You invited her."

"I gave her my card. It was an error in judgment."

"You don't make errors in judgment. And we need an aristocratic chit under our protection like a dog needs diamonds."

"She's not under our protection for long."

"No. Soon she will be your victim. Along with Ewan."

"No heirs," Devil said. "You remember the deal."

Whit's lips flattened into a straight line. "I do. I also know there are cleaner and safer ways of getting what we want than buying a wallflower a new fucking frock."

Devil was growing irritated. "Like what?"

"Like slicing our brother's face to match your own."

Devil shook his head. "No. This way is better." Whit did not reply, and Devil heard the tacit disagreement in the silence. "Fists are a threat. This way is a promise. This way, we remind Ewan that his future belongs to us. Just as ours once belonged to him."

A pause, and then, "And the girl? What happens when you have to take her future from her?"

"I'll pay handsomely for it. I'm not a monster."

Whit gave a little huff of laughter.

Devil looked to him. "What does that mean?"

"Only that you're mad if you think that paying for the girl's ruination isn't monstrous. She'll not only care; she'll come for you."

The idea of Felicity Faircloth, plain, aging spinster, coming for a Bareknuckle Bastard was ludicrous. Devil forced a laugh of his own. "Let the kitten try to gut me, then. I shall keep my sword at the ready."

"I heard she punched Reggie."

Pride flared at the memory, chased away immediately by rage at the same. "She missed."

"You should teach her to throw a punch."

"As she'll never be in the Garden again, it's unnecessary." Indeed, if the other evening in the dark streets of Covent Garden had done anything, it had convinced her to stay far away from the neighborhood.

Never mind that she'd thought those streets beautiful.

Good Lord — when she'd pointed at those gleaming cobblestones and expounded on their beauty, Devil had had half a mind to tell her they were just as likely to be soaked in rain as they were to be running with blood.

Even if she was right — they were beautiful.

Which he never would have noticed if she hadn't said so, dammit.

Whit grunted, then, "I think you mean, as she now bears the protection of the Bastards, it's unnecessary."

"She's not coming back," Devil said. "Christ. I nearly killed a man in front of her."

"But you didn't."

That man had touched her. That cretin had felt the silk of Felicity's hair before Devil had. The hand on his cane itched to do damage. Best, because when it itched to do damage, it wasn't itching to touch her again. It wasn't itching to draw her close again. He wasn't itching to kiss her again.

Lie.

He shook his head. "I should have killed him."

Whit turned back to the ballroom windows. "But you didn't. And that's going to make 'em talk."

"It's certainly made *you* talk."

Thankfully, that silenced him.

They watched in silence for long minutes, and Whit bounced on the balls of his feet lightly, the movement uncharacteristic for a man so often still and solid. Uncharacteristic, unless you knew what it meant. Devil said, "Is there a bout tonight?"

"Three."

"Are you fighting?"

He shrugged. "If I'm tempted."

There were two kinds of fighters — those who played by the rules and those who fought to win at all costs. Whit was the second kind, and he only ever sparred when he couldn't stop himself from doing it. He preferred to run the bouts and train the fighters. But when he did enter the ring, he was near unbeatable.

It had only ever happened once.

Another memory flared — Whit on the ground, covered in dirt and blood, unconscious. Devil covering him with his own body, taking what felt like a dozen blows himself. A hundred. Protecting his brother.

Until they'd escaped.

"Grace has been asking about your girl."

Devil looked to Whit. "You haven't told her who she is."

"No, but our sister's no fool, and she has

her own runners — every one better than ours." Grace's employees — save for precious few — were female, and the girls could move quickly and beneath notice through most of London.

Devil was saved from answering by a flash of golden fabric inside. Felicity. His gaze tracked her through the throngs of people, drinking her in, like sunlight. "She's here," he said, unable to keep the softness from his tone. "She's wearing it."

Whit grunted. "Then we go."

No.

Devil swallowed the word and shook his head. "No. I have to be certain they meet."

His brother's gaze moved to the windows of the ballroom, and he let out a low whistle. "Ewan will lose his mind when he sees that dress."

Devil nodded. "I want him to know I'm ahead of him. That I shall always be ahead of him."

"I'll say this. Lady Felicity tidies up nicely."

"Bollocks off," Devil said, tempted to put his fist into his brother's face for the comment. But doing so would have required him to look away from Felicity, and he wasn't interested in doing that. He wasn't certain he *could* do it, if he was being honest.

She was impossible to ignore.

She looked as though she were dressed in liquid gold. He'd known the dressmaker would serve her well, but this was magnificent. The bodice was cut low, revealing a stunning expanse of skin — enough to make men around the room take notice. Which Devil supposed was the point, but he found he didn't care for men around the room taking notice. "That line is too low."

"You're mad," Whit said. "Even Ewan won't be able to look away from it."

Devil couldn't look away from it, either. That was the problem. The sleeves were fitted to her shoulders, a perfect cap, leaving long, lovely arms too soon hidden away beneath gloves in golden silk that made him think thoroughly nefarious things.

Things like how a man might like to peel them off her.

Things like whether they were long enough to use to tie her wrists to the bedposts. Whether they were strong enough to hold her while he wrung pleasure from her again and again until they were both lost to sin.

And all that before Devil remembered what had been delivered with the frock and gloves. His heart pounded with twin threads of knowledge and curiosity, the thrumming made worse as Felicity was set upon by a collection of black-clad men — several of whom Devil recognized as young scoundrels who should not be allowed in a ballroom, let alone near a woman looking as much like perfection as she was.

A particularly impertinent one fingered the ivory-handled fan dangling from her wrist — hang on. The fan? Or was he touching her wrist?

Devil growled low in his throat, and Whit looked to him. "You're right. There's nothing at all wrong with this plan."

Devil scowled. "Enough." Felicity eased away from the touch, removing the fan from her wrist and passing it to the man in question. "Who is that?"

"How would I know?" Whit made it a point to stay as far from the aristocracy as possible.

"I intend to break his hand if he touches her again. She clearly doesn't like it."

The man inside was writing on her fan, then passing it to the next man in their circle, then the next, then the next. "What are they doing?"

"Some ridiculous aristocratic ritual, no doubt." Whit yawned, loudly. "The girl is fine now."

She didn't look fine. She looked — surprised. She looked young and perfect and uncertain and surprised, as though she hadn't expected the dress to change anything. As though she'd really believed that most men had brains in their heads enough to see a woman for her true value without a garment that cost a fortune. Or a cake of powder. Or a pinch of rouge. If they'd been able to do that as a gender, then Felicity Faircloth would not be on the shelf. She'd have been happily married long ago, to a proper man with a proper past and not a hint of revenge to be seen.

But men weren't and so she wasn't, and she was surprised and perhaps a bit unsettled, and Devil found he wanted to go to her, to remind her that she was there for a reason — to bask in the glow of this attention and find herself the place in society to which she so desperately wished to be restored.

To embrace the promise of a future with a man who might one day love her as she deserved.

"Ewan is here."

A promise that would never be delivered.

Devil swallowed back guilt and, with difficulty, tore his attention from Felicity, finding the duke in the crowd. He watched as Ewan searched the throngs of revelers. Though he inclined his head in acknowledgment as an older woman with an enormous turban spoke to him, his search did not stop.

Ewan was looking for Felicity.

"Let's go," Whit said. "I fucking hate Mayfair."

Devil shook his head. "Not until he sees her."

And then the duke found his surprise bride, in her gown shot through with gold thread, and Devil watched as his brother — the handsomest man Felicity Faircloth had ever seen — did a double take, his gaze narrowing on her.

"There," Whit said. "The message was received. The gold frock was inspired."

It had been calculated to summon Ewan's attention, and his memories. To remind Ewan of a promise made, long ago. One that he had never made good on. One that he would never make good on.

The gold dress would send a message — all without Felicity Faircloth knowing — that Devil had been there first. That he was ahead of his brother in this game. That he would win.

Marwick watched her for a long moment,

and all Devil wanted to do was steal her away.

He was saved from the instinct by a different man, the one who had touched her wrist earlier. He indicated the orchestra and extended his hand. An invitation to dance. Felicity put her hand in his and he led her onto the dance floor, away from Ewan.

Away from Devil.

Whit grunted. "I'm leaving."

"Go, then," he said. "I'm staying."

"With her?"

Yes. "With *them.*"

After a long silence, Whit said, quietly, "Good chase, then," and left Devil in the darkness, watching her as she was passed from partner to partner, spinning across the ballroom again and again. He watched as she smiled up at one escort after another, silently cataloguing each one's missteps — a hand too low on her waist. A too lingering glance at her bosom. A whisper too close to her ear.

As he watched the performance, Devil began to ache with it, with the keen distaste for the men who were able to touch her, to hold her, to dance with her. And he quietly imagined punishing them the way he'd punished Reggie the night before. Banishing them from her presence. For a moment, he imagined what would happen if he could do that — if he could banish one after another after another, until the only man left was him.

A man unworthy of her, as he fully intended to use her to ruin another before leaving her in ruin herself.

But there had been a time, decades earlier, when it might have been Devil inside that room, dressed in finery, watching his betrothed, clad in finely spun gold, happily pulling her into his arms and dancing her through the room.

There had been a time when he might have been the duke. When he might have been able to give Felicity Faircloth the life of which she dreamed.

And for a fleeting moment, he wondered what he might have done to open that door if he'd known she was on the other side.

Anything.

Blessedly, the dancing stopped, and she was alone at the edge of the ballroom, behind a potted fern, stepping through a door left open to the night beyond.

The night, where he reigned.

CHAPTER ELEVEN

Felicity had spent much of her twenty-seven years at the center of the *ton*. She'd been born with immense privilege, the daughter of a rich marquess, sister of an even richer earl, cousin to dukes and viscounts.

She'd been smiled upon by society, and, when she came out, it was to be immediately welcomed by the most powerful children of the aristocracy. Women invited her to the gossip of ladies' salons, men scraped and bowed and battled their way to refreshment tables to fetch glasses of champagne.

She'd never been belle of the ball, but she'd been belle of the ball adjacent, which meant dancing every dance and flirting with gentlemen and summoning the vaguest of pity for those who stood at the edge of the ballroom.

And she'd never quite noticed what it was to be at the center of the ballroom, because she'd always been there.

That is, until she was banished from it. Then, like an opium eater, all she'd wanted was to return.

Devil had promised her that return and, somehow, he'd delivered it. As though he were magic, after all. As though he really could make the impossible, possible.

She'd arrived that evening in the gown he'd sent, which looked as though it were made of spun gold, and she'd been instantly surrounded by smiling, welcoming faces, each more complimentary than the last, each wishing to speak a kindness to her. To make her laugh. And all because her lie had somehow not been revealed. In their minds, she was the next Duchess of Marwick, infinitely more valuable that night than she had been a week earlier — and they welcomed her with open arms.

But it was not as sweet a homecoming as Felicity had imagined.

Because she was no different than she had been a week earlier.

And now, halfway through the ball, having danced a half-dozen dances and flirted not at all effortlessly, having had trouble knowing when to laugh and when a laugh might be taken as a great insult, and having been terrified that she might say or do something wrong and ruin her one chance at saving her family, Felicity Faircloth knew the truth.

Being a darling of the *ton* was a fireplace filled with wood left out in the rain — hopeful and worthless. All of London minced and simpered after her because the duke had not denied their engagement and did not seem interested in doing so tonight. London seemed to have rediscovered Felicity Faircloth, plain, spinster, wallflower, and renamed her fascinating, affianced, bon vivant.

Which she wasn't, of course. She was no different today than she had been a month ago, except today she was to marry a duke. Supposedly.

And her reentry into society because of that — it wasn't nearly as rewarding as she would have expected.

Escaping the crush, Felicity tucked herself behind a potted fern beyond a blessedly open door. All she wished to do was to step over the threshold and flee into the darkness, to hide until it was time to leave.

But she couldn't do that, as she still had three dances left on her dance card.

Three dances, and none with the Duke of Marwick, who was supposedly her fiancé. At least, he hadn't denied the engagement, and he'd sent notice to her father that he would soon come to discuss the details of an impending marriage, which had sent her mother into fits of pleasure and set Arthur to smiling once more. Even Felicity's father had grunted his pleasure at the turn of events, and the Marquess of Bumble rarely had time for domestic matters, let alone time for articulating his pleasure with them.

No one seemed concerned that the duke had not thought it necessary to darken Felicity's doorstep at any point.

"Surely, he'll turn up eventually," her mother had replied when Felicity had pointed out the odd progression of events and her alleged fiancé's invisibility. "Perhaps he's simply busy."

Felicity rather thought that a man who had time to send correspondence relating to an engagement would find the time to set the thing in motion, but that seemed beside the point.

All that, and Devil had promised her that the dress she wore would lure the duke, would put him in her path and help to win him, but so far, there had been no inkling of such a triumph. She wasn't even certain the duke was in attendance. Was it possible he'd left London altogether? And if so, what was Felicity to do — continue to brazen it through and lie to all the world?

At some point, the Duke of Marwick

would have to realize that they were not, in fact, engaged. And no frock — sent by the Devil or otherwise — was magic enough to protect her from the truth once she had to stare down the Duke of Marwick himself.

Not even *this* frock, which seemed more magical than any she'd ever imagined.

It was perfect.

How he'd done it was a mystery — but he'd promised her a perfectly fitted dress, and one had arrived that morning, as though crafted by magical beings. It had been crafted, in fact, by Madame Hebert, London's most renowned modiste, despite Felicity not having been to the dressmaker in months — the product, she now realized, of her family's penny pinching as much as her own disinterest in frocks now that she wasn't welcome at the center of this world.

It seemed, however, that Hebert knew what kind of gown would be of interest. And it was a most definitely interesting one, Felicity had to admit. Even if Arthur's brows hadn't shot up when she'd appeared in it, Felicity had known the moment she'd opened the great white box embossed with a gold H that it was going to be the most beautiful gown she'd ever worn.

It hadn't been a dress alone, however. There had been shoes and stockings and gloves and undergarments — she blushed at the memory of them, each piece edged with ribbons in a pink so vibrant it seemed scandalous.

I like pink, she'd told him earlier in the week.

It felt sinful to wear those underthings, silk and satin and stunning, knowing they came from him. Nearly as sinful as wearing the dress itself, because she hadn't been able to stop herself from thinking of wearing it for the man who had sent it, rather than for all the men who had seen it tonight.

She'd even left the door to her balcony open all day, thinking perhaps he would sneak in once more. That he might wish to see her in it. That he might wish to see that she looked something like pretty in it.

But he hadn't come.

He'd kissed her in the darkness, giving her a taste of wickedness and sin, tempting her with its power, promised to see her in three nights' time, and then . . . deserted her.

It wasn't as though a man who lived in Covent Garden and carried a weapon in his walking stick had been invited to a ball hosted by one of the longest standing titles in Britain. Even if Felicity wished it so.

"He didn't come, the bastard," she whispered to herself and the inky blackness beyond.

"Such language, Felicity Faircloth."

Her heart began to pound as she spun around to face him. "Are you an actual devil? Have I summoned you with my thoughts?"

His lips twisted in a wry smile. "Have you been thinking of me?"

Her mouth dropped open. She'd had too much champagne if she was admitting that. "No."

The smile became a wolfish grin and he backed away into the shadows. "Liar. I heard you, my talkative wallflower. I heard you curse my not coming. Was I expected in your rooms?"

She blushed, grateful for the darkness. "Of course not. I keep my doors locked, now."

"It's a shame I don't know a lockpick, then." She coughed, and he laughed, low and dark and delicious. "Come into the darkness, Felicity, lest you be caught cavorting with the enemy."

Her brows knit together but she followed him nonetheless. "Are you the enemy?"

He rounded the corner, where the light from the ballroom gave way to dark. "Only to everyone in Mayfair."

She drew closer to the shadow of him,

wishing she could see his face. "Why is that?"

"I am all they fear," he said, low and dark. "Everyone has a sin, and my trick is knowing it. I can read them on people."

"What is mine?" she whispered, her heart pounding, at once eager to hear his answer and terrified of it.

He shook his head. "Tonight, you are too aflame for sin, Felicity Faircloth. You've burned it all away." She smiled, the words making her breathless. "And so, tell me. Have you reentered the aristocratic fold?"

She spread her hands wide. "Wallflower no more."

"Pity," he said.

"No one wants to be a wallflower," she said.

"I've always thought the wallflowers the best in the hothouse," he replied. "But tell me, my potted orchid, which moths have you lured?"

She wrinkled her nose. "You are mixing metaphors."

"Careful, your wallflower past is showing. No darling of the *ton* would ever dream of criticizing a man's grammar."

"No darling of the *ton* would ever dream of clandestinely meeting a man like you."

His lips pressed together in a firm line,

and for a moment, she felt a pang of guilt at the words before he leaned back against the side of the house. "Tell me about the incident in the bedchamber."

She went still. It shouldn't be a surprise that he knew about it — everyone knew about it. But he didn't know about the other scandals in her life, so why would he know about this one?

Why did he have to know about this one? She swallowed. "Which incident?"

"The one that made you a woman of questionable eligibility."

She winced at the description. "How did you know about that?"

"You will find, my lady, that there are few things about which I do not know."

She sighed. "There's nothing to be said. There was a ball. And I found myself in a man's bedchamber by accident."

"By accident."

"Mostly," she hedged.

He watched her for a long moment, and then asked, "Did he touch you?"

The question surprised her. "No — he — in fact, he was quite outraged to discover me there, which I suppose I should be grateful for, as if he hadn't been I might have —" She stopped and tried again, "I'm not the world's greatest beauty to begin with, and to add to it —" She stopped.

"What?"

"Nothing."

"I don't think *that's* true."

She sighed again. "I was crying."

A beat. "In a stranger's bedchamber."

"Might we be finished with this conversation?"

"No. Tell me why you were crying." There was an edge to his voice that she hadn't noticed before.

"I'd rather not."

"Need I remind you that you owe me for that pretty frock, Felicity Faircloth?"

"I was under the impression that the frock was part and parcel with our original arrangement."

"Not if you're not going to tell me why you were crying, it isn't."

He was an irritating man. "I'd rather not tell you, because it's silly."

"I don't mind silly."

She couldn't help the laughter that came at the words. "Excuse me, but you seem to be the kind of person who minds silly *exceedingly.*"

"Tell me."

"I was — part of a group. I had friends."

"The vipers from the other night?"

She shrugged. "I thought they were my

215

friends."

"They weren't."

"Yes, well, you weren't there to tell me that, so . . ." She paused. "At any rate, that was why I was . . . in a state. We'd been inseparable. And then . . ." She paused, resisting the knot of emotion that came whenever she thought of that time, when she'd been a society darling, and the world had seemed to bend to her will. "Like that . . . we were not. They still sparkled and glittered and loved each other. But they did not love me. And I did not know why."

He watched her for a long time. "Friendship is not always what we think. If we are not careful, it often becomes what others desire."

She looked to him. "You don't seem the kind of man who — loses friends."

He raised a brow. "I think you mean that I don't seem the kind of man who has them to begin with."

"Do you?"

"I have a brother. And a sister."

"I should like to be your friend." The confession shocked them both, and she wished she could take it back.

Even more so when he replied, "Felicity Faircloth, I'm no kind of friend for you." He wasn't wrong, but it smarted nonetheless. "Shall I tell you why your so-called friends left you?"

"How would you know?"

"Because I'm a man of the world and I know how it turns."

She believed him. "Why?"

"They deserted you because you were no longer useful. You stopped laughing at their idiot jests. Or stopped simpering after their faded frocks. Or stopped encouraging the cruelty they directed at everyone else. Whatever it was, you did something to make them realize you were no longer interested in licking their boots. And there is nothing like the loss of a sycophant to anger gasbags like those four." She hated the reasoning, even as she knew it was correct. Even as he added, "Every man and woman inside that room is a parasite, Faulk, Natasha Corkwood, and Lord and Lady Hagin included. And you are best rid of them, my pretty flame."

At the words, she looked back into the ballroom, watching scores of revelers chatter and gossip and dance and laugh. They were her people, were they not? That was her world, wasn't it? And even if she'd had the same thought earlier, though not in so many words, she should defend her world to this man — this outsider, she supposed.

"Not all aristocrats are parasitic."

"No?"

"I am not."

He came off the wall then, rising to his full height, and she tilted her face up to meet his gaze. "No. You're just so very desperate to be part of it again that you're willing to make a deal with the Devil to do it."

What if I changed my mind?

She resisted the whisper of a thought. "I need to save my family," she whispered, her cheeks blazing. *I don't have a choice.*

"Ah, yes. Familial loyalty. That is admirable, but it seems to me that they could have told you their situation before throwing you to the marriage-seeking wolves."

She hated him a little then. Hated him for speaking the words that she barely dared think. "I shan't be a bad wife."

"I never said you would be."

"I will keep his house and provide him heirs."

His gaze found hers instantly, hot and focused in the darkness. "Is that the dream, then? Mothering the next Duke of Marwick?"

Felicity considered the question for a long moment. "I've never had aspirations to ducal motherhood, but I should like children, yes. I think I would make a fine mother."

"You would." He looked away. Cleared his throat. "But that's not the only dream, is it?"

She hesitated, the soft question swirling around them. The secrets it seemed to understand. The desire to be accepted by these people. To take a place among them again. "I don't wish to be alone any longer."

He nodded. "What else."

"I wish to be wanted." The truth hurt as it emerged, leaving an ache in her throat.

He nodded. "That's why you lied at the start."

"And why I agreed to our deal," she said, softly. "I want it all. I told you. So much more than I can have."

"You are worth all of them combined," he said. "But hearing it from me is not enough, is it?"

It was more than he knew, it seemed, from the warmth that spread through her at the words. And yet, it wasn't enough. "You don't know what it was like. What it *is* like."

He watched her for a long moment. "As a matter of fact, my lady, I know precisely what it is like to lose people you think you can rely upon. To be betrayed by them."

She considered the words and what she knew of this strange, wicked man's life —

the kind where betrayal might live behind every corner. She nodded. "It does not matter, does it? None of the men I've danced with care for me; there's no reason to believe the duke shall."

"They seemed to care for you when they swarmed you to hold your fan for whatever reason."

She reached for the item in question, spreading it out to show the names written on each of the pine sticks there. "Dance card. And they only care for me because they think I'm to be a —"

"You have an unclaimed dance." He had the fan in hand, and she was tethered to him.

Her breath caught as he tugged on it, pulling her a step closer. "I — I thought I should save one for my fictional fiancé." She paused. "Not so fictional if you read my father's correspondence. How did you do it?"

"Magic," he replied, the scar down the side of his face white in the shadows. "As I promised." She started to press him for a better answer, but he continued, refusing to let her speak. "He shall claim that dance soon enough."

Her attention lingered on the empty slat in the fan, the way it seemed to shout her falsehood to the world. For a single, wild moment, she wondered what it might be like if Devil claimed it. She wondered what might happen if he wrote his blasphemous name across it in black pencil.

What might happen if he stepped into the ballroom with her, took her into his arms, and danced her across the room. Of course, a man like Devil did not know how to dance like the aristocracy. He could only watch from the shadows.

The thought inspired her. "Wait. Have you been watching me all evening?"

"No."

It was her turn to say, "Liar."

He hesitated, and she would have given anything to see his face. "I had to be certain you wore the dress."

"Of course I wore the dress," she said. "It's the most beautiful dress I've ever seen. I wish I could wear it every day. Though I still do not understand how you were able to get it. Madame Hebert takes weeks to produce a design. Longer."

"Hebert, like most businesswomen, is willing to work quickly for a premium." He paused. "That, and she seems to like you."

Felicity warmed at the words. "She made my wedding trousseau. Or, rather, all the clothes I brought with me to win myself a husband last summer." She paused. "To lose myself one, I suppose."

A beat, and then, "Well, without those, you would not have this gown. And that would be a proper crime."

She blushed at the words — the most perfect thing anyone could have said. "Thank you."

"The duke could not keep his eyes from you," he replied.

Her jaw dropped and she looked over her shoulder. "He saw me?"

"He did."

"And what now?"

"Now," he said, "he comes for you."

She swallowed at the promise in the words. At the vision they invoked, of a different man coming for her. No kind of duke. "How do you know?"

"Because he shan't be able to resist with the way you look in that gown."

Her heart pounded. "And how do I look?"

The question surprised her with its impropriety, and she nearly took it back. Might have, if he hadn't replied. "Are you searching for compliments, my lady?"

She dipped her head at the soft question. "Perhaps."

"You look just as you should, Felicity Faircloth — the fairest of them all."

Her cheeks blazed. "Thank you." *For saying so.* "For the gown." She hesitated. "And . . . the other things." He shifted in the darkness, and she was keenly aware of this secret spot — so close to all the world and somehow private for them alone. She didn't know what one was to say after thanking a virtual stranger for undergarments. "My apologies. I'm sure we should not be discussing . . . those."

"Never apologize for discussing those." Another pause, and then he said, wicked and soft, "Are they pink?"

Her mouth dropped open. "I don't think I should tell you that."

He did not seem to care. "You like pink."

She'd never been so grateful for the shadows in her life. "I do."

"And so? Are they?"

"Yes." She could barely hear the whispered word.

"Good." The word came on a ragged growl, and she wondered if it was possible that he was as moved by the conversation as she was.

She wondered if he had thought of her wearing the clothes he'd sent half as much as she had thought of wearing them for him. Of him kissing her in them.

"Men seem to like the line," she said, her

223

satin-covered fingers running along the edge of the gown even as she knew she shouldn't draw attention to it. Even as she wanted him to notice it. What did this man do to her? *Magic.* "My mother thought it was . . . unsuccessful."

Immodest was the word the Marchioness of Bumble had used before insisting Felicity fetch a cloak *immediately.*

"Your mother is far too old and far too female to be able to judge the success or failure of that frock. How did you explain its arrival?"

"I lied," she confessed, feeling as though it were a thing she should whisper. "I said it was a gift from my acquaintance Sesily. She's quite scandalous."

"Sesily Talbot?"

"You know her?" Of course he did. He was a red-blooded human male and Sesily was every man's dream. Felicity did not like the thread of jealousy that coursed through her with the thoughts.

"The Singing Sparrow is two streets from my offices. It's owned by an acquaintance of hers."

"Oh." Relief flared. He didn't know Sesily. At least, not in the biblical sense.

Not that it mattered whom he knew biblically.

Felicity didn't care.

Obviously. It had nothing to do with her.

"At any rate," she said, "the dress is beautiful. And I've never felt so close to beautiful in my life as I do wearing it." The confession was soft and honest, and easy because she spoke it to his silhouette.

"Shall I tell you something, Felicity Faircloth?" he said softly, taking a step toward her. The words wrapped around them, making Felicity ache. "Shall I give you a piece of advice that will help you lure your moth?"

Will it lure you?

She bit back the question. She did not want to lure him. The darkness was addling her brain. And whatever his answer was . . . that way lay danger. "I think I should go," she said, turning away. "My mother . . ."

"Wait," he said sharply. And then he touched her. His hand came to hers, and she would have given anything to have her golden glove disappear. Just once, just to feel his touch.

She turned back to him and he moved into the light, taking care that they were not able to be seen. She could see his face now, the strength of it, the slash of scar down his cheek, his amber gaze gone black in the darkness, searching hers before he raised his hand to her face, running a thumb along her jaw, across her cheek, his silver ring a cool counter to the warmth of his skin.

More, she wanted to say. *Don't stop.*

He was so close, his eyes raking across her face, taking in all her flaws, discovering all her secrets. "You are beautiful, Felicity Faircloth," he whispered, and she could feel the breath of the words on her lips.

The memory of their kiss on the streets of Covent Garden rioted through her, along with the aching frustration he'd left her with that night. The way she'd dreamed of him repeating it. He was so close — if she went up onto her toes, he might.

Before she could, he let her go, leaving her wanting it. Wanting him. "No," she said, hot embarrassment flaring in the wake of the exclamation. She shouldn't have said it. But didn't he want to kiss her again?

Apparently not. He took a step back, the irritating man. "Your duke shall find you tonight, my lady."

Frustration flared. "He is not my duke," she snapped. "In fact, I think he might be closer to yours."

He watched her for a long moment before saying, softly, "You can win every one of them. Any one of them. The aristocratic moth of your choosing. And you chose your duke the moment you pronounced him yours. When he is drawn to you tonight, you shall begin to win him."

And if I do not want him?

If I do not want any aristocratic moth?

If I want a moth who belongs nowhere near Mayfair?

She didn't say the words, instead saying, "How shall I win him?"

He did not hesitate. "Just as you are." It was nonsense. But he did not seem to care. "Good night, my lady."

And then he was moving, returning to the shadows, where he belonged. She followed him to the top of the stone steps leading down to the gardens beyond the house. "Wait!" she called, searching for something to return him to her. "You promised to help! You promised magic, Devil."

He turned back at the bottom of the steps, white teeth flashing in the shadows. "You have it already, my lady."

"I don't have magic. I have a beautiful gown. The rest of me is entirely the same. You've sent a hog to the milliner. It's a lovely hat, but the pig remains."

He chuckled in the darkness, and she was irritated that she couldn't see the smile that came with the sound. He didn't smile enough. "You're not a hog, Felicity Faircloth."

227

With that, he disappeared, and she went to the railing, setting her hands to the cool stone to watch the gardens, angry and frustrated and wondering what would happen if she followed him. Wanting to follow him. Knowing she couldn't. That she had made her bed, and if she or her family had any chance of surviving it, she must lie in it. Behatted swine or not.

"Dammit, Devil," she whispered into the darkness, unable to see him and still somehow knowing he was there. "How?"

"When he asks about you, tell him the truth."

"That's the worst idea I've ever heard."

He didn't reply. He'd placed her in full view of London, promised her a match for the ages, and left her alone with terrible advice and without making good on the promise. As though she were the flame he'd assured her she'd be.

Except she wasn't.

"This is the worst mistake ever made. In history," she said to herself and the night. "This is up there with accepting the gift of a Trojan horse."

"Are you giving a lecture on Greek mythology?"

She spun around at the words, and found

the Duke of Marwick standing not three feet from her.

Chapter Twelve

Because she wasn't entirely certain what one was to say to a man whom one had proclaimed her fiancé, Felicity settled on, "Hello."

She winced at the decidedly unmagical word.

His gaze flickered to the dark gardens where Devil had disappeared, then back to her. "Hello."

She blinked. "Hello."

Oh, yes, this was all going quite well. She was all flame. Good God. It was only a matter of time before he ran back to the ballroom, stopped the orchestra, and denounced her publicly.

But the duke did not run. Instead, he took a step toward her, and she pressed back to the stone balustrade. He stopped. "Am I interrupting something?"

"No!" she said altogether too forcefully. "Not at all. I was just . . . here . . . breathing." His brows rose at the words, and she shook her head. "Breathing air. Taking air. I mean. It's quite warm in the ballroom, don't you think?" She waved a hand at her neck. "Very warm." She cleared her throat. "Hot."

His gaze slid to her wrist. "It was good foresight for you to bring something to combat it."

She looked down at the wooden fan dangling from her wrist. "Oh." She snapped it open and fanned herself like a madwoman. "Yes. Of course. Well. I have excellent foresight."

Stop talking, Felicity.

Those brows rose again. "Do you?"

Her brows narrowed. "I do."

"I only ask because it seems to me that someone uninformed of that particular quality might find you to have the opposite of foresight."

She caught herself before her jaw dropped open. "How is that?"

He did not immediately reply, instead coming to stand next to her at the balcony railing, turning his back to the gardens, crossing his arms over his chest and watching the revelers inside the beautifully lit ballroom. The light made his fair hair gleam gold as it harshened the angles of his face — high cheekbones and strong jaw; something about him whispered familiarity, though she couldn't place it. After a long silence, he said, "One might argue that telling the world you are engaged to a duke when you've never met him lacks foresight."

And, like that, the truth of her act was between them. Felicity was not riddled with the embarrassment or the shame she might have imagined. Instead, she was consumed with an immense relief. Something near to power — close to the way she felt when she picked a lock, as though the past was behind her and what was to come was all possibility.

Which was, of course, a kind of madness in itself, because this man held her fate and that of her family in his hands, and the future he might mete out was dangerous indeed. Madness seemed to reign, nonetheless. "Why did you confirm it?"

"Why did you say it?"

"I was angry," she said quietly. She lifted a shoulder. "It's not a good excuse, I know . . . but there it is."

"It's an honest excuse," he said, returning his attention to the ballroom. "I, too, have been angry."

"Did your anger result in tacit engagement to a person you'd never met?"

He looked to her, and it was as though he

was seeing her for the first time. "You remind me of someone."

The change of topic was jarring. "I . . . do?"

"She would have adored that dress; I promised to keep her in spools of gold thread, someday."

"Did you deliver on that promise?"

His lips flattened into a cold, straight line. "I did not."

"I am sorry for that."

"As am I." He shook his head, as though to rid himself of a memory. "She is gone now. And I find myself in need of an heir to . . ."

Felicity could not help her little huff of surprised laughter. "I say, you've come to the right place, Your Grace, as there's nothing London likes more than a duke in your precise predicament."

He met her gaze, and that eerie familiarity echoed. "If we are to be engaged, you ought to understand my purpose."

"Are we? To be engaged?"

"Aren't we? Did you not make that decision five nights ago at my home?"

"Well, I wouldn't call it a decision," she said softly.

"What would you call it?"

The question didn't seem relevant, so

instead, Felicity asked, "How did he convince you?"

He looked to her. "Who?"

"As I've said, you could have denied me and chosen another without hesitation. What did he threaten you with to make you choose me?" She didn't think Devil the kind of man who would threaten bodily harm, but she supposed she didn't really know him, and he *had* climbed her trellis and entered her bedchamber uninvited, so perhaps he had less of a conscience than she thought.

"What makes you think I had to be threatened?"

The duke was an excellent actor, clearly. Felicity almost believed that Devil hadn't convinced him to marry her. Almost.

And then said, "I accepted your proposal, did I not?"

"But why? We've never met."

"We met several minutes ago."

She blinked. "Are you mad?" It was an honest question.

"Are you?" he countered.

Felicity supposed that was fair. "No."

He shrugged one shoulder. "Then perhaps I'm not, either."

"You don't know me."

He looked to her. "You would be surprised

by what I know of you, Felicity Faircloth."

A thread of unease passed through her at the way he said her name, an echo of another man. *The fairest of them all.* "I'm sure I would, Your Grace, as I am surprised you were even aware of my existence."

"I wasn't honestly, until late in the evening on the night of my ball, when a half-dozen doyennes of the *ton* — none of whom I knew existed, either, by the way — waylaid me on the way to the water closet to confirm my engagement to — what was it they called you? — poor Felicity Faircloth. It seemed they wanted to be certain I knew precisely what sort of cow I was purchasing."

"Hog," she corrected, immediately regretting the words.

He looked to her. "I'm not certain that's more flattering, but if you prefer it." Before she could tell him she was not enthralled by either descriptor, he pressed on. "The point is, I narrowly escaped the gaggle of women and then the ball — I should thank you for that."

She blinked. "You should?"

"Indeed. You see, I no longer had need of it, as my work had been done for me."

"And which work is that?"

"The work of finding a wife."

"And an heir," she said.

He lifted a shoulder. Dropped it. "Precisely."

"And you thought a madwoman who pronounced you her fiancé was a sound choice for the mother of your future children?"

He did not smile. "Many would say a madwoman is my best match."

She nodded. "Are you a madman, then?"

He watched her for a long moment, until she thought he was not going to speak again. And then, "Here is what I know of you, Finished Felicity. I know you were once a perfectly viable option for marriage — daughter to a marquess, sister to an earl. I know something happened that landed you in the bedchamber of a man to whom you were not married, and who refused to marry you —"

"It wasn't what you —" she felt she had to explain.

"I don't care," he said, and she believed him. "The point is, after that, you became more and more curious, an oddity on the edges of ballrooms. And then your father and brother lost a fortune and you became their only hope. Unbeknownst to you, they took your freedom from you, and shipped you off to — do I have this right? — vie in a competition for a married duke's hand?"

236

"Yes," she said, cheeks blazing.

"That sounds like the plot to a ridiculous romantic novel."

"It wasn't ridiculous. And it was terribly romantic for the woman already married to the duke."

"Hmm," he said. "So, I have it all right? Impoverished spinster wallflower?"

Felicity rather hated to be boiled down to three unflattering words, but, "Yes. You have it right. Except for the bit where I proclaimed to be affianced to a duke whom I had never met."

"Ah. Yes. I had nearly forgotten that." The words weren't dry. They were honest. As though he had forgotten why they were conversing altogether.

He *might* be mad.

Felicity pressed on. "I'm sorry, Your Grace, but why on earth would you — a young, handsome duke with a clear past — choose to remain affianced to *me*?"

"Are you trying to convince me *not* to remain affianced to you?"

Was she?

Of course she wasn't. He was, after all, a young, handsome duke with a clear past, was he not? She'd falsely proclaimed him her fiancé, plunging herself and her family into certain social and financial ruin, and here he was, offering her rescue.

I promised you the impossible, did I not?

For a strange, wild moment, it occurred to Felicity that it was not the duke offering rescue at all — it was the Devil, with his outrageous offers and his wild deals and his wicked deeds.

A ducal moth, straight to her flame.

And here it was.

Magic.

"But . . . why?"

He looked away then, turning back to the dark gardens, his gaze searching, as hers had done before he'd appeared. "What do they call it? A marriage of convenience?"

The words settled between them, simple and unsatisfying. Of course, the offer of a marriage of convenience should have sent Felicity into convulsions of pleasure. It meant she'd save her family's reputation, and her own. It meant money in her father's coffers, the restoration of the estate, the protection of the name.

And that was all before she became a duchess, powerful in her own right, welcome once more in the bright, glittering ballrooms of London. No longer strange or scandalous, but valued. Returned to the place she'd been before — plain, but empowered. Duchess of Marwick.

It was all she'd ever wanted.

Well, not *all.* But *much.*

Some.

"Lady Felicity?" the duke prompted once more, pulling her from her thoughts.

She looked up at him. "A marriage of convenience. You get an heir."

"And you get a very rich duke. I'm told that's a precious commodity." He said it as though he'd just learned the fact earlier that day, as though all of recorded history hadn't been predicated on women being forced to find wealthy matches.

Her mother would be beside herself with pleasure.

"What say you?" he prompted.

She shook her head. Was it possible it was so simple? A single meeting, and her lie made true? Her gaze narrowed on the duke. "Why?" she repeated. "When you could have any of them?"

She waved a hand at the open door to the ballroom, where no less than a half-dozen women openly watched them, waiting for Felicity to misstep, and for the duke to realize his mistake. Frustration flared, alongside that familiar indignation — the emotion that had set this insanity in motion. She resisted it as his gaze followed hers, lingering on prettier, younger, more entertaining unmarrieds, considering them.

When he turned back to her, she expected him to have realized that she was not the most qualified bride for him. She was already imagining the disappointment in her mother's eyes when this false engagement was no longer. She was already scrambling for a solution to Arthur's empty coffers. To those of her father. Perhaps she could convince the duke to break off the engagement without revealing her stupid mistake. He did not seem a bad man. He simply seemed . . . well, frankly, he seemed uncommon.

Except he did not break off the engagement as she'd expected. Instead, his eyes met hers and, for the first time, it seemed as though he *saw* her. And, for the first time, she saw him, cool and calm, not at all unsettled by the fact that she was there, and they were about to be engaged. He seemed not to care at all, actually. "I don't want them. You turned up at the right time, so why not you?"

It was ridiculous. Ducal marriages did not happen like this. Marriages in general did not happen like this — on empty balconies with no more than a vague whim born of convenience.

And yet . . . this was happening.

She'd done it.

No, Devil had done it. Like magic.

The words whispered through her, at once true and terribly false. Devil hadn't worked magic. This duke was no moth. Felicity was not flame. She was *convenient.*

And there was nothing magical about convenience.

"Have you room on that fan for another dance?" the duke said, interrupting the rush of awareness that flooded her at the thought.

She looked down at the fan, at the empty slat that remained. An echo came from earlier. A vague imagining of another man marking that slat. Claiming that dance. A man who disappeared into the darkness, replaced with this one — who reigned in the light. She tried a smile. "I do have room, as a matter of fact."

He reached for the fan, stopping before he touched it, waiting for her to offer it to him. Devil hadn't waited. Devil wouldn't have waited. She extended her hand to the duke and he lifted the fan, taking the little pencil dangling from it in hand and writing his name across the bare stick. *Marwick.*

Felicity imagined she should feel breathless at the action — but she didn't. Not even when he released the fan and claimed her hand instead, lifting it in a slow, deliberate motion, until his full, handsome lips grazed over her knuckles.

She most definitely should have felt breathless at that. But she was not, and neither was he. And as she watched the Duke of Marwick — her proclaimed fiancé turned real — lift his head, a single thought rioted through her.

The duke's wings remained unsinged.

Which meant the Devil had not made good on his deal.

CHAPTER THIRTEEN

Devil was already spoiling for a fight the next night when he stepped through the well-guarded door to the Bastards' warehouse — so much so that the sound of the lock turning in the great slab of steel did not comfort him the way it should have.

He'd spent much of the day attempting to focus on his ledgers, telling himself that it was more important than everything else — that he had plenty of time to seek out Felicity Faircloth and discover precisely what had happened between her and Ewan.

In fact, he knew what had happened. His watch had seen her home only two hours after he left her — along with her mother, deposited there by her brother — after which, no one had left Bumble House, not through any of the ground-level egresses, nor down the trellis beyond Felicity's bedchamber. This morning, the ladies of the house had spent the morning in Hyde Park with the marchioness's dogs and returned for luncheon and tea and note writing or whatever it was that ladies did in the afternoons.

Absolutely nothing out of the ordinary had come to pass.

Except Felicity had met Ewan. Devil had watched from the shadows as they'd spoken, resisting the instinct to go to her and stop their conversation. And then Ewan had kissed her — on her gloved hand, but kissed her nonetheless — and Devil had gone stone-still and somehow turned his back on the scene rather than giving into his second, baser instinct, which was to destroy the duke, carry Felicity off to Covent Garden, lay her down, and finish the kiss they'd started the last time she was there.

But she wasn't for him. Not yet.

Not until it was time to thieve her away from his brother and remind him of how easily he could be raised up only to be dropped, hard and fast, to the ground, ensuring Ewan never again considered flying too fast or too far.

That was why Devil had been so kind to her. So complimentary. Because Felicity Faircloth was a means to a very specific end. Not because he actually thought she was beautiful. Not because he actually cared if she was wearing pink undergarments. Not because he actually wished her to believe in her own worth.

He didn't. *He couldn't.*

And so, he told himself that it was nothing more than general curiosity that sent him to the warehouse to find Whit in shirtsleeves, hook in hand, overseeing the distribution of the shipment that had been sitting in the ice hold for more than a week, waiting to move.

General curiosity in the business and not the memory of Ewan's lips on Felicity's knuckles. Not remotely.

After all, Devil told himself, a smuggling empire did not run itself, and there were workers to be paid and deals to be inked and a new shipment to arrive next week, laden with liquor and contraband, which they wouldn't have room for if they didn't get rid of the one in the hold.

General curiosity, and not a keen need to resist the urge to go to the Faircloth home this afternoon, climb the damn trellis, and talk to the girl.

He was a businessman. What mattered was the work.

Inside the warehouse, two dozen strong men moved in unison, muscles straining under the weight of the crates they passed from down the line, from the hole in the floorboards to one of five caravans ready to move the product overland: two to a score of locations in London; one west, to Bristol; one north, to York; and the last to the Scottish border, where it would be redistributed for delivery into Edinburgh and throughout the highlands.

There were any number of moments in the life of a smuggler that brought danger and uncertainty, but these were the worst, knowing that once the goods left the warehouse, the transport was in more danger than ever. No one could prove the Bareknuckle Bastards were smuggling goods inside the ice ships they worked; there was no way to check the contents of the ships as they entered the harbor, nearly sinking for all the melted ice in their holds. In this moment, however, with untaxed, undeclared goods in the hands of their loyal men, no one would be able to deny the criminal activity.

On nights when they moved product, every able body in the organization helped to get it done as quickly as possible. The longer night hung over the rookery, the safer the product, and all their futures.

Devil made for Whit and Nik, shucking his coat and waistcoat, exchanging his walking stick for a great, curving box hook. He moved to the hole, coming alongside Whit heaving crates up and passing them to another man, then another, and another, and a second row of men immediately followed him, forming a new line, doubling the pace of the work.

Nik was down in the hole, marking boxes and barrels with white chalk as they passed, calling out their destinations and marking them into the small ledger that never left her pocket. "St. James's. Fleet Street. Edinburgh. York. Bristol."

It wasn't the business of smuggling that made for salacious news; crates of contraband weren't interesting until they were opened and used. But the purchasers of those crates? The most powerful men in government, religion, and media? Suffice to say, the world would be eager for even a glance at the Bareknuckle Bastards' client list.

Devil hooked a barrel of bourbon headed to York Cathedral, and lifted it up with a loud grunt. "Christ, those things are heavy."

Whit didn't hesitate in pulling up a crate, his heavy breathing the only indication that the grueling task was impacting him. "Weakling."

Nik snorted a little laugh, but did not look

away from her list. Devil reached down for the next box, ignoring the way the muscles of his shoulders strained when he pulled it up and passed it to the man at his back. He returned his attention to Nik. "I'll have you know that I'm the intelligent brother."

She looked up at him, eyes twinkling. "Are you?" She marked a box. "Bank of London."

Whit grunted and leaned into the hole. "And the books he insisted on reading when we were children continue to keep him warm at night."

"Oi!" Devil said, hooking another barrel. "Without those books, I'd never have learned about the Trojan horse, and then where would we be?"

Whit didn't hesitate. "I imagine we would have had to devise for ourselves that we could smuggle one thing inside another thing. However would we have done that?" he asked with a little grunt as he pulled up a cask of brandy. "Thank goodness for your primitive knowledge of the Greeks."

Devil took advantage of his empty hook and offered a rude gesture to his brother, who turned to the men assembled with a wide, white grin and said, "You see? Proof I am right." Whit looked back to Devil and added, "Though not at all a sign of intelligence, one might point out."

"What happened to you being the brother who does not talk?"

"I'm feeling out of sorts today." Whit heaved up a heavy crate. "What brings you out, bruv?"

"I thought I'd check on the shipment."

"I'd've thought you had other things to check on tonight."

Devil gritted his teeth and reached down for a crate of playing cards. "What's that to mean?"

Whit didn't reply.

Devil straightened. "Well?"

Whit shrugged a shoulder beneath his sweat-dampened shirt. "Only that you've your master plan to see to, no?"

"What master plan?" the ever-curious Nik asked from below. "If you lot are planning something without me . . ."

"*We're* not planning anything." Whit reached back into the hole. "It's just Dev."

Nik's keen blue gaze moved from one brother to the next. "Is it a good plan?"

"It's a shit plan, actually," Whit said.

Unease threaded through Devil, and his retort stuck in his throat. It was a good plan. It was the kind of plan that punished Ewan. *And Felicity.*

There was only one way to respond. Another rude gesture.

Whit and Nik laughed, before she interjected from her place below, "Well, as much as I am loath to end this fascinating conversation, that's the last of it."

Devil turned to watch the men on the line tuck the last of the product into the large steel wagons as Whit nodded down and said, "All right then. Tell the lads to send up the ice."

Passing his hook down to Nik, Devil received another, cold as the product it held — the first of the six-stone blocks of ice. Turning, he passed the hook and its capture to the next man in line, who handed him an empty hook, which Devil passed down to catch its frozen prey. The second block was passed up, and Devil passed down another empty hook, and so it went, rhythmic and backbreaking, until the backs of the steel caravans were filled to the roof with blocks of ice.

There was a pleasure in the grueling work, in the line of men working in unison, toward a common, achievable goal. Most goals were not so easily reached and, too often, those who aspired to them found themselves disappointed in the reaching. Not this. There was nothing so satisfying as turning to discover the work finished well, and the time ripe for an ale.

But there was no satisfaction to be had that day.

He was reaching down into the hole when John shouted out for him; turning, he found the big man crossing from the back entrance to the warehouse, a boy trailing behind him. Devil's gaze narrowed in recognition. Brixton was one of Felicity's watch.

He dropped the hook to the dusty floor, unable to keep himself from moving toward them. "What's happened to her?"

The boy lifted his chin, strong and proud. "Nuffin'!"

"What do you mean, nothing?"

"Nuffin', Devil," Brixton replied. "Lady's right as rain."

"Then why are you off your watch?"

"I weren't, until this stroker pulled me off it."

John cut the boy a warning glance at the insult, and Devil turned to the head of the warehouse's security. "What were you doing in Mayfair?"

John shook his head. "I wasn't in Mayfair. I've been on guard outside." They were moving a shipment tonight, so the roads leaving the rookery were monitored by a team of men in their employ. No one came in or out without the Bastards' approval.

Devil shook his head. He couldn't have

understood. It wasn't possible. He narrowed his gaze on the boy. "Where is she?"

"At the door!"

His heart began to pound. "Whose door?"

"Yours," John said, finally allowing the smile that had been threatening to break through. "Your lady's tryin' to pick the lock."

Devil scowled. "She's not my lady. And she sure as hell shouldn't be in the rookery."

"And yet, here we are." This, from Whit, who had appeared behind Devil. "Are you going to get the girl, Dev? Or are you going to leave her out there like a lamb to the slaughter?"

Goddammit.

Devil was already heading for the back door. A low rumble of laughter behind him that could not have been his brother's, as Whit surely did not want murdering.

He found her crouched low at the door to the warehouse, a sea of barely visible pale skirts billowing around her, and the flood of relief at discovering her unharmed quickly dissolved into irritation and then unwelcome interest. He pulled up short just around the corner of the building, not wanting to alert her to his presence.

Giving her a wide berth, he approached her from behind. Her head was bowed toward the lock, but not to see it — it was the dead of night and even if it hadn't been cloudy, the moonlight wouldn't have been enough for her to see her workspace.

Lady Felicity was talking to herself again.

Or, rather, she was talking to the lock, presumably without knowing that it was un-pickable — designed not only to guard, but to punish those who thought themselves better than it.

"There you are, darling," she whispered softly, and Devil froze to the spot. "I shan't be rough with you. I'm a summer breeze. I'm butterflies' wings."

What a lie that was. She threatened to incinerate every butterfly in Britain.

"Good girl," she whispered. "That's three and —" She fiddled with the picks. "Hmmm." More fiddling. "How many have you got?" She fiddled again. "More impor-tantly, what is so important inside this building that something as beautiful as you is protecting it . . . and its master?"

A thrum of excitement went through Devil at the words. Here, in the darkness, she spoke of him, and while he might not admit it to others, or even to himself, Devil liked that very much.

Even though she shouldn't be here, finery in filth.

Here she was, nonetheless, her soft whispers in the darkness, as though she could coax the lock open, and Devil almost thought she might. "Once more, darling," she whispered. "Please. Again."

He closed his eyes for a moment, imagining that whisper in his ear, cloaked in a different darkness, in his bed. *Please.* He imagined what she might plead for. *Again.* He grew hard at the possibilities. And then . . .

"Ah! Yes!" Another thing he'd like to hear her cry in different circumstances. His fingers ached to reach for her, the muscles of his arms and back no longer weary from the work inside, now more than willing to try their hand at lifting her up, against him, and laying her down somewhere soft and warm and private.

"Oh, bollocks."

He certainly didn't intend for anything like that disappointed utterance, however. The frustrated words pulled him from his imaginings and his brows rose.

"How did —" Felicity jiggled the lock. "What —"

It was his cue. "I'm afraid, Felicity Faircloth, that that particular lock is immune to your charms."

He would be lying if he said he didn't love

the way her shoulders straightened and her neck elongated. She did not come up out of her crouch, however — did not release the picks in the lock.

"Though they were pretty whispers, I must confess," he added.

She barely turned her head. "I suppose this looks rather damning."

He was grateful for the darkness, as it hid the twitch at his lips. "That depends. It looks as though you are attempting to break and enter."

"I wouldn't say that," she said, all calm. Felicity Faircloth, ever willing to brazen it out.

"No?"

"No. Well, I mean, I certainly am attempting to enter. But I never intended to break."

"You should stop entering my buildings uninvited."

She was distracted by the lock again. "I thought this was what we did with each other." She rattled the picks. "It appears I have unintentionally damaged this lock."

"You didn't."

She looked to him. "I assure you, I'm quite good with locks, and I've done something to this one. It's stuck."

"That's because it's supposed to be, my little criminal."

Understanding dawned. "It's a Chubb."

Something close to pride burst at the words, alongside something like pleasure at the reverence in her words. He didn't like either emotion in relation to Felicity Faircloth. He redoubled his efforts to remain aloof. "It is, indeed. How is it you are never in possession of a chaperone?"

"No one in my family expects me to do anything near this," she said, vaguely, as she returned her attention to the lock, perfectly set into the heavy steel door. "I've never seen a Chubb."

"I am happy to be of service. Your family ought to know better. What on earth possessed you to enter a London rookery in the dead of night? I should call the authorities."

Her brows rose. "The *authorities*?"

He inclined his head. "Thievery is a serious offense."

She gave a little laugh. "Not so serious as whatever you've got going on in here, *Devil.*"

Too smart for her own good. "We import ice, Lady Felicity. It's all very aboveboard."

"Oh, yes," she scoffed. "*Aboveboard* is one of the top three adjectives I would use to describe you. Immediately following *proper* and *uninteresting.*"

He smirked. "Those three words all mean

256

the same thing."

She gave a little, breathy laugh, and the June night went unseasonably warm. "Do you have the key to unstick the lock?"

Chubb locks were known for their perfect security. They were unable to be picked because at the first sign (or, in Felicity's case, the umpteenth sign) of picking, they locked up, and could only be reset with a special key. "As a matter of fact, I do."

He extracted the key from his trouser pocket, and she shot to her feet, reaching for it. "May I?"

He snatched it back. "So you might learn my secrets? Why would I allow that?"

She shrugged her shoulder. "As I shall learn them anyway, I see no reason why you shouldn't save me some time."

Christ, he liked this girl.

No. He didn't. He couldn't. If he liked her, he wouldn't be able to use her as needed.

He held the key straight up toward her, waiting for her to reach for it. When she did, he snatched it back again. "How did you find the warehouse?"

She met his gaze. "I followed you."

What in — "How?" It was impossible. He would have noticed someone following him.

"I imagine the normal way one follows

another. From behind."

If he hadn't been so consumed with thoughts of the ball the night before, he would have noticed. *Christ. What had this girl done to him?* "No one stopped you."

She happily shook her head.

He paid men a great deal of money to ensure that he wasn't killed on the streets of Covent Garden. You'd think one of them would think to apprise him of this woman shadowing him through the rookeries. "You could have been killed." Worse.

She tilted her head. "I don't think so. I think you made it more than clear that I was untouchable. Just before I was given free rein of your turf."

"You were never given free rein of my turf."

"How was it you put it?" Placing her hands on her hips, she lowered her voice to a register he assumed was supposed to sound like his. *"No one touches her. She belongs to me."* She relaxed her arms with a smile. "It was rather primitive, that, though, I'll admit, fairly empowering."

Goddammit. "Why are you here?"

"I'll tell you if you give me the Chubb key."

He laughed at her attempted negotiation. "No, no, kitten. You haven't the power here."

She tilted her head. "Are you sure?"

He wasn't, if he was honest. He pocketed the key once more. "No one has power here but me."

Her gaze lingered on the place where the key had disappeared and for a long, terrifying moment, he thought she might come for it. Terrifying, because in that moment he wanted her to do just that.

But damn if the woman didn't turn her back to him and crouch once more at the lock. Reaching into her coif, she extracted another hairpin. "Fine then. I shall do it myself."

Stubborn woman. He watched as she straightened the pin and kinked it at the end. "The Chubb is unpickable, darling."

"So far, it is, yes."

"You intend to pick it in the dead of night?"

"I do, indeed," she said. "What I know is that your key works in the reverse of normal keys, no? It resets the tumblers. In which case, if I can pick the sticking mechanism, I can learn how the lock works."

He watched as she inserted her newly made pick into the lock alongside a second tool, and came around to lean against the door, crossing his boots and his arms and watching her. "Why did you follow me?"

She scraped the inside of the lock. "Because you were leaving when I arrived."

"And why did you come see me in the first place?"

Again, a futile effort. "Because you didn't come to see me."

He stilled at that, at the implication that she'd wanted him to come and see her. "Did we have an appointment?"

"No," she said, calmly, as though they were in Hyde Park in the middle of the day and not in one of London's most dangerous neighborhoods in the dead of night. "But I would have thought that you would have checked in on me."

He had checked in on her. He had a watch checking in on her every minute of the day. "To what end?"

"To see if your promise was made good upon."

"My promise?"

"The Duke of Marwick, mad for me."

He gritted his teeth, remembering Ewan's lips on her silk-covered knuckles. She wasn't wearing gloves now, and Devil wanted to burn away any memory of Marwick's touch with his own lips. On her bare skin.

"And was it?"

She didn't reply. She was distracted by her pins in the lock.

"Felicity Faircloth," he repeated.

"Hmm?" She paused. Then, "Ah, I see." Another pause. "I beg your pardon, was what?"

"My promise. Was it made good upon? Did you meet your duke?"

"Oh," she said again. "Yes. We met. He was very handsome. And possibly . . . well . . . what they say about him might be true."

"What do they say about him?"

"That he is mad."

Ewan wasn't mad. He was obsessed.

"He danced like a dream."

Devil shouldn't be irritated by that statement. Wasn't this what he wanted? Ewan thinking he'd won Felicity? So it hurt more when Devil stole her away?

He wanted to put a fist through a wall at the idea of them dancing. He couldn't resist scoffing. "Like a dream?"

"Mmm," she said distractedly. "He has lovely form. Makes you feel as though you're a cloud."

"A cloud," Devil said, working to keep his teeth from clenching.

"Mmm," she said, again.

He was so irritated with the vision of cloudlike dancing that he snapped, "You don't just come to see me, Felicity."

"Why not? I've something to discuss with you."

"It doesn't matter. When we've things to discuss, I shall find you. You don't just turn up in the rookery."

"Is this a rookery? I've never been to one."

He would have laughed if it weren't all so laughable. Rookeries were full of stink and filth, death and destruction. They held the worst of the world — too often given to those who deserved the best of it. Of course, Lady Felicity Faircloth had never been to a rookery. She'd as likely have been to the moon.

"It's very quiet. I would have thought it would be otherwise."

"It's quiet because you're deep within the most protected part of it. But you could have easily lost your way."

"Nonsense. I followed you." She leaned toward the door and whispered, "That's it, darling."

Devil went hard as a rock. He straightened, coming off the door and shoving his hands into his pockets to keep her from noticing his untimely affliction. Clearing his throat, he said, "Giving you my direction was a grave mistake, as you seem unable to deliver a written message to my offices like any other normal human female." He paused. "Is it possible you are unable to write? Has your brother's poverty limited the amount of ink in your home? The quantity of paper?"

"Paper is not exactly the least expensive commodity," she offered.

Click.

Devil's jaw dropped. *Impossible.*

"Gorgeous, gorgeous girl. Well done." Felicity Faircloth stood up and raised her arms, deftly returning her hairpins to their proper seats. "Shall we see just how *above-board* you are, then?"

CHAPTER FOURTEEN

She'd shocked him.

The unmovable Devil, all powerful and controlling, impenetrable and domineering, and she had shocked him. She knew it, because his eyes went wide and his jaw went slack, and for a heartbeat she thought he might have swallowed something too large. He looked to her, then the lock, then back again. "You did it."

"I did," she said, happily.

He shook his head. "How?"

She couldn't control her proud grin. "Be careful, Devil. I shall begin to imagine you thought me without use."

"You're supposed to be without use!"

"I beg your pardon," she said. "Ladies are *not* supposed to be without use. We're supposed to speak several languages, and play the pianoforte, and needlepoint with aplomb, and lead a house party in a rousing game of blindman's buff."

He looked away and took a deep breath, making her think he might be searching for calm. "All so useful. Do you do all that?"

"I speak English and imperfect French."

"And the rest?"

She hesitated. "I'm quite good at needle-point." He cut her a look, and she added, "I hate it, but I'm fairly decent at it."

"And the pianoforte?"

She tilted her head. "Less so that."

"Blindman's buff?"

She shrugged a shoulder. "I can't remember the last time I played."

"So, we are left with lockpicking."

She grinned. "I'm very good at that."

"And is it useful?"

Not knowing where she summoned the brash courage, Felicity set her hand to the handle of the great steel door she'd just unlocked. "Let's see, shall we?" She didn't wait, too eager to see inside the warehouse and too afraid he'd stop her. She pulled at the door, using her whole weight to open it a half inch before he did just that.

The door slammed shut, one of his enormous hands splayed wide at her head. She fixed her gaze on that hand, its silver rings glinting in the dark, when he leaned in to her ear and said, "You should not have come."

She swallowed, refusing to let him win. "Why not?"

"Because it is dangerous," he said quietly, sending a shiver of belief through her. "Because the rookeries are no place for pretty girls with a breathless anticipation of adventure."

She shook her head. "That's not what I am."

"No?"

"No."

He waited for a long moment, and then said, "I think it is exactly what you are, Felicity Faircloth, in your pretty frock with your pretty hair high up on your pretty head, in your pretty world where nothing ever goes wrong."

The words grated. "That's not what I'm like. Things go wrong."

He tutted. "Ah, yes. I forgot. Your brother made a bad investment. Your father, too. Your family's poor enough to fear social exile. But here's the rub, Felicity Faircloth — your family will never be poor enough to fear poverty. They'll never wonder when their next meal will come. They'll never fear for the roof over their heads."

She turned her head then, almost looking at him, hearing the hint of truth in his words; he knew what that poverty was.

He continued before she could speak. "And you —" His voice grew lower. Darker. Thickly accented. "Silly gel . . . you come into Covent Garden like the fucking sun, thinkin' you can take a walk wiv us and still stay safe."

She did look at him then, cursing the shadows at his eyes, which made him a different man. A more frightening one. But she wasn't frightened. If she were honest, the low voice and the dark profanity made her feel something very different than frightened. She squared her shoulders and replied, "I am safe."

"You're nothing close to safe."

She might not know this place — she might never have known a life like the ones lived here — but she knew what it was to want beyond what she could have. And she knew that, right now, she had it in her reach — even if it was just for the night. Defiance flared and she lifted her chin. "Then we'd best get inside, don't you think?"

For a moment, she thought he might turn her away. Stuff her into a hack and send her home, just as he'd done before. But instead, after a long stretch of silence, he reached behind her and opened the enormous door with virtually no effort, his hand coming to rest on her waist to guide her into the cavernous room beyond. It was best he did keep his hand there, as she came up short in the doorway, eyes wide and disbelieving.

She'd never seen anything like it.

What, from the outside, seemed like a large building, from the inside seemed to be the size of St. James's Park. Around the outer edges of the single, massive room were racks of barrels and boxes stacked six or seven high. Inlaid in the ceiling at the outer edge of the racks were huge iron hooks, each attached to long, steel beams.

It was magnificent. She looked to Devil, who was watching her, more carefully than she should have liked. "It's yours?"

Pride lit in his eyes, and something tightened in her chest. "It is."

"It's magnificent."

"It is."

"How long did it take you to build it?"

And like that, the pride was gone — extinguished. Replaced with something darker. "Twenty years." She shook her head. Twenty years would make him a child. It wasn't possible. And yet . . . she heard the truth in the words.

"How?"

He shook his head. That was all she would get from the Devil on that front.

She changed tack — moved back to safe

ground. "What are the hooks for?"

He followed her gaze. "Cargo," he said, simply.

As she watched, a man approached one of the hooks and swung a rope over it, pulling it toward the ground as two other men lifted a rope-wrapped crate up onto the hook. Once secured, they pushed it through the room with what looked like no effort at all. At the other end of the room, the crate was removed and placed inside one of the five wagons that stood closest to Felicity, each tethered to six strong horses. Surrounding them were dozens of men, some carrying bales of hay to the open ends of each wagon, others checking the hitches for the horses, and still more hurrying back and forth from the back end of the warehouse — which was too dark to see — holding great metal hooks carrying massive blocks of —

"It *is* ice," she said.

"I said as much," Devil replied.

"For what? Lemon treats? Raspberry?"

He smirked. "Do you like sweets, Felicity Faircloth?"

She blushed at the question, though she couldn't for the life of her say why. "Doesn't everyone?"

"Mmm."

The low murmur rumbled through her, and she cleared her throat. "Is it all ice?"

"Does it appear that there is anything but ice in those wagons?"

She shook her head. "Appearances are not reality."

"Lord knows that's true, Felicity Faircloth, plain, unassuming, uninteresting wallflower spinster lockpick." He paused. "What do your unfortunate, terrible friends think of your hobby?"

She blushed. "They don't know about it."

"And your family?"

She looked away, heat and frustration flaring. "They . . ." She paused, thinking twice about the answer. "They don't like it."

He shook his head. "That's not what you were going to say. Tell me the first bit. The true bit."

She met his eyes, scowling. "They are ashamed of it."

"They shouldn't be," he said simply. Honestly. "They should be bloody proud of it."

She raised her brows. "Of my criminal tendencies?"

"Well, you won't find criticism of criminal tendencies here, love. But no. They should be proud of it because you've got the future in your hands every time you hold a hair-pin."

She stopped breathing at that, her heart pounding at the calm assessment of her wild, wicked skill. He was the first person who had ever, ever understood. Not knowing how to respond, she changed the subject. "What else is in the wagons?"

"Hay," he said. "It insulates the ice at the back, near the door openings."

"Oi! Dev!"

Devil's attention snapped to the growl from the darkness. "What is it?"

"Tear yerself from the girl and 'ave a look a' the manifests."

He cleared his throat at the impertinent question and turned to Felicity. "You. Stay here. Don't leave. Or commit any crimes."

She raised a brow. "I shall leave all crime committing to you lot."

His lips pressed into a flat line and he crossed into the darkness, leaving Felicity alone. Alone to investigate.

Ordinarily, if this were, say, a ballroom or a walk in Hyde Park, Felicity would have been too afraid to approach a location so teeming with men. Aside from pure good sense — men were too often more dangerous than they weren't — Felicity's interactions with the opposite sex rarely ended in

271

anything that was not an insult. Either they rebuked her presence or they felt entitled to it, and neither left a woman interested in spending time with a man.

But somehow, now, she'd been made safe among them. And it wasn't simply that Devil had wrapped her in the mantle of his protection; it was also that the men assembled didn't seem to notice her. Or, if they did, they didn't seem to care that she was a woman. Her skirts weren't interesting. They weren't judging the condition of her hair or the cleanliness of the gloves she was not wearing.

They were working, and she was there, and neither thing impacted the other, and it was unexpected and glorious. And full of opportunity.

She headed for the wagons, larger than most, and made not of the wood and canvas that was so commonly found on London streets, but of metal — great slabs of what looked to be flattened steel. She approached the nearest conveyance, reaching up to touch it, rapping at it to hear the sound of the full cargo beyond.

"Curious?"

Felicity whirled to face a tall man behind her. No, not a man. A woman, incredibly tall — possibly taller than Devil — and whipcord lean, lean enough to be mistaken for a man as she was, dressed in men's shirt and trousers, and tall black boots that only served to elongate her, so that it seemed as though she could reach her arms over her head and touch the clouds themselves. But even without the height, Felicity would have been fascinated by this woman — by her easy stance and her obvious comfort. By the way she seemed to stand in the dimly lit warehouse and claim it as hers. She did not need to pick a lock to gain access . . . she possessed the key.

What must it be like to be a woman such as this, head now tilted to one side, staring down at Felicity. "You can look, if you like," the woman said, one hand waving toward the back of the wagon, her voice carrying a strange, soft accent that Felicity could not place. "Devil brought you here, so he must trust you."

Felicity wondered at the words, at the certainty that Devil would do nothing to harm this place or the people who worked within it, and something flared in her — something startlingly akin to guilt. "I don't think he does trust me," she replied, unable to keep herself from looking in the direction of the woman's wave, wanting nothing more than to follow it and look inside this great steel wagon. "I brought myself here."

A smile played at the other woman's lips. "I promise you, if Devil didn't want you here, you wouldn't be here."

Felicity took the words at their face, and moved toward the open back of the wagon, her fingers trailing along the steel, which grew colder as she reached her destination.

The woman turned to a man nearby. "Samir, this one is ready for you. You stay on the North Road and you don't stop until daylight. Keep to your planned stops and you'll see the border in six nights. There, you'll be met by three others." She handed the man a handful of papers. "Manifests and directions for the other deliveries. Understood?"

Samir, who Felicity imagined was to drive the wagon, tipped his cap. "Aye, sir."

The woman clapped her hand on his shoulder. "Good man. Good chase." She turned back to Felicity. "Devil will be back in no time. He's just checking the loads."

Felicity nodded, rounding the corner of the wagon to discover a wall of hay, loaded up to the top. She looked to the woman. "They don't have a better way to bring ice to Scotland than through London?"

The woman paused, then said, "Not one we know of."

Felicity turned back to the wagon and reached out to touch the coarse straw hiding whatever was inside. "Strange no one has realized that Inverness is directly across the North Sea from Norway." She paused. "Which is where ice comes from, no?"

"Is she bothering you, Nik?" Felicity pulled back her hand and spun toward the question, spoken altogether too close to her ear. Devil had returned to inspect the open wagon, and Felicity, it seemed.

"No," the woman named Nik replied, and Felicity thought she might hear laughter in the other woman's voice, "but I'm imagining she's going to bother you quite a bit."

Devil grunted and looked to Felicity. "Don't bother Nik. She's work to do."

"Yes, I've heard," Felicity retorted. "Ensuring your ice is shipped the hundreds of miles back toward its origin." He looked over her shoulder at that, and she followed his gaze to Nik, who was smirking at him. Excitement flared. "Because it's not ice, is it?"

"See for yourself." He reached past her, pulling a bale of hay down from the wagon, revealing a block of ice behind. He frowned.

Felicity's brows rose. "Are you surprised?"

Ignoring her, he reached for another bale, and another, pulling them down to reveal a

275

wall of ice the length of the wagon and rising nearly to the top of it. He looked to Nik, the wicked scar on his face gone white in the dim light. "This is how we get melt."

The woman sighed and called into the darkness, "We need another row here."

"Aye," came a chorus of men from the darkness.

They came almost instantly, carrying great metal tongs, each bearing a block of solid ice. One by one, they passed the blocks to Devil, who'd climbed up onto the wagon and was fitting them carefully into the void left at the top of the shipment, ensuring as little space as possible was left.

Felicity would have been fascinated by the process if she weren't so fascinated by him, somehow hanging off the edge of the wagon, heaving great blocks of ice up nearly to above his head as though he were superhuman. As though he were Atlas himself, surefooted and holding up the firmament. He wasn't wearing a topcoat or a waistcoat, and the linen of his white shirt stretched and flexed over his muscles as they did the same, making Felicity wonder if it might tear beneath his strength.

Everyone was always on about women's décolletages and how corsetry was growing more salacious by the minute and skirts clung too close to women's legs, but had any one of those people seen a man without a coat? Good God.

She swallowed as he put the last block into place and leapt down, raising a strange, steel lip from the base of the wagon — approximately twelve inches high and so tightly fitted to the sides of the vehicle that the scrape of it screamed through the warehouse.

"What's that for?" she asked.

"Keeps the ice from sliding when the melting begins," he said, not looking at her.

She nodded. "Well, anyone peeking into this wagon would think that you were a very skilled ice deliverer, that is certain."

He did look at her then. "I am a very skilled ice deliverer."

She shook her head. "I would believe it, if it were ice."

"Do your eyes deceive you?"

"They do, in fact. But my touch does not."

His brow furrowed. "What's that to mean?"

"Only that if this entire steel wagon were filled with ice, the entirety of the outside would be as cold as the rear two feet."

Nik coughed.

Devil ignored the words, reaching to swing the large rear door to the wagon closed, latching it in three separate places. Felicity watched carefully as he closed the locks and delivered their keys to Nik. "Tell the men they're ready."

"Aye, sir." Nik turned to the men assembled. "That's a go, gentlemen. Good chase."

At the words, the men scrambled, the drivers leaping up to their blocks, seconds joining them. Felicity watched as the one closest to her slid a pistol into a holster attached to his leg. Two other men hefted themselves up onto the rear step of the wagon, pulling wide leather straps around their bottoms.

Felicity turned to Devil. "I've never seen anything like those — seats for outriders? To keep them from having to stand the whole trip?"

He watched as one of the men lashed himself to the wagon with the strap. "Partially for comfort," he replied, turning to accept something from the man to his left. "Partially because they might need their hands for something other than to hang on." Moving forward, he handed a rifle up to the outrider, and another to the man's partner.

"Ah, yes. I see now that it is all ice," she said dryly. "Why else would it require so many armed men?"

He ignored her. "Aim true, boys."

"Aye, sir." The reply came in unison.

"Yourselves above all," Devil said, and her gaze snapped to his face, registering the seriousness of his words and something else — something like concern. Not for the cargo, but for the men. Felicity's chest tightened.

"Aye, sir." They nodded, strapping the weapons across their chests and checking the fastenings on their seats before banging on the side of the wagon.

Down the line, other young men were similarly preparing, lashing them to the wagons and strapping rifles to their chests. Metallic thuds echoed through the great room, until every wagon was ready to leave. A great scrape sounded as several men slid an enormous steel door open — large enough to pull a wagon through.

"The border," Nik called, and the wagon closest to Felicity leapt to movement, pulling through the open door and into the night. She backed into Devil, his arm coming around her waist to steady her as Nik said, "York." Another wagon moved, and it occurred to Felicity that she should step away from his touch. That another woman certainly would do so. Except . . . she didn't want to.

Next to him, with the horses stomping their feet and the men shouting their orders, she felt like the lady of a medieval keep, skirts billowing in the Scottish wind as she stood next to her laird and watched her clan prepare for war.

"London First," Nik shouted above the racket of wagon wheels.

It seemed a little like war. Like these men had trained together, becoming brothers in arms. And now they sojourned together in service to a greater purpose.

To Devil.

Devil, whose arm held her closer than it should. Stronger than it should. And precisely as she found she wished. As though she were his partner, and he hers.

"Bristol," Nik called, spurring another wagon to motion. "London Second."

Before the last of the vehicles left the warehouse, the door was sliding closed, several men moving forward to place a great wooden beam against it to prevent it being opened from the outside. At the thunder of the heavy lock, Devil released her, stepping away, as though his hold had been nothing more than a fantasy.

She tried for levity. "And so, your ice is beyond your control."

"My ice is well within my control until it

reaches its destination," Devil said, watching as another man approached, this one dark-haired, with golden-brown skin. "I would remind you, my lady, that I am able to wield considerable power with or without physical presence."

The words, a low rumble, sent a shiver through her — reminding her of the way he had seemed to exude power from the moment she met him. He'd somehow prevented the duke from denying her claim of their engagement. He'd discovered her family's secrets without even trying. He'd made her safe in Covent Garden even when he wasn't with her. Perhaps he was the Devil, after all, all-powerful and omniscient, manipulating the world without struggle, collecting debts along the way.

But he hadn't yet collected her debt.

The duke might have offered her marriage, but a marriage of convenience was not her plan. And so she was here in this magnificent place like nothing she'd ever seen, ready to face the Devil once again. And remind him that his end of the bargain had not been met.

"Not enough power," she replied.

He snapped his attention back to her, his narrow gaze setting her heart racing. "What did you say?"

Before she could reply, the other man joined them, also in shirtsleeves, rolled up along his forearms, revealing a pattern of black ink that Felicity would have considered more seriously if the man hadn't stepped into a pool of golden light that revealed his face — beautiful beyond measure. The kind of face that painters assigned to angels.

She couldn't hold back her gasp.

Both men looked at her.

"Is there a problem?"

She shook her head. "No. It's just — he's very —" She looked to the man, realizing it was rude to speak of him as though he weren't standing directly in front of her. "That is, sir, *you're* very —" She stopped. Was it appropriate to tell a man he was beautiful? Her mother would no doubt dissolve into conniptions. Though, to be fair, her mother would likely dissolve into conniptions if she knew her daughter was anywhere near Covent Garden — let alone deep in one of its rookeries. So she was long past any semblance of understanding of what was appropriate.

"Felicity?"

She did not look at Devil. "Yes?"

"Do you intend to finish that thought?"

She remained transfixed by the newcomer.

"Oh. Yes. I'm sorry. No." She cleared her throat. "No." Shook her head. "Definitely not."

One black eyebrow rose, curious and assessing.

And familiar.

"Brothers!" she blurted out, looking from him to Devil and back again, then took a step toward him, sending him back a half step, his gaze flying to Devil's, giving her a chance to inspect his eyes — the same mysterious color of Devil's — somehow gold and somehow brown, and with that dark ring around them, and altogether, thoroughly unsettling. "Brothers," she repeated. "You're brothers."

The beautiful man inclined his head.

"This is Beast," Devil said.

She gave a little laugh at the silly name. "I suppose that's meant to be ironic?"

"Why?"

She looked over her shoulder at Devil. "He's the most beautiful person I've ever seen."

Devil's lips flattened at that, and she thought she heard a little growl of amusement from the man called Beast, but when she returned her attention to him, he hadn't moved. She pressed on. "Your eyes are the same. The bones of your cheeks, your jaws.

The curve of your lips."

The growl seemed to come from Devil then. "I'll thank you to stop considering the shape of his lips."

Her cheeks grew warm. "I'm sorry." She looked to Beast. "That was quite rude of me. I shouldn't have noticed."

Neither brother seemed to care about the apology, Devil already moving away, no doubt expecting her to follow. She supposed no one was going to stand on ceremony in a Covent Garden warehouse and make introductions, so she decided to do it herself. She smiled at Devil's brother. "I am Felicity."

That brow rose and he stared at her outstretched hand, but he did not take it.

Really. Were the brothers raised by a mother wolf? "This is the bit where you tell me your real name; I know it isn't Beast."

"Don't talk to him," Devil said, his long legs already eating up the ground as he headed across the warehouse.

"But you believe his name is Devil?" The question came low and graveled, as though the Beast was out of practice using his voice.

She shook her head. "Oh. No. I don't believe that at all. But you seem more reasonable."

"I'm not," he replied.

Felicity probably should have been unsettled by the answer, but instead, she found she rather liked this second, quiet brother. "I wasn't noticing your lips you know," she offered. "It's just that I've noticed his and yours are the same . . ." She trailed off when both his brows rose. She supposed she shouldn't have admitted to that, either.

He grunted, and Felicity imagined that it was supposed to set her at ease.

Oddly, it did. Together, they followed Devil, who had already disappeared into the shadows of the warehouse — hopefully far enough away that he hadn't heard her. As they walked, she searched for a topic that might make the unsocial man more willing to converse. "You've been running ice for a long while, then?"

He did not reply.

"Where does it come from?"

Silence.

She searched for something else. "Did you design the transport wagons yourselves? They're very impressive."

Again, silence.

"I must say, Beast, you do know how to put a woman at ease."

If she weren't paying such close attention to him, she might not have heard the little catch in his throat. A laugh of some sort.

285

But she did, and it made her feel triumphant. "Aha! You are able to respond!"

He said nothing, but they'd reached Devil by then. "I told you not to talk to him."

"You left me with him!"

"That doesn't mean you should talk to him."

She looked from one brother to the other and sighed, then waved a hand at the men dispersed around the enormous room. "These are all your employees?"

Devil nodded.

Beast grunted.

Felicity heard it and turned on his brother. "That. What does that mean?"

"Don't talk to him," Devil said.

She didn't turn back. "I think I shall, thank you very much. What did that noise mean?"

"They are his employees." Beast's gaze slid away from her.

She shook her head. "That's not all it meant, though, is it?"

Beast met her eyes, and she knew whatever he was about to say was important. And true. "The kind of employees who would walk through fire for him."

The words fell in the darkness, filling the warehouse, reaching the corners and warming them. Warming her. She turned back to

Devil, who stood several feet away, his hands thrust into his trouser pockets, a look of irritation on his face. But he wasn't looking at her. He couldn't.

He was embarrassed.

She nodded, then said, softly, "I believe that."

And she did. She believed this man who called himself Devil was the kind of man who could engender deep, abiding loyalty from those around him. She believed he was a man with whom one did not trifle, and also a man of his word. And she believed that he was the kind of man who held up his end of the bargain.

"I believe that," she repeated, wanting him to look at her. When he did, she realized his eyes were not the same as his brother's. Beast's gaze did not make her heart pound. She swallowed. "So, they help you smuggle cargo?"

Devil's brow furrowed. "They help us move ice."

She shook her head. She didn't believe for a second that these two men, with the way they fairly oozed danger, were mere ice traders. "And where do you keep this alleged ice?"

He straightened his arms and fisted his hands in his pockets, rocking back on his heels and looking at the ceiling. When he replied, his words were filled with frustration. "We've a hold full of it downstairs, Felicity."

She blinked. "Downstairs."

"Underground." The word rang forbidden in the dimly lit room, spoken low like sin, as though he were the Devil, inviting her not only underground — but so far underground that she might never return.

It made her want to experience everything it promised. It made her ask for that experience, without hesitation. "Show me."

For a moment, no one moved, and Felicity thought she had asked too much. Pushed too hard. After all, she hadn't been welcome here; she'd picked the lock to make her way in.

But she had been welcome here. He'd let her pick the lock. He'd given her free rein of the warehouse, let her stand among his men and see the operation and, for a moment, he'd let her feel something other than alone. He'd given her access to his world in a way no man ever had before. And now, drunk on the power that came with that access, she wanted all of it. Every inch.

More.

"Please?" she added in the silence that followed her demand — as though politeness would impact his answer.

And it did. Because Devil looked to his brother, who revealed none of his own thoughts as he passed a large brass key ring to Devil. Once the keys were in hand, Devil turned away, making for a great steel plate set into the ground nearby, reaching down and opening it up, revealing a great black hole in the ground. Felicity approached as he reached for a nearby hook, bringing down a coat. "You'll need this," he said. "It will be cold."

Her eyes went wide as she reached for it. It was happening. He was going to show her. She swung the great heavy cloak around her shoulders, the scent of tobacco flower and juniper encircling her, and she resisted the urge to bury her nose in the lapel. The coat was his. She looked to him. "Won't you be cold?"

"No," he said, reaching for a lantern nearby and dropping into the hold.

She came to the edge and looked down at him, his face shadowed by the flickering light. "Another thing you control? Cold does not bother you?"

He raised a brow. "My power is legion."

She turned and climbed down the ladder inlaid into the side of the hatch, trying to remain calm, trying not to notice that her world was changing with every step. That the old, plain, wallflower Felicity was being left behind, and in her place was a new, strange woman who did things like pick locks that opened doors instead of closing them, and visit smuggler's caches, and wear coats that smelled of handsome, scarred men who called themselves Devil.

But truth such as that was impossible not to notice.

There was something to be said for being in league with the Devil.

When Felicity reached the dirt ground, she spoke to the rungs of the ladder. "I am not certain you wield the power you think, sirrah."

"And why is that?" he asked, his voice quiet in the dark.

She turned to face him. "You made me a promise, and you have yet to deliver."

"How is that?" Had he moved closer? Or was it the darkness playing tricks? "From what you've said, it sounds like your duke is won. What was it you said? He dances like a dream? What more would you like?"

"You didn't promise me a duke," she insisted.

"That is precisely what I promised you," he said as he climbed several rungs of the ladder and pulled the door to the hold closed behind them, throwing them into darkness.

She blinked. "Is it necessary to shut us in?"

"The door stays closed at all times. It prevents melt, and the curiosity of anyone who might be interested in what we do inside the warehouse."

"No, you promised me a moth," she said, not knowing where the bravery came from. Not caring. "You promised me singed wings and passion."

His eyes glittered with his attention. "And?"

"The duke is under no risk of bursting into flames, you see," she replied. "And I thought it only right that I inform you that if you are not careful, *you* are at risk of finding yourself in *my* debt."

"Hmm," he said, as though she'd made an important business point. "And how do you suggest I change that?"

"It's quite simple," she whispered. He *was* closer. Or maybe it was that she wanted him closer. "You must teach me to lure him."

"To lure him."

She took a deep breath, his warmth around her, tobacco flower and juniper drugging her with power. With desire.

"Precisely. I should like you to teach me to make him want me. Beyond reason."

CHAPTER FIFTEEN

The idea that any human male would not want Felicity Faircloth beyond reason surpassed understanding. Not that Devil intended to tell her that.

It was important to note, however, that when the thought crashed around him in the dark hold beneath the Bareknuckle Bastards' Covent Garden warehouse, Devil did not count himself in that particular group of human males.

Obviously, *he* had plenty of reason when it came to Felicity Faircloth. *He* wasn't near beyond it. Not even when she stood mere inches from him, wearing his coat, and speaking of burning men to cinders.

He was immune to the lady's charms.

Remember the plan. The words echoed through him as his hands itched for her, fingers flexing, wanting nothing more than to reach for the lapels of his coat and pull her to him, close enough to touch, until she couldn't remember the Duke of Marwick's name, let alone the way the man danced.

Like a dream, my ass.

He cleared his throat at the thought. "You want a love match. With Marwick." He scoffed. "You're too old and too wise for simpering, Felicity Faircloth."

She shook her head. "I didn't say anything about a love match; I want him to want me. I want passion."

It should be illegal for a woman like Felicity Faircloth to say the word *passion*. It conjured images of wide expanses of skin and beautiful, mahogany locks across white sheets. It made a man wonder how she would arch her back to his touch, how she might ask for it. How she might direct it. How her hand would feel on his, moving his fingers to the precise location she wanted them. How her fingers would feel against his scalp as she moved his mouth to the precise location she wanted it.

Thank God they were standing fifteen feet from a hold full of ice.

In fact . . . "This way." He raised the lantern and moved down the long, dark corridor, toward the ice hold, forgetting, for the first time, ever, that he didn't care for the dark. Grateful for the distraction, he

294

spoke as they walked. "You wish for passion."

Remember the plan.

"I do."

"From Marwick."

"He is my future husband, is he not?"

"It's only a matter of time," he said, knowing he should be more committed to the endeavor, considering that Ewan and Felicity had to be engaged before Devil could steal her away from the engagement. The engagement was part of the plan. A part of Ewan's lesson. Of course Devil wanted it.

"He asked me last night."

He just hadn't wanted it so quickly, it seemed.

He turned to her. "He asked you to do what?"

Her hair glittered copper in the candlelight as she smiled up at him. "To marry him. It was really quite simple. He introduced himself, told me he was happy to marry me. That he was in the market for a wife, and I had . . . how did he put it? Oh, it was terribly romantic." Devil's teeth clenched as she searched for the words and then found them, dry as sand. "Oh, yes. I had *turned up* just at the right time."

Good Lord. Ewan had never been a brilliant wordsmith, but that was particularly bad. And proof that the duke, too, had a plan. Which meant that perhaps Felicity Faircloth's request was not such a terrible idea after all. "Terribly romantic, indeed," he said.

She shrugged. "But he is very handsome and dances like a dream, as I said."

It didn't seem possible that she was teasing him. How could she possibly know how the words would grate? "And that is a thing all women look for in their husbands."

She grinned. "However did you know?"

She was teasing him. She was teasing him, and he liked it. And he shouldn't. "You want the man mad for you."

"Well, I remain unconvinced that he is not mad in general, but yes," she said. "Doesn't every wife want that from her husband?"

"Not in my experience, no."

"Do you have a great deal of experience with wives?"

He ignored the question. "You don't know what you're asking for," he said, turning back down the corridor.

She followed him. "What does that mean?"

"Only that passion isn't a thing one toys with — once the wings are singed, the moth is yours to deal with."

"As the moth shall be my husband, I

imagine I will have to deal with him anyway."

But he won't be your husband. Devil resisted the urge to say it. Resisted, too, the
emotion clawing at him as he thought the
words. The guilt.

"You promised me, Devil," she said softly.
"You made me a deal. You said you'd make
me flame."

He didn't have to do anything to turn her
to flame. She burned too brightly already.

They reached the exterior door to the
hold, and he crouched low, placing the
lantern on the ground as he reached for the
ring of keys. She came to his side, reaching
out for the row of locks, her fingers tracing
over one of them as though she could pick
it by touch alone. And with the way she'd
tackled the Chubb earlier, he half believed
she could.

Cold seeped through the steel door, and
he hunched his shoulders, sliding the key
into the first lock. "Why do you lockpick?"

"Is that relevant?"

He threw her a sidelong look. "I'm sure
you can see how it would be of interest."

She watched as he worked the second
lock. "The world is full of doors." Lord
knew that was true. "I like being able to
open my own doors."

"And what do you know of locked doors, Felicity Faircloth?"

"I wish you would stop doing that," she said. "Treating me as though I have never wanted for anything in my life. As though it has all been mine for the taking."

"Hasn't it been?"

"None of the important bits, no. Not love. Not . . . friendship. Barely family."

"You're better off without those friends."

"Are you offering to be a new one?"

Yes.

"No."

She huffed a little laugh, reaching to take one of the padlocks from the door as he continued his work. Out of the corner of his eye, he could see her turning it over and over in her hand. "I pick locks because I can. Because there are very few things in the world I can control, and locks are something I am good at. They are a barrier I can clear. And a secret I can know. And in the end, they bend to my will and . . ." She shrugged. "I like that."

He could imagine bending to her will. He shouldn't imagine it. But he could. He opened the first, heavy door, frigid air washing over them as the second door came into view. He set to work on the next row of locks. "It's not the kind of skill one expects

298

a woman to have."

"It's exactly the kind of skill we *should* have. Our whole world is built by men. For them. And we're simply here for decoration, brought in at the end of everything important. Well, I grow tired of ends. Locks are beginnings."

He turned to look at her, consumed with a desire to give her infinite beginnings.

She kept talking, seemingly mesmerized by his keys as he worked. "The point is, I understand what it is to want to be on the other side of the door. I understand what it is to know that the room isn't mine for the taking. So many doors are closed to all but a fraction of us." He opened the last lock, and she finished, softly, "Why should others be the ones to decide which doors are for me?"

The question, so honest, so forthright, made him want to break down every door she came to from now until the end of time.

Devil settled on the one in front of them, pushing it open to reveal the ice hold. A wall of cold greeted them, and beyond it, darkness. Unease thundered through him — resistance to the darkness, an all too familiar urge to run.

Felicity Faircloth had no such urge. She stepped right into the room, wrapping her arms about her. "So, ice it is."

He followed her, holding the lantern high, even as the cavernous space swallowed the light. "You still did not believe me?"

"Not entirely."

"And what did you think I was planning to show you down here?"

"Your mysterious, underground lair?"

"Underground lairs are highly overvalued."

"They are?"

"No windows, and they're hell on the boots."

Her little laugh was a flicker in the darkness. "I expect I shall have some explaining to do tomorrow when my maid sees the hem of my skirts."

"What will you tell her?" he asked.

"Oh, I don't know." She sighed. "Late night gardening? It doesn't matter. No one expects me to do anything like explore the underground caverns of Covent Garden."

"Why not?"

She paused, and he would have given anything to see her face, but she was too busy peering into the darkness. "Because I'm ordinary," she said simply, distractedly. "Terribly so."

"Felicity Faircloth," he said, "in the few days I've known you, I've learned one, unimpeachable truth. You are no kind of ordinary."

She turned back to him at that, fast and unexpected, and in the lantern light he discovered her cheeks pinkening from the cold, which made her rather . . . fetching.

Whit would eat him for supper if he knew Devil had even *thought* the word *fetching.* It was a ridiculous word. The kind of word used by fops and dandies. Not by bastards who carried cane swords. And she wasn't fetching. She was a means to an end. An aging, wallflower, spinster means, in his orbit for a sole purpose — his brother's end.

And even if she weren't all those things, she absolutely wouldn't be for him. Felicity Faircloth was the daughter to a marquess, the sister to an earl, and so far above his station she should have a different climate. Her porcelain skin was too perfect, her hands too clean, and her world too grand. Her wide-eyed delight at his Covent Garden warehouse and her smirking pride at cracking the lock to his criminal life only proved the point. Lady Felicity would never know what it was to be common.

That, alone, should have been enough.

Except she smiled before he could stop this mad game, and the candlelight played tricks, because she went from fetching to fucking beautiful. And that was before she said, breathlessly, "No kind of ordinary; I think that might be the nicest thing anyone's ever said to me."

Christ.

He had to get her out of there. "Well, now you've seen the hold."

"No, I haven't."

"This is all there is to see."

"It's dark," she replied, reaching for the lantern. "May I?"

He relinquished it reluctantly, a thread of unease coiling through him at the idea that he was no longer in control of the light. He took a deep breath when she turned away from him and moved deeper into the hold to discover the stacks of ice within.

The ship's cargo had been moved carefully, through a long, straight path cut by removing blocks of ice, revealing the center of the hold, which only hours ago was full of casks and crates and barrels and boxes now on their way to myriad locations throughout Britain.

Damned if Felicity Faircloth didn't head straight for that path, as though she were attending a tea party at the center of a labyrinth. She called back, "I wonder what I shall find *inside* the ice?"

He followed her.

No. He followed *the light.* Not the girl.

He didn't care what happened to the girl. Let her explore the hold all she liked. Let her get frostbite for how she lingered inside it. "More ice," he said, as she found the center of the space, along with its cold, muddy ground.

"I'm not so sure." The light disappeared as she turned the corner and it went out of view, darkness crawling over him from the rear. He took a deep breath, keeping his gaze on the hazy shadow of her head and shoulders above the ice . . . until it, too, disappeared, dropping out of sight. She'd no doubt slipped in the wet slop of the hold — a danger of working with ice.

"Be careful," he cautioned, picking up speed, turning into the empty center of the room to discover her crouched low, holding the lantern in front of her with all the skill of a Thames tide-picker, searching for treasure.

She looked up at him. "There's nothing here."

He exhaled. "No."

"Nothing but footprints of what was here before," she said with a wry smile. She pointed. "A heavy box, there." Changed direction. "And there, a barrel of some kind."

His brows rose. "Bow Street is missing your cunning investigative instincts."

The smile became a grin. "Perhaps I'll stop there on my way home. What was it?"

"Ice."

"Hmm," she said, "I'm guessing it was something alcoholic. And I shall tell you what else . . ."

He crossed his arms over his chest and replied dryly, "I wish you would."

She pointed a finger at him triumphantly. "I'm guessing it was something that came into the country untaxed." She was so proud of herself that he almost told her it had been American bourbon. He almost did a lot of things.

He almost pulled her to her feet and kissed the detective work from her lips.

Almost.

Instead, he rubbed his hands together and blew into them. "Excellent deductions, my lady. But it's bloody freezing in here, so shall we head back so you might perform a citizen's arrest for your accusations — for which you haven't a lick of proof?"

"You should have worn a coat." She waved him off and went back to the wall of ice blocks. "What do you do with the ice now?"

"We ship it throughout London. Homes and butcher shops and sweet shops and restaurants. And you're wearing my coat."

"That's very kind of you," she replied. "Did you not have a waistcoat?"

"We turn a profit on the ice, or we wouldn't deal in it," he said. "I typically don't dress for manual labor."

"I noticed," she said, and Devil snapped to attention at her low, soft words.

"You noticed."

"It was virtually indecent," she said, her voice louder, defensive. "I'm not certain how I was not to notice."

He approached her, unable to stop himself, and she pressed back, away from him, against the ice. Reaching out, she set a hand to the fabricated wall, instantly removing it when the cold registered.

"Be careful," he said.

"Are you worried I'll freeze?"

He told the truth. "I'm worried you'll melt it."

She raised a brow at him. "You forget I have not yet learned to be a flame."

For the life of him, he'd never know why he didn't stop at that. Why he didn't snatch up the lantern and take her away. "You and your desire to incinerate us all, Felicity Faircloth; you are terribly dangerous."

"Not to you," she said softly as he drew nearer, the quiet words like a siren's call.

"You'll never get close enough to burn."

He was already close enough. "You'd best keep your sights on another, then."

No. Set them on me.

We can burn together.

He was close enough to touch her. "Then you'll teach me?"

Anything. Anything she asked for.

"You'll show me how to make men adore me."

God, it was tempting. She was tempting.

If Ewan adores her, it will hurt him more when you take her away. If he's impassioned, you'll punish him more.

But that wasn't all of it. Now, there was Felicity. And if she allowed herself to feel passionately about Ewan, she wouldn't only be ruined by the dissolution of their courtship, she'd be devastated by it.

She'd be a casualty of this war, decades in the making, that she'd had nothing to do with. She'd be wounded in the balance; that was never the plan.

Bullshit. That was always the plan.

The plan was to show Ewan that Devil would always be able to pull the strings. That Ewan lived by his bastard brothers' benevolence and nothing else. That they could end any marriage he thought to begin. That they could end *him.*

Teaching Felicity Faircloth about passion would be the easiest way for Devil to put his plan into action. He could woo the girl even as she wooed the duke, and then, just as they were to marry, seduce her away and send his clear message — *no heirs. No marriage. No free will. Never for you.*

That was the arrangement they'd made, was it not? The promise the brothers had sworn in the dark of night as their monstrous father had manipulated and punished, never once thinking of them as anything more than candidates to be the next in a long line of Marwicks.

The three boys had vowed never to give their father what he asked.

But Ewan had won the contest. And after he'd taken the title, the house, the fortune, the world their father had offered . . . he'd broken ranks and tried for even more. An heir to a dukedom that should never have been his to begin with.

An illegitimate son, once willing to kill for legitimacy, now come for it on another path. One he had vowed he would never travel.

And Devil would teach him a lesson.

Which meant Felicity would have to learn it, too.

He lifted the lantern from her hands and set it on the block next to her, the light flickering over the cloudy ice, setting it to a strange, grey-green glow. He could see the pulse racing in her neck as he did it, he was so close to her.

Or maybe he couldn't. Maybe he only wanted her pulse to race.

Maybe it was his pulse he sensed.

He met her gaze, eager and beautiful, and leaned toward her. "Are you sure you wish this door opened, Lady Lockpick?" he said, hating himself for the words. Knowing that if she agreed, she would be ruined. He would have no choice but to ruin her.

She didn't know that, though. Or, if she did, she didn't care. Her eyes sparkled, candlelight flickering in their deep brown depths. "Very sure."

No man on earth could resist her.

And so he did not try.

He reached for her, his hand coming to her cheek, fingers grazing over the impossibly soft skin of her jaw, tracing the bones of it into her hairline, threading there, catching in the thick mahogany curls, trapped by her hairpins, bent into lockpicks, locking him to her. Her lips fell open at the touch, a soft, stunning intake of air revealing her excitement. Her desire.

Revealing his.

With his free hand, he touched the other

side of her face, exploring it. Reveling in the silk of her skin, in the way her cheeks rose and hollowed, in the little crease at the corner of her mouth, where a dimple flashed when she teased him. He leaned toward her, fully, madly intending to put his lips to that crease. To taste it.

"Blindman's buff," she whispered. "Your hands . . . It's like the game."

A child's game. A country house whim. One player blindfolded, trying to identify another by touch. As though Devil wouldn't know Felicity Faircloth by touch for the rest of time. "Close your eyes," he said.

She shook her head. "That's not how the game is played."

"I'm not playing a game."

Her gaze found his. "Aren't you?"

Not in that moment. "Close your eyes," he repeated.

She did, and he moved closer, leaning in, putting his lips at her ear. "You tell me what you feel."

He could hear the way he impacted her — the breath that caught in her chest, shuddered through the long column of her throat as she exhaled, thin and reedy, as though it were difficult for her to get the air in.

Devil understood the feeling, even more so when one of her hands rose to hover above his shoulder — teasing him without touching him. He spoke again, letting his breath fan the high arc of her cheek, where he wanted to kiss. "Felicity, fairest of them all . . ." he whispered. "What do you feel?"

"I —" she started, and then, "I don't feel cold."

No, he didn't imagine she did. "What do you feel?" he asked again.

"I feel . . ." Her hand lit upon his shoulder, the weight of it like fire. He bit back a groan. Grown men did not groan at the brush of a hand against their shoulder.

Not even if it was a flame, hot and impossible in the frigid room.

"What do you feel?"

"I think it must be . . ."

Say it, he willed, the words a prayer to a God that had forsaken him decades ago if he'd ever been blessed to begin with. *Say it, so I may give it all to you.*

It was possible he said the words aloud, because she replied to them, her beautiful brown eyes, black in the darkness, finding his, her fingers tightening at his shoulder, her free hand coming to rest high on his chest as she whispered, full of surprise and somehow certainty, "Want."

"Yes," he said, leaning close, tightening his grip and pulling her to him, somehow finding the strength to keep his kiss from hers. "I feel it, too."

Her eyes closed, long dark lashes a sooty slash against her skin, luminous in the ethereal, icy light for half a moment before they opened again, found his. "Unlock me," she whispered.

The words were strange and perfect and irresistible, and Devil did as she commanded, his fingers sliding into her hair, his thumb stroking over her cheek, sipping at her lips, once, twice, gently, savoring the taste of her — soft and impossibly sweet.

He lifted his head, leaving a minuscule space between them, enough for her to open her eyes. Her fingers curled into the fabric of his shirt, tugging at him, to bring him back. "Devil?"

He shook his head, unable to stop himself. "When I was a boy," he whispered, leaning in for another taste, a little, lingering lick, "I stole into the May Day fair in Hyde Park." Another kiss, this one longer, ending on her sigh, pretty as sin. He pressed a kiss to her cheek, another to the corner of her lips, where that dimple lay, letting his tongue linger in the space until she turned toward him. He pulled back, suddenly wanting her to hear the story. "There was a stall filled with sticks of spun sugar, white and fluffy

311

as clouds — I'd never seen anything like them."

She was watching him, and he leaned in to kiss her gently, unable to keep himself from licking at her full, lower lip, loving the way it went slack at the touch, the way she opened to him. "Children clamored for those treats," he whispered, "and parents, lost in the festivities, were more generous than usual."

She smiled. "And did someone buy one for you?"

"No one ever bought anything for me."

Her smile fell.

"I watched as dozens of others received their treat, and I hated them for knowing what those white clouds tasted like." He paused. "I nearly stole one."

"Nearly?"

He'd been run off by fairground guards before he could. "For years, I've told myself that the idea of that treat was far better than however it might have tasted."

She nodded. "Tell me the idea of it."

"It couldn't possibly taste near what I imagined it to be, you see. It couldn't be as sweet, or as sinful, or as delicious." He drew closer to her, his words barely a breath over her lips. "But you —" He let his lips slide over hers, a silken touch. "You, Felicity Faircloth, just might be all those things." Another slide, the little whimper that escaped from her making him want to do wicked, wonderful things. "You just might be more."

Her fingers tightened, threatening to shred the linen of his shirt. "Devil."

"I'm going to steal you, instead," he said then, knowing she'd hear the words as part of the story and not as she should — as the truth. "I'm going to steal you," he confessed again. "I'm going to steal you and make you mine."

"It's not theft if I allow it," she whispered.

Silly girl; of course it was. But it wouldn't stop him.

CHAPTER SIXTEEN

She was so sweet, heady and lush and soft
like that spun sugar from all those years ago.
She was sin and sex and freedom and
pleasure and something more and something worse, and he was lost in the feel of
her lips and the taste of her when she
opened to him like she'd been waiting her
whole life for him.

Felicity Faircloth was perfection — the
first taste of it Devil had ever had.

She tasted like a promise.

She sighed and he groaned, pulling her
tighter to him, his fingers tangling in her
hair as hers came to the rough stubble of
his cheek, her nails scraping across it until
she was pulling his head down to her, as
though she'd been waiting all her life for
this kiss, and she meant for it to be worth
it.

Goddammit, he wanted to make it worth it.

He wrapped an arm around her, pulling

her tight against him so quickly, so thoroughly, that she gasped. He released her lips and said, "I wanted to hold you like this earlier, when we were watching the cargo move," he said.

Christ, why was he telling her that?

She came up on her toes and pressed her forehead to his. "I wanted you to hold me like this," she whispered.

How could he resist that?

He returned to her lips, playing over them gently, softly, teasing her with his tongue until she sighed, opening to let him in, all sweet, silken heat and lush promise. And then Felicity Faircloth, plain, spinster, wallflower, kissed him back, meeting his tongue, matching him, like a fallen angel.

Like a fucking goddess.

And he reveled in it, in her pleasure, in her sighs and moans and the shiver that went through her when he opened her coat — no, *his* coat — and put his hands to her. She broke their kiss on a gasp. "Devil."

"Are you cold?" Goddammit, of course she was cold. They were surrounded by ice.

"No." She panted the response, her hands clutching his shirt in one fist and pulling him closer. "No, I'm blazing."

Her grasp almost undid him — she was magnificent, a queen in the darkness. He

315

knocked the lapels of his coat aside, resisting her pull to watch his hands on her, on that pretty white and pink frock that didn't belong anywhere near this place that was too dark and too dirty and too sinful for her. Felicity didn't belong here, but it didn't stop him from touching her.

"You are blazing," he said, his gaze tracking the movement of his hands, up the sides of her bodice to the neckline, where silk gave way to impossibly soft skin. He touched her there, where breath came hard and fast, revealing her pleasure. "You don't need lessons in fire. You're an inferno."

She nodded. "I feel it."

He almost smiled. "Good."

"Would you —" She stopped, and then, "Would you kiss me again?"

Yes. Christ. Yes. "Where?"

Her eyes went wide. "Where?"

"Shall I show you where you might like it?"

Her lips curled in a magnificent smile. "Yes, please."

Far be it from him to deny a lady. Returning his hands to her waist, he pulled her closer, putting his lips to her jaw, letting his tongue slide along the line of it. "Here, perhaps?"

"Oh, yes." She sighed. "That's quite nice."

"Hmm," he said. "I think we can do better than quite nice." He ran his teeth down the long column of her neck. "How about here?" Her fingers slid up over his tightly shorn hair, her nails raking over his scalp, sending shivers of pleasure through him as he sucked at the place where her neck met her shoulder, knowing he must be careful. Knowing he couldn't mark her. Wanting desperately to mark her. She whimpered, and he lifted his head. "What does that mean?"

She slid her gaze to his, and the look in her eyes nearly brought him to his knees there in the hold. "That's *very* nice."

The woman was teasing him. And it was delicious. He was hard as steel, and he loosened his tether, grasping her waist and lifting her to sit on the ice behind her. When she squeaked her surprise, he slid between her legs, her heavy skirts making it impossible to get too close, which was probably best.

Definitely best.

And also the fucking worst.

"This isn't —" She cut her own breathless words off.

He reached for her again. "It isn't the kind of thing ladies do."

She shook her head, bit her bottom lip.

"No, but I find I do not care."

He did laugh then, a short, unwelcome bark of laughter.

"It is delicious. Show me another place." And his laughter dissolved into a groan.

He pulled her closer with one hand, setting the other to her soft, bare ankle beneath her skirts. "You are not wearing stockings," he whispered at her ear.

"It's June," she said.

"And in June ladies are able to dispense with stockings?"

She dipped her head, and he adored her embarrassment. "I did not expect anyone to see."

"I can't see," he whispered, letting his frustration fill the words, loving the laugh he summoned with the words.

"I most certainly didn't expect anyone to touch."

"Mmm," he replied, letting his hand climb higher. "That's the problem with being flame, Felicity . . . moths want to touch."

"Show me," she whispered.

God help him, he did, taking her lips and letting his hand climb higher, pushing her skirts up, over her knee, revealing a long, soft expanse of leg. He took her thigh in hand, lifting her leg, pressing closer, and damned if she didn't come to the edge of the ice block to meet him. He pressed a line of kisses to her shoulder and down the slope of one breast to the neckline of her dress. "Here?" he whispered, playing at the place where her breast rose from the lacy white fabric. He raised a hand, tugged at the bodice, baring more skin, enough to reveal the upper edge of a nipple. "Here?"

He licked at the soft skin, loving the way it puckered beneath his touch. She hissed at the sensation and he pulled back from her. "Are you cold?"

She shook her head. "No. No. No. No." Her fingers tightened at his head and she rose toward him, closing the distance between them. "Again, please."

Anything she wants. Everything.

He groaned and pulled the line of the dress lower, revealing her nipple for his lips and tongue, scraping it with his teeth as he tucked his hard length against her, his trousers suddenly too tight. She cried out when he suckled, light and then harder as she whispered his name in the darkness. "Devil."

Devon, his mind whispered back, and he pushed the thought aside, refusing to allow it purchase. No one called him by his given name. Certainly no woman. And he wasn't about to let Felicity Faircloth be the first.

But he would let her do other things — he would let her touch him, let her direct his mouth to where she wanted it, let her press closer to the long, throbbing length of him even when she didn't know what she was tempting. What she was asking. "I want —"

"I know," he replied, rocking against her, letting her taste the pleasure he could give her. She quickly got the hang of it, and Devil let her use him. He growled and sucked deeper, loving the cry she let loose against his hair as he worked her with tongue and lips. As she worked herself on him. She was fire.

And he was aflame.

All he wanted was to lie her back on this slab of ice and worship her with his hands and mouth and cock until she'd learned the thousand ways he could bring her pleasure. She would let him. She was lost to pleasure, rocking against him, begging him for it. "Please." She sighed.

Not tonight.

He stilled at that, raising his lips from her breast, staying the movement of his hand on her thigh where it played at the seam of her undergarments.

Not yet. Banns haven't been posted.

The whisper came from deep within, from

320

the place that had planned revenge against his brother. From the place that had hated his brother for twenty years. From the place that had hated his father for far longer.

Hate had no place with Felicity Faircloth.

It would. There would be a time when she would hate him.

A heavy pounding on the steel door to the room punctuated the thought, and they both turned toward it. It wasn't locked, but Whit and Nik would know better than to enter without permission. They'd also know better than to knock in the first place unless something had gone wrong.

He pulled away abruptly, her fingers releasing his head as he lowered her skirts, dropping them over her legs and stepping back — putting room between them as their heavy breaths echoed through the cavernous space.

She reached for him, like a goddess.

He shook his head, somehow finding the will to refuse her. "No," he whispered. "No more tonight, Lady Flame."

"But —" He heard the frustration in the word — the same frustration that crawled through him. She wanted him. She wanted all of it. But Felicity Faircloth didn't know how to ask for it, thank God, and so she settled on, "Please."

Christ, he wanted to give it to her.

Not tonight. Too soon.

He shouldn't give it to her ever.

A knock again. Urgent and unwilling to be ignored.

He righted her bodice and pulled his coat tight around her when she shivered, the cold finally finding her. "Come," he said, and she did, following him back through the ice to the steel door.

Behind it, Nik. "It's London Second. Again."

Devil cursed. "It's been what, an hour?"

"Long enough to clear the rookery," she said. "They were waiting for us. Stopped just before crossing Long Acre. Headed for Mayfair."

They were already through the steel door, letting it clatter behind them, unlocked as they headed down the long, dark corridor to the hatch that let them up into the warehouse.

"What's happened?" Felicity asked at his elbow. "Is it the Crown?"

He looked to her, half grateful she knew the truth and half irritated she knew the truth. "What would the Crown want with ice?" Then, without hesitating, he looked back to Nik. "The boys?"

"Dinuka is returned." One of the outriders. "He fired on them. Thinks he winged one. Niall and Hamish are shot."

"Goddammit, we changed the route." It was the third hijacking of the same delivery in two months.

Felicity's gasp drowned out his curse at the news. "Shot by whom?"

Nik looked to her. "We don't know."

If they knew, Devil would have run them through already. He swore again as Nik reached the ladder and set to climbing. Niall was one of the Bastards' best drivers; the Scotsman had been with them since he was a boy. Hamish was his brother — barely out of boyhood, hadn't even grown his first beard.

"Alive?" he shouted up to Nik as she turned to help Felicity out of the hold.

The Norwegian looked down at him. "We don't know."

Another curse as he passed up the lantern, Felicity leaning down to take it from him as though she'd done this a hundred times instead of once. "Devil," she said, softly, and he hated the pity in her tone, as though she understood the rioting emotions in him. These were his boys. Every one of them, his to keep safe.

And tonight, three of them had been threatened.

He turned away from her gaze, looking back toward the ice hold.

Mistake.

There was darkness everywhere now that he'd handed up the lantern, and its nearness, the way it crept into the corners of his consciousness, was too much. He scrambled up the ladder, desperate to escape it. Except he'd never been able to escape it. He lived in darkness.

But there, on the surface, was Felicity, light and hope and everything he would never have. Everything he'd once been promised. Everything he'd once imagined might be his, in a brilliant, beautiful package.

The concern in her eyes was nearly his undoing.

He barked an order to Nik to close the hatch to the ice hold.

What had he been thinking?

What had he been *doing*?

She didn't belong here — in this place or in his life. He shook his head once and started across the warehouse, toward the door she never should have come through, where Whit stood sentry, dark eyes seeing everything, lingering at a place near Devil's thigh. Devil's hand flexed under his brother's watchful gaze, and he realized Felicity's was in his grasp.

He hadn't even noticed.

Devil dropped her hand, catching the cane sword Whit tossed before he was through the door and calling for John, who leapt down from the roof, rifle in hand. Waving back at Felicity without stopping, Devil ordered, "Take her home."

Felicity's inhale was loud as a gunshot in the warehouse courtyard. "No."

Devil didn't look at her.

John nodded. "Aye, sir."

"Wait!" She chased after Devil. "What's happened? Where are you going? Let me come. I can help."

She had to leave here. She was in more danger every moment she lingered. She was more danger to him every moment she lingered. What if she hadn't been here? Perhaps he would have decided to drive the rig. Then Niall wouldn't have a bullet in him.

His gaze met Whit's, calm and collected and absent of judgment, but Devil felt the judgment anyway.

What the hell was he doing, playing at passion in the ice hold while men with lives and families and futures were shot at in his name? Christ. He never should have let her in. Hadn't Whit said it? Hadn't Devil known it?

What a fucking mess.

He repeated his order to John. "Take her home. Shoot anyone who gets in your way."

"Aye," John replied again, reaching for her arm. "My lady."

She pulled away. "No." The word was firm and John hesitated. "Devil. I can help. If it's the Crown — no one hurts a marquess's daughter."

Devil stopped then, turning to her, unable to keep his frustration from rising. "You think for a moment that if someone comes at you with a rifle, they'll care if you're a marquess's daughter? You think they'll care that you're a lady who embroiders and speaks two languages and knows where to put the goddamn soup spoon and is engaged to a fucking duke?"

Her eyes went wide, and he should have stopped, but he didn't. He was angry. At himself, but at her as well, for her fresh-faced innocence and her certainty that the world wasn't bitter and cruel. "They won't. Not for a second. In fact, they'll aim for you, looking like sunshine and smelling like jasmine, because they know men raised in the dark will do anything for light." Her jaw dropped, and he cut her off before she could speak. "You think you can help us?" He gave a little, humorless laugh. "What will you do, pick their locks?"

Her back went stick-straight, and he hated the thread of guilt that came with the hurt in her eyes. "You're no kind of help. You think this is a game; you think the darkness a shining new toy. Well, here is your most important lesson — the darkness isn't for princesses. It is time for you to return to your storybook tower. Don't come back."

He turned his back on the wallflower, leaving her in silence and taking to the horse at the center of the yard, saddled and waiting for him.

Felicity Faircloth wasn't ready for silence.

"So you renege?" she called after him, her voice strong and steady, a siren's call. He wheeled the mount around so he could see her in the shadows of the lanterns strewn about the yard, wind rustling her skirts and several locks of errant hair he'd released from their moorings when he'd kissed her.

His chest tightened at the image — at the straight line of her shoulders and the proud jut of her chin. "You have your duke, don't you?"

"Not the way you promised."

Fucking passion, like nothing he'd ever experienced. He never should have come near that request, because right now, he was willing to do anything to keep her from sharing air with his brother — let alone sharing herself with him. "You should know better than to believe the promises of a man like me. The deal is done. Go home, Felicity. You are not welcome here."

For a long moment, she watched him, and every inch of him knew that he should turn from her before she spoke again. But he couldn't. And then she spoke, her words taunting and as stinging as a whip. "Tell me, Devil, what shall you do to keep me away? Lock the doors?"

What in . . . Was she *provoking* him? Did she have any idea who he was? What kind of man he was? He moved to dismount. To approach her and —

Christ. He wanted to kiss her senseless.

What the hell had he done?

"Devil," Whit warned, atop his own mount, staying Devil's movement.

There were more important things than teaching Felicity Faircloth a lesson. He stared down at her from his great black horse — delivering her the cold, icy look that had terrified larger, stronger men.

Not stronger.

"Take her home," he said, without looking at John.

She did not look away from him as his man approached her. Indeed, one mahogany brow rose in beautiful defiance.

Devil spun his horse around to face Whit, who was watching him, stone-faced. "What?" Devil snarled.

"Smelling like jasmine?" Whit said, his tone dry as sand.

Devil's curse was lost in the wind as the Bastards spurred their horses into motion, heading for Fleet Street to rescue their fallen men.

CHAPTER SEVENTEEN

"He could be dead."

Felicity stabbed her needle into her embroidery hoop two mornings later with a violence that matched the thought, barely missing drawing her own blood — not that the threat served to slow her next stitch. Or the next. "I don't care if he's dead," she added, speaking to the Bumble House sunroom at large despite it being empty of living creatures. "He was unkind, and it won't matter a bit if he's dead."

Except, before Devil had been unkind, he hadn't been unkind at all.

Before Devil had been unkind, he'd been altogether the opposite of it.

He'd kissed her and touched her and made her sigh in ways she did not know a person was able to sigh. He'd made her feel things she'd never felt before. "Not that any of that matters, as he ultimately became very unkind and is likely dead," she repeated, stabbing her needle into her embroidery hoop again, with wicked force.

He wasn't dead.

The words whispered through her mind as she continued her project, resisting the urge to find a piece of paper and send him a note telling him in great detail what he could do with himself if he were dead. Resisting the more pressing urge to toss her whole embroidery hoop into the fire and make her way back to Covent Garden in broad daylight and see his dead body for herself.

It occurred to Felicity that a woman should be able to sense the death of a man if she'd nearly ruined herself with him in an ice hold beneath a warehouse mere hours earlier. And yet she sensed no such thing. The universe was frustrating, indeed.

She set her hoop on her lap and heaved a sigh. "He'd better not be dead."

"Goodness, Felicity, of course he's not dead!" her mother sang from the doorway, her trio of dachshunds barking excitedly to punctuate the declaration, startling Felicity from her talkative reverie.

Felicity turned. "I beg your pardon?"

The marchioness waved a hand in the air and laughed in that way that mothers laughed when they didn't want their daughters embarrassing them. "He is decidedly not dead! He's clearly had business to attend to since last you saw him."

Felicity blinked. "I'm sorry, Mother. Who is it who is not dead?"

"The duke, of course!" her mother said, and one of the dachshunds barked, then promptly tipped over Felicity's embroidery basket and began to gnaw upon the handle, prompting the marchioness to add, in dulcet tones, "No, no, Rosie, that's not good for you."

The dog growled and continued to chew.

"I wasn't suggesting the duke was dead," Felicity said, "but I might say, Mother, that it's not an impossibility. After all, we haven't seen the duke in several days, and so we don't *know* he is alive."

"We do assuming he hasn't perished in your father's study in the last five minutes," the marchioness replied before reaching down to pluck the dog from the basket — which did not work as planned, as the dog simply tightened her grip and brought the whole thing with her into her mistress's arms.

"Father is here?" Felicity's brows rose. If the Marquess of Bumble was at home, something serious was happening, indeed.

"Of course he is," Felicity's mother said.

"Where else would he be with your marriage in the balance?" She tugged on the basket and the dog growled. "Rosencrantz. Drop it, darling."

Felicity rolled her eyes and stood, needlepoint in hand. "Is that what they're discussing? My marriage?"

Her mother smiled. "Your duke is arrived to save us from a life of poverty."

Felicity stilled at the words, honest and somehow flippant. An echo of Devil's words two nights earlier. *Your family will never be poor enough to fear poverty.*

She had been defensive when he'd said it, as though he didn't take her seriously.

But here, as the words echoed beneath her family's roof, as they wore their fashionable frocks surrounded by her mother's dogs, who ate better than the children in the rookery where Devil made his life and were safer than the boys who worked for him — she understood them.

What had his life been like?

She might have been manipulated in recent months — pushed to marry without being told why, leveled with disappointment without reason — but she'd never doubted her family's love for her. She'd never feared for her safety, or her life.

But Devil had — she knew that as clearly

as she knew his kiss. As she knew the feel of his touch. And the thought consumed her.

Who had saved Devil from his past?

Or had he been forced to save himself?

Her mother interrupted the thoughts. "Well done. Landing the hermit duke is a cracking good job. I knew you could do it."

Felicity's attention snapped to the marchioness. "Well, if one is thrown into the path of enough dukes, one is bound to win one of them, I suppose."

Her mother's brows rose. "Surely you aren't unhappy about the match. This one is infinitely better than the last."

"We don't know that," Felicity replied.

"Don't be so silly," the marchioness huffed. "The last one was already *married.*"

"At least the last one showed emotion."

"He offered to marry you, Felicity." Her mother's tone was getting more and more curt. "That's emotion enough."

"As a matter of fact, he didn't offer," she replied. "He said I was convenient. That I made the search for a wife easier."

"Well. I don't see the lie in that. Indeed, it might be the first time you've ever been accommodating," the marchioness retorted. "And lest you forget, it's not as though you're a *trial* . . . you are daughter to a marquess, sister to an earl!"

"And I've excellent teeth."

"Precisely!" the marchioness replied.

But she was more than that. Didn't her mother see? She wasn't simply the wall-flower at the ball, desperate to do whatever necessary to win herself a husband and save her family's finances. *She looked like sunshine and smelled like jasmine.*

The thought sent a wave of heat through her. When he'd said it two nights ago, it had taken all she had not to make him explain himself. It hadn't seemed like a compliment even as it had sounded like the most beautiful compliment she'd ever heard.

Men raised in the dark will do anything for light.

She wondered if he realized how much she wanted to explore the darkness.

Except she couldn't. Her desires were second to the needs of her family. She was their only hope — and it did not matter that she'd never be free of the yoke they wished for her. It did not matter that she'd just had a glimpse of the dark and she was losing her taste for the light.

It did not matter that she had no interest in summoning the duke to her flame. That she wished another moth. A different set of singed wings.

A moth that seemed to have no interest in

flying near her.

And so she was left here: not flame. Merely Felicity.

Her family's last chance.

She met her mother's gaze. "The duke is here for me?"

"Well, he's here to meet your father. And your brother. To sort the ins and outs of your marriage."

"He is here to fill our coffers once more."

Her mother inclined her head — tacit acknowledgment. "He's rich as the devil, I'm told."

Felicity refrained from telling her mother that she knew the Devil, and he was richer than anyone she'd ever known. It didn't matter, of course, because Devil's money would never be the saving grace of the Marquessate of Bumble. It would never rescue her brother from certain ruin.

And what of her? Could he rescue her?

No. Devil's money wasn't for saving Felicity. And neither was the man.

Don't come back.

His words echoed through her, cold and clear.

So, she was left here, with the duke. The duke Devil had promised her. The duke he'd somehow delivered. Somehow . . . without telling her how. Without telling her *why.* Surely there was a reason, wasn't there? But it wasn't important enough for her to know, just as it hadn't been important enough for her family to tell her their plans. To tell her their fears. To tell her how she was intended to save them.

Just as it wasn't important to the Duke of Marwick to tell her why he was so willing to marry her in the first place.

Another locked door.

This time, she would unlock it.

Felicity sighed again. "I suppose I should go greet him." She was out of the sitting room, her mother sputtering behind her, and in front of her father's closed study door in moments.

She rapped firmly, already turning the door handle when her father barked out his "Come!"

Her brother came to his feet as she stepped inside. Her father remained behind his desk, but it took Felicity a moment to find the Duke of Marwick, standing at the long French doors on the far end of the room.

"Felicity —" Arthur began.

"No! No! Accident!" her mother sang from the hallway, a trio of dachshunds scrambling behind. "Accident!!" This as she pushed her way into the room with a wave

337

of a hand. "Felicity did not realize men were meeting, Your Grace."

The duke turned at that, finding Felicity's eyes. "What did you think was happening?"

He wasn't ordinary, this man. He didn't seem dangerous — but rather . . . uncommon. "I thought you were here discussing our marriage and its relationship to my brother and father's financial situation."

He nodded once. "That is, indeed, what we are discussing."

Was he inviting her in? Did it matter? "Then I'm certain you won't mind if I join you."

Her mother was nearly apoplectic. "You can't do that. This conversation isn't for women!"

"Girl," her father warned from behind his desk.

Without looking away from the duke, Felicity said, "I rather think it should be for women, as its entire purpose is to put a price on one, is it not?"

"Watch it, Felicity," her father cautioned, and it occurred to Felicity that in the past, she might have left at that cold, unmoved caution. For propriety's sake. To retain the label of good and obedient daughter to a man who'd never paid much attention to her. Not even when she was his only hope for redemption.

But she found she wasn't much for propriety at the moment.

Nor was she in the market to let her family make decisions about her future any longer. Not when she was their sole bargaining chip.

She was saved from having to say any of that, however, by the duke. "Of course you should stay." And with that, the decision was made. He turned back to the window, and Felicity noticed that his hair gleamed gold in the room, as though the man traveled with his own light source.

She supposed another woman might find him beautifully handsome. She had, in the past, hadn't she? Hadn't there been a time when she'd called him the handsomest man she'd ever seen? It had been a lie, of course. Told to another, handsomer man.

A man who shouldn't be so handsome, but was, in fact, so handsome it made her want to spit with how irritating he was.

"Where did you leave off?"

"We were discussing the terms of our marriage."

She nodded. "Without me."

"Felicity . . ." her mother said before turning to the duke. "Your Grace, forgive her. We raised her to be less involved."

"That's only because you preferred not to tell me anything about your plans for my future," Felicity said.

"We didn't want to worry you," Arthur replied.

She looked to her brother. "Shall I tell you what worries me?" He didn't reply, but she saw the guilt flash over his face. Good. "The fact that even after everything that has happened, you still cannot see beyond your own problems."

"Dammit, girl. This is how it's done," her father interjected. "Women like to think marriage is about love. It's not. It's a business. We're discussing business."

She looked to her father, then back to Arthur. "Then you will surely understand that it worries me that you thought I was a commodity to be traded without my consent."

"One might argue that you consented when you told half of London that we were to be married," the duke pointed out — not incorrectly.

She started across the room, toward him. "Nevertheless, Your Grace will surely understand that I have a vested interest in the terms to which you've agreed?"

Her fiancé was calmer than ever, his attention fixed to a hedgerow in the distance. "I certainly do understand, as they are more the terms to which *you've* agreed."

Felicity hesitated. Was it possible this man was an ally? It was difficult to imagine what he might be with how impenetrable he was. "Of course. I forgot that my father and brother speak with my voice."

"Felicity —" Arthur began.

The duke cut him off. "I'm not certain anyone in the world speaks with your voice."

"Is that an insult?" she asked.

"No, as a matter of fact."

He was a strange man. "And so? To what have I agreed?"

"The banns will be posted immediately, and we will marry in three-weeks' time. After which, you have agreed to live here in London, in the house of your choosing."

"Have you more than one London home?"

"I do not, but I am very rich, and you are welcome to purchase another home should you find one you prefer."

She nodded. "And you aren't interested in where we live?"

"As *we* will not live there, I am not."

The words surprised her. She looked to her father, jaw set in irritation, then to her mother, whose jaw dropped just slightly, then to Arthur, who appeared to be trans-fixed by the carpet. She returned her atten-tion to the duke. "You mean, as *you* will not live there."

He inclined his head and returned his attention to the gardens beyond the window.

She watched him for a moment. "You've no interest in marrying me."

"Not particularly," he replied absently.

So much for moths and flames. "But you will, nonetheless."

He was silent.

Her gaze narrowed. "And what then?"

One side of his mouth kicked up in a little wry smile. "You'll be very rich, Lady Felicity. Surely you'll find something to do with yourself."

Her mouth opened. Her mother gasped. Her father coughed. Arthur was silent.

The words weren't cruel. The duke wasn't angry or bitter or punishing. He was simply forthright. And there was something in that truth that spoke to Felicity . . . just long enough for her to wonder what, precisely, he was planning. "This isn't going the way I thought it would."

"And how did you think it would?"

"I thought you would want —" She stopped.

"Did you think we would love each other?"

No. Love had never been a part of it. At least, not with him. With another man, perhaps, when she was younger. Another faceless husband. Tall and dark and with golden eyes and lips that had been forged in sin.

She pushed the thought aside. "No."

He nodded. "I didn't think so." His gaze lowered to the embroidery hoop she continued to clutch in her hand. He tilted his head. "Is that a fox?"

She lifted the project, looking down at it, surprised. She'd forgotten what she'd been doing before he'd arrived here and everything had gone to pot. "It is."

"With a hen?"

It was, indeed. The orange and white animal held a silky brown chicken in its mouth. "Yes."

"Good Lord."

She looked up to him. "I'm quite good at needlepoint."

"So I see." He stepped forward, not lifting his gaze. "The blood is rather . . ."

She considered the hoop, then offered, "Gruesome?"

He nodded. "Gruesome."

"I was angry when I started it."

Devil had exiled her from his world and rushed off, armed, to Lord knew where. He might be dead.

He wasn't dead.

Did it matter? He'd sent her home and

told her never to return. He might as well be dead for all he was rid of her. She didn't like the way her chest constricted at the thought. She wasn't ready to be rid of him. Or the world in which he lived, or the hints of magic he'd shown her.

But he was ready to be rid of her, and here she was, negotiating the terms of a loveless marriage with this strange duke who proposed nothing like magic.

Here she was, alone once more.

"Is this how you show your emotions?" Marwick pressed on, curious, "Needlepoint?"

"I also talk to myself."

"Christ, girl . . . he'll think you mad."

She didn't look to her father. "That's fine, as I think him rather mad myself."

"Felicity!" Her mother threatened the vapors, no doubt. One of the dogs barked and attacked the clawed foot of her father's desk.

"Dammit, Catherine," her father shouted at her mother.

"Gilly! Stop it! No biting! Guildenstern! Enough!"

The dog continued.

Arthur stared up at the ceiling and sighed.

The duke did not seem to mind the chaos. His eyes went to the windows again. "Then we are settled?"

She supposed they should be. She looked to her brother, meeting the brown eyes as familiar as her own. Saw the pleading in them. The hope. And she couldn't stop the irritation that flared at it. "And so we have it. I marry and you live happily ever after."

Her brother had the grace to look guilty.

"You deserve it," she said, unable to keep the sadness from her voice. From her mind. "You and Pru and the children. You deserve everything you've ever wished. You deserve happiness. And I shall be glad to give it to you. But I'm not sure I'll ever stop begrudging you for it."

Arthur nodded. "I know."

She turned to find the duke watching her for the first time, something more than boredom in his face. Something like longing. Which was impossible, of course. This mad duke did not seem a type that *longed.* And certainly not for her. For the life of her, she'd never understand why she asked him, "Would you like to see the gardens?"

"No," her father interjected, his frustration evident. "We're not done."

"I would, as a matter of fact," the duke said, before turning to the marquess. "We can discuss the rope I shall toss you both to keep you from drowning when I return."

With that, he set his hand to the door handle and opened it to the balcony beyond. Standing aside, he allowed her to exit before he followed her out, closing the door firmly behind them.

Felicity hadn't gone three feet when he said, "I don't care for your family."

"Neither do I, at the moment," she replied. Then, supposing she should offer a defense, she said, "They're desperate."

He passed her, heading for the stone steps leading down into the gardens, clearly expecting her to follow. "They don't know what desperation is."

The words were so familiar — an echo of Devil's rant at the warehouse — but in the wake of the place and man who had said them first, they seemed ridiculous, and Felicity found herself irritated by them. "What does a duke rich as a king know of desperation?"

He turned to her then, something in his eyes unsettling enough to stop her in her tracks. "I know that your father is a marquess and your brother is an earl, and even if they never married you off, they'd fail to understand the level of want that men can achieve. And I know that if they have even an inkling of love for you, they will regret sacrificing you for their own happiness."

She inhaled sharply at the words, clear and filled with honesty. She opened her mouth. Closed it. Then tried again. "They are my family. I wish to protect them."

"They should be protecting you," he replied.

"From you?"

He seemed to struggle with the reply, finally settling on, "You've nothing to fear from me."

She nodded. "Especially since you've no intention of our interacting once we're married. What would I fear . . . becoming lost in your piles of money?"

He did not smile. "Did you expect us to interact?"

The question shouldn't have summoned a vision of two nights earlier — of the interaction Devil had offered her. Of the kiss that had stolen her breath and her thoughts for longer than it should have. If *that* was a commonplace interaction between married couples, she had most certainly not expected it. Pressing her hands to her cheeks to will away the flush that came at the memory, she replied, "I don't know. I never expected any of this." He did not reply, and she asked, "Why marry me, Your Grace?"

"I would prefer you not call me that."

She tilted her head. "Your Grace?"

347

"I don't like it."

"All right," she said slowly, surprised less by the request than she was by the simple way he made it, as though it were perfectly ordinary. "Why marry me?"

His gaze did not leave the hedge at the far end of the garden. "You've asked before. The answer has not changed; you're convenient."

"And I positively swooned," she said, dryly.

He cut her a look and she smiled. He did not. "Why do you sacrifice yourself for your family?"

"What choice do I have?"

"The choice that ends with you having the life you wish."

She smiled, softly. "Does anyone really have that life?"

"Some of us have the chance of it," he replied, distracted again.

"Not you, though."

He shook his head. "No."

She wondered what had made this man — a prince among men, handsome and rich and titled, so lost to his own future that he chose a loveless marriage over the chance of a life he wished. "Have you family?"

"No." The answer was clipped and unemotional.

She knew his father had died years earlier, but, "No mother?"

"No."

"Siblings?"

"Gone."

How tragic. No wonder he was so odd. "I'm sorry," she said. "I might be irritated with Arthur right now, but I do care for him."

"Why?"

She thought for a moment. "Well, he is a good brother and a good husband. A good father."

"I've seen no evidence of his husbanding or fathering, but I can tell you he does not seem a good brother."

She pressed her lips together at that assessment.

Silence fell, until Felicity almost thought he'd forgotten she was there. He watched the hedgerow in the distance, his stare blank. And then, after a long moment, he said, "It must be nice," he said, "having a partner in the past."

It was. Arthur drove her mad, and she was irate that he'd kept the secret of their family's finances from her, even more so that he'd attempted to manipulate her future for it. But he was her brother and her friend, and she had trouble believing he didn't wish the best for her. Even shrouded in uncertainty, she knew her family wished her well — they hadn't forced this marriage, after all; she had.

Even though, now, she did not wish it.

Even though, now, she wished for something else indeed.

Even though, now, she wished for a different partner. A different future. An impossible one. But it was not impossible for him, and she felt she had to point it out. "You realize that without me . . . you might still find a partner in the future?"

As though he'd been far away, he returned to her then, and she realized how close he was, recognized the conflict in his eyes, a beautiful golden brown — a strange, unsettling echo of another pair of eyes that had threatened to consume her.

Before she could allow her thoughts to wander to Devil, the duke spoke. "I can't find her."

"I am not she." Felicity offered him a small smile.

"And I am not he."

No. You're not.

She took a breath. "And so?"

"And so, banns shall be posted, and I shall send an announcement to the *News* for Monday." It was as simple as that. "And in three weeks, you may begin anew, a duchess, with your family returned to money, power, success. On one condition," the duke said, absently, his attention returned to the hedge. "One kiss."

She stilled. "Excuse me?"

"I think I was clear," the duke said. "I should like a kiss."

"Now?"

He nodded. "Precisely."

Her brows stitched together. She did not know much about men, she would allow, but there was no doubt in her mind that this one did not wish to kiss her. Not really. "Why?"

"Does it matter?"

"Considering you have made it more than clear that you've no interest in passion with me, yes, honestly. It does."

He closed the distance between them. "Fair enough. My reason is that I wish it."

"I —" She stopped. "One kiss?"

He lowered his head toward her, blocking her view of the gardens with his broad shoulders and his handsome face. "Just one."

Why not? she thought. Why not kiss him and see if kisses were all as magnificent as the one Devil had given her in the ice hold?

The duke was near. "I shan't kiss you if

you don't allow it."

Her gaze flew to his. Perhaps the kisses with Devil hadn't been special. Perhaps it had been plain old ordinary kissing. "Why wouldn't all kissing be the same?" she whispered. She wouldn't know it unless she kissed another man, and she just so happened to have one.

"You are speaking to yourself," he said, watching her, his amber eyes seeing far more than she'd like. "I won't be your first kiss, will I?"

"I don't see how that's your business," she said, pertly. "I shan't be your first kiss, either."

He didn't reply, instead setting his hands to her arms and turning her so that her back was to the hedge he'd found so fascinating all afternoon. Once she was positioned carefully — for whatever reason — he returned his attention to the matter at hand, leaned in, and pressed his lips to hers.

It was . . . uneventful. His lips were firm and warm and utterly unmoving. And not only in the sense that the kiss itself did not move her. He also, quite literally, did not move. He set his lips firmly against hers, and kissed her as though he were a statue. A handsome statue, she would allow, but a statue nonetheless.

It was nothing even in the same realm as the kiss she'd received from Devil.

The realization had barely formed when he lifted his head and released her, like he'd been burned — and not in a mothy, singey way. In the kind of way that ended with medical treatment.

He looked down at her and said, "Fate is a cruel thing, Lady Felicity. At another time, in another place, you might have had another duke who would have loved you beyond reason."

Before she could respond, he was pushing her out of the way and bounding for the hedge, moving branches aside and reaching one long arm into it.

He was mad.

Clearly.

She took a tentative step toward him. "Um . . . Duke?"

He grunted his reply, half inside the bush.

"At the risk of being impertinent, may I ask why you are so interested in the hedgerow?"

She didn't know what he would say. She supposed he might tell her it reminded her of someone or something — whatever it was that had turned him into this odd man. She might have imagined that he would tell her he had an affinity for nature — after all, he was a notorious London recluse, having spent his whole life in the country. It would not have surprised her if he'd told her he cared for a particular species of bird in sight, or a weed sprouting below.

But she absolutely did not expect him to extract a boy from the hedge.

Felicity's jaw dropped as the Duke of Marwick stood up and hauled the young man to his feet. "Do you know our spy?"

The child looked to be no more than ten or twelve, long and thin like a bean, with a sooty face and a cap low on his brow. She stepped forward and lifted the brim to see his eyes, blue as the sea and just as defiant. She shook her head. "No."

The duke commanded the boy's attention. "Are you watching me?"

The boy didn't speak.

"No," the duke said. "You wouldn't be in the gardens if you were watching me. You'd be out front, waiting for me to leave. You're watching Lady Felicity, are you not?"

"I ain't tellin' you nuffin'," the young man spat.

Felicity's heart began to pound. "You're from the rookery."

The duke's brows rose, but he did not speak.

Neither did the boy, but he didn't have to.

Felicity did not need confirmation. Something like panic was thrumming through her. Panic and desperation. "Is he alive?" she asked, watching the boy consider not answering her. She leaned down, staring directly into his eyes. "Is he?"

A little nod.

A wave of relief. "And the others?"

A defiant lift of the chin. "They've holes in 'em, but yeah."

She closed her eyes for a moment, collecting herself. Then, "I've a message for your employer," she said, looking to the duke. "You tell him that I am soon to be married, and therefore do not require his attention — or yours — any longer. Do you understand?"

The boy nodded.

"What's your name?" she asked gently.

"Brixton," he said. Her brows furrowed at the name, and the boy grew defensive. "It's where 'e found me."

She nodded, hating the way the words tightened her chest. "You'd best get back, Brixton." She looked to the duke. "Let him go."

Marwick looked to the boy, as though he'd just discovered that he was holding a child aloft, and said, "Be sure to tell him about the kiss." He set Brixton down without

355

hesitation, and the boy was gone like a flash, over the hedge and into the world beyond. She stared after him for longer than she should, wanting to follow him more than she should.

Wanting, full stop.

Finally, she turned to the duke, who appeared not at all surprised by the turn of events. Indeed, there was a light in his brown eyes that had not been there before. Something that looked like satisfaction, though it made no sense whatsoever why that would be. She took a deep breath. "Thank you."

"Would you like to tell me about the boy's employer?"

She shook her head. "I would not."

He nodded. "Then tell me this. Was I right or wrong?"

"About what?"

"About the kiss being a worthy report for our little watchman."

For a moment, Felicity allowed fantasy to roll through her — the idea that Devil might care that the duke had kissed her. That he might care that banns would be posted. That he might care that she'd returned home after he'd tossed her out and decided to get on with her life with another man. That he might regret his actions.

But that was all it was — a fantasy.

She met her fiancé's gaze. "You were wrong."

CHAPTER EIGHTEEN

He came to tell her that she couldn't use his boys as messengers.

He came to tell her that he had more important things in his life — responsibilities that far outweighed that of a bored wallflower lockpick for whom he had little time and even less interest.

He came to tell her that he didn't belong to her, and she should not for a moment think he did.

He did not come because Ewan had kissed her.

And if he did come because Ewan had kissed her, it wasn't because of Felicity. It was because he knew his brother well enough to know that Ewan was trying to prove a point. Trying to send his own message to Devil, that he had his marriage and his heir well within his grasp.

Either way, he didn't come for Felicity.

At least, that's what Devil told himself as

he crossed the back gardens of Bumble House mere hours after Brixton returned to the rookery with news of the kiss, his subsequent discovery, and the fact that Felicity Faircloth had returned him to deliver a scolding to his employer.

Devil tucked his walking stick beneath his arm and began to climb the rose trellis beneath her window. He was a handful of feet above the earth when she spoke from below.

"I thought you were dead."

He froze, clinging to the slats and vines for longer than he'd like to admit, loathing the way her voice had his breath catching in his chest and his heart beating slightly faster than it should. It wasn't because of her, he told himself. It was because he was still on edge from the last time he saw her. From the news that the Bastards' shipment had been hijacked and their men hurt. From the fact that he'd been with her instead of taking care of his men.

That was all.

He looked down at her.

A mistake.

The sun was setting over the Mayfair rooftops, sending rich rays of copper-tinted light into the gardens, catching her dark hair and setting it aflame, along with the satin of her gown. Pink again, now the color of an inferno thanks to a trick of the light. Not that Devil should have noticed that it was pink. He shouldn't have. He also shouldn't have wondered if she was wearing the undergarments he'd purchased her days ago. He certainly shouldn't have wondered if the undergarments came with pink satin ribbons like he'd asked.

Asking for those was another thing he shouldn't have done.

Christ. She was magnificent.

He shouldn't notice that, either, but it was impossible not to, what with how she looked like she'd been forged in fire and sin. She was beautiful and she was dangerous. She made a man want to fly right to her. Not like a moth. Like Icarus.

The only thing he should notice was that this woman was not for him.

"I'm not dead, as you can see."

"No, you're quite hale."

"You needn't sound so disappointed," he replied, climbing down a foot or two before letting himself drop to the ground and taking his stick in hand.

"I thought you were dead," she repeated, as he turned to face her, her velvet brown eyes a wicked temptation.

She was too close, but his back was up

against a trellis, and he couldn't move. "And were you very pleased?"

"Oh, yes, I was over the moon," she said, pertly. And then, after a moment, "You addlepated cabbagehead."

His brows shot up. "Excuse me?"

"You sent me away," she replied, speaking slowly, as though he were a child who could not remember the events of two nights earlier. "You climbed up onto a horse with your idiot weapon — which is no kind of protection from bullets, I might add — and rode off into the darkness without a second thought for me. Standing there. In the courtyard of your warehouse. Certain you would be killed." Her cheeks were flushed, her nostrils flaring, the pulse in her throat racing. She was more beautiful than she'd ever been. "And then your henchman packed me into a carriage and took me home. As though everything was fine."

"Everything was fine," Devil said.

"Yes, but I didn't *know* that!" she said, her voice high and urgent. "I thought you were dead!"

He shook his head. "I'm not."

"No. You're not. You're simply a bastard." With that, she turned on her heel and left him, giving him no choice but to follow her, like a dog on a lead.

He didn't care for the comparison, nor its aptness, but follow her he did. "Be careful, Felicity Faircloth, or I shall start to think you concerned for my well-being."

"I'm not," she said without looking back.

The sulk in the words made him want to smile, which was strange in itself. "Felicity?"

She waved a hand in the air as she crossed into the high, labyrinthine shrubbery at the rear of the garden. "You shouldn't be here."

"You summoned me," he said.

She whirled toward him at that, her earlier frustration tipping over into anger. "I did no such thing!"

"No? Didn't you send my boy packing to fetch me?"

"No!" she insisted. "I sent Brixton packing because your *spies* are not welcome in my hedgerow."

"You sent him with a clear message for me."

"It wasn't clear at all if you think I meant to summon you."

"I think you always mean to summon me."

"I —" she began, then stopped. "That's ridiculous."

He couldn't stop himself from approaching her, from drawing near enough. "I think you issued a challenge in the yard of my warehouse, looking like a queen, and when

I did not rise to it, you thought to bring me to you. You imagined that I'd turn up here, desperate for you."

"I have never imagined you desperate for me."

He leaned in. "Then you are not as creative as I thought. Did you not pronounce to all assembled two nights ago that you were not through with me?"

"No, as a matter of fact. I pronounced that I was not through with Covent Garden. That's quite a different thing altogether."

"Not when Covent Garden belongs to me."

She turned away, heading deeper along the hedge path. "I hate to disabuse you of your pompous self-worth, sirrah, but you were not in my thoughts, except to let you know that I was prepared to deliver on my debt to you."

He stilled, not liking the words. "Your debt."

"Indeed," she tossed over her shoulder. "I thought you'd like to know that your lessons worked."

Of all the things she could have said, those were the words most likely to set Devil off. "Which lessons?"

"Your lessons in passion, of course. The duke was here this morning to discuss the

363

terms of our marriage, and I took matters in hand."

His grip tightened on his cane sword, instinct making him wish he could unsheathe it and set it to his bastard brother's neck. "What matters?"

She turned, still moving deeper into the gardens, spreading her hands wide as she walked backward, cheeks flushed. "Kissing, of course." And then, as though she'd remarked upon the weather, she completed a full circle and continued away from him. "Did Brixton not report back?"

Devil tapped his walking stick in his hand twice. A thread of unease whispered through him. Brixton had reported that Ewan had kissed her, of course. But when Devil had pressed the boy for more information, he'd been told that the caress was short and perfunctory — the very opposite of what had happened with him in the ice hold two nights ago.

There was nothing perfunctory about the way he and Felicity had come together.

So what had happened after Ewan had sent the boy packing? She wasn't wearing gloves. Had they touched? Skin to skin? *Had* he kissed her with passion?

Good God. Had *she* kissed *him*?

Impossible. And yet . . .

I took matters in hand.

Devil followed her, coming around a corner to see her headed for one end of an enormous, curved stone bench that must have been twenty feet long. "You kissed him."

"You needn't say it like you're shocked. Was that not the purpose of your lessons?"

No. Their kiss might have begun as education but it had ended as eroticism — pure, unfettered pleasure. Pleasure that Devil would refuse to believe she'd been able to echo with Ewan.

Pleasure he imagined he might never be able to echo with anyone ever again.

But Devil did not say any of that. Instead, he asked, "And? Were you satisfied with the outcome?"

She seated herself, spreading her skirts wide and lifting an embroidery hoop from the bench. "Quite."

His blood was rushing in his ears — loud enough to make him wonder if he was going mad. "What did you do?"

She tilted her head. "What did I *do*?"

"How did you win him over?"

"What are you suggesting? That I shan't singe his wings after all? What happened to *You're not a hog, Felicity Faircloth*? With such a rousing assessment from you, how could I not have won him over?"

"You're not a hog," he replied, feeling like an ass. Feeling off balance. "But that's not the point. You'll never get passion from Marwick."

"Perhaps I won his heart with my remarkable kiss." Her lips curved in a perfect bow, making him wish they weren't talking about kissing, but doing it, instead.

"Impossible." Her face fell, and he hated himself for the way he stripped her power from her. Wanting, instantly, to return it, even though he shouldn't. Even though returning it would only make her more dangerous.

"Is it? Did you not promise me he would? Did you not say I would have him slavering after me? Singeing his wings?"

He tapped his cane against his boot. "I lied."

She scowled. "Somehow, I find myself unsurprised."

"Marwick is not a man who can give you passion."

"You don't know that."

"In fact, I do."

"How?"

Because I've seen him turn his back on it without a second thought.

She narrowed her gaze on him. "No one

in London knows him. But you do, don't you?"

He hesitated. "Yes."

"How?"

"It's not important." What a lie that was.

"As he is going to be my husband, it seems quite important."

He's not going to be your husband. He couldn't say that to her, and so he stayed quiet.

"I should have realized it from the beginning," she said. "From the moment you promised him to me. Who is he to you? Who are you to him? How do you have such control over him?"

"No one has control over the Duke of Marwick." That much was true. That much he could tell her.

"Except you," she said. "Who is he? A rival in business?" Her brow furrowed. "Is he the reason your men were shot?"

"No." At least, Devil did not think so.

She nodded once, lost to the memory of the night in the rookery. Her gaze found his, full of concern. "Your men. Brixton said they were not —"

His chest tightened at the realization that even now, even as she released her rage at him, she worried for the well-being of his men — boys she did not know. "The ship-

367

ment is gone, but the men live." The two men had been lucky, all things considered. He and Whit had found them unconscious, not from blood loss, but from cracks to the skull. He'd been awake for nearly two straight days, threatening doctors to ensure they remained alive. "They shall heal."

She released a breath. "I'm grateful for that."

"Not so grateful as I."

She smirked up at him. "A pity all your ice was stolen. Strange thing to be on a thief's list."

He raised a brow at her observation. "People like to keep things cold."

"Of course," she said. "However would they do that without — what is it they call you? — the Bareknuckle Bastards?"

He nodded.

"Why do they call you that?"

A memory flashed — his first night in London, after three and a half days without sleep — he, Whit, and Grace huddled together in a corner in the rookery, hungry and scared, with nothing but each other and the lesson their father had taught them — fight as dirty as you can. "When we arrived in the rookery, we were the best fighters they'd ever seen."

She watched him from her seat. "How old

were you?"

"Twelve."

Her eyes went wide. "You were children."

"Children learn to fight, Felicity."

She thought for a moment, and he wondered if he was in for a soapboxing — a treatise on children's rights and how he should have had a better childhood, as though he didn't know all that already. He stiffened, preparing himself, but she didn't give it. Instead, she said, "But they shouldn't have to."

God knew that was true.

She stood then, and his gaze went to her embroidery hoop. "Good God. Is that a fox mauling a hen?"

She tossed it to the bench. "I was angry."

"I can see that."

She stepped toward him. "So, you and Beast were young and you learned to fight."

"We were young and we were *already* fighters," he corrected her. "We fought for scraps on the streets for a few weeks before we were discovered by a man who ran a fight ring." He paused. "The three of us owned it. And then we owned Covent Garden."

"The three of you?"

"Beast, Dahlia, and me."

"Dahlia fought?"

Devil smirked, the memory of Grace in her grimy dress and then in her first pair of beautiful, shiny boots — bought with her winnings. "She fought harder than the rest of us combined. Collected enough winnings to start her own business long before we started ours. We were Bareknuckle Babes in comparison. Dahlia . . . she was the original Bareknuckle Bastard."

Felicity smiled. "I like her."

He nodded. "You are not alone."

"But now, you don't fight with fists," she said, her gaze lowering to where his bare hand held his cane sword. Her own hand moved, and he wondered if she might touch him. He wondered if he'd let her.

Of course he'd let her.

He tapped his stick twice against the toe of his boot. "No. Once you learn to use a steel, you don't go back to flesh." You did what you could to keep yourself safe. Your brother and sister. Your crew. And a blade was more powerful than a fist.

"But you do still fight." Felicity was still staring at his knuckles, and he was growing more unsettled by the second.

He flexed his fingers. Cleared his throat. "Only when I need to. Beast is the one who likes the show."

Her gaze flickered to his. "Did you fight

the other night?"

He shook his head. "By the time we got there, the goods were gone."

"But you would have." She reached for him, and they were both transfixed as her fingers traced his knuckles, white under the tight grip he held on his cane, crisscrossed with scars and marks, badges earned in the rookery. "You would have put yourself in danger."

Her touch was pretty poison, making him want to give her everything she wanted, everything he had. He should move. "I would have done what was necessary to keep mine safe."

"How noble," she whispered.

"No, Felicity Faircloth," he said. "Don't go painting me a prince. There's nothing noble about me."

Her beautiful brown eyes found his. "I think you're wrong."

Her thumb stroked back and forth over his knuckles, and it occurred to Devil that he'd never realized how sensitive the hand was. How powerful a touch there could be. He'd only ever felt pain in his knuckles and here she was, ruining him with pleasure, making him want to haul her into his arms and show her the same.

Except, he wasn't supposed to want her.

He moved his hand from beneath her touch. "I came to tell you that you cannot summon me."

Her rich brown gaze did not waver. "I cannot come to you, and I cannot summon you to me."

"No," he said. "There's no need for either."

She shook her head and spoke softly, her voice low and lush like a promise. "I disagree."

"You can't," he said, as though it meant something.

It didn't. In fact, it meant so little that she changed the subject, her gaze tracking over his face as though she were attempting to memorize him. "Do you know, I've never seen you in the sunlight?"

"What?"

"I've seen you in candlelight, and in the eerie glow of your ice hold, in the dead of night outside and in the evening starlight on a ballroom balcony. But I've never seen you in the sunlight. You're very handsome."

She was so close. Close enough that he could track her gaze as she explored his face, taking in all the faults and angles. Close enough that he could explore hers — perfection to his flaw. And somehow, he couldn't stop himself from saying, "It's

strange. All those times we've met in darkness, and I've only ever seen you in sunlight."

Her breath caught, and it took all his
energy not to touch her.

Which didn't matter, as she reached up in
that moment and touched him, her fingers
like fire on his skin, coasting along his
cheekbone and down to his jaw, where she
traced the sharp angles of his face before
finally reaching her goal — his scar. The tis-
sue there was strange and sensitive, the
nerves unable to distinguish pain from
pleasure, and she seemed to know that, her
touch remarkably gentle. "How did you get
this?"

He did not move; he was too afraid that if
he did, she might stop touching him. Too
afraid, also, that she might touch him more.
It was agony. He swallowed. "My brother."

Her brow furrowed and her gaze flew to
his. "Beast?"

He shook his head.

"I didn't know you had another brother."

"There are many things you don't know
about me."

She nodded. "That's true," she said, softly.
"Is it wrong that I would like to learn them
all?"

Christ. She was going to kill him. He took

a step back, and the loss of her touch threatened the same. He looked away, desperate for something to say. Something that did not involve kissing her until neither of them remembered all the reasons they could not be together.

Reasons that were legion.

He cleared his throat, focusing on the strange shape of the bench behind her. "Why is this bench curved?"

For a long moment, she seemed too busy watching him to reply, her focus making him curse the daylight and wish there were shadows in which he could hide.

He should leave.

Except she answered him. "It's a whispering bench," she said. "The acoustics of it are designed so that if someone is whispering at this end, the person on the other end can hear them. It's said to have been gifted to one of the ladies of the house by her gardener. They were . . ." She blushed, beautiful and honest, then cleared her throat. "They were lovers."

That blush nearly killed him.

He considered the bench, then moved to the far end, leaning back, his thighs wide, draping one arm over the back of it, forcing himself to seem casual. "So if I sit here . . ."

She moved on cue, resuming her spot on

the opposite end. She looked down at her lap. And then she spoke, the words in his ear as though she were next to him. As though she were touching him. "No one would ever know what we are to each other."

It was rare that Devil was surprised, but the bench surprised him. Or perhaps Felicity's words surprised him. Perhaps it was the idea that they might hold weight — that the two of them might be something to each other. He immediately looked to her, but she remained transfixed by her embroidery hoop.

"No one would ever know we were speaking," he said.

She shook her head. "The perfect meeting place for spies."

His lips twitched at that. "Do you notice a great deal of clandestine visits to your gardens?"

She was not so hesitant with her smile. "There's been an uptick in the use of my rose trellis recently." She looked to him and whispered, "One must be prepared for anything."

He was transfixed by the shape of her — by the straightness of her spine and the rise and fall of her breasts, the softness of her jaw and the swell of her torso. She was Rubens's Delilah, making him wish he were

Samson, at her feet, draped over her sun-kissed skirts.

Willing to give her anything, even his power. "Do you know the story of Janus?"

She tilted her head. "The Roman god?"

He leaned back, extending his legs far in front of him. "The god of doors and locks."

"They have a god?"

"And a goddess, as a matter of fact."

"Tell me." The whisper was full of anticipation, and he turned to look at her, finding her warm brown gaze spellbound.

He couldn't help his smile. "All the times I've tried to tempt you, Felicity Faircloth, and all I had to do was tell you about the god of locks."

"You've done quite well tempting me without that, but I should like to hear anyway."

Devil's heart pounded at her honesty, and it was an exercise in control to stay where he was. "He had two faces. One always saw the future, the other always the past. There wasn't a secret in the world that could be kept from him, because he knew the inside and the outside. The beginning and the end. His omniscience made him the most powerful of the gods, rivaling Jupiter himself."

She was leaning toward him, and his gaze flickered to the place where her skin, freckled in the sun, rose up from the silk of her dress. The bodice was pulled tight with the angle of her body, and Devil was only a man, after all; he lingered there, watching her breasts strain for freedom. It was beautiful, but nothing like the look in her eyes as she repeated her request. "Tell me."

The words made him feel like a king. He wanted to tell her stories for the rest of time, to entertain her, to linger in her presence and learn the ones that fascinated her . . . the ones that struck to the very core of who she was, his beautiful lockpick.

Not his.

He put the thought aside and continued. "But seeing the future and the past is as much curse as a gift, you see, and for every beautiful beginning, he also saw the painful end. And this was Janus's devastation, because he could see death in life, and tragedy in love."

"How awful," Felicity whispered in his ear from too far away.

"He did not sleep. Did not eat. He found pleasure in no one and nothing, as he spent all his time — an eternity of time — guarding the past, warding against the inevitable future. Where other gods rivaled and battled for access to each others' power, none warred with Janus . . . they saw the pain he suffered and steered far clear of it."

She leaned forward, that dress pulling even more, tempting even more — like the future that could be seen and not warded against. "I imagine he was not a cheerful deity."

He gave a little bark of laughter. "He was not." Her eyes widened and she sat up. "What is it?"

"Nothing, only you laugh so rarely." She paused. "And I like it."

His cheeks warmed. Like he was a goddamn boy. He cleared his throat. "At any rate. Janus could see the future, and knew it brought only tragedy. Except there was one thing he could not see. A thing he could not predict."

Her brown eyes twinkled. "A woman."

"What makes you say that?"

She waved a hand in the air. "It's always a woman if it's unpredictable. We're changeable like the weather, did you not know? Unlike men who always act with clear and logical purpose." She ended with a dry harrumph.

He inclined his head. "It was a woman."

"Ah. You see?"

"Would you like me to tell you the story or not?"

She leaned back against the bench, cradling her face in her hand. "Yes, please."

"Her name was Cardea. And he could not see her coming, but once she was there, he saw her in bright, vivid color. And hers was the greatest beauty he had ever known."

"Aren't they always the greatest beauty, these unpredictable women?"

"You think you are so smart, Felicity Faircloth."

She grinned. "Am I not?"

"Not in this case, because, you see, no one else could see her beauty. She was plain and uninteresting to the rest of the gods. She'd been made so before birth, as punishment to her mother, who had crossed Juno. And so the daughter was punished with mediocrity."

"Well, I certainly can understand that," she said quietly, and it occurred to Devil she had not meant for him to hear the words. He wouldn't have, if not for the bench.

"But she was not plain. And she was not uninteresting. She was beautiful beyond measure, and Janus could see it. He could see the beginning of her and the end of her. And in her, he saw something he had never allowed himself to see."

Her full lips opened on a tiny inhale. *He had her.* "What did he see?"

"The present." He would have stayed there, forever, on that bench, imprisoned by her rapt attention. "He'd never cared for it before. Not until she arrived."

Not until she showed him what it could be.

"What happened?"

"They married, and on the consummation of their marriage, Janus, the god with two faces, became the god with three. But only Cardea saw the third face — it was for her alone, the face that experienced happiness and joy and goodness and love and peace. The face that saw the present. Only Cardea was gifted a look at the god in his full, glorious form. As only Janus was gifted a look at his goddess in the same way."

"She unlocked him," Felicity whispered, and the words threatened to bring Devil to his knees.

He nodded. "She was his key." The words came like wheels on gravel. "And because she had gifted him the present, he gave her what he could of the past and future, of beginnings and ends. The Romans worshipped Janus for the first month of the year, but by his will, they honored Cardea on the first day of every month — the end of what had been, the beginning of what was to come."

"And then? What became of them?"

"They reveled in each other," he replied. "Gloried in having finally found the other being in all the world who could see them for who they were. They are never apart — Janus, forever the god of the lock, Cardea, forever the goddess of the hinge. And the Earth keeps turning."

She slid toward him for just a moment, just until she realized what she was doing — that she shouldn't be moving. That it wasn't proper. Not that anything between them had ever been proper.

He wanted her near him. Touching him. This bench was a torture device. "Did you like the kiss?"

He shouldn't have asked it, but she replied nonetheless. "Which one?"

He raised a brow. "I know you liked the one we shared."

"Such modesty."

"It's not conceit. You liked it." He paused. "And so did I." She inhaled sharply, and he heard it as well as saw it, the way she straightened. Perhaps it was the ease of whispering, but he couldn't stop himself from adding, "Has anyone ever told you that you have a beautiful blush?"

Red crept to her cheeks. "No."

"You do — it makes me think of summer

berries and sweet cream."

She looked down at her lap. "You shouldn't —"

"It makes me wonder what I can't see that has gone pink. It makes me wonder if all that pink tastes as sweet as it looks."

"You shouldn't —"

"I know your lips are sweet — your nipples, too. Did you know they are the same color? That pretty pink perfection."

Her cheeks were flaming. "Stop," she whispered, and he could swear he heard the sound of her breathing along their secret stone pathway.

He lowered his voice to a whisper. "Do you think we offend the bench?" She gave a little laugh, and he went hard at the sound, so close and with her so impossibly far away. "Because I imagine that when this bench was gifted to the lady of the house, her lover sat on the far end and said much worse."

She looked to him then, and he saw the heat in her gaze. The curiosity. Felicity wanted to hear worse.

Better.

"Shall I tell you what I imagine he said?" he asked.

She nodded. Barely. But enough. And, miraculously, she didn't look away. She wanted to hear more, and she wanted to hear it from him.

"I imagine he told her that he built this place inside this web of hedgerows so that no one would see. Because, you see, Felicity Fairest, it's not enough that we can whisper and not be heard . . . because you reveal everything you think and feel on your beautiful, open face."

She lifted one hand to a cheek, and he continued his soft litany. "I imagine the lady's lover adored the way her emotions played across her face — the way her lips fell open like temptation incarnate. I imagine he marveled at the pink of them, wondering at the way they matched the perfect tips of her round breasts, and the pink perfection of somewhere else entirely." She gasped, her eyes flying to his. He smirked. "I see you are not as innocent of thought as you would like others to believe, love."

"You should stop."

"Probably," he replied. "But would you prefer I continue?"

"Yes."

Christ, that word alone, the glory of it, rioted through him. He wanted to hear it from her again and again as he talked and touched and kissed. He wanted it as her fingers scraped through his hair, as they clutched his shoulders, as they directed his

383

mouth wherever she wanted him to go.

He made to rise, to go to her and continue with his hands and his lips, but she stayed him. "Devil." He met her gaze. "You lied to me."

A hundred times. A thousand. "About what?"

"Marwick was never going to singe his wings."

"No." Not that Devil would have let it get that far. Not once he realized how hot she burned.

"I still want the singed wings."

The sun was leaving, and the darkness was falling and with it, his ability to resist her. He shook his head. "I can't make him want you."

I won't.

What a fucking mess he'd made. He'd lost control of all of it. Ceded all his power to this woman, who had no understanding of how she wielded it.

She shook her head. "I don't want Marwick."

She was twenty feet away, and the whispered words sounded like gunfire in his ears, but he still didn't believe he'd heard them correctly. "Say it again."

Felicity was watching him from her end of the bench, her velvet-brown eyes unwavering. "Marwick isn't my moth."

"Who, then?"

"You," she whispered.

He was already moving toward her, fire already consuming him, knowing he'd never survive it.

CHAPTER NINETEEN

She wanted him.

Not this moment, on the whispering bench in the gardens, though that, too.

She wanted him, forever.

And not only because she didn't want the strange duke who seemed uninterested in marriage and even less interested in the trappings of it. No, she wanted him because she wanted a man who kissed her like she was everything he would ever want. She wanted a man who teased her and then bewitched her with long-ago stories. She wanted a man who made promises to her that only he could keep.

She wanted this man. Devil.

She didn't know his name or his past, but she knew his eyes and his touch and the way he saw her and listened to her, and she wanted him. For a partner. For a future.

Here, in the gardens of her family home. In Covent Garden. In Patagonia. Wherever he liked.

And when he went to his knees in front of her, like he'd been there a thousand times before, placing one hand on her hip and the other around her neck to pull her to him and kiss her, she wanted him even more, and not only because his kiss made her want to live here, on this bench, his whispered temptation in her ears, his lips on her skin, for the rest of her life.

"Felicity Faircloth, you shall ruin me," he whispered, taking her mouth, stealing kisses between his words. "I swore I would come here . . . to tell you to leave me alone . . . to tell you to forget about me."

Her hands came to his shoulders, clutching the fabric of his shirt as he slid his lips across her cheek, taking the lobe of her ear between his teeth and worrying it. "I don't want to leave you alone," she whispered. "I don't want to forget about you."

I don't want to marry another.

He pulled away, putting enough distance between them that he could search her face. "Why?"

How could he ask her that? How could she find the answer?

"Because I want to see all of you," she replied, the echo of the story he'd just told her. "I want to see your past and your future."

He shook his head. "I'm not a god, Felicity Faircloth. I'm the very opposite of one. And you're too good for my past or my future."

What of your present? she wanted to ask him, desperately. Instead, she pulled him to her and he came, kissing her again, growling low in the back of his throat, licking over her lips until she opened for him and he could tease inside, tempting her. She sighed, and he rewarded the sound by deepening the kiss, one hand scrambling her hairpins as the other found her ankle, smooth and bare beneath her skirts. His warm fingers wrapped around her ankle, strong and firm, then began to tease up the inside of her leg. "Again, no stockings," he said. "My wicked wallflower."

"Wait," she gasped, and he did, his touch stilling instantly when she pulled back from him, wanting to see his eyes — those beautiful amber eyes, ringed in black. "Why do you lie to me?"

"Do I lie to you?"

She searched his face for a long moment before she said, "I think you do, you know. I think you lie every time you look at me."

"I lie every time I look at anyone."

"Tell me something true," she said.

"I want you." The words were instant, and she saw the honesty in them. Pleasure thrummed through her.

It wasn't enough. "Something else."

He shook his head. "There is nothing else. Not right now."

"Another lie," she whispered, but she leaned in and kissed him anyway, feeling his desire. Matching it with her own. When the kiss ended, they were both panting. He wrapped a large, firm hand around the back of her neck and pressed his forehead to hers. He closed his eyes and said, achingly soft, "It's the only truth. I want you. I've never in my life even dreamed of wanting something like you. Something pristine and perfect." His eyes opened, finding hers instantly. "It's like wanting sunlight."

This man was going to be the end of her. He was going to ruin her for all others.

"You can't hold sunlight, though," he whispered. "No matter how much you wish to touch it, it slips through your fingers, chased away by the dark."

She shook her head. "You're wrong. Sunlight is not chased away by dark. It fills it up." And then she kissed him again, and he took control, tempering her eagerness with his superior skill — making the caress slow and long and deep, his fingers tracing up the inside of her leg.

She let him touch her, let him tease her knee, made room for his touch on that skin that had never been touched before. She gasped as he moved higher, his touch like a whisper, barely there and consuming her nonetheless.

He broke the kiss. "So soft," he said, pressing warm, full kisses down the column of her neck as she gasped her pleasure. "Like silk." He stroked up her thigh, leaving fire in his wake until he reached a satin and lace edge. He fingered the ribbon he found there, and she willed it gone. "Are these . . ."

She nodded, knowing she should be more embarrassed. Not caring. "The ones you gave me."

"If I were to look —" He tugged on the tie, loosening the pant leg, and she closed her eyes at the sensation. "They would be pink?"

She nodded.

"May I?"

Her eyes shot open. "May you what?"

"May I look?"

Only if you promise to touch, as well.

Somehow, she refrained from saying the words. But she could not refrain from nodding, knowing she shouldn't. Knowing that she wanted everything he promised.

The moment she did, he moved, sitting back to lift her skirts and reveal her. Her cheeks blazed as he reached for the pink silk ribbons. "I will remember these pretty pink ribbons," he said softly, to himself more than her as his warm fingers slid beneath along her thigh, beneath the fabric, "for the rest of my life."

She leaned back, giving him more access. "I will remember *this*."

His gaze flickered to hers. His hand moving up to her waist, to another pink ribbon, one he could not see but undid effortlessly nonetheless. "This?"

She gasped. "Yes."

He clasped the waistband. "Shall I give you other memories, love?"

"Yes," she whispered, and he tugged, removing the undergarment with efficiency. "Please."

Tossing it to the side, he returned his hands to her legs, now fully bare, draped in the pink silk of her dress. "So much prettier without the ribbons," he whispered, pressing a soft kiss to her knee, the caress sending heat rioting through her. "Open for me, love."

Perhaps it was the feel of the command against that skin that no one had ever touched.

Perhaps it was the sound of it — the growl that set her heart to pounding.

But it was very likely the rest that had Felicity opening her thighs to the air and the sun and this magnificent man.

It was the endearment. *Love.*

He was dangerous indeed.

Because the moment she did as he asked, his strong, warm, work-hewn hands came to the insides of her knees and held her open, his gaze locked to the shadowed space between her thighs, his throat working as though he were holding himself back from —

She reached for him, her fingers trailing down the side of his face, running over his scar, stark white but for the muscle twitching beneath it. "You look as though . . ." He met her eyes, and what she saw there took her breath. "You look . . ."

"Hungry." His hands moved then, beautifully, sliding up her thighs, pushing her skirts as far back as they would go. "I am hungry for you, Felicity Faircloth. I am starved for you." His fingers reached the dark curls that shielded her sex. "I want to touch you, love. And I want more. I want to taste you."

The words might have shocked her, but he punctuated them with a gentle stroke, a slow slide as he parted her. "I want to know every inch of you. What gives you pleasure." A movement. A deep, delicious groan. "You're so wet for me."

A blush rose on her cheeks, and he shook his head, coming up on his knees to steal a kiss. "No," he whispered. "Never be embarrassed of that. You want it, don't you? My touch?"

She closed her eyes. "Yes." More than anything.

"You want my kiss."

She pulled him to her. Took his lips. "Yes."

"Greedy girl. You may have it any time you ask."

The words sent a flood of liquid fire through her. "I want it now."

He laughed at the words, low and rough. "I want to give it to you." He stroked, and she gasped. "You like that?" She nodded, lifting her hips toward his touch. "Here?" A long, lingering touch. "Or here?" A slow circle, firm and gentle. She gasped. "Ah . . ." he said. "There."

Another circle, and her spine went straight, her fingers tightening on his shoulder, her eyes closing, her mouth dropping open. "Yes. There. Please."

"Hmm." The circular strokes continued, lazy and perfect, and thought scrambled.

She reached down to grasp his hand, her fingers circling his wrist. "Do you wish me to stop?"

"No!" She gasped. "Yes. I don't . . ." He did, and she hated him a little for it. Her eyes opened. "Don't stop."

He leaned in and kissed her again, then said, "I think I should show you something else."

"But I liked that!" she protested.

"You shall like this more," he whispered.

She arched toward him as his fingers retreated. "Devil, please."

"Devon."

She met his gaze, clear and beautiful and full of something she did not quite recognize. "What?"

"Call me Devon."

Her heart threatened to pound from her chest, her hand sliding up over his cheek. "Devon."

In response, he lowered his head to her thigh, as though in worship. Which was mad, of course. He was the one who deserved worship. She stroked his hair, her fingers trembling with need for him. For his kiss, yes. His touch, yes. But *him.* "Devon," she whispered again.

The name unlocked him, and he pressed a soft kiss to her thigh, and another, and another, chasing the soft skin to her sex, her hands still stroking his smooth, short hair. He parted her folds, opening her to his gaze, and, for a moment, she struggled, embarrassed by his actions.

Until he spoke, his breath hot and devastating against her. "So beautiful." He pressed a kiss directly above her sex, inhaling deeply, as though summoning strength. "I shouldn't have told you. Now you own me."

If only it were true. And still. . . . "Devon."

He looked up at her then, his eyes all she could see. "Show me what you like."

She shook her head. "I don't know . . ."

"You will." And then he was kissing her, and she was lost, gasping her pleasure as he pressed his tongue into her softness and made love to her with those slow, languid circles he'd discovered she liked so much. Felicity was undone, her hands at his head as his tongue stroked over the swollen, aching center of her, sending wave after wave of pleasure through her.

Her fingers tightened, holding him against her. She moved against him, and Devil — Devon — groaned, letting her use him, savoring her, impossibly, like she was all he'd ever desired. At the sound, Felicity released him, embarrassed, and he lifted his head instantly, ending her pleasure. *No!* She shook her head, raising her hands. "I'm sorry — I didn't —"

He reached for one of them, pressing a kiss to the center of her palm as he returned it to his head. "Don't ever apologize for taking what you want, love. For showing me how to give you pleasure."

She closed her eyes, horrified by the words, certain that women *did not* do such a thing.

Devil returned to his task, his tongue flickering just barely at the core of her. Too lightly. Barely there. She opened her eyes. "Devon." The name came on a whine. His eyes met hers over the long expanse of her torso, and she saw the mischief in them. "Please," she said. "More."

"Show me," he said, continuing his teasing. She knew what he wanted from her. Could she do it?

He leaned back and blew a long, slow stream of air over her. Gentle. Useless. Dammit. She lifted her hips. He rewarded the movement with a little suck to her straining flesh. She gasped.

And then, the monster, he returned to his barely-there touch. "Do it!"

He lifted his head, and gave her a look of pure challenge. "You do it."

God help her, she did, guiding him to her, lifting her hips, taking her pleasure. In response, he wrapped his arms around her hips, pulling her closer, holding her tight and firm, feasting at her as she sighed his name again and again, writhing against him. He moved one hand to add to her pleasure, sliding it inside her, finding a spot that made her see stars. "Devon!"

His response was a growl, the vibration adding to the immense pleasure he wrung from her, the command in it making her grasp tighten, her hips rise, her pleasure crest. And Felicity was lost, unable to do anything but give herself up to this magnificent man and his magnificent touch, pulsing against him, crying out his name as the world tilted and everything she knew changed.

And somehow, as she flew apart, she began to laugh.

It was uncontrollable — an exclamation of deep, nearly unbearable euphoria, rolling through her as he summoned pleasure from her, as she moved against him and let herself go. She laughed and laughed and reveled in this man, his kiss, his touch, her fingers scraping through his tightly shorn hair.

Soon, his mouth softened, his fingers stilling as she quieted. He turned his head, setting his lips to her thigh once more, softly. She caressed his head and face, the back of his neck and his beautiful wide shoulders, not wanting to let him go. "Was that —"

He looked up at her, and she could read the desire in his eyes, dark and sinful. "It was glorious."

She blushed. "I didn't expect . . . I didn't mean to laugh."

"I know."

Was it normal to laugh? She couldn't ask him. So instead she said, "I've never felt that way."

Something flashed across his face, there and then gone before she could read it, replaced by a sly smile, one side of his beautiful mouth tilting up. "I know, love. I was there. I felt you against me. Tight around my fingers. Pulsing against my tongue. And that laugh . . . it was the most erotic thing I've ever heard. For the rest of time, I shall hear that laugh in my dreams."

And then he stood, stroking the palms of his hands down his thighs, the last rays of sun turning the sky bloodred behind him.

He was gone. Still there, but gone from her, as though he'd never been there to begin with. She came forward on the bench. "Devon?"

He shook his head, barely glancing at her. "I shouldn't have told you that."

"Why not?"

"Because it's not for you."

The words stung like a blow. She stiffened.

He swore, low and dark, running his hands over his perfectly formed head. She hated that she noticed that perfection. Hated that she noticed everything about him — the dark slash of his brows, low over his eyes, the furrow between them. The straight line of his nose and the barely-there indentation at the tip of it. The shadow of beard on his cheeks, as though he could not shave enough to keep its darkness at bay. And that scar, wicked and beautiful because it was his.

Not for you.

Never to be hers.

He was the lock she would never pick.

It didn't matter that he seemed to know a dozen ways to open her.

"You asked me for something true," he said, gruff edge in his voice. "Earlier."

She stood, wanting to be free of the bench that would never be hers again, because it would always be his. "Yes. And you lied."

"I didn't," he said. "I told you I wanted you."

For a moment, not forever. She didn't say

it, and she was proud of herself.

"And I didn't lie when I told you that my name wasn't for you, either."

He didn't have to say it twice. It didn't have to sting twice. "Yes, *Devil*. I am not addlebrained. I understand your birth name is too precious to share with me."

He looked away again. Cursed again. "For Christ's sake, Felicity. When I say it isn't for you, it's because it's not precious at all. Because it defiles you to speak it."

She shook her head. "I don't —"

"It's not my birth name; I don't have a birth name. I was found, days old, wrapped in swaddling clothes and screaming on the banks of the River Culm, a note pinned to me, with instructions that I was to be sent to my father."

Dear God.

Her chest tightened at the words. At the vision of him, a child. A babe. Left. "Who would do such a thing?"

"My mother," he said without emotion. "Before she filled her pockets and walked into the water, thinking me better off without her." Felicity felt ill. What must that poor woman have been facing? What fear must she have carried? What sadness?

And then he added, "She thought he would accept me."

400

Of course she'd thought that. Who wouldn't accept him, this pillar of a man, proud and strong and brilliant and bold? How could any man not love such a son?

How could anyone not love such a man?

How could anyone leave him?

The thought rioted through her on a flood of recognition. She loved him. Somehow, she'd fallen in love with him. What was she going to do?

She stepped toward him, reaching for him, wanting to show him. Wanting to love him. "Devil."

He shook his head at the whispered name and stepped back, refusing her touch, his words unfeeling. Miraculously so. "He did not come for me. And no one in town wanted a bastard castoff — so they sent me to an orphanage. I had no name, so they named me Devon Culm — for the county from whence I came and the river where my mother died."

She reached for him again, only to have him pull away again. "Your father . . . he must not have known . . . the letter must not have found him . . . he would never have left you."

"You will make a lovely mother someday," he said. "I told you that once before, but I want you to know I mean it. There will

401

come a time when you will have beautiful, mahogany-haired daughters, Felicity, and I want you to remember that you will be a remarkable mother."

Her eyes stung with tears at the words — at the invocation of those children that she did not want if they were not shared with a man she loved. With *this* man, whom she loved.

"You wanted the truth, Felicity Faircloth, and there it is. I am so far beneath you that I soil you with my very thoughts."

She lifted her chin. "That's not true." Did he not see he was magnificent? Did he not understand that he was ten men? Stronger and wiser and smarter than anyone she'd ever known?

He reached for her then, his fingers trailing over her cheek in a caress that felt too much like a farewell. She reached up to capture his hand. "Devil," she repeated. "It's not true."

"I made a mistake," he said, so softly it was almost carried away on the wind. The words made Felicity ache with sadness.

"This isn't a mistake," she said. "This is the best thing I have ever known."

He shook his head. "You'll never forgive me," he said, looking at her. "Not if I take you from the life you deserve. Don't seek me out again."

He dropped his hand and turned away. She watched him go, willing him to turn back. Telling herself that if he turned back, it would mean something. If he turned back, he cared for her.

He didn't.

And her frustration and irritation simmered over.

"Why?" she called after him, getting angrier by the moment. Hating the way he had stripped her bare and made her believe that she *mattered* — and then left her as though she were nothing but an afternoon distraction. As though she were nothing at all.

He stopped, but did not look at her.

She did not move, refusing to chase him. Even a wallflower had pride. But she let her frustration ring out. "Why me? Why give me a taste of this? Of you? Of your world? Why let me have it and then snatch it away?"

It was becoming more difficult to see him in the dimming light, and she wondered if he would answer her. When he did, it was soft enough that she wondered if he meant her to hear it. If he realized that the breeze would carry the words to her just as the bench had done earlier.

"Because you are too important."
And he was gone, into the darkness.

CHAPTER TWENTY

Felicity had heeded his instructions.

She had not sought him out, nor had she broken into his offices or his warehouse, nor had any of his watches seen her in Covent Garden. In fact, Brixton, returned to his post outside Bumble House, had reported virtually no activity from Felicity at all since Devil had left her in her gardens.

She had not even resorted to sending him a note.

It had been three days, and Felicity had left him in peace, and Devil found he was more and more consumed with her with every passing second.

Perhaps he could have avoided it if he hadn't answered the summons she'd sent via Brixton. Perhaps he might have been able to ignore her if he hadn't kissed her in the gardens. If he didn't remember the sound of her voice carried along that whispering bench. If he didn't know she laughed when she came.

She laughed when she came.

He'd never known a woman to give herself over to pleasure like that. So fully, so completely that her pleasure poured from her in pure, unadulterated joy. For the rest of his life, he would remember the sound of her laughter in that garden, shared with him and the setting sun and the trees and nothing else.

For the rest of his life, he would dream of the taste of her pleasure and the sound of it. He was ruined by her.

He'd spent three days pretending to ignore the memory of her pleasure, of her glorious, rolling laughter, and finally, in failure, had left his offices to meet the latest ice shipment on the Thames. The sun had barely set — sending gold and purple streaks across the sky above London — and it was high tide.

Devil crossed over Fleet Street, toward the docks, checking his watch as he walked — ten past nine. He noted the quiet of the taverns frequented by London's dockworkers, most of whom would have found work that evening, seeing ships in and out of the moorings on the river while tide was high and the boats could be controlled. Once tide ebbed, it would be twelve hours before the ships could be moved — and time in shipping was funds.

Crossing down to the river's edge, walking stick in hand, he followed the docks for a few hundred yards to the large berth the Bastards leased on evenings when they received shipments. A massive ship loomed ink black against the grey sky, just docked, half-sunken in the high water because of its cargo — one hundred and fifty tons of ice, a good portion of it melted inside the hold.

Whit was already there, black hat low on his brow, greatcoat waving in the wind, with Nik by his side. The Norwegian was leafing through lading papers under the nervous gaze of the ship's captain. "It's all here, according to the papers," she said. "But we can't be sure until we get to it."

"How long?" Whit asked, lifting his chin in acknowledgment of Devil's approach.

"If we're lucky, Wednesday night." Two nights hence. "If we start draining the melt from the hold tonight, the moment the tide begins to ebb, it might be finished before then."

"Two nights and no more," Whit growled. "We can't risk it sitting without full guard for longer." A dozen men would be posted to protect the cargo while the water was drained from the ship's hold, because there was no other option — it was impossible to access the hold while it was filled with ice melt — but the docks were low ground, and, while on them, the guard could protect neither the cargo nor themselves as well as the Bastards liked.

"Two nights, then. I shall have the boys prepare for wet boots." Nik nodded to the captain, releasing him to his ship once more.

"We'll want extra guards on the move to the warehouse, as well," Devil said, tapping his stick against the boards of the dock. "I don't want to see another load compromised."

"Done."

"Excellent work, Nik."

The Norwegian dipped her head in a barely-there acknowledgment of the praise.

"Especially since Devil had nothing to do with this one," Whit added.

Devil looked to him. "What does that mean?"

"You've spent two weeks mincing after the girl."

"Why in hell are you tracking me?"

Whit looked away, down the dock. "As long as he is here, I'm having everyone tracked."

Ewan. "If he wanted us, he would have come for us."

"He wants Grace."

"Between her cover and her guard, she's well protected."

Whit grunted, low and full of grit. "I'm surprised you knew we *had* a shipment coming in today, with all the time you've had with your girl."

What a fucking bastard his brother was. "I had to convince her to trust me if we were going to use her to punish him."

Whit grunted. "That still the plan, is it?"

"No," Devil replied instantly, knowing that he was begging for trouble, but he rejected the idea of using Felicity as a pawn in their game so thoroughly now that he could not find the strength to pretend otherwise.

Christ, he'd made a hash of it.

"Bad plan after all, innit?" Whit said, and Devil resisted the urge to put his fist into his brother's face.

"Bollocks off."

Whit shared a sidelong glance with Nik, who spoke for them both. "If that isn't the plan, then what have you been doing all this time?"

"You worry about the ship," Devil said. "This isn't your business."

She shrugged and turned away.

" 'S a fair question, bruv."

It was. But that didn't mean Devil had to

answer it. "Tonight, you find your tongue?"

"Someone's got to help you sort out your idiocy."

"I'm handling it," Devil said.

He was.

He would.

All he had to do was stop thinking about her goddamn laugh.

"You. Fucking. Fools."

Devil turned toward the words. "Excellent." He looked to Nik. "Leave while you still can."

The Norwegian made her way up the gangway to begin her assessment of the hold as Grace neared, tall and proud and perfectly turned out in a tailored scarlet coat. She was flanked by two lieutenants — women in similarly cut black coats. All that was visible beneath the trio's outerwear were black boots, but Devil knew they were all wearing trousers — which made for fast walking and even faster running, should they need to avail themselves of the skill. The guards stopped ten yards from them as Grace approached.

Whit's brows rose and he looked over his shoulder at their sister for a long moment before returning his attention to the half-sunken ship in the water. "Evenin', Dahlia."

Grace narrowed her gaze on Whit. "What

the hell has you so chatty?" Before he could answer, she turned to Devil. "The two of you together have the sense of an addle-brained hedgehog."

"I am routinely amazed that London's best and brightest find you charming," Devil said.

"Did you think I wouldn't discover it? Did you think it could happen beyond my notice? Is it possible that the two of you have suffered simultaneous blows to the head and forgotten that I am smarter than you both put together?"

Whit looked to Devil. "She seems unhappy."

"Unhappy?" With lightning speed, Grace boxed Whit's ear.

"Oi!" Whit danced backward, a hand at the offended body part. "Fucking hell!"

"You shouldn't talk when you are so out of practice, Beast." She stepped toward him, a finger raised at his nose. "*You* should have told me."

"Told you what?" Whit asked in a frustrated near-whine.

She'd already turned her back on him, however, rounding on Devil, who held up his walking stick to keep her from getting too close. "And you . . . I ought to have you tossed into the river. You deserve to reek of

411

it for days. You deserve whatever perverse creature would find its way into you from the muck."

Devil lowered his stick, recoiling at the words. Grace had always been the best of them at verbal threats. Devil was better at making good on them. "Good God. That's grim."

"Do you know what day it is?"

"What?"

"Do you know. What day. It is."

"It's Monday." Devil grew nervous.

"It is, indeed, Monday." She reached into her coat and extracted a newspaper. "And do you know what is printed in Monday's newspaper?"

"Shit."

Whit let out a low whistle.

"Ah. And so we return to my original assessment."

"Addlebrained hedgehogs," Whit said.

Grace spun around and raised one black-gloved finger at him. "Hedgehog. Singular. One infinitesimal brain for both of you to share." She turned back to Devil.

"I don't know what you're on about," he said, brazening it through.

"Don't you even try denying it. And don't play the fool, though you obviously are one." She paused and took a breath. And when she spoke, the words were softer than he expected. Full of more emotion than she expected. "Banns were posted yesterday at St. Paul's. The announcement of the Duke of Marwick's engagement is in today's *News*."

Devil reached for the paper. "Dahlia —"

She rapped his hand with the rolled up print, and he recoiled. "When were you going to tell me?"

"We didn't think you would —" He looked to Whit, who offered no assistance. He returned his attention to Grace and cursed.

"What did you think I would do? Toss myself off the nearest bridge?"

Devil looked away. "No. Of course not."

"Rend my clothes?"

He tried a small smirk. "Perhaps."

She cut him a look. "My clothes are far too expensive for rending."

He gave a little huff of laughter at that. "Of course they are."

"What, then?"

"Well, murder wasn't an impossibility," Devil replied. "And the last thing we need is a dead duke."

Whit grunted. "It's not like we haven't had one of those before."

Grace ignored them both. "I'm not here because he's to be married. I'm here for you to explain why my girls tell me his fiancée is under the protection of the Bare-knuckle Bastards."

He froze at the words.

Grace noticed, as she noticed everything, one red brow rising.

"Did I not just finish pointing out that the last thing we need is a dead aristocrat? I had to protect the girl. She wants into the Garden as much as anyone here wants out of it."

"What is the daughter of the Marquess of Bumble doing in the Garden, Dev?" his sister asked.

Whit made things worse. "Devil likes the girl."

Grace did not look away from him. "Does he?"

I like her too much.

"This is the plain girl I met in your offices, correct?"

"She's not plain."

The words garnered both Whit and Grace's attention. Whit grunted, and Grace said, thoughtfully, "No . . . I don't suppose she is."

Devil felt like an idiot, but did not reply.

Grace changed tack. "Why wouldn't you tell me that you're trying to manipulate him?"

"Because we agreed that you would never meet again. Because we agreed that nothing about him is safe for you." Grace was too valuable. The duke could never know where she was. Grace was proof of a past that Ewan would do anything to keep secret.

If Grace were discovered, Ewan would hang.

A long silence followed the words, and she said, "We agreed that decades ago."

"It's no less true now, and you know it. He's come for you. He remembers the deal. No heirs. And he wants a trade."

Understanding flared in Grace's blue eyes. "A trade? Or does he want both?"

"He gets neither," Devil replied.

She looked from one of her brothers to the other. "We're not children any longer." Whit shoved his hands in the pockets of his greatcoat as she continued. "You don't have to protect me any longer. I can go toe-to-toe with Ewan any day. Let him come for me and I shall show him the sharp end of my blade."

It wasn't true. Ewan was ever Grace's weakness. Just as she was his.

And fate was a cruel bitch to make them each the demise of the other.

"Grace —" Devil began softly.

She waved off the rest. "And so, what?

What game are you playing, Dev? You're not planning on letting the girl marry him, are you?"

"No." Christ. No.

"What, then? You planned to end the engagement and send him a message? No heirs?" She looked to Whit.

Whit spread his hands wide. "I wanted to beat him bloody and send him back to the country."

Grace smirked. "That's still idiotic, but less so. Christ, you two." She grew serious. "I should have been in on the plan," she said softly. "I should be in on it from here on out."

"Why?"

"Because he didn't steal my future."

"That's a fucking lie," Whit said.

"He stole your future the moment he drew breath. Yours more than ours," Devil agreed. And her past. And her heart — but they never discussed that. "You were the heir."

Grace went still, every inch of her steeling at the words. She shook her head. "I was never heir."

She'd been a girl. Not that it had mattered, as the Duke their father had already set his terrible plan in motion. Devil pressed on. "You were born of the Duchess, baptized the future Duke. And Ewan stole your future as keenly as our father did."

Grace looked away, the wind from the Thames whipping the full fabric of her scarlet coat around her legs. "Your father hated me from the start," she said, loud enough to be heard over the wind. "I expected *his* betrayal; I never counted for more than that with him." She shook her head. "But Ewan . . ."

Devil hated the confusion in his sister's voice. "He betrayed all of us. He stole future from all of us. But you are the only one from whom he stole past."

She looked to him, her gaze tracking the scar on his cheek. "He nearly killed you."

"He nearly killed us all," Devil replied, the mark tight on his skin.

"He still might," she said. "And here's the other reason I should be in on the plan; I'm the one who knew him best." That much was true. "And Ewan can't be manipulated; he does the manipulating."

"Not this time."

"He's no fool; he knows I'm the keeper of all his secrets," she said. "My knowledge — my *existence* — sees him at the gallows. He won't rest until he finds me. He hasn't rested in twenty years."

"We tell him you're dead," Whit said. "That was always the plan if he got close enough to scent you."

She shook her head. "You don't put me in the ground until I'm cold, boys. He's too close not to find me."

"We'll never give you up."

"And when I grow tired of hiding?" Whit growled, and she turned to him. "Poor Beast. Always looking to put your fist through something." She looked to Devil, letting the Garden into her voice. "No worries, bruvs. He won't be the first duke we've fought and won." She paused, and then said, "Stop worrying about me, and worry about the deal. No heirs."

Whit grunted, and Grace turned to him. "What?"

"Devil's mucked the whole thing up."

Devil gritted his teeth. "I haven't mucked it up. I've a plan."

Grace looked to him. "What kind of plan?"

"Yeah, bruv." Whit looked to him. "What kind of plan? We know you shan't hurt the girl."

He should thrash them both. "I'm getting her out of it."

"Of the marriage?" Grace replied. When he didn't reply, she added, "How? If he leaves her, she's damaged. If she leaves him, she's damaged. There is no scenario where the girl isn't destroyed and you knew that

418

going in."

"She was damaged goods before he ever got near her," Whit said.

Devil turned on his brother. "She was not."

A pause. Then Grace said, "I heard the same. Something about being found in a bedchamber that was not her own?"

"How do you know that?"

Grace raised one red brow in his direction. "Need I remind you that I am the one with the network of decent spies? Shall I tell you what I've heard about you and Finished Felicity Faircloth?"

He ignored the taunt. "The point is, she's not damaged. She's —"

Perfect.

Well. He couldn't say that.

"Oh, dear," Grace said.

Whit removed his hat and rubbed a hand over his head. "You see?"

"See what?" Devil asked.

"You care for the girl."

"I don't."

"Then throw her to the wolf. Get her to the edge of the altar and ruin her. Prove to Ewan that he'll never marry as long as you live. Or, if he does, he'll be as cheated of real heirs as his own father was. That you will eliminate the possibility of any heir he

419

might find. Make good on your vow."

He looked away from his sister. "I can't."

"Why not?"

"Because she will be ruined in the balance. At my hands."

"My girls on the ground tell me she's ruined already, Devil. Half the Garden saw you kiss the girl on the night you told the world she was off-limits."

He never should have touched her that night. Nor any of the nights since. But that wasn't the kind of ruination he meant. Not the silly ruination that came with a clandestine kiss. A night of pleasure — stolen moments that meant nothing. For Devil's plan to work, he would have had to have done it publicly. In front of all the world.

And Felicity would be exiled for it. She'd never be a jewel of the *ton.* She'd never return to a place of honor. Never be at the center of that world for which she longed.

Grace smirked at his lack of response. "Tell me again that you don't care for the girl."

"Fuck." Of course he did. She was impossible not to care for. And he'd made a proper hash of it from the start, from the moment he saw her on the balcony. From the moment he veered from his plan to send his brother packing, and instead lingered with her . . . made promises to her he had no intention of keeping. Made promises he could not keep even if he wanted to.

"You've already thrown her to the wolves, Dev," his sister said. "There's only one way to save her."

He turned on her, unable to keep the cold rage from his voice. "Ewan doesn't get heirs. And he definitely doesn't get them from Felicity Faircloth."

She's mine.

A red brow rose. "Not Ewan."

His brow furrowed. "Who? Who do we know who is good enough for her?"

Grace smiled then, full and open and uncalculated. She looked to Whit. "Who, indeed."

"Beast?" Devil thought he might lose his mind at the idea of his brother touching Felicity.

"Oh, for God's sake," Whit growled. "You just might have the intelligence of a hedgehog. She means you, Dev. *You* marry the girl."

For a heartbeat, emotion rioted through him, the force of it sending him back. Excitement and desire and something dangerously, impossibly close to hope.

Impossibly close, and impossible.

He closed out the emotions. "No."

"Why not?"

"She doesn't want me." Lie.

Marwick isn't my moth. You are.

"Do you want her?"

Yes. Of course. He couldn't imagine how any man wouldn't want her. His grasp tightened on the silver lion's head in his palm.

Grace ignored the answer. "You could marry her. Save her from ruin."

"It wouldn't be saving her. It would be trading one ruin for another. What's more ruinous for a highborn lady than life as a Mrs. in the Covent Garden muck? What sort of life would she have here?"

"Please," Grace scoffed. "You're rich as a king, Devil. You could buy her the western edge of Berkeley Square."

"You could buy her the *whole* of Berkeley Square," Whit added.

It wouldn't be enough. He could buy her Mayfair. A box at every theater. Dinners with the most powerful men in London. Audiences with the king. He could clothe her in the most beautiful frocks Hebert could fashion. And she'd never be accepted by them. Never be welcomed back. Because she'd be married to a criminal. One with whom they happily consorted, but a crimi-

422

nal nonetheless. A bastard, raised in an orphanage and bred in the rookery.

If only he'd been the one to win the dukedom, it might be different. He shook his head, hating the thought — one he hadn't had in two decades, since he was a boy, aching with hunger and desperate for sleep somewhere other than on the streets.

Behind them, footsteps clattered, fast and furious. A girl, no more than twelve, blond and reed-thin, stopped in front of Grace's lieutenants. "One of mine," Grace said, raising her voice and waving her forward. "Let her come."

The girl approached, a square of paper in hand. Dipped a knee. "Miss Condry."

Grace extended a hand to receive the message and opened it, her attention no longer on Devil.

Thank God. He'd already said enough to sound like a love-sick fool.

Perhaps it was an important enough message for her to stop asking him about Felicity.

She dug into her pocket, delivering a coin to the messenger, who was already turning for the darkness. "Off you go. Safely." Grace returned her attention to him. "It occurs that the lady's ruin should be her own decision, don't you think?"

Perhaps it was not enough, and Grace would talk about Felicity forever, like perfect torture. "She's already made the decision. She lied about marrying a duke to return herself to society. She chose Marwick, a duke she'd never met."

I wanted to punish them, she'd told him. *And I wanted them to want me back.*

"I made a mistake bringing Felicity Faircloth into this battle."

Whit grunted.

"God knows that's true," Grace agreed.

"I shall get her out of it, and save her future in the balance."

Grace nodded, returning her attention to the slip of paper she'd been delivered. "I'm not so certain you're in control of her future anymore."

"I'm not so certain he's ever been in control of it," Whit said, bracing himself against the wind.

He scowled at them. "The two of you can go to hell."

"Tell me." Grace did not look up. "As part of your arrangement, did the lady ask to be schooled in the art of temptation?"

Devil stilled. How would Grace know that? "She did. Yes."

His sister looked to him. "And you were unable to provide said instruction?"

"I instructed her fine." Whit's brows went up at that, and Devil had the distinct impression that the wheels were coming off the cart. "But it wasn't about tempting just anyone. It was about tempting the untempt-able. It was about tempting *Ewan,* for Christ's sake. To get back into society. To rise to its full height. She wants her reputa-tion restored, along with that of her family. Have you not been listening?"

"The girl doesn't seem to care a bit about her reputation, Devil," Grace said. "I might go so far as to say she's absolutely no inter-est whatsoever in what society thinks of her."

"How would you know that?" he snapped. "You've met her one time."

She brandished the note. "Because she's at the club right now."

He froze. "Which club?"

A perfectly arched red brow rose as she replied, all calm, "My club."

There was a beat, followed by Whit's quiet, "Fucking hell."

Or perhaps it was Devil who said it. He wasn't certain, as he was distracted by the wash of fury that came over him at the words.

He was gone in an instant, disappearing into the darkness without farewell, long legs eating up the ground until he became unsatisfied with his speed and began to run.

Grace and Whit stood on the docks, watching their brother disappear into the darkness before she turned to him and said, "Well. This is all unexpected."

Whit nodded once. "You realize that Ewan won't like it when Devil wins."

"I do."

He looked to her. "You've got to get gone for a bit, Gracie."

She nodded. "I know."

CHAPTER TWENTY-ONE

Felicity was fairly certain that 72 Shelton Street was a bordello.

When she had knocked at the entrance an hour earlier, a small inlaid door had slid open, revealing a set of beautifully kohl-lined eyes. And when she'd told those eyes that Dahlia had invited her, the small door had given way to the larger one, and she'd been welcomed inside.

A tall, raven-haired beauty in deep sapphire had met her in a lovely receiving room, explained that Dahlia was not in at the moment, and invited Felicity to wait. As Felicity's curiosity was impossible to deny, she had, of course, agreed.

At that point, she'd been provided with a mask and escorted to a larger room, oval in shape, wrapped in silk and satin and appointed with a dozen or so settees, armchairs, and tufted cushions. Refreshments had been offered.

And then the men had arrived.

Or, rather, they'd begun to arrive.

The room boasted a half-dozen doors, all closed, except to herald the entry of what must have been some of the handsomest men in Britain. And they'd kept coming, these charming men, offering more wine, more cheese, candied sweets, and sweet plums. They sat close and regaled her with stories of their strength, telling her delightful, diverting jokes, and generally making her feel as though she were the only woman in the world.

Making her forget, almost, the reason she had come in the first place.

What was remarkable was this — the charming assembly of men made her feel the center of their world despite the presence of any number of other women, all of whom entered wearing masks, whose comings and goings appeared to be for the purpose of pairing off with one (and in some cases, more than one) of these gentlemen.

No doubt for lovemaking.

It occurred to Felicity that there was a time when she might have felt uncomfortable with the goings-on inside 72 Shelton Street, but now she was more than thrilled with her decision to accept Dahlia's invitation, because if anyone could teach her how to woo a man such as Devil, it was these men, who were so impressively charming.

A tall, handsome man was entertaining her; he'd introduced himself as Nelson — *like the hero, but better-looking* — with a smile in gentle eyes that had lovely wrinkles at their corners, and made him seem the kind of man with whom one might like to spend a lifetime, not just an evening.

After showering her in compliments, Nelson began to regale her with the story of a cat he'd once known — one who had a penchant for attending regular church services, and not simply attending them: "She was particularly fond of climbing the pulpit and spreading herself across the Book of Common Prayer. Needless to say, the vicar did not care for it, and routinely had to put the cat out to get on with his sermon."

Felicity laughed at the image as Nelson added, dark eyes twinkling, "I always thought it cruel treatment. The sweet pussy only wished for a pet."

The double meaning in the words did not escape Felicity, and her eyes went wide at the flirt. Was it considered a flirt if it was so overt?

Before she could suss out the answer, two

raps sounded, and she felt the vibration in the floorboards as Nelson's gaze flickered to a spot behind her, up, up until his eyes were also wide, and he was scrambling to his feet.

Felicity knew before she turned what she would find there.

Or, rather, *whom* she would find.

It did not change the way her heart began to pound when she discovered Devil in his tall darkness, clad all in black, walking stick in hand, storm clouds in his eyes. Her breath caught as he searched her face, the muscle in his jaw ticking wildly, making her want to reach up and touch it. Soothe it.

No. There would be none of that.

Instead, she straightened her spine and said, "What are you doing here?"

"This place is not for you."

She immediately resisted the words. "I cannot fathom how you are in any position to say so."

If possible, the angles of his face grew sharper, his eyes darkening. "Because this place is in Covent Garden and I own Covent Garden, Felicity Faircloth."

She smirked. "Well. Then I suggest you think very carefully before you give a fairy-tale princess free rein of your property."

"Goddammit, Felicity," he said, his voice low enough as to not draw attention from the others in the room. "You cannot hie out of Mayfair whenever you like."

"It seems I can, though, can't I?" Thank goodness for being a spinster; no one ever thought to make sure you remained in your bedchamber after you retired to bed. It made one feel quite chuffed when one did escape one's home.

And even more so when one was able to give a proper set-down to an arrogant man who deserved it. Feeling quite proud of herself, she turned on her heel and crossed the room, opening one of the beautiful mahogany doors and walking straight through it — as though she had any idea where she was going.

She would worry about that bit once she was rid of him.

Felicity closed the door behind her on the sound of his curse. Blessedly, there was a key in the lock, which she turned and pocketed. She looked about. She was in a stairwell, dimly lit and covered in gold and scarlet satin wall coverings, narrow wooden stairs climbing up to whatever was above.

The handle to the door rattled. "Open the door."

"No," she said. "I don't think I will."

A pause. And then, again, "Felicity. Open the door."

Excitement threaded through her. Excitement and a sense of freedom like she'd never felt before. "I would imagine you rather wished you had a talent with locks right now, don't you?"

"I don't need a talent with locks, love."

Love. The endearment filled the small, quiet space. She shouldn't let it warm her, but it did. She shouldn't let *him* warm her. Hadn't he hurt her? Hadn't he sent her away? Sworn her off him?

She gave a little huff of frustration.

And still, she wanted that endearment.

And still, she wanted the man.

Felicity turned on one heel and took off, up the steps, and quickly, as she wanted to put distance between them before he found a key and came after her. Or perhaps she wanted to put distance between herself and her feelings for him. It didn't matter anymore. She imagined she had a minute or two before the beautiful woman who had met her at the door provided him with a key.

She was three-quarters of the way up the staircase when the door flew in, ricocheting against the wall only to be caught by Devil's strong arm as he stepped through the doorway. Her mouth fell open as she stilled on the steps. "Are you *mad*? I could have

432

been standing there!"

"You weren't," he said, coming for her.

She backed up the steps, her heart pounding. "You broke your sister's door."

"My sister is very rich. She will repair it." He kept coming. "I'm not happy with you right now, Felicity Faircloth."

She continued up the steps, one hand lifting her skirts to allow for freedom of movement. "I can see that, *as you just broke down a door.*"

"I would not have had to do that if you hadn't turned up in Covent Garden."

"This has nothing to do with you." She retreated.

"It has everything to do with me." He advanced.

"You told me not to seek you out again." He was closing in on her. And she found she enjoyed the way her pulse thrummed with every measured footstep.

"So you seek out a fucking bordello?"

She paused, putting one hand to the wall to steady herself. "I had an inkling that was what this was!" Now she was rather regretting not exploring a bit more.

"An *inkling*?" Devil looked to the ceiling as though for patience. "What in hell else would it be? A second White's? Special for the Covent Garden set?"

She tilted her head. "It had occurred to me that it might be a . . . you know . . . but it hadn't quite felt so . . . bordello-esque." He had nearly reached her. "Why are all the ladies masked?"

"Are you through storming away from me?"

She tilted her head. "For now."

"Only because I've piqued your interest and you want answers."

"Why are all the ladies masked?"

He stopped on the step below her, and the difference in height brought them eye to eye. "Because they don't want to be recognized."

"Isn't that the point? Don't the clients wish to see the women's faces?"

"Felicity . . ." He paused, a ghost of a smile on his lips. "Darling, the women *are* the clients."

Her mouth went perfectly round with surprise. "Oh."

It was a bordello — *in reverse.*

"Oh," she repeated. "That would explain why Nelson was so very charming."

"Nelson is very good at his work."

"I can imagine," she said, softly.

"I'd prefer you not." Devil gave a little growl.

Her eyes went wide. Was it possible he

was . . . jealous? No. That was impossible. Men like Devil did not experience jealousy over women like Felicity Faircloth.

He interrupted her thoughts. "What are you doing here?"

I came to learn how to win you. "I have an invitation."

"Yes, and my sister is lucky I did not decide to put her into the Thames for extending it to you." He was so close, and speaking so quietly in the shadows. "Now I'm going to ask you one more time, my lady, and you'd do best to tell me the truth. What are you doing here?"

For the first time in her life, as she heard the words *my lady,* she wondered what it would be to actually, honestly be someone's lady. What might it be like to stand by his side? To touch him at will? To have him touch her?

She wanted it.

But instead of saying so, she said, softly, "You told me I couldn't come to you any longer."

He closed his eyes a breath longer than he should. "Yes."

The reply grated. "You want to have your cake and eat it, too, and I shan't allow it. You may either wash your hands of me or attempt to be my keeper, Devil, but you may not have both. And I'm not in the market for a keeper, anyway."

"As you are standing in the middle of a Covent Garden bordello, I think you absolutely should be."

"I am in the middle of a Covent Garden bordello because I am through with keepers, and there is a wide world of things I'd like to learn."

"You should go home."

"And what will I learn there, how to be a sacrificial lamb? How to marry a man I do not love? How to save a family I find I resent more than I should?"

Another low growl. "And what do you think this place will teach you?"

How to win you.

She swallowed. "All the things you refuse to."

He narrowed his gaze on her. "Do you remember what I told you about passion, Felicity? I told you it is not like love — it is not patient or kind or whatever else Scripture likes to tell us. It is not want. It is *need.*"

Heat was coming off him in waves, wrapping itself around her with the promise of his words. What would it be like to be needed by him? Would it be as heady as how it felt to need him?

Because she was beginning to feel she needed him.

Surely that was why it had hurt so much when he'd left her.

Not because she loved him.

And then he added, "Passion comes with the worst of sin far more than it comes with the best of virtue."

She heard the guilt in his words, and could not stop herself from lifting her hand, from putting her fingers to his cheek, wishing her gloves gone. Wishing she could feel him, skin to skin. "You know about sin, don't you, Devil?"

He closed his eyes, leaning into her touch, sending a flood of pleasure to the core of her. "I know more about sin than you could possibly dream."

"You told me once you could see my sin," she said.

His beautiful eyes opened again, dark and knowing. "It is envy. You envy them their place. Their lives. Their acceptance in society."

Perhaps that had been the case once. Perhaps there had been a time when she would have done anything to have the life the rest of society had. The happiness. The acceptance. No longer. "You're wrong. That isn't my sin."

It was his turn to lift a hand. To touch her, his magnificently warm fingers against her cheek. "What is it, then?"

"It is want," she said, the words barely there.

He cursed softly in the darkness, so close. So impossibly, beautifully close.

She pressed on, knowing she shouldn't. Unable to stop. "I want *you,* Devil. I want to woo *you.* I want to be *your* flame. But I fear . . ." She paused, hating the way he watched her, as though he saw every word that was coming before she formed it. And perhaps he did. It didn't matter. "I fear I am your moth, instead."

His fingers moved, sliding to the back of her neck, into her hair, pulling her to him, and setting her on fire.

There was nothing tentative about the kiss — which only added to the heady fog that came over her with it. One moment, she was sure that he wanted to be rid of her, and the next, he was stealing her breath and thought and sanity, one hand cradling her face, the other arm wrapping around her back to keep her steady and pull her close to the heat of him. His mouth played over hers, sending wave after wave of sensation rocketing through her, rough and perfect, his tongue warm and lush against her own.

It might well be the last time he kissed her, and it was *magnificent*.

She could happily live here, in his arms, in this stairwell, forever.

Except a throat cleared behind him, from what seemed like a mile away, and panic flared at being discovered. She pushed at his shoulders, and Devil lifted his lips from hers in a slow, lingering disengagement, as though he had no reason whatsoever to disengage.

"What?" he asked, without looking away from her.

"You've broken my door," Dahlia said from below.

He grunted his acknowledgment of the words, still not looking away from Felicity, whose cheeks were blazing. His free hand ran down her arm to take her hand in his.

"We've rooms for things like that, you know," Dahlia added.

Devil's beautiful lips flattened into a straight line. "Bugger off." He leaned in and kissed Felicity again, quick and thorough, leaving her breathless when he lifted his head and said, "Come with me."

As though she could do anything but that.

They climbed the stairs, one flight, and the next. He didn't hesitate — didn't slow his pace, not even when Felicity craned to see down the beautiful, mysterious hallways that promised adventure and sin. Instead, he led her higher and higher, Felicity's heart pounding harder and harder until he stopped in an almost pitch-black narrow stairwell, with nowhere else to go.

He released her then and set his hands to the ceiling, rings gleaming in the darkness mere inches above his head, and pushed open an inlaid door, lifting himself up and out, leaving Felicity gaping at his beautiful body, silhouetted against the starlit sky.

When he reached back and offered her a hand, she did not hesitate, and he pulled her out into the night, where he reigned.

CHAPTER TWENTY-TWO

He took her to the rooftops.

He knew he shouldn't. He knew he should pack her into a hack and return her to Mayfair — untouched, to the home that had been in her family for generations. He knew he was wrong to bring her to this world that was all his and nothing of hers, that would do nothing but soil her with it.

But if Felicity's sin was want, so was Devil's. And Christ, he wanted her.

He wanted her more than he'd ever wanted anything, and Devil had spent much of his youth hungry and cold, poor and angry. He might have been able to resist his desire — but then she'd confessed her own: *I want you. I want to be your flame . . . but I fear I am your moth instead.*

And all Devil wished was to take her somewhere so they might burn together.

He closed the door after he pulled her up onto the roof of Grace's club — rising from the task to discover her staring out into the night, the city below and the stars above, as clear as his view of the future.

The one he would spend without her.

But tonight, he would share this world with her, even as he knew he would regret it forever. How could he resist?

Especially when she reached up and removed the mask she'd been given inside, revealing herself to the warm night. She turned in a slow circle, eyes wide as she took it in. And then she raised her gaze to his, and the breathless smile on her face threatened to send him to his knees. "This is magnificent."

"It is," he said, his own breath coming harshly.

She shook her head. "I never think of the rooftops."

He extended his hand to her. "They are the best way to travel." She settled her hand in his, giving her trust over to him before he led her from one building to the next, down a long, curving city street, up and over the roofs, from ridge to ridge, around chimneys and over broken tiles.

"Where are we going?"

"Away," he said.

She stilled at the words, releasing his hand. When he looked to her, she was facing away from him, toward the city. As he watched, she spread her arms wide and turned her face to the sky, breathing in the night, a small smile playing over her lips.

Devil froze, unable to keep his eyes from her, from the joy in her eyes, the wash of excited color on her cheeks, the swell of her breasts and the curve of her hips, her hair gleaming silver in the moonlight. For a heartbeat, she was Cardea, unseen by all the world except him — the beginning and the end, the past and the future. The present.

As beautiful as the night sky.

"I love this," she said, the words strong and full of passion. "I love the freedom of it. I love that no one knows we are here, secrets in the darkness."

"You like the darkness," he said, the words coming out graveled, like wheels on the cobblestones below.

She looked to him, a twinkle in her eye. "I do. I like it because you wrap yourself in it. I like it because you so clearly love it."

He tightened his grip on his walking stick, tapped it twice against the toe of his boot. "I don't love it, as a matter of fact."

Her brows rose and she lowered her arms to her sides. "I find that difficult to believe, as you reign over it."

He climbed to the peak of the roof, making a show of considering the drop to the next one, so that he did not have to look at her when he said, "I feared the dark as a child."

A beat, and then her skirts rustling over the roof tiles as she approached. Without turning, he knew she wished to reach for him. To touch him. And he did not think he could bear her pity, so he kept moving, down to the roof below, and up the iron steps to the next. And all the while, speaking — more than he'd ever said to anyone before — thinking to stop her from touching him. To stop her from ever wanting to touch him again. "Candles were expensive, and so they did not light them at the orphanage," he said, stilling on the next rooftop, his gaze fixed on a lantern swinging outside a tavern far below. "And in the rookery, we did everything we could to avoid the monsters that lurked in the darkness."

Still, she advanced, his name like a prayer on her lips.

He tapped his walking stick on the red roof tiles marking the gable of the roof beneath his boot, wanting to turn and face her, to say, *Don't come closer. Don't care for me.*

"It was impossible to keep them safe," he said to the city beyond.

She stopped. "Your brother and sister are lucky to have you. I've seen the way they look at you; whatever you did, you kept them as safe as possible."

"That's not true," he said, harshly.

"You were a child, too, Devon," she said at his back, the words so soft he nearly didn't hear his name in them. *Lie.* Of course he heard it. His name on her lips was like salvation.

One he did not deserve. "Knowing that does not help the regret."

She reached him then, but did not touch him, miraculously, instead, she sat at his feet on the roof's peak, staring up at him. "You are too hard on yourself; how much older could you possibly be?"

He should end the conversation there and take her down, through the door inset in the roof below, to his offices. He should send her home. Instead, he sat next to her, facing in the opposite direction. She put her gloved hand to the roof between them. He took it in his own, pulling it into his lap, marveling at the way the moon turned the satin to silver.

When he replied, it was to that silver thread, somehow magically spun in this darkness he loved and hated. "We were born on the same day."

A beat. "How is that —"

He traced her fingers slowly through the glove. Up and down, like a prayer. "To different women."

Her fingers twitched beneath the touch. Beneath the words. "But the same man."

"Not Grace."

"Grace," she said, her brow furrowing. "Dahlia."

He nodded. "She has a different father. Which is likely why she is better than the rest of us combined." His fingers found the buttons on her glove and began to work at them.

Together, they watched the skin of her wrist revealed, before Felicity said, softly, "I thought you said you did not know your father."

"I said my father did not wish to claim me when my mother died."

"But later?"

He nodded, refusing to look at her face, instead removing the satin glove in a long, slow slide that made his mouth water. "Later, we became useful." He paused. "When he realized Grace was all he would get."

She shook her head. "I don't understand.

She wasn't his daughter."

"He was married to her mother, though. And willing to accept her as his, so desperate he was for an heir."

An heir meant . . . "He was titled."

He nodded.

It took all her energy not to ask him which title they discussed. "But . . . he had sons. Why not wait? Why not try for another? A legitimate one?"

"It wasn't possible. He'd never get another."

Confusion flared. "Why?"

She had the most beautiful skin. He turned her palm up and traced circles in it. "Because he couldn't sire heirs after Grace's mother shot him."

Her eyes went wide. "Shot him where?"

He did look to her then. "In a place that made it impossible to sire heirs."

She opened her mouth. Closed it. "And so he was left with a girl. No heir."

"Most men would have given up," he said. "Let the line die out. Pass to some distant cousin. But my father was desperate for a legacy."

Her hand closed around his finger, capturing it with her warmth, making him wish she would stay with him forever and keep the cold at bay. "You and Beast."

He nodded. "Whit."

She offered a small smile at Whit's real name. "I prefer that, if I am honest. Devon and Whit," she said, releasing his fingers and raising her bare hand to his face. He closed his eyes, knowing what she was thinking before she touched him, letting the soft pads of her fingers trace down the long white scar on his cheek. "And the one who did this."

"Ewan." He captured her hand in his, leaning into the touch as he told the story for the first time in his life — at once hating himself for resurrecting the past and taking remarkable pleasure in speaking of it, finally. "I thought I was saved when he turned up at the orphanage — my father." She nodded, and he went on. "My mother had left a few coins, but the family that took me in while they waited for word from him took room and board."

"For a babe?" Her shock was palpable, and it occurred to Devil that there were some things he would never tell her — things he would protect her from ever knowing existed in the world.

He reached into his trouser pocket and extracted a scrap of fabric. Threadbare and worn. Her gaze fell to it as he rubbed his thumb over the embroidery, the tin pin attached. She wanted to take it, he knew. To investigate it. But she didn't, and he was torn between giving it to her and hiding it away — at once wanting to share it and terrified of it, of the proof that he would never be enough. He settled for holding it in his palm, revealing the once-fine red M, now faded to brown and barely able to hold together. His talisman.

His past.

He wanted her to understand. "I was ten when he came — at night, ironically. They came to fetch me from the boys' quarters and I can still see the light of the dean's candle." He squeezed her hand without knowing. "I thought I was saved. My father brought me to the country, to an estate that rivaled anything I'd ever dreamed. He introduced me to my brothers." He paused, then repeated, "And I thought I'd been saved."

Her grasp tightened, her fingers threading through his own, as though she could already see the past.

"I hadn't been," he said. "I'd exchanged one kind of darkness for another."

Devil could feel Felicity's keen focus, razor-sharp and without cease. He did not look at her. He couldn't. Instead, he continued to speak to her hand, turning it over, running his thumb over her knuckles, savoring the feel of the peaks and valleys of them. "The day of our birth should have been an embarrassment of riches for a father. Four children. Three boys and a girl." He shook his head. "I should not take glee from it, knowing as I do how the story ends, but I am proud to say that all my father wanted that day was an heir, and he did not receive one. The only one he might have been able to pass off as heir was born a girl. And the others —" He looked to the starlit sky. "We were all bastards."

He tried to release her, but she wouldn't have it. Her hand clasped his ever more tightly as he continued. "But my father was nothing if not shrewd. And for him, name was more important than fortune. Or future. Or truth. And he claimed an heir had been born. A son."

Felicity's eyes went wide. "That's illegal."

Not just illegal. Punishable by death when the heir would inherit a dukedom.

"No one discovered it? No one said anything?" It was impossible to believe, Devil knew. Late at night, he often struggled with the memory of it, certain he had it wrong. The house had been filled with servants. So many should have noticed. Should have spoken up.

But he'd been there. And the memories

did not lie.

He shook his head. "It never occurred to anyone to go looking. Grace was kept in the country — never brought to town, something her mother was more than happy to allow, as Grace, too, was a bastard. A handful of old, loyal servants were allowed to stay with them. And my father had a plan. After all, he had three sons. By-blows, certainly, but sons nonetheless. When we were ten, he collected us. Brought us to the country house, and told us his plan.

"One of us, you see, would be heir. Rich beyond measure. Educated in the best schools. He would never want for anything. Food, drink, power, women, whatever he wanted."

Her grasp threatened to stop the circulation of his blood through his fingers. "Devil," she whispered.

He looked to her then. "Devon."

It was important she remember that now, the name that he'd inherited not from a family, but from nothing. Important, too, that he remember it, here with her as pure temptation — making him wish he could take her for his own. He hadn't won the competition. He was not the duke. He was still nothing.

Memories swirled. Whit, reed-thin and

451

small, with too many teeth in his little face, his impish smile big and bright. Grace, tall and sturdy, with sunken sad eyes. And Ewan, all long legs and sharp bones, like a foal. And with a monstrous determination.

"One of us would inherit everything. And the others, they would receive a different fate. A lesser one."

"How?" she whispered to him. "How did he choose?"

Devil shook his head. "He would tell you he didn't choose. He would tell you we chose."

"How?"

"We fought for it."

She exhaled at the revelation, harsh and low. "Fought how?"

He looked to her then, finally able to meet her gaze. Eager to see the horror in it. Ready for her to understand from where he had come. And how. Ready for her to see what he had known from the start — that he was so far beneath her that he might as well be in hell.

When she was gone from his life, he would be in hell.

"However he asked."

She clutched his hand, her grip stronger than he would have imagined it could be. "No. That's madness."

He nodded. "The physical challenges were easy. First sticks and stones. Fists and fire. But the mental ones — those were the ones that destroyed us. He'd lock us up, alone in the dark." He hated telling her, but somehow, couldn't stop the words from coming. "Tell us that we could be set free, into the light, if we'd choose another to fight."

She shook her head. "No."

"He gave us gifts, took them away. Sweets. Toys . . ." He paused, a memory teasing at the edge of his mind. "He gave me a dog. Let it keep me warm in the dark for days. And then told me I could keep it forever if I traded it for one of the others."

She pressed closer to him. Wrapped her arms around him, as though she could ward off the memory. "No."

He shook his head and looked to the sky, sucking in air. "I refused. Whit was my brother. Grace my sister. And Ewan . . ."

Ewan had been the only one allowed to keep his dog.

What had Ewan done?

Felicity shook her head. Pressed her face into his arm. "No."

His arm came around her, stroking over her hair, pulling her tight against him. *Ewan would never have Felicity.*

"He wanted the strongest of us for his

453

heir. The hungriest." He wanted the son who would give him a legacy. "At some point, I stopped competing. I simply tried to keep the others safe."

"You were children," she whispered, and he heard the wound in her voice, as though she'd never imagined such torture. "Surely someone tried to stop his crimes."

"They are only crimes if they are discovered," he said quietly. "We found ways to stay together. Ways to keep sane. We made promises to each other, never to let him win. Never to let him take us from each other."

Felicity was looking down at her lap now, and he knew this was the ending. That she wouldn't return to Covent Garden after this story. She wouldn't return to him. He forced himself to finish. "But when it came down to it . . . we weren't strong enough." The scar on his cheek burned with the memory of Ewan's blade, sharp and unpleasant. With the order that had caused it. His father's voice ringing out in the darkness.

If you want it, boy, you must take it from the others.

Ewan coming for him.

He exhaled, extinguishing the memory. "We had no choice but to run."

She did not look up. "Here."

He nodded.

"How long were you there?"

"Two years. We were twelve when we left."

Her breath came on a harsh exhale. "Two years."

He pulled her close and pressed a kiss to her temple. "We survived it."

She looked to him, long enough for her beautiful gaze to set his heart to racing. "I wish I could give those years back."

He smiled and stroked his thumb across her soft cheek. "I would take them." Tears welled in her beautiful eyes. "No, love." He shook his head. "No tears. Not for me."

She dashed one away. "There was no one you could trust."

"We trusted each other," he said. And it was the truth. "We vowed we would grow strong and powerful, rich as royalty. And we would mete out a single, endless punishment — my father always wanted heirs. As long as we lived, he would never get them."

Her eyes glistened in the starlight, her mouth set in a firm, straight line. "I want him dead."

His brows shot up.

"I know it's wrong. I know it's a sin. But your father — I hate even calling him that — he deserves nothing short of death."

It took a moment for him to find his reply.

"He received it."

She nodded. "I hope it was painful."

He couldn't help his smile at that. His magnificent lockpick, known to all of London as a wallflower, was a lioness. "If he weren't dead, you're enough to make me wish I could bring him to you as a trophy."

"It's not a jest, Devon," she said, her voice wavering with emotion. "You didn't deserve it. None of you did. Of course you are terrified of darkness. It was all you ever had."

He pulled her tight to him, whispering into her hair. "Believe it or not, love, now it is impossible to remember the way the darkness terrified me. As it is impossible to imagine that I will ever think of darkness without thinking of tonight. Without thinking of you."

Felicity turned toward him, her hand coming around his waist, pulling him tight to her as she bent her legs and wrapped herself against his side. The movement, immediate and without artifice, consumed him, and he could not resist mirroring her contortion, bending toward her, wrapping his arm around her, pulling her close. Pressing his face to her neck and inhaling her delicious scent. Jasmine was ruined for him. It would always be tied to this magnificent woman, with her soft skin and her lush body and the hint of it — enough to make his mouth water.

It was only then, as they curled together, as he breathed her in, that he felt her tears, the dampness on her neck, the ragged breath in her lungs. He pulled back and pressed a kiss to the damp tracks on her cheek. "No, sweet girl. No. No tears. I am not worth them."

Her fist clenched at the edge of his waistcoat, pulling the fabric and him closer. "Stop saying that," she whispered. "Stop trying to convince me you lack value."

He lifted her bare hand to his lips, kissing her palm. "I do."

"No. Shut up."

He grazed his teeth over the full flesh at the base of her thumb. "You are a princess compared to me. A fairy queen. Don't you see?" He licked the soft skin there. "My past is without value. My future, too. But yours . . ." His breath was hot against her palm. "Like Janus, I see your future. And it is glorious."

Without me.

She heard the words he did not say. "You're wrong. Your past is who you are — it bears infinite worth. And my future is nothing without you. The only thing that is glorious is our present."

"No, love. Our present . . ." He gave a little huff of laughter. "Our present is torture."

"Why?"

He reached for her, wrapping his fingers around her neck, pulling her close. Holding her still so he could watch her eyes when he told her the truth. "Because my present is only you, Felicity Faircloth. And you cannot be my future."

Her eyes closed at the words, stayed that way for an impossibly long time as her lips twitched with frustration and emotion and her throat worked and her breath came in harsh, angry pants. When she finally, finally opened them, there were tears glistening in their beautiful brown depths. Tears, and anger, and something he recognized because he knew it was mirrored in his own.

Need.

"Then let us live in the present," she whispered.

And she kissed him.

CHAPTER TWENTY-THREE

For the rest of her life, Felicity would remember his warmth. His warmth, and the way he slid a hand into her hair when she kissed him. His warmth, and the way he scattered her hairpins across the roof and pulled her into his lap to afford them both better access to each other and to the caress.

She slid her hands inside his open coat, loving the dark, luxurious heat she found there, the breadth of his chest, the rise and curve of the muscles of his sides and back, the way he allowed her access to him, a low growl of pleasure rolling through him, vibrating against her as he opened his delicious lips and reseated them on her own.

His kiss was slow and deep, as though they had the rest of time to explore. And it seemed, in that long, drugging caress, as though they did — as though that rooftop in Covent Garden, under the moon and stars, was for them alone, as private and perfect as the kiss itself. When he released her lips, she opened her eyes and found his, watching her, seeing her pleasure, taking his own in it. And then, he said, "You never had to be taught to be the flame, Felicity."

And she reached up to pull him down to her again.

"It was always in you," he whispered against her lips, and she sighed her pleasure, letting him capture the sound for a long moment before he added, "You are the most remarkable woman I've ever known, and if I have only this moment — this present — with you, then I wish to make you burn until you've made the stars jealous of your heat."

The words were fire through her, fast and furious, making her head light and her breath shallow as he brushed his lips across her cheek, leaning down to her ear. "Would you do that? Would you burn for me? Tonight?"

"Yes," she replied, a shiver of pleasure sighing through her as he worried the lobe of her ear. "Yes, please."

"So polite," he said, low and delicious. "Shall we go inside? I have barely slept in my bed for the memory of you upon it."

She pulled back and met his eyes, unable to keep surprise and delight from her tone.

"Really?"

He gave her a little smile. "Really. Your hands on my counterpane, your pretty pink slippers dangling from your toes. I imagine —"

"Tell me," she said when he stopped himself.

"I shouldn't."

"Please."

He leaned in with a little groan, stealing a kiss. A lingering lick. "I cannot deny you."

"You deny me all the time."

He shook his head. "Not this. Never this, love." He kissed her again, slow and perfect, and then he put his forehead to hers and said, "I imagine coming to my knees there, at your feet, removing those slippers and exploring my way up your body." His hand traced the line of her leg beneath her skirts. "I am tired of imagining what is under these pink gowns, my lady. And when I lie in bed and chase sleep, I imagine stripping you of your clothes and basking in you, soft and curved and silk and perfection."

She let out a long, trembling breath. "I want that."

"I shall give it to you, my wicked flame. I shall give you whatever you wish."

He stood, reaching down to her, pulling her up to standing, above him on the roof,

461

just high enough that their lips were even. He kissed her again, then whispered, "I shall always give you whatever you wish."

It was a lie, of course, and she knew it.

Tell me something true.

He lifted her in his arms to give her what he promised, but she set a hand to his chest. "Wait."

A gust of wind swirled around them as Devil stilled, whipping his coat behind him and wrapping them both in her skirts. He stilled, unmoving, holding her as though she weighed nothing at all, his eyes on hers as he waited for her to continue. "Anything."

"I don't want to go inside."

He closed his eyes at the words, his grasp tightening around her for a heartbeat before he nodded and said, softly, "I understand. Let's get you home, my lady."

Felicity's heart skipped a beat as he moved to set her down. "No," she whispered. "You don't understand. I don't want to go inside . . ." She ran her fingers over his tightly shorn hair, loving the way it feathered over her skin. "Because I want to stay here." Her fingers toyed at his ear, and she loved the way he dipped his head toward her touch, as though he couldn't resist her. Lord knew she could not resist him. "In your world," she whispered. "In the darkness. Beneath the stars."

He remained still for another moment, the muscle in his cheek the only evidence that he'd heard her. And then he climbed down from the peak, not releasing her until they reached the flat roof below. He set her down and stepped back, shucking his coat and swirling it away, spreading it wide at his feet.

Once that was done, he extended a long, strong arm to her, palm up. An irresistible invitation.

She moved instantly, coming down the tiled roof into his waiting arms, and the next time he lifted her, it was to lie her down on the soft wool of his coat, which enveloped her with his warmth and his scent before he lowered himself down atop her, set his lips to hers, and began to slowly strip her of her sanity. And her clothes.

"That first night, on the balcony at the Marwick ball . . ." He stripped her of her pelisse. "It was too dark to see the color of your gown . . ." He pressed a kiss to the soft skin at her jaw. "And I imagined you were cloaked in moonlight."

Her hands were stroking over his head. "You make me feel like that's possible."

"Anything is possible," he promised, stealing her lips again.

Between long, languid kisses, he untied

the ribbons at the front of her bodice, separating fabric to reveal her corset, her breasts rising above it. He released her lips, his tongue tracing the cords of her neck to nip at her shoulder. She gasped her surprise and pleasure to the stars.

"You like that?" he said softly to her skin.

"Yes," she said, her fingers curling at the back of his head, holding him there.

And then he'd worked magic at her corset, and her breasts spilled into the night, the cool air rushing across her imprisoned skin. Another gasp, this one drawing a little laugh against her shoulder as he moved, stroking and circling the straining tips before he lifted his head, his searing gaze finding hers for an instant before flickering lower. His lips softened as he took her in, and she arched toward him, asking for more of his attention. More of his touch.

More of him.

He gave it, lowering his head, circling one peaked nipple before his lips closed around it and he sucked gently, working the hardened tip until she cried out, her fingers flexing against the perfection of his head, holding him there, as though she might never let him go.

She might not have let him go, not if he hadn't growled through his long, rhythmic sucks. Not if he hadn't slid his hand higher beneath her skirts. Not if she hadn't lifted her hips to meet his touch, rocking against him. Not if the movement hadn't shaken him from his task, caused him to release her from his kiss, panting wildly. "Christ, Felicity. You taste like sin." His hips rocked against her, and an ache pooled in her core — an ache made worse and better by his nearness.

"Devon." She sighed. "I need . . ."

"I know, love." He lifted his weight from her and made quick work of her dress and his waistcoat before returning to her, his hands sliding over her bare skin. "Are you cold?"

She laughed. She couldn't help it. The idea of being cold with him — "No," she said. "I'm burning."

His lips found hers again. "God knows that's true."

She caught his hand in hers, sliding her fingers over his, pulling away when she found the cool metal there. Running a thumb gently over each of the cool silver bands, she said, "Where did these come from?"

He followed her gaze down, surprise on his face, as though he hadn't thought about the rings in years. He smiled. "There was a

465

man in the Garden, used to make them. No one had the money for gold — but silver, a man could buy that. All the fighters wore these rings . . . a show of their might. Of their success in the ring." He pointed to the one on his thumb. "That one is from the first time I broke a nose." To the second on his ring finger. "That one is from the first time I knocked a bloke out." And he pointed to the third, on his forefinger. "That one is from the last bout I ever fought because I had to."

He flexed his hand once, twice, curling his fingers into a heavy fist. "I don't even think about them any longer."

She lifted her hand to her lips, pressing a kiss on each of the silver rings. "Proof of your mettle."

He growled, pulling her to him for a proper kiss then, and she took the opportunity to trace her own hands over his shirt, tugging it from the waistband of his trousers, itching for him. She slid her hands beneath the hem, finding his warm, smooth skin, desperate to be closer to him. Immediately. "Devil."

"I know," he repeated. And he did. He knew her body better than she could dream. He knew the places that ached for his touch, the skin that wanted his kiss. His fingers plucked at the hard tip of one breast as he licked at her neck, once, twice, sending thick arcs of pleasure through her.

She cried into the night, frustrated and eager and desperate for him.

He stilled at the noise, and she opened her eyes. He watched her, something magnificent in his beautiful amber gaze. "The roof was an excellent choice."

Her brow furrowed. "Why?"

He leaned down and sucked the tip of her breast into his mouth, hot and warm and wonderful. And when she was crying her pleasure, he released her, pressing his forehead to hers as he replied, "Because when you scream your pleasure to the night, you can be as loud as you like."

She flushed at the words. "I shan't scream."

He lowered his hips to hers, notching his hard length against the softest part of her. "Perhaps not. Perhaps you'll laugh."

The flush turned to flame. "I didn't mean to laugh . . ."

Devil shook his head. "Don't you dare apologize for that, love. I will die with the sound of that laughter in my ears. The pure pleasure of it. It was glorious." He kissed her again. "All I want to do is summon it again."

She closed her eyes at that, embarrassment and desire warring in her.

Desire won out. "I want you to summon it again." She lifted her hips again, enjoying the hissing curse that came from him at the movement. If it was possible, the hard length of him grew harder. Longer. "But you are wearing legions more clothes than I would like."

He growled his pleasure at that, rolling off her and coming to his feet to remove his shirt, following it with boots and trousers. The movements lacked any artifice, as though he was immensely comfortable with his body — and how could he not be? He was perfection. She could spend hours watching him.

When he stood once more, nude, and turned to return to her, she held out a hand. "Wait."

He stilled, his gaze hungry and hot. "What is it?"

She sat up, pulling his coat around her. "I want to look."

The words changed him. He dipped his head, running a hand over his tightly shorn hair, the movement at once deeply endearing and a striking display of the perfection of his arms and shoulders. Felicity's mouth went dry as his hand wrapped around his neck and slid over his chest, rubbing back and forth before dropping to his side. "Look your fill, then, my lady."

She waved a hand lazily in the air, like a queen, indicating that he should turn, and like a miracle, he did. A smirk on his lips as he returned to his original position. "Have you decided what to do with me?"

The memory of the first night, in her bed-chamber, teased over her. *I've never quite understood what one does with exceedingly perfect men.*

She met his eyes. "I'm still not sure what one does, but I find I'm willing to brazen it through."

He raised a brow. "I'm very happy to hear that."

Dear God. He was splendid — the play of moonlight over his skin, the dusting of hair over his chest. The sculpture of his muscles, ridges at his hips, the delicious curve of his backside, the heavy cords of his thighs. And between them, the straining length of him, hard and beautiful and throbbing. "When I saw you in your bath . . . below . . ." she began, unable to tear her gaze from the hard length of him. "I wanted to look at you . . . It was all I could do not to come to the edge of your bath and see . . ."

"Fuck, Felicity." He groaned.

Her gaze flew to his face at the groaning curse. "What?"

He looked to the sky, letting out a long, beautiful breath. "Forgive me," he said, so softly that it occurred to her that he might not wish her to hear it. And then he looked back to her. "You licked your lips, love."

Her hand flew to her mouth. "I did?"

He grinned, his white teeth flashing, and her first look at his wicked smile was enough to steal her breath. "Don't you dare be ashamed of it. I just — Christ — I just want this to be perfect for you, and when you look at me like that — like you want it . . ." He trailed off as her gaze lowered again, to the straining length of him, and then — dear God — his hand moved, and he was taking himself in hand, caressing that magnificent length, and her mouth was watering and there was only so much a woman in her position could manage.

She stared at his hand, at his slow, languid movements, and swallowed. He was so perfect. "I do want it."

The sound he made — low and dark — sent desire coursing through her, pooling deep in places she had only just discovered. And when he moved, coming toward her, her heart began to pound. "I'm going to make you say that a thousand times before we are through," he growled, coming to his knees beside her, reaching for the coat she'd wrapped around her nudity.

She clutched it tighter.

He tilted his head. "Felicity?"

Her gaze flickered over him again, taking in his raw beauty. "I'm —" She stopped.

Devil waited with infinite patience.

She tried again. "I'm — not like you."

He sat back on his heels, as though he were entirely comfortable. As though he could live his whole life without clothing and never think twice. His gaze softened. "I know that, love. That's a large part of why I'd like to remove this coat."

"I mean —" She swallowed. "I've never been nude before. With a man."

He offered her a little smile, crooked and gorgeous. "I know that, too."

"I'm not — I don't —"

He let go of the fabric. Waited.

"You are perfect," she said. "But I — I am all flaws."

He watched her for a long time. An eternity. Seconds stretched between them like miles. And then, just when she thought it was all over, he said, quiet and certain, "Here is something true, Felicity Faircloth, wallflower, lockpick, and wonder; there isn't a single thing about you that is flawed."

She blushed. And somehow, for a fleeting moment, she believed him.

"Please, love. Let me show you."

As though such an offer could be denied. She dropped the coat. Revealed herself.

He studied her like she was a master's painting, eventually coming to her side and bringing her down so that they lay together, hands and mouths exploring, his hands on her skin, her fingers raking through the dark hair on his chest. His lips seeking out the dimples in her round belly as her legs parted in a slow slide along his straining length.

"Tell me again," he whispered to her stomach, one hand sliding along the soft skin of her inner thigh.

She understood instantly. "I want you." She explored the curves of his muscles, the hills and valleys of his body.

He rewarded the words with another kiss. A suck. A lick. A slide.

And all the time, his hands moved closer to his goal.

Hers, too.

"Where do you want me?"

She squirmed against him, embarrassed by the question, and he nipped at her skin again, a little sting, enough to make her gasp and want him even more. How did he know that? That a delicate bite could seduce as well as a kiss? Before she could ask, he parted the folds beneath her thighs and said, low and delicious, "Here?"

Another gasp. "Yes."

He stroked against her pulsing flesh, soft, then firm, swirling and stroking. "Tell me again. I'll give you everything you want — all you have to do is ask for it."

"I want it," she panted. She rocked against him, aching for more of his touch. "Please. I want —"

His thumb worked a tight circle, setting her ablaze. "Shall I give you the words, love?"

"Yes," she said. "I want every word. All the wicked ones."

He exhaled on another curse. "You are going to destroy me, Felicity Faircloth."

"Not before you give me the words." She sighed, loving that he was as moved as she was.

"You want to come," he said. "You want me to make you come."

Another press, another stroke. And another, and another. "Yes."

"You want my fingers here." He moved, and she cried out as he began to fill her, magnificently, her hands coming to his head, pushing him lower and lower. He growled again. "And wicked girl, you want my mouth, too."

"Yes," she said again. "Yes, I want it."

He gave it to her, setting his tongue to her soft heat, savoring the taste of her as his fingers continued their movement, making love to her with slow, savoring strokes, his free hand lifting one of her legs over his shoulder, opening her to him. She could not stop herself from pressing her hips to him, and did not wish to — crying out that single word again and again, her only purchase her hands in his hair, holding him to her until she found her orgasm, shouting his name to all the world as he worked her with hands and mouth and tongue until all she knew was pleasure.

As she came down from her pleasure, his tongue gentling, his fingers stilling as she pulsed against him, she pulled him up to her, his name hoarse on her lips, eager for more.

Eager for all of it.

He followed her touch, climbing over her, stealing her lips in a long, sweet kiss that stoked fire once more before she pulled back and set her hands to his torso, sliding them down over the ridges and planes of his body to find the part of him that had transfixed her.

When her fingers touched his straining

length, he jerked his hips away from her. "Wait, love."

She opened her eyes. "Please," she whispered. "Please, let me touch you."

He growled and kissed her again. "I don't think I can have that, sweet," he said at her lips. "I don't think I can bear it. I don't want it to be over."

She stilled. It couldn't be over. She wanted the rest.

She wanted all of it.

Every touch, every kiss, every movement that would tie them together.

She nodded, refusing to relinquish his gaze, and smiled.

His eyes flickered to her lips, then back again. "That's a wicked smile, my lady."

"I am your lady," she said softly, her hand moving slightly, just enough to encircle him. To tentatively explore.

He hissed his pleasure. "Yes. Fuck. Yes." And then he reached for that roaming hand and returned it to his chest, a safer place.

"Someday," she said, "you'll let me touch you."

He looked away, then back. The movement was barely there. Less than a second. Less than that. And still, it was enough. Felicity knew the truth. There would be no someday. No tomorrow, no next week, no next year. There wouldn't be another night here, on the roof of his offices, or in his rooms, or in the ice hold at his warehouse. Tonight was it. She'd played her game, and tonight was it.

Tonight was all they'd have.

And tomorrow, he would be gone.

She lifted her hips to him again, loving the way his length stroked through her wet folds, slick and smooth and hot as the sun. Her cry of pleasure was met with his low groan, until he pulled away, lowering himself once again. "You wish to come again, love?"

Where was he going?

"Wait," she said.

His lips, again on her torso. Felicity tried to sit up. "Wait, Devon."

He rubbed the rough shadow of his beard over her skin. "I shall take care of you. Lie back. I intend to taste your pleasure a dozen times tonight. A hundred."

But not the way she wished. Not with his whole self.

"Wait," she repeated, this time lifting her knee, pressing it against him. Pushing him away as she scrambled to sit up. "No."

He stopped instantly at the word, reeling back, his warm hand on her thigh. "What is it?"

"I don't want that."

His thumb stroked at the warm, soft skin of her thigh, and her breath caught in her chest, followed by a flood of warmth when he said, low and dark, "You don't?"

Of course she did. My God, the man was magnificent. "I mean, I don't want it alone. I want it with you. I want us . . ." She hesitated. And then, into the breach. "Together."

He released her, instantly. "No."

"Why?"

"Because if I touch you like —" He stopped and looked away, to the buildings in the distance, dark against the starry sky. And then back to her. "Felicity . . . if I fuck you . . . you're ruined."

The coarse language was meant to scare her. It only made her want him more. "You told me you would give me what I want. I want that. I want tonight. With you. All of it. All of you."

"Not that. I shall give you everything but that." He looked hunted.

"Why?"

"Felicity." He began to rise. "I am not for you."

She came up on her knees, following him. "Why not?"

"Because I was born in God knows where, and was reborn here, in the Covent Garden filth. I am soiled beyond repair. And I am so far beneath you that I have to strain to look at you."

"You're wrong," she said, reaching for him, not knowing what else to do. He pulled away. "You're wrong."

"I assure you — I am not. The things I have done . . ." He paused, running a hand over his head. "The things I will do . . ." He backed away from her. "No, Felicity. We are through. Get dressed, and I will bring you home."

"Devil," she said, knowing that if she left that rooftop, she'd lose him forever. "Please. I want you. I . . ." Another hesitation. And then, the only words she could find. "I love you."

His eyes went wide, and the hand at his side moved. Reaching for her? Please, let it be reaching for her. "Felicity . . ." Her name was ragged on his lips. "No . . ."

She resisted the tears that threatened. Of course he did not love her back. He was not the kind of man who would love her. And still, she could not stop herself from adding, "You are all I wish for. You. This. Whatever is to come."

He shook his head. "You think London will have you back if you tie yourself to me? You think you'll resume your place in

Mayfair ballrooms? Have tea with the queen or whatever it is you people do?"

"I don't want to have tea with the queen, you idiot man," she replied, letting her frustration take hold. "I am tired of having my life chosen for me. My family decides where I go, what I do, whom I should marry. The aristocracy tells me where I belong in a ballroom, what I can hope for as a woman, where the limitations are for my desires.

"Don't ask too much, they caution. *You are too old, too plain, too strange, too imperfect.* I shouldn't want more than what I should be grateful to receive — the scraps of the rest of the world."

He reached for her then, but she was busy with her rage. "I am not too old."

He shook his head. "You are not."

"I am not too plain."

"You are nothing close to plain."

"And we are all imperfect."

"Not you."

Then why won't you have me?

She hugged her knees to her chest and confessed her sin. "I don't want to save them."

"Your family."

She nodded. "I am their last hope. And I should want to sacrifice everything for them. For their future. But I don't. I resent it."

"You should resent it," he said.

"They care nothing about me," she whispered to her knees. "They love me, I suppose, and they tolerate me, and they would miss me if I were gone, but I'm not sure they would notice for quite a while, honestly — my mother hasn't noticed I've taken to spending my evenings in Covent Garden, and Arthur's so worried about his own marriage, he hasn't time to think for a second about mine. And my father . . ." She trailed off. "He's barely a character in this play. He's deus ex machina, popping in at the end to sign the papers and take the money."

She looked up at Devil. "I don't want that."

"I know."

"I never wanted to win the duke. Not really."

"You wanted more than that."

"Yes," she whispered.

"You wanted the marriage, the man, the love, the passion, the life, the wide world."

She considered the words — perfectly encapsulating what she wanted. But not Mayfair. No longer Mayfair. Here. Now. Covent Garden. With its king.

More than she could have. Always more.

"Shall I tell you something true?"

He exhaled on a long, harsh breath, her name in it like a prayer. "No."

"Well, I'm going to, considering I've already told you the worst of it," she said, unable to stop the words from coming. "I hate tea. I want to drink bourbon. The kind you won't admit to smuggling in from America with all that ice. I want to make love to you in your ice hold and bathe in your enormous bathtub. While you watch. I want to wear trousers like Nik and learn every inch of Covent Garden. I want to stand by your side here on the roof and there in the street below, and I want you to teach me to wield a cane sword as well as I wield a lockpick." She paused, enjoying the dumbfounded look on his face nearly as much as she hated it. "But more than all that . . . I want you."

"This world is all sin, Felicity, and I am the worst of it."

She shook her head. "No. This world is locked away. You are locked away. Like something precious." She met his gaze. Held it. "And I want in. Tonight." *Always.*

"There is no way this ends without your ruin."

"I am already ruined."

He shook his head. "Not in any way that

matters."

She thought that was rather a semantic argument. And then, like a promise, memory surged. Wild and mad, just as she was when she grasped it. "I'll never win the duke, you know. The banns are posted, yes, but even if I were to marry him, I wouldn't win him. I don't want him. And he doesn't want me. Not with passion. Not with purpose."

"It's not important to him," Devil said. "He doesn't know about passion."

"But you do," she replied.

He cursed in the darkness. "Yes, dammit. Yes, I know about passion. It's consuming me here, tonight, naked on a roof in Covent Garden where anyone could stumble upon us."

She smiled at the words, pride and love rioting through her. This magnificent man. She reached for him, and he let her, let her touch his thigh, let her come closer, even when she softened her words and said, "And if someone were to stumble upon us?"

"I'd have to kill them for seeing you naked."

She nodded. Dear Lord. She would never love anything the way she loved him. "Devil . . ." she whispered, her hand sliding up his bare chest, flirting with the skin there.

He caught it in his own. "Felicity . . ." She hated the resignation in his tone.

"We made a deal all those nights ago," she said, leaning in, pressing a kiss to the corner of his full, beautiful lips. "I was promised slavering."

He saw where she was going. Shook his head. "Felicity —"

"No. That was the deal. You wouldn't renege, would you?"

He considered it. She watched the battle wage on his beautiful face, his scar gone stark white on his cheek as he fixed his gaze over her shoulder on a faraway rooftop. She took the opportunity to lean in and press a soft kiss to his cheek.

"Devil," she whispered at his ear, loving the shudder that went through him at the word. "By the details of our arrangement, you still owe me a boon."

His hands settled on her. His arm encircled her. Pulled her close. "Yes."

"That's a marvelous word."

He laughed at her ear, low and graveled and without humor, his hands. "Indeed, it is."

"My boon, then?"

Pleasure washed over her as he stroked the bare skin of her back. "Ask."

She put her lips to his ear. "I want to-night."

Before the words had disappeared, Devil was turning her, laying her down again, looming over her, cradling her face in his strong hands and ravishing her with his kiss — long and lush, making her body sing — her breasts, her thighs, that soft place between them that he'd loved so well and still ached for him.

Felicity lifted her thighs and rocked against him, and he tore his mouth from hers with a hiss, throwing his head back to reveal the long cords of his neck. When he looked down at her again, his beautiful amber eyes were filled with desire and something close to pain. "One night," he said. "One night and then you leave me. One night and you take your place in the world where you belong."

As though one night would ever be enough. "Yes," she lied.

"I shall make it right," he whispered. "I shall keep you safe."

She nodded. "That's what you do." This beautiful man, who had spent a lifetime as a protector.

He met her gaze. "You'll have it all."

Not you, though.

She pushed the thought from her head,

reaching for him. "Please." She lifted her hips to him. "Don't stop."

He exhaled on a breathless laugh, leaning down to suck on the tip of one breast until it was hard and straining. "I have no intention of stopping, my greedy girl." His fingers found their way to her core, stroking and lingering, stretching and petting, her breath coming faster and faster, pleasure coursing through her. She strained to keep his hand against her, even as his touch gentled.

"More," she said. "I want it all."

"I do, too," he whispered, putting his forehead to hers and kissing her once again. "God, I am going to love being inside you when you come."

"Yes." She kissed him. "Please."

"So greedy."

She nodded. "Wanton."

He huffed a little, strained laugh. "You shouldn't know that word."

"You have taught me worse," she said.

"That's true," he replied, the words sounding strangled as he rocked against her.

"You can't have them back," she said, spreading her thighs wide to accommodate him as the tip of him settled at the opening of her, hot and smooth and, "Oh . . ."

"Mmm," he said harshly. "Oh . . ."

And then he was sliding into her with

485

perfect control, slow and smooth, and it occurred to her that the sensation might make her mad. He was so hard, and so full, stretching her beyond anything she could have imagined, not pain or pleasure but some unbearable, glorious combination of the two. No. Pleasure. So much pleasure. She gasped.

He froze. "Felicity? Talk to me."

She shook her head.

"Love . . ." He kissed her gently. "Sweetheart, say something."

Her eyes flew to his. "Oh . . ."

"Something more than *oh*, love. I don't want to hurt you."

She flexed against the full shape of him, and he sank deeper into her channel. He groaned, his eyes sliding closed.

"Oh, my . . ." she said.

He laughed again, hoarse and perfect. "Sweetheart, if you don't say something other than some variation on *oh*, I'm going to stop."

Her eyes flew open. "Don't you dare."

His brows rose. "Well. That's something other than *oh*."

She reached for his shoulders, smoothing her hands over his muscles, each one more tense than the last. "You wish more words?"

"I need them," he said softly. "I need to

know it's good for you."

She smiled at that, and then leaned up and stole his mouth for a lingering kiss. When it was over, she curled her hand behind his neck, looked into his eyes, and said, "I want it all."

And he began — blessedly — to move. Long, slow strokes sent pleasure curling through her, again and again.

"Tell me how it feels, love."

She wanted to, but it was impossible — she'd lost her words again. He'd stolen them with his kiss and his touch and the delicious length of him, stroking, guiding, pleasuring her. His movements were slow and delicious, enough to chase away the last hints of pain that had lingered, leaving only sighs and gasps and a perfect rhythm — one she was happy to match.

And when she did, he opened his eyes, meeting her gaze, and she lost her words again at the pure, unadulterated desire in them. She reached for him, running her fingers along his jaw, where his scar ran jagged and white. "You want it all, too."

"Yes . . ." He hissed his pleasure. "Fuck, yes, I want it all."

And then his hips rolled beautifully and she cried out as he knocked against a magnificent place. He stilled, raising a brow.

"There?" He repeated the movement.

She clasped his shoulders. "Yes."

Again.

"Please."

Again.

"Devil," she gasped.

"Tell me again," he growled, driving her higher and higher. "Give me the words again."

Her eyes flew open to find his on hers. "I love you," she whispered as he thrust into her.

"Yes."

"I love you." She clung to him, the words a prayer. A litany. "I love you."

"Yes." He held her gaze through it all, whispering that single, beautiful word, again and again, as he gave her everything she'd ever wanted. Everything she'd ever dreamed. As she whispered her love and they careened toward pleasure, hard and fast and perfect, like truth. And when pleasure coursed through her like a wave, he captured first her cries and then her laugh with his kiss. And only then, the sound of her riotous pleasure in his ears, did he find his own release, deep and powerful, her name on his lips.

Minutes later, hours, perhaps, they lay in silence beneath the stars in the stunning wake of what they'd done. Devil had reversed their position, draping Felicity across his chest, where her head lay and her fingers danced circles on his skin.

He held her tight against him, his arms and coat keeping her warm, his fingers sifting through her hair in a delicious, rhythmic caress, and for that brief eternity, she imagined that the night had changed him as much as it had changed her.

She closed her eyes, the steady beat of his heart against her thoughts — the quiet, domestic fantasy that ended with his taking her hand in his and pledging himself to her, forever. She inhaled, overcome with the scent of him, tobacco flower and juniper and sin, and she imagined that, forever, any hint of it would summon the false memories she wove in his arms.

A Covent Garden wedding, a raucous celebration filled with wine and song, and a night to follow on this very roof — a repeat of tonight, but better, because it would not end with him leaving her.

It would end with a life together. A marriage. A partnership. A line of children with beautiful amber eyes and strong shoulders and long, straight noses. Children who would learn that the world was wide and good, and the aristocracy was nothing compared to the hardworking men and women who built the city in which they lived and made it better every day.

Men like their father. Women like the one she hoped to become by his side.

She closed her eyes and imagined those children. Wanted them. Loved them, already.

Just as she loved their father.

"Felicity." He said her name, low and perfect, and she lifted her head to meet his gaze. "Dawn approaches."

Dawn, ready to burn away the dark and with it, those precious, unmade memories.

Don't send me back. Keep me here. I belong here.

She didn't say the words, but he seemed to hear them anyway. He exhaled, the sound broken. "You deserved more than this," he said. "You deserved a wedding night. With a man ten times what I am. With a man who can give you *ton* and title, name and fortune, a Mayfair townhouse and a country estate that's been in the family for generations."

Anger flared. "You're wrong."

"I'm not."

"I don't want those things."

He watched her for an age. "Tell me again why you were crying in that bedchamber, the day you picked the lock. The day your friends turned their backs on you. Tell me again what you mourned."

Hot embarrassment flared. "It's not the same," she protested. "*I'm* not the same. I don't care about Mayfair and balls."

"If I believed that . . ." He looked away, back to the stars. "I'd crawl to you without hesitation, but if I did, you would never have that life. Nor the acceptance."

"Would you love me?" she whispered, the sound barely there, barely different than the wind rustling over the tiles on the rooftop. The sound of skin brushing against skin. The sound of their breath mingled.

The sound of hope.

He exhaled, long and jagged. And then he told her something true. "Not enough."

And there, under the stars in this place she had come to love, Felicity resolved to prove him wrong.

CHAPTER TWENTY-FOUR

Everything had changed, Felicity realized, as she alighted from her family's carriage the next evening, her mother following immediately behind, her rich pink satin skirts swirling around her.

A year ago, a month ago, two weeks ago, Felicity had longed for this exact moment. It was mid-June and summer had arrived, all of London preparing to pack up and leave for the country, but the best of the city's gossips wouldn't dream of leaving before this particular ball — the Duchess of Northumberland's summer herald, the most glamorous ball of the season.

A year ago, a month ago, two weeks ago, Felicity couldn't have imagined a more desirable event than this one, climbing the steps to Northumberland House, the manor windows glittering with candlelight, her mother fairly vibrating her pleasure at Felicity's elbow, the handful of guests assembled outside and clustered around the door acknowledging her without hesitation.

Welcoming her.

Claiming her.

Except everything had changed.

And not simply the fact that she was no longer odd, wallflower, spinster Felicity.

Nor that she was, to all assembled, the future Duchess of Marwick.

Oh, that was certainly why the aristocracy believed everything had changed. But Felicity knew better. She knew that what had changed, summarily and irrevocably, was that she had fallen in love with the world beyond this, and with the man who had revealed it to her. And that truth betrayed another: This world she had once cared so much about was nothing in comparison to his. To *him.*

Which he did not believe, and so, without recourse, Felicity had come to this place, filled with these people, to prove it to him.

The knowledge straightened her spine and squared her shoulders. It kept her chin high, as she was suddenly unwilling to allow this place — these people — to hold dominion over her. There was only one person who held her in his sway. And only one hope of winning him.

Which meant she had to find her fiancé.

"Your engagement has already made the world take notice!" the marchioness said excitedly as they stepped into the great Northumberland foyer, throngs of people surrounding them. She looked to the main staircase, filled with revelers, and gave a little squeak. "We weren't invited last year; we weren't welcome. Because of — well, you know."

Felicity slowed and looked to her mother. "I don't, as a matter of fact."

The marchioness looked to her and lowered her voice. "Because of your scandal."

"You mean the scandal of my being trotted off to the Duke of Haven's marriage mart?"

Her mother shook her head. "Not only that."

"The scandal of my aging spinsterhood?"

"That might have been a bit of it, as well."

"Is it more or less a bit of it than my being exiled from the inner circle of the jewels of the *ton*?"

"Really, Felicity." Her mother looked about with a too loud laugh, clearly afraid that someone might overhear them.

Felicity was less interested in that eventuality. "I would have thought that the scandal that eliminated our names from the guest list was Father and Arthur losing all the family's money."

Her mother's eyes went wide. "Felicity!"

Felicity pressed her lips together, knowing now was neither the place, nor the time, but not particularly caring. Turning, she made her way up the stairs, toward the great ballroom. "It's no matter, Mother. After all, we're here tonight."

"Yes," the marchioness said. "That's the important bit. As is the duke. And we shall be here next year. And all the years after."

I shan't be.

"Even your father plans to make an appearance tonight."

Of course her father would, now that he felt he could show his face with the family coffers nearly filled once more.

Felicity focused on the top of the stairs. "I must find the duke."

She had not made it ten paces when a voice called out from somewhere above, "Felicity!"

The voice was familiar enough that she hesitated in her movement, turning instantly to meet Natasha Corkwood's bright eyes, glittering with interest as she waved from the top of the stairs, bobbing and weaving to keep contact with Felicity. She turned to say something to her companion, and Jared, Lord Faulk, looked over his shoulder to follow her gaze, recognition and something else flaring in his eyes. Something predatory.

Felicity looked away immediately, redoubling her movements up the stairs.

When she reached the top, Natasha called out again, closer than Felicity would like. "Felicity!"

"Darling, we should stop. Lady Natasha and Lord Faulk are your friends." As simple as that, her mother swept the past away, as though eighteen months of shame and sadness and confusion was nothing.

Friendship is not always what we think.

Devil's words echoed through her, tempting her to turn her back and leave them there, in front of every Londoner whose good opinion they courted. Instead, she turned to face them.

"Felicity!" Natasha said, breathless, face full of a false smile. "We've been waiting for you!" Her hand settled on Felicity's arm.

Felicity's gaze settled on the offending touch for long enough that Natasha removed it, at which point Felicity looked up and said, "Why?"

Color washed over Tasha's cheeks and she blinked, a little nervous laugh accompanying her surprise. "Why — because we have missed you!" Her eyes flickered to her brother. "Haven't we, Jared?"

Lord Faulk grinned, revealing large teeth, nearly too big for his mouth. "Of course."

As though the past had never happened. As though they'd had a vague disagreement after too much champagne instead of the lot of them pretending that Felicity did not exist for eighteen months. As though they were still her people.

As though she ever wanted them to be again.

Unfortunates.

Devil's word again, low and dark, whispering in her ear, its memory bringing her strength.

"Your gown is *stunning.*" Natasha was still talking, and Felicity's hands moved of their own volition to her skirts, full and fuchsia, as pink as pink came. The gown had arrived that morning from the dressmaker Madame Hebert — along with a little note from the Frenchwoman, thanking Felicity for her business with *once and future dukes . . . and any others who might happen along and enjoy you in pink.*

And it was stunning, lavish beyond anything she'd ever worn before, with a low-cut neckline revealing a wide expanse of shoulders, along with magnificent pink skirts shot through with deep eggplant silk thread, the whole thing giving the gown the look of sunset.

Or better, the Devon sky at sunset.

She wished Devil could see it.

Devil would see it, of course. The moment she finished with the duke, whom she could not find in the crush of people. The thought set her heart pounding, and Felicity went looking for her fiancé, pressing further into the ballroom.

"Thank you, Natasha — you always look so beautifully turned out, as well," the marchioness offered at the edge of her attention, filling the silence when Felicity did not.

Tasha dipped into a curtsy. "Thank you, my lady. And my congratulations to you as well — on your soon-to-be son-in-law!"

The marchioness tittered.

Natasha tittered.

Jared grinned.

Felicity looked from one face to the next and said, "Am I mad, or are you attempting to befriend me once more?"

Color rose high on Natasha's cheeks. "I beg your pardon?"

"Felicity!" her mother interjected.

"I'm quite serious, Natasha. It seems as though you would like to pretend that we never fell out. That you never *exited* me from your group — isn't that what you called it?"

Natasha's mouth opened and then closed.

Felicity ignored her former friend, remarkably uninterested in her — for the first time in possibly ever. She searched the sea of revelers headed for the ballroom. Freedom. Without farewell, she said, "I must find the duke."

"Oh, of course she must," the marchioness said overexcitedly, for some reason all too eager to keep their hangers-on hanging on. Sotto voce, she added, "Engaged couples wish to be in each other's company as much as possible, you must know."

"Oh, of *course,*" Natasha fawned for the benefit of all assembled. "We're still *so* impressed you managed to land him! After all, Felicity isn't exactly the kind of wife a *duke* comes for."

"I didn't land him," Felicity said absently, pressing forward.

Natasha took on the look of a wild barn cat, mouse in sight. "You *didn't?*"

Silence followed, then her mother's too loud laughter. "Oh, Felicity! What a jest. Of course, the banns have been read! There was an announcement in the *News!*"

"I suppose so. Well, either way, I would not take such interest in it, Tasha . . ."

499

Felicity said, turning a cool gaze on the other woman, "as even if I did land him, you'd never be welcome in our home, anyway."

Tasha's mouth fell open at the words, and Felicity's mother gasped her horror at Felicity's rudeness. Blessedly, Felicity was saved from having to continue by the discovery of her fiancé, a blond head taller than anyone else in the ballroom, on the other side of the mad crush. The moment she saw him, her heart began to pound. She broke away from her unwelcome companions, weaving through the crowd to get to him.

To get free of him.

He was alone when she reached him, stick-straight and staring aimlessly at the crowd. She placed herself directly in front of him. "Hello, Your Grace."

His gaze flickered to her, then back to the ball. "I asked you not to call me that." He paused. "Who is that woman?"

She looked over her shoulder to find Natasha simpering nearby, playing the wide-eyed victim.

"Lady Natasha Corkwood."

"What did you say to her?"

"I told her she'd never be welcome in our home."

He met her eyes. "Why not?"

"Because she hurt me. And I find I'm through with being hurt."

He shrugged. "Fair enough."

"Not that it matters, as we shan't share a home."

"No," he agreed. "But it's a fine figure of speech, and I'm sure it helped get your point across."

She took a deep breath. "That's not what I meant, though."

He looked to her, and she saw understanding in his gaze. Understanding and something else. Something like . . . respect? "What is it?"

It seemed fitting that an engagement begun in front of all the world ended in front of it. At least Felicity was ending it to the duke's face, instead of to a collection of maddening gossips. "I'm afraid I cannot marry you."

That got his attention. He watched her for a long moment, and then said, "May I ask why?"

Half the world was watching, and Felicity found she did not care. But surely the duke cared. "Would you like to find a place where we might . . . talk?"

"Not particularly," he said.

That gave her pause. "Your Gr—" She stopped. "Duke."

"Tell me why."

"All right," she said, her heart pounding. "Because I love another. Because I think he could love me. All I have to do is convince him that I want him more than I want this world."

He met her eyes. "I don't imagine your father will be thrilled with your decision."

She shook her head. "I don't imagine so. I was something of a last hope for him."

"For your brother, as well," he pointed out. "They were more than happy to take my money."

"In exchange for a loveless marriage," she said. She shook her head. "I don't wish that."

"And what do you know of love?" he asked, the words a quiet scoff.

I would walk through fire for him. Whit had used the words in the warehouse the other night, explaining the loyalty of Devil's employees. She understood it now. She loved him. She looked to the duke. "Enough to know that I want it more than I want the rest."

He smirked at that.

"And you should, too," she added. When he did not reply, she added her plea, tentatively, "I wonder if I might convince you to invest with my brother in some way? He's

502

very knowledgeable in business, despite —"

He cut her off. "Tell me what it looks like."

She hesitated. He was asking about . . . love? "It's impossible to describe."

"Try."

She looked away, her gaze settling on a dancing couple, the woman in a beautiful sapphire gown. They were mid-turn, her back in a perfect arch over his strong arm, her skirts flaring out behind her. She stared up at him, smiling, and he, down at her, rapt, and in that moment, they were perfect enough to steal breath. Not because of her dress or his coat or how they moved or the fact that when they stopped that turn, her skirts would swirl around them both, and he would feel their heavy weight on his legs, and wish for a lifetime of the sensation.

Sadness and desire and resolve warred within her when Felicity returned her attention to the duke. "You find your match. You find your match, and you let them love you."

"It is not that easy." The words were gruff.

"Well," she said. "You could start by looking for her."

"I've been looking for her for twelve years. For longer. For as long as I can remember." The words were impossible to misunderstand. The duke was not speaking of a nameless, faceless woman with whom he might live out the rest of his days. He was looking for someone specific.

She nodded. "She is worth the wait, then. And when you do find her, you will be happy for this moment."

"When I find her, I shall be the most unhappy I have ever been."

A vision flashed. Of Devil, the night before, telling her he could never love her enough. Of his seeing her home as light began to streak across the sky. Of the soft kiss he gave her in the gardens, before she sneaked through the door to the kitchens. Of how it felt like farewell. Of the tears that had come, unbidden and unwelcome but there, nonetheless, until she'd decided that she was through having the world manipulate her, and that it was her time to manipulate the world.

"Would you like to dance, Lady Felicity?"

Her brow furrowed. "What?"

"We are at a ball, are we not? It's not an unimaginable eventuality."

She didn't wish to dance.

He went on. "That, and all of London is watching, and you are not the least emotive person I have ever met."

It wasn't all of London, though. It was a tiny fraction of London, and one she was finding less and less tolerable. Nevertheless, she let him lead her to the center of the ballroom and collect her in his arms. They danced for several long minutes in silence, before he said, "So you think my brother in love with you."

Felicity pulled back at that, or as far away as she could while dancing. She certainly had misheard. He clearly hadn't said — "I — I beg your pardon?"

"There's no need for you to play the fool, my lady," he said. "He's been after you from the start, has he not? From the night you announced our engagement to the world?" She missed a step at the words, and his arms tightened around her, lifting her off the ground for a heartbeat as she regained her footing.

Confusion flared, her gaze flying to his. He couldn't be speaking of Devil.

Devil, whose eyes were that same, beautiful amber color as the duke's — which she should have noticed earlier. Which she would have noticed earlier if Devil's weren't so full of heat, and these weren't so cold.

Realization dawned.

Dear God.

Devil's father had been the Duke of Marwick.

Which made the man with her — "Ewan."

To an outside observer, the name appeared to have no impact on him. But Felicity was in his arms, scant inches from him, and she saw the way it struck him as clearly as if she'd clenched a fist and sent it right into his jaw. Every inch of him tightened. His jaw clenched. His breath stilled in his chest. His hand went to stone in hers, and his arm became steel at her back. And then he looked at her, his eyes full of truth and something she should have been afraid of.

But Felicity was not afraid. She was confused and shocked, and half a dozen other emotions, but she could not find room for fear, as she was too full of fury. Because if she was right and this man was Ewan, the third brother, kidnapped to the country to vie for a title in some kind of monstrous game, then he was the winner of the game. And instead of keeping his brothers close and caring for them as they should have been cared for — as they *deserved* to be cared for — he'd left them to scrape and fight in the streets, never knowing where they would find their next kindness. Never knowing where they would find kindness, at all.

And for that alone she loathed him.

"He told you about me," he said. Surprise in the words. Something close to awe.

She vibrated with anger. She made to stop the dance. He refused to allow it. She pressed back against his arm with all her strength. "Let me go."

"Not yet."

"You hurt him."

"I hurt a lot of people."

"You took a blade to his face."

"I assure you, I didn't have a choice."

"No. Clearly this world was worth more than your *brother*." She shook her head. "You were wrong. I'd choose him over this place any day. I choose him now. Over you."

The duke's eyes flashed. "You won't believe me, but it had nothing to do with this world."

"No, I'm sure not," she scoffed. "Not the title or the houses or the money."

"Believe what you like, Lady Felicity, but it is true. He was a means to an end." The words weren't cruel. They were honest.

Her brow furrowed. "What kind of end would require such means?" She loathed this man. "You should be thrashed for what you did to him. He was a boy."

"So was I." He paused. Then, casually, "If only you'd been with us then, Lady Felicity. Maybe you could have saved him. Maybe you could have saved us all."

"He does not need saving," she said,

softly. "He is magnificent. Strong and brave and honorable."

"Is he?"

Something about the question unsettled, as though the duke were a chess master, and he could see her inevitable end. She pushed against him again, wanting away from this man turned monster. "I thought you were odd. You're not. You're horrible."

"I am. As is he."

She shook her head. "No."

His response was instant, filled with darkness. "He is not without sin, my lady. Aren't you curious as to how you came to know him? As to how he came to have an interest in you?"

She shook her head, thinking back. "It was by chance. I lied — about our engagement — he overheard."

He did laugh then, the sound sending cold through her. "In our lifetime, nothing has ever happened to us by chance. And now you are a part of us, Felicity Faircloth. Now you are tied to us. And nothing will ever happen to you by chance again. Not engagements. Not the breaking of them. Not golden ballgowns or spies in hedgerows. Even the birds you hear sing to you in the nighttime do not warble by chance."

Felicity went cold and the room spun with

revelation — that this man, this odious, horrid man, was inexorably tied to Devil. That he'd been so for years and, worse, that he knew the extent of her interactions with him. That he'd used her in spite of them. That he'd used her *because* of them, manipulating her without effort.

"You were using me to get to him."

"I was. Though, to be fair, I did not set out to use you, specifically. That bit *was* chance, as a matter of fact." He turned her, moving her through the room, and to an outside observer, they must have looked riveted to each other — a perfect match. No one could see the way she pushed against him, wishing to be far from him and whatever it was he was about to say.

"I have searched for them for twelve years, did you know that? To no avail. I'd a line on a pair of brothers in Covent Garden. Ice dealers. Possibly smugglers. But they ran the streets, paid well for loyalty, and were well protected. I had no choice but to try a new tack. I came to town, broadcasting the news of my search for a bride."

Understanding dawned. "To summon them from shadows."

He inclined his head, surprise in his eyes. "Precisely. They might hide from me, but they would never stay quiet if they thought

I was to renege on our only deal." His gaze fixed on a point beyond her shoulder.

"No heirs."

More surprise. "He told you that, as well?"

"He never intended for you and I to marry," she whispered.

The duke barked a laugh, and those around them turned at the unexpected sound. He didn't care. "Of course he didn't. We were cut from the same cloth, my lady. You proved very useful to me . . . and exceedingly useful to him, as well."

"How?"

"You were a message. I am not allowed happiness. I am not allowed a future. As though those things were ever in my cards."

Her gaze went to his, her heart pounding in her ears alongside the cacophony of the room. "I don't understand. You didn't want me. I wasn't going to bring you happiness."

"No. But you might have brought me heirs. And those, he would not have allowed. That was the only punishment we could give our father. No heirs. The line ends with me, you see. And I know my brother well enough to know Devon would make certain of it."

We would mete out endless punishment.

And Felicity was the weapon he'd chosen.

The weapon, it seemed, they had both chosen.

And then he added, "And the promise of you would deliver Devon to me."

She slowed to a stop and the duke allowed it, her skirts swirling around her, even as the rest of the assemblage continued dancing. Heads turned toward them, whispers already beginning. Felicity didn't care. "I'll give him his due; he did his work well." He paused. "I'm guessing he's already had you. I'm guessing he expected you to come here tonight and end our arrangement. Which of course you did, because you fancy yourself in love with him. Because you fancy yourself able to convince him that he loves you, as well."

The room whirled around them, the realization that Devil had betrayed her coming hard and fast and making her want to simultaneously cast up her accounts and do physical harm to the arrogant man before her. And then he added in a tone absent of emotion, "Poor girl. You should have known better. Devon cannot love. It's not in him. He, like all of us, and like our father before us, can do nothing but ruin. I hope yours was at least enjoyable."

The words threatened to break her. To return her to Forlorn Felicity. Finished

Felicity. But she would not allow that. She came to her full height, her shoulders straight and her chin proud, refusing to acknowledge the tears that threatened. She would not have tears. There was no time for them.

Instead, she took a step back, putting distance between them, and the nearest couples slowed, craning their necks to see. They did not have to crane when she let her hand fly, nor did they have to strain to hear the wicked crack of her palm against his cheek.

He took the blow without a word, and the entire room felt its ripple.

CHAPTER TWENTY-FIVE

Devil spent hours that evening in the muck of the Thames, working the hook, the best way for him to keep his mind off what he'd done. He'd hauled and lifted until his muscles were raw, until his clothes were drenched with sweat and it felt as though the skin from his shoulders had been flayed. Only then did he find it in him to return home, aching and stinking and tired enough to have a promise of a bath and sleep before he woke, hard and hot and reaching for the one thing he could not have.

Christ. It had been barely a day and he missed her like air.

He cursed and unlocked the door to his offices, the building heavy with silence.

Letting exhaustion come, he climbed the stairs and extended a key into the lock, only to discover that no key was necessary. Someone had unlocked the door to his chamber and, while there were half a dozen plausible possibilities, there was only one person he wished it to be, even as he wished for it to be anyone but her.

He pushed the door open, the hinge groaning beneath the slow movement.

Felicity was standing at the center of his offices, in the most beautiful pink gown he'd ever seen — the kind of gown any man would kill to remove — still and straight and serene, her eyes instantly on his, as though she'd been standing there forever, waiting for him. As though she *would* stand there forever, until he returned.

Past and future and glorious, impossible present.

He entered, closing the door behind him, steeling himself for what was to come. Summoning the strength to send her packing again. "I would ask you how you got into the building, but I don't think I would like the answer." He lifted his chin at her dress, unable to stop himself from pointing out the finery. "Covent Garden has never seen a frock such as that, my lady."

She did not look down at it. "I came from the Northumberland ball."

He whistled, long and low. "Did you give the nobs my regards?"

"I did not, as a matter of fact," she said. "I was too busy ending my engagement."

The words rioted through him. He moved toward her without thought. False. There was a single thought. *Yes.* Yes, she was free, and could finally, finally, be his.

Except she couldn't. "Why?"

"Because I did not wish to marry the duke, or anyone else in the aristocracy."

Marry me.

She went on. "Because I thought that if I did it there — if I ended my engagement publicly, in front of all the *ton* — then you would see that I was willing to turn my back on that world and join you here, in this place."

His heart began to pound.

"You see, after that . . . after striking the duke in public —"

"You hit him?" He reached for her. "Did he —"

She recoiled from his touch and he stilled, dread and something else settling, instantly, in his gut. *Fear.* "I did, as a matter of fact. At the center of a ballroom in the seat of one of the most powerful dukedoms in history. I'm well and truly ruined now."

He didn't care about ruination. He cared about *her.* "Why did you hit him? Did he hurt you?"

She laughed, the sound bitter. "Did he hurt me? No."

"Then why —"

"I suppose some might be hurt by discovering they'd been betrayed by the man they are to marry . . ." She watched him for a long moment, unspeaking. "But I was never to marry him, was I? Not from the beginning?"

The question settled between them like ice.

"Was I, Devil?"

He pressed his lips together, suddenly off-kilter; the ground was shifting beneath his feet. "No."

"Interestingly, he had no intention of marrying me, either, so for once, you and your brother were not at odds." Blood rushed in Devil's ears.

Brother. She knew.

"How did you know?"

A beat. And then, "I know because you are the same."

No. "We are nothing like the same."

Her gaze narrowed on him. "Bollocks. You are more alike than you can imagine." She didn't know how the words would sting. How they would rage in him. How they would whisper truth.

"Neither of you thought twice before using me. Him, to summon you from the darkness, to find you after twelve years of looking. But here is the truth of it . . ." She paused, and he knew the blow was coming. Knew, too, that he could not escape it. "I don't care about him. I didn't trust him. I didn't bare myself and worse — my heart — to him. And so, while his past sins are no doubt monstrous . . . while he more than deserved the blow I delivered . . . while I wish him ill beyond measure . . . his sin is nothing in comparison to yours."

She turned away from him then, rounding his desk and going to the window at the far side of the room, the sound of her skirts brushing against the carpet like gunfire. He hated watching her leave him. Hated the way the air seemed to cool with every one of her steps, as though he might be left cold and frozen without her.

And he would be.

She stilled at the window, lifting a hand to a mottled pane of glass, small and barely transparent. It wasn't worth filling Covent Garden windows with decent glass, and watching Felicity dressed like a queen and running her fingers down the windowpane only underscored everything Devil knew to be true. He could not have her.

Her discovery tonight was for the best.

She was not for him.

"Do you love me?" The question, so

517

forthright, came like a blow. "I ask because two nights ago on the roof of this very building, you told me you could not love me enough to marry me. And I thought it was a shield you'd thrown up to protect yourself from your silly belief that I wanted that world instead of this one."

It had been. Christ. He should have told her then, when he had the chance.

Except they'd still be here. And it would hurt all the more.

As though it could hurt more.

"So I ask you now, tonight, do you love me at all?"

He would not survive this. "Felicity."

He moved toward her, coming around the desk, but she did not look at him. She remained at the window, looking out at the distorted Covent Garden rooftops, all he could give her. "I begged you to love me. I begged you to believe I was enough for you. That I was enough for this place."

You are. You always were.

"Felicity." Her name was like gravel in his throat.

"Of course," she said, a smile on her lips. Ashamed. "I asked all of that because I did not know the truth. I did not know how well I had played into your plans."

His heart stopped, then roared to a thunder. "Felicity."

"Stop saying my name," she said, the words cold and angry. "You don't have the right to my name."

That much was true.

"*Felicity Faircloth,* you whispered when you came into my bedchamber all those nights ago and made me promises no man would ever be able to keep. You mocked my fairy-tale name, telling me you could give me the fairy tale. Promising it to me. Knowing it was all I ever wanted."

"I lied," he said.

She laughed, harsh and unamused. "So I have divined. You thought you could tempt me into your game with promises of being loved again. Of being accepted again. Of being a part of that world. And I went, blindly. Happily. Because I believed you."

He loathed the words. The affirmation of her desire to return to her tower and play princess once again.

"And then you made it worse. You showed me a wide world that I wanted more than anything I'd had before. You showed me a life worth living. And you presented me with a man worth —"

She stopped, but he heard the end of the sentence nonetheless. *A man worth loving.* He heard the words she would never give him. Not now that she knew the truth.

She shook her head. "You are worse than them all. I would rather have the cut of every member of the aristocracy than your lies. Your manipulative promises. I wish —" She shook her head and stared out the window. "I wish you never knew my name. I wish it had been a secret. Like yours."

"No longer a secret," he said. "I told it to you."

"Yes. You did. Devon Culm. Named for the past."

"That is the truth."

She nodded. "He told me you intended to seduce me out from under him. To use me to teach him a lesson."

He nodded. "I did."

She laughed without humor. "I shall tell you this, you are the only person I have ever met whose truth is all lies. You didn't tell me your name because you cared I know it." It wasn't true, but he didn't say it. "You didn't tell me for any reason but to tempt me further. To make me your pawn. You knew the story would break me. You knew your past would link me to you. And you preyed upon me with that knowledge, all while you planned my demise." She paused, anger and regret warring in her eyes. The first, Devil could manage — he'd always been able to manage anger. But the latter — it was a knife to the gut to think of her regretting him. "All while making me love you."

The words threatened to crush him.

"Our arrangement. All those nights ago. You were to have given me the duke, and I was to have given you a favor. What was the debt you planned to collect?"

"Felicity."

"What was it?" Her fury was like a blow.

"One night." Christ, he felt like a monster. "Your ruination."

A beat. Then, softly, to herself more than him, "No heirs." She laughed, humorless. "I don't know which is worse," she said, and he heard the sadness in her voice. "The fact that you intended to ruin me for sport, or . . ."

"It wasn't sport."

"Revenge is sport. It isn't important. Nothing changes in the end, and double the wrongs have been committed." She paused. "And innocent people have been hurt. I have been hurt." Guilt slammed through him as she spoke, as she turned her beautiful brown eyes on him and said, "I have been hurt a thousand times, and none of them have mattered in comparison to this . . . in comparison to you. Devil, indeed."

He ran a hand over his chest, where an ache had settled — one he did not expect to ever be rid of. "Felicity, please . . ."

She did not hesitate. "What is worse than that, though — than your stupid plan — is that I would have given you a thousand nights. And all you had to do was ask." She looked away from him. "What a fool I was, thinking I could go up against the Devil."

"Felicity."

"No." She shook her head. "You've made me foolish long enough. You and your pretty words. *You are important, Felicity . . .*"

Christ, she was.

"*You're beautiful, Felicity . . . You're so far above me I can barely see you, Felicity . . .* What utter rubbish."

Except it wasn't. God, he hadn't meant for it to be.

"And then . . . *No, Felicity, we can't. I shan't ruin you . . .*" She paused. "That one is my favorite. How very, very rich, when that was the plan all along. To ruin my engagement. My future. *Me.*"

No. Not on the roof. By then . . . all I wanted was to protect you.

By then, all he wanted was to love her.

She turned and looked at him, her eyes

glistening with anger and frustration and unshed tears. "You know, I actually started to believe it. I started to believe that I was more than all of it. I started to believe that Finished Felicity could be Fearless Felicity. That Mayfair Felicity could be reborn on the rooftops of Covent Garden. At your hands."

Every word was a blow, like Whit's knives, thrown one after another, into his chest, making him want to get down on his knees and tell her the truth. Except, she was giving him the chance to give her the life she deserved. All he had to do was stomach losing her. All he had to do was choose her over himself.

Sadness edged into her gaze, and he willed himself not to look away. Not to reach for her. Not to move. "I worked the plan for you, didn't I? I made the decision for you. I chose ruination, thinking it was going to bring me happiness." She scoffed. "Thinking I could convince you, in it, that we could be happy. That I didn't want any of that if I could have this. If I could have you. How you must have laughed. How you must have rejoiced."

No. Christ, no. Nothing about the night on the roof was about revenge. None of it was about his brother. It had been about her, and about him, and about the knowledge that she was all he'd ever wanted, laid bare before him. Forever.

She hadn't been the one reborn on the roof, he had been.

But if he told her that, she would stay. And he couldn't have her stay. Not here. Not when he could give her the rest of the world.

Sadness gave way to anger. Good. Anger was good. She could channel anger. She could survive it. And so he would stoke that anger. "Shall I tell you something true?"

"Yes," she said, and he hated the word on her lips . . . that word that had echoed in his ear as he'd made love to her. That word that meant they were together. That they were partners. The word that marked her pleasure and their future.

But there was no shared future. Only hers. He could give her a future. He could give her the present. And she deserved it. She deserved all time.

"Tell me," she said, letting the words come, angry and forceful. "Tell me something true, you liar."

So he did the only thing he could do. He cut her loose from this world that did not deserve her. He set her free.

He lied.

"You were the perfect revenge."

She went still, her eyes going narrow with a hot loathing that was nothing close to the one he had for himself — the one that seeped through him, settling in muscle and bone and stealing every shred of happiness he might ever have.

Loathing was good, he told himself. Loathing was not tears.

But it also was not love.

He'd stolen that from her, like a thief. No, not from her. From himself.

And his love, his beautiful, spinster, wallflower lockpick, she did not cry. Instead she lifted her chin and said, calm as a queen, "You deserve the darkness."

And she left him to it.

Chapter Twenty-Six

The next morning, instead of heading to the warehouse to oversee the movement of the ice from the shipment that had just come in, instead of preparing for that evening's delivery of nearly two tons of untaxed, illegal goods, instead of heading for the docks of the Thames or the Bastards' rookery warehouse, Devil donned his coat and hat and went to see Arthur, Earl Grout, heir to the Marquessate of Bumble.

He was, it would come as no surprise to anyone, turned away at the door by a butler who could have stepped out of any number of toffs' houses for the skill he exhibited in looking down his nose at a man no fewer than six inches taller and five stone heavier than he was.

The Earl Grout, Devil was told, was not receiving.

Which, no doubt, was the result of Devil's calling card saying just that. *Devil.*

"Fucking Mayfair," he grumbled as the door shut firmly in his face, nearly removing his nose. Did no one on this side of town realize that men like Devil were often richer and more powerful than they could dream, and therefore good allies?

Not to Felicity.

He pushed the thought to the side.

Goddammit. He had to find another way in. For her.

Walking around the back of the house, he investigated a variety of different avenues: he could break a window to enter the ground floor; he could climb the ivy-covered back wall to God knew what was in the third-floor window above; he could go back to the door and strongarm the butler; or he could climb the tree that had a prominent branch leading to a second-floor balcony.

A balcony not unlike Felicity's at Bumble House.

As he'd had good luck with that particular balcony, Devil chose the tree, making quick work of scaling it before setting down gently on the wrought-iron Juliet, quietly testing the door, which was open.

All aristocrats were idiots. It was a miracle no one had robbed this house blind.

Just before he stepped into the room, he heard a woman's voice from within. "You

527

should have told me."

"I didn't wish you to worry."

"It did not occur to you I would begin to worry when you started leaving the house before I woke and returning after I took to bed? It did not occur to you that I would notice that something was terribly wrong when my husband stopped speaking to me?"

"Dammit, Pru — it's not for you to worry about. I told you, I would take care of it."

Devil closed his eyes and turned his face to the sky. He appeared to have discovered a bedchamber, in which Grout and his wife were having a lovers' quarrel.

"Not for me to worry about . . . you're mad if you think that I shan't take interest in our life."

Devil remained quiet, listening. By all accounts Devil had found in his reconnaissance on Felicity's family, Lady Grout was quite dull, largely interested in books and watercolors, but one half of a long-time love match. Grout had married her when they were both twenty, after which they'd lived happily in town while he amassed a fortune in good investments, before they had their first child, a son, five years earlier. The lady was increasing once more, Devil had been told.

"You can't take care of this, Arthur. Not

by yourself. You're at a loss. And while I haven't two crowns to rub together, I've a brain in my head and a willingness to help, despite your cabbageheaded decision to keep secrets from me."

The bit about Lady Grout being dull appeared unreliable.

"I have shamed us! And my parents! And Felicity!"

"Oh, idiot man. You made a mistake! As did your father. As did your sister, I might add, though I imagine she had more than a decent reason to strike the duke and I would dearly like to know it."

There was a long pause, and then a quiet, gutted "This is my job, Pru. To keep you happy. Safe. Comfortable. To provide for you. That's what I agreed to when we married."

Devil understood the frustration in the words. The sense of desperation that came with wanting to keep one's love safe. Was that not why he was here? To keep Felicity safe?

"And I agreed to obey! But I am rather through with doing that, I'll tell you, Arthur." Devil's brows rose. The lady was not happy. "We are either partners in life or we are not. I do not care if we are poor as church mice. I don't care if all of London refuses us entry to their homes. I don't care if we're never invited to another ball as long as we live, so long as we are together in it."

I'm not the same. I don't care about Mayfair and balls.

"I love you," the countess said, quietly. "I've loved you since we were children. I've loved you rich. And now I love you poor. Do you love me?"

Do you love me?

The question had been echoing through Devil since Felicity had asked it, six hours earlier. And now, spoken on another set of lips, it threatened to put him on his knees.

"Yes," said the earl within. "Yes, of course. That's why I have made such a hash of everything."

Yes.

Yes, of course he loved her. He loved everything about her. She was sunlight and fresh air and hope.

Yes. He loved her wildly.

And he'd ruined that. He'd used her and lied to her and turned her against him. He'd betrayed her and her love. And he would suffer his own damnation by living his days wildly in love with her, and living without her.

Which was likely best, because love did not change the fact that Felicity would always be Mayfair, and he would always be Covent Garden. He would never be good enough to stand in her sunlight, but he could absolutely protect her from the darkness.

More than protect her. He could give her everything she'd ever dreamed.

It was time for Devil to walk into a second Faircloth bedchamber and offer its inhabitants everything they wished. And this time, he did not intend to fail.

When he was through speaking to the earl and countess, Devil returned to the warehouse, where he continued his bruising work, preparing the hold for a new shipment, grateful for the ache in his muscles — his hair shirt for sins committed against the woman he loved.

Punishment for his lies.

He worked tirelessly, alongside half a dozen other men who were rotating in shifts to avoid spending too long in the freezing temperatures. Devil embraced the cold as he did the darkness and the pain, accepting it as his punishment. Welcoming it as such. The dozen or so lanterns hung high against the ceiling were not enough to keep the darkness at bay, and he ignored the thread of panic that came every now and then when he looked the wrong way and found infinite blackness, just as he ignored the sweat soaking his clothes. Not long after he'd begun to work, he removed his coat and draped it over one of the high ice walls to allow greater freedom of movement.

Long after he'd lost the ability to recall how many shifts had rotated through the hold, Whit arrived, closing the great steel door behind him to keep the cold in. He wore a thick coat and hat, and boots to the knee — which had been helpful as he'd spent his day in the ice melt at the dock.

Whit watched Devil hook and lift several immense blocks of ice before he growled, "You need food."

Devil shook his head.

"And water." Whit extended a skein toward him.

Devil moved to the pile of ice at the center of the hold and picked another cube. "I'm surrounded by water."

"You're soaked with sweat. And the cargo is on its way. The men will need you strong enough to help when it arrives."

Devil did not reveal his surprise at the information; if the cargo was on the move, the sun had set and darkness had fallen in truth, making it near midnight, hours since he lowered himself into the dark hold and began his work.

"I shall be strong enough when it gets here. I've built the whole fucking hold, haven't I?"

Whit's assessing gaze tracked the room. "You have."

Devil nodded, ignoring the chill that ran through him — perspiration cooling him the moment he paused in his work. "Then let me get back to it. And you worry about your own strength."

Whit watched him for a long moment, and then said, "Grace is gone."

Devil stilled, turning to his brother. "For how long?"

"Long enough for us to get Ewan under control. He won't like that you've won the girl."

"I haven't won the girl."

"I heard she clocked him." Whit paused. "Felicity Faircloth, name like a storybook princess, right hook like a prizefighter."

Devil didn't reply. He didn't think he'd be able to find words around the tightness in his throat at his brother's pride in the woman he loved.

After a long stretch of silence, Whit added, "At least put your coat back on. You know what happens in the cold, Devil; you can't save the girl if you're dead."

Devil looked to his brother, letting his fury into his gaze. "I've already saved the girl."

Whit's brows rose in silent question.

"You don't see her anywhere near the Garden, do you? Now get the fuck out."

Whit hesitated, as though he might say something, and then turned to leave. "They'll be here in thirty minutes. Then the real work begins."

And it did, right on time, a line of strong, strapping workmen heaving boxes and barrels, crates and casks — the largest shipment the Bastards had ever imported — into the hold. After that, more ice. Thousands of pounds of it, and Devil stayed, ignoring the thirst and hunger that teased around his edges, ignoring the pain in his shoulders and the burn of the work.

He'd take all of that over what awaited him above in a world without Felicity.

The men made quick work of their load — a valuable skill that had come with years of practice. The hold was only useful if the cargo was brought in and hidden as quickly as possible, preventing too much melt and, by extension, possible discovery.

An hour before dawn, as the sky outside edged from black to grey, Devil came up from the hold, lantern in hand, to confirm that the delivery was complete. The work crew was clustered together upstairs — sixty men and boys in total, plus Nik and a handful of young women from the rookery who worked for her, keeping the business running smoothly.

On the other side of the warehouse, Whit climbed up on one of the massive wooden scaffolds to address the men. A ripple went through the group; Whit was not one for grand speeches. Or any speech at all. And yet, here he was.

"This was a good night's work, lads" — he found the women in the crowd, looked each one in the eye — "and lasses. It stays here until we're sure we can move it and keep you all safe. As you know, we lose money every day we keep cargo in the hold . . ." He shook his head and met as many of his men's eyes as he could, the accent of the rookery edging into his words. "But don't for a moment think you lot ain't the most important fing in this buildin'. Devil and I — we know that better than any. And while we're at it, might as well point to our darlin' Annika, with a brain smart as 'er mouth."

A cheer rose up from the group, and Nik gave an elaborate, flourishing bow before straightening and cupping her hands to her mouth. "You talk too much, Beast! When

535

can we drink?"

Laughter followed, the corners of Whit's eyes crinkling with satisfaction as he looked over the crowd. When he found Devil in the back, he lifted a chin in acknowledgment before saying, "Calhoun is keepin' the Sparrow open for us, as a matter of fact. Ale is on the Bastards this morning, bruvs."

Another raucous cheer sounded as Whit leapt to the ground, weaving through the men, aiming for Devil, who tipped his head and said, "You're as good as Wellington with your rousing speeches."

"Ending with drink helps. Come with us?"

Devil shook his head. "No."

"Fair enough." Whit clapped Devil on the shoulder, and he hissed in pain. Shocked, Whit immediately released him. "You're going to hurt in a few. You're soaked through with sweat. It's a miracle you're still standing; go home and get them to pull you a hot bath."

Devil shook his head. "In a bit. I've got to finish the last of the wall and lock the hold. The men deserve the celebration."

"You worked all day down there. You did more work than any of us. You deserve the rest." When Devil said nothing, he added, "I'm going to send word home. They're going to pull you a bath in one hour. Be there for it."

He nodded, not wanting Whit to know the truth — that he didn't want to go back to that building that was full of memories of how he'd hurt her. "Go. I shall finish up and find a bed."

"I don't suppose it will be a bed warm with Felicity Faircloth?"

The idea stung. "I prefer you not talking."

"Next time you take the girl to the roofs, Dev, call off the watch."

He cursed roundly. "There'll never be a word about Felicity Faircloth from the watch."

"Of course not. Besides, once they hear she decked Marwick in front of the Duchess of Northumberland, they'll love her even more."

"Even more?"

Whit's eyes darkened. "There are whispers that she makes you happy, bruv."

She does. God above, Felicity made him happy — happier than he'd ever been, if he was honest. He wasn't the kind of man who was afforded the luxury of happiness, except in her arms. And in her eyes. "I don't wish to discuss Felicity Faircloth. And I'll sack anyone else who does. She's not for the Garden."

His brother watched him for a long moment, unmoving, before he nodded once and turned away.

The group made quick work of leaving, the first group of watchmen making their way to the roof. No one would get into the building without a bullet in him first. Not without express permission from the Bastards themselves. So Devil was alone when he lowered himself from the dark warehouse into the dark hold, where a single lantern had been left burning.

He was alone when he took the hook to the final row of ice, lifting and moving until the blocks were even in a perfect wall, topping seven feet, this exertion, on top of the rest of the day's, was a great deal, and his breath was harsh and labored by the end of his task. He moved slowly to the door, collecting the lantern, and let himself out of the hold, setting the lamp to the floor and closing the interior steel door behind him, eager to work the locks quickly and be rid of the darkness.

As though he'd ever be rid of the darkness now.

Before he'd even touched the first lock, a voice sounded from it. "Where is she?"

Devil spun to face Ewan in the shadows. "How did you get in here?"

His brother came closer, into the dim light of the lantern, fair-haired and tall and broad — too broad to be an aristocrat. It was a miracle no one had noticed his lack of refinement — a mark of his baseborn mother — though Devil imagined the aristocracy saw what they wished to see.

Ewan ignored the question. Repeated his own. "Where is she?"

"I'll gut you if you've hurt another one of my men."

"Another one?" the duke said, all innocence.

"It's you, isn't it? Thieving our shipments?"

"Why would you think that?"

"The toff on the docks, watching our ships. The timing — thefts began just before you announced your return. And now . . . here you are. What, it is not enough that you threatened our lives? You had to come for our livelihood, as well?"

Ewan leaned back against the wall of the dark tunnel. "I never came for your lives."

"Bollocks. Even if I didn't remember the last night at the manor house, when you came at us with a blade sharp enough to end us, you've been coming for us for years. We met the spies, Ewan. We ran them off. We raised a generation in the rookery on one, single rule. No one talks about the Bastards."

Silver flashed, and Devil's gaze flickered to his brother's hand, where he held Devil's walking stick. His heart began to pound, and he forced a laugh. "You think to silence me? You think you're still the killer among us? I've twenty years in the rookeries on you, toff."

Ewan's lips flattened.

Devil pressed on. "But even if there were a chance of you taking me, you wouldn't."

"And why is that?"

"For the same reason you let us escape all those years ago — because if you kill me, you'll never know what happened to Grace."

Nothing changed in the duke at the words, not the cadence of his breath or the straightness of his spine, but Devil did not need proof that he'd struck true. There had been a time when he'd known Ewan like he knew himself. And he still did. They were plaited together, the three of them. The four of them.

"I found you," Ewan said, finally.

The words sent a chill through Devil that rivaled the ice hold. "Yes. But not her."

"You made a mistake, Dev." He'd made a dozen of them, and this consequence was nothing compared to the others. "You should have been more careful with Felicity Faircloth."

Tell me something true.

"I heard she hit you."

Ewan raised a hand to his cheek. "She wasn't happy to discover my ulterior motives."

"Nor mine."

I would have given you a thousand nights. And all you had to do was ask.

"I told her she should have been with us at the manor." The country house where they'd been trained and tested, where Ewan had won his title and their father had won his heir.

If she'd been at the manor, Devil would never have survived it. He would have been too busy protecting Felicity to protect himself. He shook his head. "I wouldn't wish her anywhere near the manor. I'd take death before she witnessed a moment of what we suffered. I don't know how you live there. I would have burned it to the ground."

"I consider it every day," Ewan replied, all calm. "Perhaps, one day, I shall do it."

Devil watched him for a long moment. Ewan had always been like this, settled and assessing, as though he simply did not feel the emotions made for the rest of the world.

As though he found them interesting in the vague way one found a cabinet of curiosities so.

Grace had been the only person able to make Ewan feel. And even then, he'd nearly killed her. Nothing stood between Ewan and what he wanted.

Nothing but Devil, it seemed. Always Devil.

"I am not the one thieving your cargo," Ewan said after a bit, the change of topic not remotely out of character. Devil believed him. After all, everything was out in the open now, and no one had reason to lie. "Earl Cheadle is thieving your cargo."

Devil's brows rose. He wasn't sure he believed the words, but Ewan had little reason to lie. "It didn't occur to you to do something about it?"

"We're all criminals in some way or another, Devon," Ewan said, simply. "And besides, your drink is not what I'm after."

"No. You're after something far more valuable. The impossible."

"She's all I've ever been after," Ewan said. "And Felicity Faircloth served her purpose to get me here. Close enough to find her. I will say, Lady Felicity was convenient . . . even more convenient than I imagined she would be, once I realized that you cared for her."

The words enraged Devil. Felicity was more than convenient. She was more than a pawn. "How dare you manipulate her to get to me."

Ewan raised a blond brow in his direction. "Say that again. This time, more slowly."

Devil swore. Yes, he had used Felicity. At the beginning. For a heartbeat, before he'd realized. The moment he'd sent her into the ballroom, a message to Ewan, he'd lost all will to follow through with his plan. He'd floundered. And he'd fallen.

"The problem is, Devon, Felicity Faircloth isn't only convenient. She is also too smart for her own good. And she knows our secret."

Devil stiffened, the words and their meaning ringing clear as a rifle's report in the darkness. He resisted the urge to wrap his hands around his brother's throat and end this now. "And now we get to it. We should have killed you when we had a chance."

"You know, brother, most days I wish you had done just that. But you're the one who always liked the deals, Devon. If there was a bargain to be had, you were the one to have it."

Not for her. Felicity was too important to bargain with.

"You touch her, you die. That is the only deal that matters."

Ewan looked down the corridor, into the darkness. "I'm surprised you found it in you to love someone, Dev. What with how certain you once were that the emotion was a fable." On another's lips, the words might have been caustic. Or they might have been kind. But on Ewan's, they were curious, as though Devil were a specimen under glass.

Ewan continued. "Tell me, when did you realize it? When I kissed her on the balcony at the ball? In her golden dress? That was a cruel touch, by the way."

Devil hated the revelation that Ewan had been manipulating him, as well. "Just a reminder that you were never enough for Grace. That you never kept your promises to her."

The duke's gaze narrowed. "Or was it when the boy in the hedge came back to report that I'd kissed Felicity in the gardens? Was that when you realized you loved her?" He paused. "She loved you by then, you know. And I think you loved her, too, what with the speed with which you came to claim her."

The words stung. And they were enraging, because it seemed a betrayal of the worst kind that the Duke of Marwick knew that Devil loved Felicity when she did not. When she would never know, because if he told her, he might not be able to resist what she did next, and she would never get the life she deserved.

"If only you had decided to love her from the start instead of manipulating her to punish me, perhaps we would have avoided all this —"

"Think very carefully before you threaten Felicity, bruv."

The duke's eyes found Devil, all calm. "Why should I do that?"

"Because I won't hesitate to destroy you in her name."

"There is nothing you would not do for her, is there?"

Devil shook his head. "Not one thing. I would happily give up everything for her happiness. I'll see the gallows for killing a duke . . . without a second thought."

"The deal is simple, Devon. You tell me where I can find Grace, and I shan't punish Felicity Faircloth for knowing what she should not know. Even better, I shan't simply let her live; I'll let her end our ruined engagement. I'll settle the money on her barely-there father. On the brother, too. I'll leave her better than I found her. Far better than she could be with you."

Rage rioted through Devil at the cold words. At the idea of Ewan anywhere near Felicity. Felicity, his fairy-tale princess.

His brother pressed on. "Magnanimous of me, don't you think?" He paused. "But if you do not give me Grace . . . I have no choice but to punish her. And you. I'll force the marriage. I'll take the girl to the country, somewhere you'll never get to her. And I'll make certain that you never see her again."

Devil stiffened. Forced himself to raise a brow. "You think there's anywhere I can't find you? I've spent years in the darkness, Ewan, while you've gone soft in the light."

A long silence. And then a simple, "Come for her, then. But if you get near, know I take things from her. Things she loves. Every glimpse you get of her will result in her deprivation of the world she's only recently come to revel in. Never forget that I learned your punishment from our father."

Memory flashed. Coming out of the dark ground, eyes red from a night of crying for the dog his father had taken from him, to find Ewan on the lawn of the manor house, playing with his own.

Ewan, who had always chosen his future over their shared past. The perfect heir.

546

"You're a fucking monster. Just like him."

Ewan did not move. "Perhaps. But you brought the girl into this, didn't you? You put her on the table as a weapon. I'm simply using her."

Devil had had enough. He threw himself across the dark hallway, fist already raised, the full weight of his body behind the blow, which connected with the wicked sound of bone on flesh. The duke's head snapped back, the movement broken by the stone wall at his back. "You think you can threaten her?"

Ewan recovered with unbearable speed, landing his own heavy blow, sending breathtaking pain radiating out from Devil's eye. Devil was already pulling his brother off the wall to deliver a series of blows in quick succession. "You think I won't leave you here to rot in this muck I've done everything to keep her from? I have given up my only chance at happiness to keep her from this. From my past. From *yours,* you fucking cur."

Ewan's eyes opened, unmoved. "And what would you do to find her if she was lost?"

Anything.

Breathing heavily, Devil threw his bleeding brother to the ground and backed away from his brother's body. At the door to the

547

hold, he searched his pocket for his keys.

"Where is she?" Ewan had pushed himself up to a seated position, back against the wall, face in the shadows, black blood running down his chin. "I've spent twelve years looking for you. And when I hear about you — about the Bastards — it's only ever about you and Whit. No women. No wives. No sister. Where is she?"

He could hear the anguish in his brother's words, and for a moment — for a heartbeat — Devil considered telling him the truth. He would follow Felicity from the shadows for the rest of time. He would watch her marry and grow old. He would watch her have children — little brown-haired lockpicks who were more than they seemed. And if he couldn't find her?

He'd no doubt grow as mad as his brother, without the woman he loved.

But a thousand years ago, when three children escaped their horrible past and made for a bright future, they'd done so because of the man in front of them. Because he'd betrayed them brutally.

Devil's scar throbbed with the memory.

And today, Devil meted out punishment with unmatched swiftness. "You tried to kill her, Ewan. Our father's last test, and you were the one to take up the blade." Ewan looked away. "She's the proof of your theft. You stole a dukedom. But worse, you stole her name."

Ewan turned to him, wild-eyed. "She never wanted it."

"You stole it anyway," Devil said. "We were children, but you two were always older by years. You were bound to each other."

"I loved her."

Devil knew that. Ewan and Grace had been too young for love, and still they'd had it. Which had made what happened even worse. "Then you should have protected her."

"I did! I let her run with you!"

Devil turned his face, showing his scar to Ewan. "Only after I stopped you from destroying her. You think I don't remember? You think I don't still feel the burn of your blade?"

Punishment and protection, two sides of the same coin. Had he not learned that lesson for himself? Had he not punished himself to protect Grace all those years ago? Hadn't he just punished himself again to protect Felicity?

Would he not take his punishment again and again for her safety?

And now he would punish Ewan. "Grace

is gone."

The lie rang through the darkness, clear and cold. And for the first time since he appeared, the duke showed himself. Ewan's inhale was loud and harsh, as though Devil had unsheathed his cane sword and put the tip right through his heart.

And he had.

"Where?"

"Where you'll never find her."

"Tell me." Ewan's low voice shook.

Devil watched his brother carefully and threw his final blow. "Where none of us can find her."

Let Ewan think Grace dead. She'd be furious at Devil for it, no doubt, but if it threw the fucking monster off her scent, he'd take his sister's heat. And besides, Ewan deserved the pain. Devil would sleep well tonight.

Except he wouldn't, because he'd be without Felicity.

He turned back to the locks, extracting his keys. Christ, he was tired of all of it. He was Janus, cursed with nothing but the broken past. The bleak future.

And, like Janus, he could not see the present.

The glint of silver from the lion's head at the tip of his walking stick came too late for him to defend himself. The blow set him to his knees, the pain excruciating.

"You were to protect her."

Devil bore the weight of his pain and lied perfectly, a lie that any good smuggler would be proud of. "You were to protect her first."

Ewan roared, his fury coming without warning. "You took her from me."

The room was spinning. "She came willingly. She came eagerly."

"You have signed your death warrant tonight, brother. If I must live without love, you can die without it."

The words were a harsher blow than the physical one Ewan had delivered.

Felicity. Devil was fast losing consciousness. He lifted a hand to his temple, feeling the telltale warm wetness there. Blood.

Felicity. He didn't want to die without her.

Not without seeing her again. Not without touching her, without feeling the soft warmth of her. Not without one last kiss.

Not without telling her something true.

Felicity. Not without telling her he loved her.

He should have told her he loved her.

He would have married her . . . *he did marry her.*

A scrape of steel sounded harsh and somehow unfamiliar.

No. No he didn't. He left her.

He married her. It was a wild, Covent Garden wedding with a fiddle and a pipe, and too much wine and too much song and he told her he loved her a hundred times. A thousand.

A slide. His body, dragged through the frigid mud into the hold.

He married her, and he made her a queen of the Garden, and his men swore her allegiance and she grew round with a child. With children. With little girls with heads for machines, just like their mother. And she didn't regret it.

And neither did he.

No. Wait. He didn't. It wasn't past. It was future.

He rolled to his hands and knees, barely able to see the flicker of lantern light in the hallway beyond. He had to get to her. To keep her safe.

To love her.

She had to know he loved her.

That she was his light.

Light. It was going away. Ewan was in the doorway. "If I must live in the dark, you can die in it."

Devil reached for the door, the infinite blackness of the hold already stealing his breath. *No, not the blackness.*

"Felicity!"

The door shut, closing out the light.

"No!"

The only response was the ominous sound of locks being thrown. One after another. Locking him into the hold.

"Felicity!" Devil screamed, fear and panic coursing through him. Forcing him to fight the haze and scramble for the door. He banged on it.

There was no answer.

"Ewan . . ." He screamed again, madness coming with the darkness. *"Please."*

He threw himself at the door, pounding upon it — knowing that the hold was too far down and too well hidden for any of the watchmen outside to hear him. And still he screamed, desperate to get to Felicity. To keep her safe. He turned, darkness everywhere, feeling along the muddy ground until he found the ice, pulling himself up on the blocks to find the pick he'd left within.

The dark closed in on him, heavy and cloying in the freezing cold, and he forced himself to take deep breaths as he searched. "Where the fuck is it?"

He found it, and taking it by the handle and crawling back to the door, he roared her name again. "Felicity!"

But she wasn't there to hear him. He'd

pushed her away.

I love you, Devil.

He pulled himself to standing and swung the hook, scarring the steel. And again. And again. He had to get to her. Again. He had to keep her safe. Again.

Do you love me?

He did. He loved her. And in that moment, as he realized the futility of his blows, he was overcome with truth — he would never have the chance to tell her just how much.

You deserve the darkness.

The final strike took the remains of his strength, and he sank to the ground and closed his eyes, letting the darkness and cold come.

CHAPTER TWENTY-SEVEN

Unable to sleep, Felicity rose at the crack of dawn and went to her brother's home, letting herself in through the kitchens and up into the family's quarters, opening the door to his bedchamber to discover him still abed, kissing his wife.

She immediately turned her back and raised a hand to her eyes, crying out, "Ahh! Why?"

While it wasn't the kindest response to the vision of marital bliss before her, it was certainly more kind than other things she might have thought or said, and it got the job done.

Pru gave a little surprised squeak, and Arthur said, "Dammit, Felicity — are you unable to knock?"

"I didn't expect . . ." She waved a hand. She looked back to find her sister-in-law sitting up in the bed, counterpane pulled to her chin. Returning her attention to the door, she added, "Hello, Pru."

"Hello, Felicity," Pru said, a smile in her voice.

"It's lovely to see you."

"And you! I hear you've a great deal going on."

Felicity grimaced. "Yes, I suppose you would have heard that."

"Enough!" Arthur said. "I'm putting locks on all the doors."

"We have locks on all the doors, Arthur."

"I'm putting more locks on the doors. And using them. Two people bursting into our private rooms uninvited in less than a day is two people too many. You may turn around, Felicity."

She did, to discover that both her brother and sister-in-law had donned dressing gowns. Pru, heavy with child, was crossing the room to a pretty dressing table, and Arthur was standing at the end of the bed, looking . . . not pleased.

"I was invited," she defended herself. "I was summoned! *Felicity. Come and see me immediately.* One would think you were king for how superior a summons it was."

"I didn't expect you to think you were summoned for this hour."

"I couldn't sleep." She didn't expect to be able to sleep ever again, honestly, for the moment she began to dream, it was of Devil, the King of Covent Garden, and the way he looked at her and the way he touched her and the way he might love her, and just when it all felt so deliciously real, she woke, and it was all horribly false, and so not sleeping seemed a better alternative. "I intended to come and see you today, Arthur. I was going to come and apologize. I know it's dreadful, and Father has disappeared, and Mother is in a constant state of vapors, but I've been thinking about what happened two nights ago and — wait. Someone else burst into your rooms?"

His brows rose. "I wondered when you would note that." He sighed. "I am unconcerned about what happened at the Northumberland Ball."

Felicity sighed. "Well, you should be concerned, Arthur. It was . . . not my best moment. I'm properly ruined."

He barked a laugh at that. "I can imagine."

"I rather think it might have been your best moment, honestly," Pru said happily from her dressing table. "Marwick sounds quite unpleasant."

"He is," Felicity said. "Mostly. But —" She stopped herself before she could point out that her decision, however freeing for herself, was the opposite for her father and

Arthur, who now had no hope for recovering their losses. If Arthur still hadn't told Pru, it would be a terrible betrayal of her brother.

Even if he deserved it.

She looked at him, the question in her eyes.

"She knows," he said.

Felicity looked to Pru. "You do?"

"That this idiot man was keeping the truth about his own ruin from us both? In fact, I do."

Felicity's jaw dropped. She never expected her sister-in-law to weep and wail in the face of financial disaster, but she also did not expect her to be so . . . well, frankly, happy. She looked to her brother. "Something has happened."

Her brother watched her for a long moment. "Indeed, something has."

Was it possible the duke was not allowing the engagement to end? He was just mad enough to do it — just to punish Devil. And as much as Felicity was irritated with Devil, and hurt by Devil, she was not interested in punishing him. "I'm not marrying Marwick. I made that very clear at the ball . . . and even if he came to . . ."

"I've no interest in you marrying Marwick, Felicity. Frankly, I despised the idea from the start. Similarly, I have little interest in discussing the ball. I should like to talk about what happened *after* the ball."

Felicity froze. *Impossible.*

"Nothing happened after the ball."

"That's not what we were told."

Felicity looked to Pru, then back to Arthur, a thread of suspicion in her. "Who burst into your rooms before me?"

"I think you know."

She went cold. "He shouldn't have come here." He'd used her. He'd betrayed her.

You were the perfect revenge.

He'd done enough damage; couldn't he leave well enough alone?

"Nevertheless," Arthur said, "he turned up here yesterday."

"He isn't important," she lied.

Arthur raised a brow.

"He seems quite important, if you ask me," Pru interjected.

No one asked you, Pru. "What did he say?" Felicity asked. He wouldn't have told Arthur the truth about the night on the roof, certainly. That ran the risk of landing him with her for a wife, and Lord knew he wasn't willing to risk that for anything.

Lord knew he wasn't willing to even consider her for a wife.

"He said a number of things, as a matter

559

of fact." Arthur looked to Pru. "Introduced himself all polite — despite the fact that he'd climbed a tree and broken in."

"He does that," Felicity said.

"Does he?" Pru asked, as though they were discussing Devil's penchant for riding.

"We're going to have to have a talk about how you know that, eventually," Arthur said. "He then tore a strip off of me for mistreating you."

Her gaze flew to her brother's. "He did?"

"He did. Reminded me that you were never a means to an end. That we were treating you abominably and that we didn't deserve you."

Tears welled, along with anger and frustration. He, too, didn't deserve her. "He shouldn't have done that, either."

"He does not seem the kind of man who can be stopped, Felicity," Pru said.

Especially when you want to stop him from leaving you.

"He was right, is the thing," Arthur said. "We did behave abominably. He thinks you ought to turn your backs on us. Thinks we're unworthy of you."

"He doesn't really believe that." Her worth had run its course the moment her usefulness in his revenge had done the same.

"For someone who doesn't believe in your

worth, he certainly was willing to pay a fortune for it."

She froze, instantly understanding. "He offered you money."

Arthur shook his head. "Not just money. A king's ransom. And not just to me — to Father as well. A hefty sum to fill the coffers. To begin again."

She shook her head. Taking Devil's money tied them together again. He could turn up any time to check on his investments. She didn't want him near her. She couldn't bear him near her. "You can't take it."

Arthur blinked. "Whyever not?"

"Because you can't," she insisted. "Because he's only doing it because he feels some kind of guilt."

"Well, one might argue that a guilty man's money spends as well as that of someone who sleeps well at night, but, leaving that aside, why would Mr. Culm feel guilty, Felicity?"

Mr. Culm. The name sounded ridiculous on her brother's tongue. Devil had never used it before with her. He loved being the opposite of a mister with a powerful passion.

And also, Mr. Culm made her remember when she wished she was his Mrs.

Which she didn't anymore. Obviously.

"Because he does," she settled on as an answer. "Because . . ." She trailed off. "I don't know. Because he does."

"I think he might feel guilty because of the *other* thing he said while he was here, Arthur."

Arthur sighed, and Felicity looked to Pru, who looked like the cat that got the cream. "What was it?"

"How did he put it?" Pru asked with a smile that gave Felicity the keen sense that her sister-in-law had committed whatever Devil had said to memory. "Ah. Yes. He loves you."

Tears came. Instantly. Tears and anger and frustration and loathing that he'd said the words she'd longed to hear to Prudence and Arthur and not to her. The person whom he ostensibly loved.

She shook her head. "No, he doesn't."

"I think he might, you know," Arthur replied.

One lone tear spilled down her cheek and she dashed it away. "No, he doesn't. You are not the only ones who treated me abominably, you know. He did, too."

Arthur nodded. "Yes. He told us that, as well. He told us he'd made enough mistakes to make it impossible for him to make you happy."

She stilled. "He said that?"

Pru nodded. "He said he would live with the regret for a lifetime. That he would remember the chance he'd had and lost."

Another tear. Another. Felicity sniffed and shook her head. "He didn't care enough about me."

Arthur nodded. "I shan't tell you otherwise; you must decide if he is a man worthy of you. But know that Devon Culm has bestowed a fortune upon you, Felicity."

"Upon *you*," she corrected. "So, what, that I may be kept? That I may be your responsibility forever? That I may belong to you, and live in sadness and silence here in this world that used to be all glitter, and is now faded paint, peeling from the rafters? All he's done is make my future a gilded prison."

"No, Felicity. I spoke correctly. Culm bestowed a fortune upon *you*. He wished you to have enough to find your own happiness." He looked to Pru. "How did he say it?"

Pru sighed. "A future wherever and with whomever you wish."

Felicity's brow furrowed. "A dowry?" The bastard. He'd just thrown up another door. She'd unlocked everything, and here she was again, surrounded by new chains. New locks.

Arthur shook her head. "No. It's yours. The money is yours. An enormous amount, Felicity. More than you could ever spend."

The shocking words settled as Pru lifted a box from her dressing table and walked it over to Felicity. "And he left you a gift."

"The money was not gift enough?" The black onyx box, longer than it was wide, barely an inch high, and tied with a pink silk bow. Her chest tightened at the pretty package it made. Pink on black, like light on darkness. Like a promise.

"He was adamant you receive this when we told you of the funds."

She slipped the ribbon from the box, wrapping it carefully around her wrist before she opened the lid to discover a thick white linen card inside. Across it, in Devil's beautiful black scrawl, were three words.

Farewell, Felicity Faircloth.

Her chest tightened at the words, tears springing again instantly.

She hated him. He'd taken away the only thing she'd ever really wanted. *Him.*

She lifted the card, nonetheless, and her breath caught at the glint of metal beneath, six straight, thin lines of shining, gleaming steel, beautifully wrought. Tears came freely

564

now, her hand shaking as she reached for the gift, her fingertips caressing the smooth metalwork. "Devil," she whispered, unable to keep his name from her tongue. "They're beautiful."

Pru craned to look in the box. "What are they? Hairpins?"

"Yes."

"What a strange design."

Felicity lifted one from the box, inspecting the jagged wave at one end. Setting it down on its black velvet cushion — the most beautiful tool chest in Christendom — she ran her finger over the L-shaped angle in another. The flat square end of a third. "They're lockpicks."

The money was one thing. But the lockpicks were everything.

You've got the future in your hands every time you hold a hairpin, he'd said all those days ago in the warehouse, when he'd told her she shouldn't be ashamed of her talent.

These picks were proof he knew her. That he put her desires first. Her passion first. That he cared more for what she chose for herself than for his own guilt.

But more than all that, they were proof that he loved her.

He'd bought her freedom — she would never again have to make choices based on

Arthur's business or her mother's home, or her own social standing. He'd freed her from Mayfair. From the world she no longer wanted. And he'd given her the future.

Just as he had on the roof, when he'd resisted her. When he'd told her that he wouldn't take her. That he wouldn't ruin her. That he wouldn't rob her of the future he could see — like Janus. In the moment, he'd let her choose him, and she had, without for a moment feeling ruined. And now, he'd ensured that she'd never be ruined again; he'd replenished her family's coffers and made her rich beyond measure. Rich in money and freedom.

Wherever and with whomever you wish.

She lifted the pins one after the other and inserted them into her hair.

She didn't want the world of the aristocracy. She wanted the world.

And he was the man to give it to her.

Not that she wasn't prepared to take it.

To no avail, Felicity banged on the great steel warehouse door a half hour later as the sun edged over the rookery's rooftops. What good was the benefit to having been given the blessing of a Bareknuckle Bastard's protection in Covent Garden if one could not enter their damn warehouse when one wished?

She was going to have to do it another way. She reached into her hair, pulling out one gleaming steel pin, and a second, each one beautifully shaped. Devil had found a skilled artisan who understood complex lockpicking, which seemed the kind of thing that should not exist . . . but he specialized in things that did not exist, and so she was unsurprised as she knelt in the dirt outside the warehouse door.

He'd better be within, or she was going to be very irritated that she'd stained her dress.

Also, he'd better be within, because she was ready to give him a firm set-down. One he richly deserved, the bastard.

After which, she intended to stay until he told her he loved her. More than once.

Before she could do the job, however, a man leapt to the ground behind her. "My lady."

She turned to face John, the handsome, friendly man who had returned her to her home the last time she was here. "Hello, John," she said, brazening through, a bright smile on her pretty face.

"Good morning, my lady," John replied in his deep baritone. "I hope you understand that I cannot allow you to pick that lock."

"Excellent," she said. "Then you shall save

me the trouble and let me in?"

John's brows rose. "I'm afraid I can't."

"But I am welcome here. I am under his protection. He gave me free rein over Covent Garden."

"Not any longer, my lady. Now we're to return you to Mayfair if we find you. No hesitation. You ain't even to see Devil."

A tightness settled in her chest. He didn't even wish to see her again.

Which of course was rubbish because obviously he wished to see her.

Obviously he loved her.

He simply had to be convinced to tell her to her face, the foolish man.

That said, this new turn of events was not ideal. Felicity tried a new tack. "I never thanked you for bringing me home that night."

"If you'll excuse me for saying so, my lady, you were too busy railing against Devil to thank me."

She pursed her lips. "I was very angry with him."

"Yes, my lady."

"It had nothing to do with you."

"No, my lady."

"He left me that night."

"Yes, my lady."

Just like he'd left her again and again. She

met John's gaze. "He left me again last night."

Something flickered in the man's dark eyes. Something suspiciously like pity. No. Felicity wasn't having anyone's pity. "He thinks to tell me what is good for me. I don't care for that."

John smirked. "I don't imagine you do."

"You shouldn't ever tell your wife what's good for her. Not if you know what's good for you, John."

He laughed at that, deep and full. Felicity kept talking, as much to herself as to him. "He's addlepated, of course, as he's more than good enough for me. He's the best of men." She looked to John again. "He's the best of men."

"Only the Bastards and Nik have keys to this lock." John watched the rooftops for a long time.

"May I convince you to at least patrol the back side of the building while I pick it, then?"

"That lock is unpickable."

She smiled. "As we become more acquainted, John, I think you'll find that I'm quite good with locks."

"I've seen you with Devil, my lady. I have no trouble believing that."

The words set her heart racing, and sadness filled his large brown eyes. He wasn't going to do it. He was too loyal to Devil to allow her in, even when he could see that her intentions were good.

"Please, John," she whispered.

"I'm sorry," he said.

A nightingale sang, and Felicity looked up at the strange sound, so unexpected here, in the yard of a rookery warehouse. When she found nothing out of the ordinary, she turned back to John, who was . . . smiling.

Her brow furrowed. "John?"

"Lady Felicity." A growl came from above and she looked up to see Whit coming down the side of the warehouse to land next to her.

"I am going to require trousers if I'm going to run with you lot, aren't I?"

He inclined his head. "It's not the worst of ideas."

His tacit acceptance of her premise filled her with joy. "I was just telling John that I love your brother quite madly." One of Whit's black brows rose. "As a result, I fully intend to pick this unpickable lock and go in there and tell him he's cabbage-brained for not loving me back. But that will take some time, and when one decides one would like to fight for the man one loves, one likes to do it as quickly as possible, you can imagine."

"I can. But he isn't here. He's at home."

She shook her head. "No, he isn't; I went there first."

He grunted disapprovingly.

"So you can see why I would appreciate it if you would let me in."

His brow furrowed. "Did you knock?"

"I did."

He raised a fist and pounded a thundering knock on the door. "And he didn't answer?"

Felicity did not like the look on his face. "No."

His key was in the lock instantly, the door opening to the cavernous warehouse in seconds. Silence and darkness greeted them. "Devil?" he called out.

No answer. Felicity's heart dropped. Something was wrong. She turned back to John. "Light. We need light."

The big man was already turning to fetch a lantern.

Whit called after him. "Did he leave?"

John's reply was firm and clipped. "No one's been in or out since you lot left."

"Devil!" Whit called out.

Silence.

John passed Felicity a lantern, and she lifted it high. "Devil?"

"He must have left," Whit said. "Goddammit, John, there's a hundred thousand pounds worth of goods down there and you lot are sleeping at the watch enough that you didn't see someone leave through the only damn door to the place."

"He didn't come through that door, Beast," John protested. "My men know their work. And they do it well."

Felicity stopped listening to the two men spar, heading deeper into the darkness to the far corner of the space. To where the door inset in the warehouse floor stood open, a yawning blackness below.

Devil had been adamant that that door never stand open. That it being open underscored that there was something below the warehouse itself.

"Devil?" She stood at the edge of the hole and called into the void for him. He wouldn't be down there. He hated the hold. He hated the darkness.

And still . . . she knew he was down there. Without question.

She was down into the darkness instantly, running along the long, dark tunnel, holding her lantern high, her heart in her throat. "Devil?" she called again.

And that's when she saw it. The flash of light on the ground in front of her. The gleam of silver. The lion's head at the handle of his walking stick. The weapon, discarded on the ground.

Next to the door to the ice hold.

She reached for the handle. Pulled. It was locked. From the outside. Six heavy steel padlocks in a neat row.

She pounded on the door in great, heavy blows. "Devil?"

No answer.

More pounding. "Devil? Are you in there?"

Again, no answer.

"Devil?" She knocked again, pressing her ear to the door, unable to hear anything over the pounding of her heart.

She dropped the lantern to the ground and reached for her hairpins without hesitation. She knocked on the door again, as hard as she could, shouting, "Devil! I am here!" before calling for Whit and John. But she could not wait for them.

Instead, she dropped to her knees and began working the locks. All the while talking to the door, hoping he would hear her. "Don't you dare die in there, Devon Culm. I've things to say to your face, you terrible, wonderful man . . ."

The first lock clicked open and she pulled it from its latch, tossing it down the corridor and immediately setting to work on the next.

". . . you think you can simply turn up at my brother's home and tell him you love me without telling me first? You think that is fair? It's not . . . and I'm going to punish you by making you tell me every minute of every hour for the rest of our lives . . ."

The second lock came loose and she immediately set her picks to the third, calling out, "Devil? Are you there? Love?" She banged on the door.

Silence. She tossed the third lock to the side.

"I love you, do you know that?" She slid her picks into the fourth lock, then the fifth.

"Are you cold, my love?" She shouted for Whit again. And John. "I'm coming," she whispered, now on the sixth lock, feeling for the latch inside the springwork within — this one different from the others. She scraped the tools together, whispering again, "I'm coming."

Done. She tossed the lock to the side and opened the door, heaving the great heavy slab to the side, the air instantly colder as she revealed the inner door, another line of locks. She immediately came to her knees in the cold mud there.

She couldn't even see the locks anymore;

she worked them by touch. Calling out to him. "Devil? Please, love — are you there?" Her heart pounded and she refused to allow the tears to come. Refused to believe she might have lost him. "Devil, please — I'm working as fast as I can. I'm here." She repeated it. "I'm here." Again and again.

And then, barely there, almost impossible to believe, she heard it. A knock. As light as butterflies' wings. As a moth's. *Her moth.*

"Devil!" she shouted, banging on the door. "I hear you! I shan't leave you. I'm never leaving you again. You'll never be rid of me."

One lock. A second. A third. Her hands were steadier than they'd ever been, the picks flying through the lockwork.

"Goddammit. No one keeps ice behind this many locks, Devil. You're definitely a smuggler. Probably a thief, too. God knows you've stolen my heart. And my future. I'm here to take it back."

The lock sprang and she was on to the fourth. At this point, any of her hairpins would have been bent or broken, rendered useless. But these pins were perfect. *He* was perfect.

"You're going to have to marry me, you know. I'm through letting you make decisions related to our mutual happiness because when you do, I am only left sad, and you are left . . ." She tossed aside the fourth. Moved to the fifth. "Well . . . locked inside ice dungeons. I assume this is the work of my former fiancé?"

A pause, while she discarded the fifth lock and set her picks to the last. "Just one more, Devon. Hold on. Please. I'm coming."

Click.

She flung the lock away and threw the heavy latch at the bottom of the door, pulling it open with all her strength. It came with a blast of frigid air and Devil, falling through the door, into her arms.

She clutched him to her and they both fell to their knees under his weight. He trembled with cold, his face pressed into the crook of her neck. He whispered one word, over and over, like a benediction. "Felicity."

Her arms wrapped around him, desperate to hold more of him. Desperate to warm him. "Thank you for my lockpicks."

"Y-you s-saved m-me." He was so cold.

"Always," she whispered, pressing a kiss to his cool temple. "Always."

"F-Felicity," he chattered her name. "I —"

She rubbed his arms with her hands, spoke to the top of his head. "No . . . don't speak. I have to get Whit."

He stiffened. "N-no." He swallowed, and

she saw the struggle of it. "It was so dark."

Tears welled. "I know. I'll leave the lantern."

His arms turned to steel, the strength of his grip surprising and immensely comforting. "N-not the lantern. You're the light. Don't leave me."

"I can't carry you," she said. "You have to let me get Whit."

His eyes opened, dark in the dim light. "Don't l-leave me ever again."

She shook her head. "Never. But love, it is so cold here. We must warm you."

"You're fire," he whispered. "You're flame. I love you."

The words thundered through her, and she could not stop touching him, stop running her hands over him, fast, furiously attempting to warm him. "Devil."

He pulled away, his gaze finding hers. "I love you."

Her heart redoubled its pounding. "Devil, I need to get you somewhere warm. Are you hurt?"

"I love you," he whispered again. "I love you. You're my future."

Her heart pounded. He'd gone mad. "My love, there is time for that once we are aboveground."

"There will never be enough time," he

said, pulling her to him, his teeth chattering, his heartbeat fast and furious. "I will never be able to tell you enough." He kissed her, his lips cold to the touch, and somehow still setting fire to her. She reached up, stroking her hand over his cheek.

When he released her, it was to press his forehead to hers and whisper, again, "I love you."

She could not stop the smile that came — here, in the dark, dank, frigid hold that had nearly killed this man, that also happened to be the most perfect place for him to tell her he loved her. "You told my brother first."

"Yes."

"I'm very angry with you about that, you know."

"So you said."

"I'm so angry, I came to tell you how angry I am about it. The money, too."

He shivered, pressing his face to her neck. "I wanted you to be free of all of it."

"I don't want your money, Devil."

"I didn't need it anymore. It meant nothing without you."

"You beautiful, ridiculous man," she said. "Then why not have me, instead?"

"Ages ago . . . you asked me why I chose you." His words were slow and measured, as though it was important that she hear them. "That night, I wanted it to be because I thought you could win him. Because you looked the kind of woman easily sacrificed."

She nodded. Forlorn Felicity. Wallflower and unfortunate.

"But it wasn't," he continued. "It never was. It was because I wanted you close. It was because I couldn't bear the idea of anyone having you. Anyone but me." He pulled her close again, his cold face at the warm skin of her neck. "Christ, Felicity. I'm so sorry."

"I am not."

He snapped to attention. "You're not?"

"No. You've a lifetime to make it up to me, and I intend to be a proper Devil's bride."

He grinned. "I shall adore every minute of that."

"I want you out of this place. I want you warm."

He pulled her close, wrapping his arms about her. "I have thoughts on how you might get me warm."

He lowered his lips to hers, and she was so grateful that he was able to think of kissing in that moment that she gave herself up to it, sliding her hands up his chest to his broad shoulders and up, up to his rough-hewn jaw and into his hair, where she discovered a wet patch.

"Well. This isn't what I expected to find down here." Whit had arrived.

Devil released her from the kiss. "Go away."

"No, don't go away, Whit," she said. "We need you."

"We do not need him," Devil said, moving to stand, sucking in a breath at the pain of the movement, making her heart ache.

She moved her hand to the light, blood shining black on her fingertips. "You're bleeding." She turned to Whit. "He's freezing. And he's bleeding."

Whit immediately came forward, catching Devil's arm over his shoulder. "What the hell happened to you?"

He put his fingers to his temple, wincing. "Ewan." He reached for Felicity. "He didn't come for you."

She shook her head. "Why would he? I ended our engagement. I hit him."

He grinned at that. "I know, love. I'm very proud of you for that bit."

"He deserved it. And more, for what he's done to you."

"Grace took to the rooftops last night."

Devil nodded. "I let Ewan think her dead." He pulled her close and kissed her temple before looking to Whit. "He's furious."

Whit nodded. "He's left. The watch reported this morning, he rode out from the Mayfair house at dawn."

Devil nodded. "He'll be back. He'll want to punish us."

Whit lifted the lantern to look at Devil's face. "Christ, he knocked you good."

Felicity scowled. "Never has a man needed punishment more than that one."

He looked at her, then to Whit. "He received it today."

Whit grunted, seeming to understand whatever that meant. Felicity did not, however, and her temper flared. "He knocked you over the head and locked you in an ice hold where you could have died. Whatever you did to him is not comparable."

"That's spoken like someone who's never been desperate for the woman he loves."

She did not hesitate. "Well, I've been desperate to get to the man I love, so I think I have an idea."

The brothers watched her for a long moment, and then Whit said, "I like her."

Devil grinned, then winced at the movement. "As do I."

She rolled her eyes. "You're bleeding from

the head. There isn't time for liking me."

"There will always be time for liking you, Felicity Faircloth."

With Whit's help, they moved Devil up into the warehouse, and then out into the courtyard, now bright with sun.

Felicity was already calling for John. "We need a hack! Or something — Devil needs a surgeon, immediately. And a decent one, not some lumbering fool with a bloodletting box." Instead of moving to help, however, John rocked back on his heels, a wide smile on his face.

Felicity's brow furrowed in confusion. "John, *please.*" And then she turned to follow the direction of his gaze, to find Devil standing perfectly still, ten paces behind her.

She flew to his side, her skirts billowing around them both. "What is it?" she said, running her hands over his arms, his shoulders. "Are you hurt somewhere else? Is it your head? Can you stand?"

He grasped her hands in one of his and pressed a kiss to her knuckles. "Stop, love. You'll make the boys think me soft."

Whit grunted. "The boys already think you soft when it comes to her."

"Only because they don't think I'm worthy of her."

"They know you're not worthy of her."

Felicity shook her head. "What is wrong with you both? He needs a doctor!"

"I need you, first," he said.

"What?" He was mad.

"You came back for me."

"Of course I did. I love you, you imbecile."

Whit coughed a laugh, and Devil pressed another kiss to her fingers. "Well, we're going to have to work on you questioning my intelligence a bit."

"I don't question your intelligence," she said. "I think you're brilliant. Except for when you think to suggest that I don't know my own mind."

"I love you, Felicity Faircloth."

She smiled. "When we are married, do you intend to call me by both of my names?"

"Only if you ask me very nicely." He leaned in close. "I think I've loved you since the moment I found you on that balcony, having picked the lock and found your way from the light to the darkness."

"To freedom," she said, softly.

"That night, in your bedchamber, I jested about rescuing the princess from her tower —"

"You did that," she interrupted.

He shook his head. "No, love. You rescued me. You rescued me from a world without color. Without light. A world without you."

He brushed a thumb over her cheek. "Beautiful, perfect Felicity. You rescued me. I wanted you from the start. It was only a matter of time before everything — *everything* — was second to me wanting you. To me keeping you safe. To me loving you." Tears filled her eyes as he continued. "And all I wanted was your happiness. Mine was nothing compared to yours."

"But my happiness is tied to yours. Don't you see?"

He nodded. "I can't give you Mayfair, Felicity. We'll never be welcome there. You'll always have gone slumming, no matter how rich we are." He paused, lost in thought, and then said, "But I'll give you everything else. The wide world. You have only to ask." His beautiful eyes glittered in the sunlight. "You rescued me from the past. You gave me a present. And now . . . I wish you to promise me the future."

"Yes," she whispered, unable to keep the tears from spilling over. "Yes."

He stole her lips in a wicked kiss that left them both breathless, and Whit grumbled, "Find a bed, will you?"

Felicity pulled away, a blush high on her cheeks, and said, "Just as soon as we find a doctor." She moved to leave the yard, to head for the street.

"Wait," Devil said. "I could swear that you insisted we marry down there, in the darkness, while you were saving my life."

She smirked. "Well, you were quite cold and are suffering from a head wound, so I wouldn't be so certain that you heard what you think you heard."

"I'm certain, love."

"Women do not typically propose to men. Certainly not women like me. Certainly not men like you."

"Women like you?"

"Wallflower spinsters. Forlorn Felicitys."

"Lady Lockpick, did you or did you not ask me to marry you?"

"I believe it was less asking and more telling."

"Do it again."

Her blush turned to flame. "No."

He pressed a kiss to her temple. "Please?"

"No." She pulled away from him and kept walking.

"So traditional," he scoffed. And then, after a moment, he called after her. "Felicity?"

She turned back to find him on his knees in the brightly lit courtyard. She took a step toward him, already reaching for him, thinking for a moment that he had fallen again.

He clasped her outstretched hand and

pulled her closer, until her skirts were billowing around him. She froze, staring down into the face of the man she loved as he said, "I haven't much. I was born with nothing, was given nothing. I haven't a name worthy of you, nor a past I'm proud of. But I vow here, in this place that I have built, that used to mean everything and now means nothing without you, that I will spend the rest of my life loving you. And I will do all that I can to give you the world."

She shook her head. "I don't want the world."

"What, then?"

"You," she said, simply. "I want you."

He smiled, the most beautiful smile she'd ever seen. "You've had me since that first night, love. Now tell me what else you want."

She blushed.

Her heart pounded when he removed the band from his ring finger, immediately transferring it to her thumb, following the kiss of warm silver with his own kiss, to the metal and then to her knuckles. There would be a wedding, no doubt, but this moment, here, in this place, felt like ceremony, blessed by sunlight and air.

And when the husband of her heart rose to his feet — towering over her with broad, beautiful shoulders, his hands coming to her cheeks, cupping her jaw, tilting her face up to his — Felicity gave him the kind of kiss a queen of Covent Garden gave her king.

When it was over, he turned to the rooftops, and Felicity's gaze followed his to the rooftops around the warehouse yard, where dozens of men stood at scattered intervals, rifles at their sides, grins on their faces, watching.

She blushed, and the blush turned to flame as he called out, as strong as ever, "My lady."

He kissed her, long and slow and deep, until the men assembled pounded their feet and shouted their congratulations down into the yard, creating a magnificent, cacophonous echo reverberating around the buildings, so thunderous that the tremors in her toes sent wild pleasure through her — pleasure that turned to fire when he pulled her close and whispered at her ear. "Your world awaits, my love."

EPILOGUE

Three months later

Felicity came to Devil's side in the court-yard of the Bareknuckle Bastards' Covent Garden warehouse as the final steel wagon left the drive, Whit at the reins.

Devil's arm pulled her tight to him as the September wind blew, sending her skirts billowing around them, and they stood, King and Queen of Covent Garden, until the clatter of the horses' hooves faded into the night. When it was gone, replaced by the voices of the watch on the rooftops above and the men who had spent the night working to get the shipment out for delivery, she tilted her face up to his and smiled. "Another day done."

He turned to face her, his hands cupping her cheeks, holding her still as he kissed her, long and deep, until they were both gasping for air. "It's late, wife," he said. "You should be abed."

"I prefer my bed with you in it," she teased, loving the little growl he gave at the words. "Call me *wife* again."

He leaned down and pressed his lips to the soft skin of her neck. "Wife . . ." He scraped his teeth at the place where her neck met her shoulder. "Wife . . ." Nipped at the curve there. "Wife."

She shivered, her arms coming up around his neck. "I don't think I shall ever tire of it, husband."

He lifted his head and met her eyes, his own dark in the moonlight. "Not even when you remember that you married into the darkness?"

The wedding, performed by special license days after Felicity had rescued Devil from the ice hold, had been perfect . . . and the opposite of everything Felicity had once imagined. Instead of a staid affair at St. Paul's Cathedral, attended by half the contents of Burke's Peerage, it had been a lively, cacophonous celebration at a different St. Paul's — a stone's throw from the Covent Garden market.

To Felicity's parents' chagrin, it had been performed by the rookery's vicar — a man who knew his ale and drank it well — to a congregation packed to the gills with the Bastards' men and their families. Arthur had been there, of course, and Pru, along with a collection of tarnished aristocrats who had taken Felicity, Devil, and the whole of the Faircloth family under their collective wing — after all, the Duchess of Haven had pointed out at the wedding breakfast that morning — scandals must stick together.

Only Grace had been missing from the celebration; she remained in hiding while the Bastards worked to find Ewan, who had disappeared after leaving London months earlier. A package had been delivered before the ceremony from Madame Hebert, however, and inside, Felicity had discovered a pair of perfectly tailored buckskin breeches, a beautiful white shirt, a pink and silver waist-coat that would rival any frock in Mayfair, and a tailored topcoat, black on the outside, with pink satin lining. Along with the clothes, a pair of tall, leather boots, fitted over the knee.

A proper ensemble, fit for a Covent Garden queen.

And with it, a message.

Welcome, sister.

That evening, there had been a riotous celebration in the Garden, where Lady Felicity Faircloth, now Mrs. Felicity Culm, had received her third name — the one she treasured the most of all: The Bastard's Bride.

It had been the perfect wedding day, Felicity thought, made better by night, when her new husband had found her in a crush of laughing well-wishers, taken her hand, and led her to the roof of his Covent Garden offices to watch hundreds of paper lanterns released into the sky from the rooftops all around them.

After she'd gasped her delight and thrown herself into his arms, he'd given her the kiss she demanded and knocked his walking stick twice upon a tin chimney nearby, dismissing the elves who had helped him before delivering his new wife to a bed of silk and fur beneath the starlit sky.

Felicity shivered with the memory of that night, and Devil pulled her closer. "Are you cold, my love?"

"No." She smiled. "Just full of memories."

He smiled into her hair. "Good ones?"

"The very best," she said, looking up at him through her lashes. "Though it occurs that it is September, and soon, we shan't be able to use the rooftops."

One black brow rose in keen understanding of what she was saying. Of what she was wanting. "I think you underestimate my power, Felicity Faircloth."

591

She smiled. "Felicity Culm, if you please. And I wouldn't dream of underestimating you, Devil . . . indeed, I cannot imagine the weather ever denying your wishes."

He nodded and leaned close, letting his voice go low and dark. "Winter on the rooftops shall be even better than summer."

Her eyes went wide. "Shall it?"

"I'm going to spread you out beneath the snow and see how hot I can make you burn, my beautiful flame."

She went hot as the sun. "I don't suppose I could lure you to a rooftop now to practice, could I, my handsome moth?"

He straightened. "No."

"No?"

"No. I've something to show you." He took her hand in his, leading her away from the warehouse and back toward the bright lights of Drury Lane. They stopped at the Singing Sparrow, full of their men, drinking and celebrating a night's hard work. Holding the door for her, Devil followed Felicity inside, with a nod to the proprietor, toward a place on the floor that had been cleared for dancing — a quartet of strings and pipes were nearby, and Devil pulled her into his arms as the musicians began to dance.

She laughed up at him when he spun her in a surprising circle. "You wished to show me this tavern?"

He shook his head. "There was a time when you told me that you didn't think I was the kind of man who danced."

She remembered. "And are you?"

"I never was before — dancing seemed like the kind of thing that people did when they were happy."

Her gaze flew to his. "And you weren't."

"Not until you."

She nodded, her fingers playing over his shoulder. And then she met his eyes and said, "Show me."

He did, pulling her close enough to scandalize Mayfair, rocking her and lifting her and swinging her and spinning her in time to the whirling, wonderful music. She clung to him, his strong arms keeping her safe and his. He spun her again, and again, faster and faster along with the music, their assembled audience clapping in time until she threw her head back and laughed, unable to do anything else.

And then he was lifting her into his arms and carrying her through the tavern and out into the street, where a fine autumn mist had turned the cobblestones gold in the light. He set her down as she caught her breath, kissing the last, lingering laugh from her lips. "Well, wife?"

She shook her head. "It wasn't like a dream." He scowled, and she laughed again, reaching for him. "My love . . . my Devil . . . it was better. It was real."

He kissed her again, long and deep. And when he lifted his head, he was smiling, wide and wicked and wonderful. She matched the smile with her own, coming up on her toes to whisper in his ear. "Love me. Past, present, and future."

His answer came like flame. "Yes."

AUTHOR'S NOTE

Two years ago, in London, I met a man who regaled me with the tales of his grandfather, who sold shaved lemon ice from an ice block he'd cart from the docks into Covent Garden. I wish I remembered your name, but wherever you are, I'm indebted to you, as I am to Gavin Weightman for *The Frozen Water Trade,* which was an invaluable resource on the history of moving ice and how it impacted the world.

Around the same time, I became transfixed by the "Perfect Security" episode of the *99% Invisible* podcast, which chronicles the invention of the unpickable Chubb Lock, and then the lock controversy of 1851, when a brash American turned up at the Great Exhibition, picked the lock, and ensured that the world would never feel safe again. Felicity Faircloth is fourteen years earlier than that American, but she picks the Chubb the same way he did, and I'm grateful to Roman Mars and his team for bringing the story to me at the perfect moment.

Felicity's Whispering Bench is a replica of the Charles B. Stover Bench in Central Park's Shakespeare Garden — the perfect place for secret-telling.

Covent Garden is a pretty posh place these days — very little like it was in the 1830s. I spent hours at the Museum of London poring over Charles Booth's extraordinary anthropological survey of "Life and Labour of the People in London," from later in the 19th century, and am so grateful to the Museum for making such a rich resource available to the public in digital format.

As always, my books are fostered and cared for by an incomparable team, and I am immensely lucky to have the brilliant Carrie Feron on my side every step of the way, along with Carolyn Coons, Liate Stehlik, Brittani DiMare, Eleanor Mickuki, Angela Craft, Pam Jaffee, Libby Collins, and all of Avon Books. My agent, Steve Axelrod, and publicist, Kristin Dwyer, are the very best.

The Bareknuckle Bastards would still be a whisper of an idea without Carrie Ryan, Louisa Edwards, Sophie Jordan, and Ally

Carter, and they wouldn't be on the page without my sister Chiara, and my mother, who teaches me every day how the world changes women, and how we change it right back.

And finally, to Eric, who takes all my research in stride, including the kind that ends with me picking the lock on a safe, getting drunk on power, and considering a life of crime: If I'm ever on the lam, I hope you'll be with me.

ABOUT THE AUTHOR

Sarah MacLean grew up in Rhode Island. She majored in European History at Smith College and later earned her Master's degree in Education from Harvard University. MacLean is the author of the series Love by the Numbers and Rules of Scoundrels. The fourth book in that series, *Never Judge a Lady by Her Cover,* made it to many bestseller lists as did *The Day of the Duchess.*